St. Martin's Paperbacks by Matt Braun

WYATT EARP
BLACK FOX
OUTLAW KINGDOM
LORDS OF THE LAND
CIMARRON JORDAN
BLOODY HAND
NOBLE OUTLAW
TEXAS EMPIRE

Coming soon

THE SAVAGE LAND
RIO HONDO

OUTLAW KINGDOM

MATT BRAUN

St. Martin's Paperbacks

OUTLAW KINGDOM

Copyright © 1995 by Matt Braun.

All rights reserved. No part of this book may be used or reproduced in any manner whatsoever without written permission except in the case of brief quotations embodied in critical articles or reviews. For information address St. Martin's Press, 175 Fifth Avenue, New York, N.Y. 10010.

ISBN: 0-312-95618-5

Printed in the United States of America

St. Martin's Paperbacks edition/January 1996

10 9 8 7 6 5 4 3 2

To
Kim and Tracey
Jesseca and Eric
Who give the world special meaning
and, as always,
to Bettiane

Author's Note

Outlaw Kingdom is based on a true story. Bill Tilghman was the prototype for the mythical gunfighter-marshal of Old West legend. Yet there was nothing mythical about Tilghman, or his exploits as a lawman on the frontier. He was the real thing.

Bill Tilghman's life on the plains spanned a time from the buffalo hunters to the oil boomtowns. His career as a lawman encompassed fifty years, ending in 1924 when he was the age of seventy. During successive eras, he served as deputy sheriff, town marshal, deputy U.S. marshal, sheriff, and chief of police. None of the lawmen fabled in Western myth—including Wild Bill Hickok, Bat Masterson, and Wyatt Earp—came close to matching his record. He was without equal among men who wore a badge.

Outlaw Kingdom deals with one era in the lifetime of Bill Tilghman. The great Land Rush of 1889 opened parts of Indian Territory to settlement, and resulted in the creation of Oklahoma Territory. Those early days of settlement gave rise to outlaw gangs who robbed and pillaged on a scale unmatched in the annals of crime. Oklahoma Territory became a battleground where deputy U.S. marshals fought a bloody and vicious war against marauding gangs. In a literal sense, the land became a killing ground.

During the era of the outlaw gangs, Bill Tilghman performed valiant service as a deputy U.S. marshal. In telling his story, fact is presented in the form of fiction, and certain license is taken with time, dates, and events. Yet there is underlying truth to the daring and courage of a man whose exploits were the stuff of legend. His record as a lawman needs no exaggeration, and his dedication to taming a raw frontier stands in a class all its own. His days on the killing ground of Oklahoma Territory were, in a very real sense, larger than life.

William Matthew Tilghman was the last of a breed. To friend and foe alike, he was known simply as Bill Tilghman, and the name alone struck fear in those who lived by the gun. Determined and deadly, sworn to uphold the law, he was a man of valor.

PART ONE

CHAPTER 1

A sea of campfires spread endlessly across the plains. Forty thousand people camping under a star-studded sky waited for the Oklahoma Land Rush.

Tilghman stood with his hands jammed in the pockets of his mackinaw. Though a brisk wind drifted down from the north, his coat was unbuttoned, and his gaze swept an inky darkness dotted with tongues of flame. His camp was located near the train tracks, and as far as the eye could see, the shadows of men were cast against the glow from thousands of campfires. Like him, they stared southward, awaiting the break of dawn.

"What're you thinking about, Bill?"

Tilghman turned to face Fred Sutton. Old friends, they were partners in certain ventures revolving around the land rush. Sutton had operated a saloon and gambling establishment in Dodge City, where Tilghman had served as town marshal.

"Way it appears," Tilghman said, "lots of folks are gonna get the short end. I calculate more people"—he motioned toward the blinking campfires—"than there are homesteads."

Sutton nodded, looking out over the mass of humanity. He was a man of medium height, square-faced and clean-shaven, a greatcoat thrown over his shoulders. He held his hands out to the warmth of the fire.

"Same old story," he said with a wry smile. "Offer something for nothing and the world beats a path to your door. Simple human nature."

"No argument there," Tilghman agreed. "Everybody and his dog turned out for this one."

Their camp was on the line separating the Cherokee Outlet from the Unassigned Lands. Tomorrow, for the first time, land would be opened to settlement in Indian Territory. By government decree, a man could claim one hundred sixty acres for a nominal filing fee. The lodestone of free land had drawn eager homesteaders from coast to coast.

Tilghman wagged his head. "Figures to be devil take the hindmost. Ought to be a helluva race."

At root was the scarcity of good farmland. The flood of settlers pouring west had already claimed the choice homestead lands; the clamor to open Indian Territory to settlement had swelled to a public outcry as western migration intensified. The primary goal of this land-hungry horde was known as the Unassigned Lands.

Embracing some two million acres of well-watered, fertile plains, it was land that had been ceded by the Creeks and Seminoles, as a home for tribes yet to be resettled. But the government eventually announced that it had no intention of locating Indians on these lands. The howls of white settlers then rose to a fever pitch, and their demands now included the Cherokee Outlet, which abutted the northern border of the Unassigned Lands.

The settlers were backed by several influential factions, all of whom had a vested interest in the western expansion. Already the Santa Fe and other railroads had crossed through Indian Territory, and competing lines had no intention of being left behind. Pressure mounted in Washington for a solution, equitable or otherwise, to the problem.

Opposed to settlement were the Five Civilized Tribes, who occupied the eastern half of Indian Territory, and a diverse group of religious organizations. The churches and missionary societies asserted that government dealings with Indians formed a chain of broken pledges and unfulfilled treaties. In that, the Five Civilized Tribes agreed vehemently. They had ceded the western part of their domain to provide other tribes with a home—not for the enrichment of white farmers and greedy politicians.

Tilghman took the pragmatic view. While serving as marshal of Dodge City, he had watched the Indians fight what was clearly a losing battle. At the forefront of the struggle was Captain David Payne. A drifter and ne'er-do-well, Payne had served briefly in the Kansas militia and the territorial legislature. Yet he was a zealot of sorts, and in the settlement of Indian lands he had at last found his cause.

Advertising widely, Payne made fiery speeches exhorting the people to action, and gradually organized a colony of settlers. Every six months or so he'd led his scruffy band of fanatics into the Unassigned Lands, and just as regularly, the army ejected them. After several such invasions, each of which was a spectacular failure, Payne's followers had become known as the Boomers. They were said to be *booming* the settlement of Indian Territory.

Though saner men deplored his tactics, Payne wasn't alone in the fight. Railroads and politicians and merchant princes, all with their own axes to grind, had rallied to the cause. That they were using the Boomers to their own ends was patently obvious. But Payne and his rabble scarcely seemed to care. Frustrated martyrs in a holy quest, they would have joined hands with the devil himself to break the deadlock.

Tilghman's woolgathering was broken by the sound of curses and shouts. Several camps down, where a fire blazed beside an overloaded wagon, two men squared off with knives. A crowd had formed a circle around them, goading the men on with guttural murmurs. Fights were common, fueled by liquor and building tension as the day for the land rush approached. But thus far no one had resorted to weapons.

No longer a lawman, Tilghman nonetheless reacted out of ingrained instinct. He hurried forward, Sutton only a step behind, as the two men slashed at one another, the steel of their knives glinting in the firelight. Shoving through the crowd, he swept his coat aside, drew a Colt Peacemaker from the holster on his hip, and thunked the nearest man over the head. The man went down as though struck by a sledgehammer.

The crowd was stunned into silence. But the other man instantly turned on Tilghman with his knife. His eyes were bloodshot from too much whiskey, his face contorted in an expression of rage. He advanced, flicking the blade with a drunken leer.

"C'mon ahead," he said in a surly voice. "Just as soon cut you as him."

Tilghman was tall, broad through the shoulders, hard as spring-steel. The firelight reflected off his cold blue eyes, showering his chestnut hair and brushy mustache with a touch of orange. He thumbed the hammer on his Colt, the metallic sound somehow deadlier in the stillness.

"Drop the knife," he said quietly. "Otherwise you won't be making the run tomorrow."

"Kiss my rusty ass!" the drunk snarled. "You got no call buttin' in on a private fight."

Tilghman stared at him. "Let's just say I made it my business. Do yourself a favor—don't push it."

"Gawddammit to hell anyway!"

The man tossed his knife on the ground. He whirled

around, bulling his way through the crowd, and stormed off into the night. Tilghman slowly lowered the hammer and holstered his pistol. He turned, nodding to Sutton, and walked back toward their camp. Sutton whistled softly under his breath.

"Jumpin' Jesus, Bill! You could've got yourself killed."

"Not much chance of that, Fred. Those boys were blind drunk."

"Yeah, but you're not wearin' a badge anymore—remember?"

"I reckon old habits die hard. No sense letting them carve on one another."

Tilghman's tone ended the discussion. At the campsite, he poured coffee into a galvanized cup and resumed staring into the night. Sutton, who understood the solitary nature of his friend, squatted down by the fire. He idly wondered if Tilghman had done the right thing by resigning as a lawman.

For his part, Tilghman dismissed from mind the knife fight. During his years in Dodge City, he had buffaloed countless drunken cowhands, whacking them upside the head with a pistol barrel. In the overall scheme of things, one more troublemaker hardly seemed to matter. His thoughts returned to tomorrow, the land rush, a new life. Oklahoma Territory.

Never had there been anything like it. President Benjamin Harrison's proclamation opening the Unassigned Lands to settlement had created a sensation. Newspapers across the nation carried stories of the "great run" and what was described as the "Garden Spot of the World." America turned its eye to Oklahoma Territory, drawn by the prospect of free land. The scintillating prose of journalists brought them hurrying westward by the tens of thousands.

Unstated in these news stories was the tale of intrigue and political skulduggery which lay behind the opening of Indian Lands. The Boomers' squalling demands, though loud and impressive, were merely window dressing. Instead, it was the railroads—and their free-spending lobbyists—who brought unremitting pressure to bear on Congress. The first step had been to declare the right of eminent domain in Indian Territory.

By 1888 four railroads had laid track through the Nations, the lands of the Five Civilized Tribes. This cleared the way for settlement, and shortly after his inauguration, President Harrison decreed that the Unassigned Lands would be opened to homesteading at high noon on April 22, 1889. But it would be on a first-come-first-served basis, a race of sorts with millions of acres of virgin prairie as the prize.

The land-hungry multitudes cared little for whose ultimate benefit it had been organized. Hundreds of thousands of immigrants were pouring into America each year, and they were concerned not so much with the land of the free as with free land. Here was something for nothing, and they flooded westward to share in the spoils.

Nearly one hundred thousand strong, they gathered north and south along the borders of the Unassigned Lands. They came in covered wagons and buckboards, on horseback and aboard trains, straining for a glimpse of what would soon become Oklahoma Territory. And of a single mind, they came to stay.

Among them was Bill Tilghman. Like thousands of others, he had come seeking opportunity, and in no small sense, a place to start over. The old life was gone, withered to nothing, and his gaze had turned toward the last frontier. A land where men of purpose might scatter the ashes of the past and look instead to the future.

A westering man, Tilghman had moved with his family in 1856 to a farm near Atchison, Kansas. At sixteen, he became a buffalo hunter, and later, operating out of Fort Dodge, he'd scouted for the army. In 1877, serving under Bat Masterson, he had been appointed a deputy sheriff of Ford County. Over the next several years he had worked closely with fellow peace officers such as Jim and Ed Masterson, brothers of Bat Masterson. During the same period, he'd developed a friendship with Wyatt Earp, assistant town marshal of Dodge City.

In 1884, Tilghman himself had been appointed town marshal, where he served for four years. Though Wyatt Earp later captured national headlines after the Gunfight at the O.K. Corral, Tilghman's fame was far greater among outlaws and in western boomtowns. He was considered the deadliest lawman of all the frontier marshals, having killed four men in gunfights. Earp and Masterson and Wild Bill Hickok got the headlines. Tilghman got the reputation as a man to avoid at all costs.

Yet, unlike many peace officers, he was a family man. He'd married a Kansas girl, and together with another old friend, Neal Brown, they had built a ranch outside Dodge City. Their principal business was raising horses, providing saddlestock for the Army as well as other ranches. Then, not quite six months past, Tilghman's wife had suddenly taken ill with influenza and died.

To Tilghman, her death somehow represented an end to that part of his life. Shortly afterward he'd sold the ranch except for the finest breeding stock, and resigned as marshal of Dodge City. The Oklahoma Land Rush was forthcoming, and he had seen that as a new beginning, a place without raw memories. Once he was settled, he planned to send for Neal Brown and the horses. His attention was now fixed on Oklahoma Territory. *A new life.*

Tilghman and Sutton had arrived early that afternoon aboard the lead train in a caravan of eleven trains organized by the Santa Fe. Their immediate goal was the townsite of Guthrie, some twenty miles south, situated along the railroad tracks just below the Cimarron River.

Tilghman had chosen Guthrie over the other major townsite, Oklahoma City, based on his assessment of the economic future of the territory. Before nightfall tomorrow he meant to have a sizable stake in that future.

Behind him in Kansas, Tilghman had left fame. Somehow, once he'd buried his wife, his reputation as a lawman had ceased to matter. The new life he envisioned was that of a businessman, a man of property and substance. Others would come along to take up the badge, enforce the law, and put the lawless behind bars. He was content to leave the past in the past.

Fred Sutton moved to stand beside him. For a moment, they stared out over the campfires, into the darkness beyond. Then, with a bemused smile, Sutton motioned southward.

"What do you see out there, Bill?"

"Nothing," Tilghman said slowly. "And everything."

What he saw was a land where a man of thirty-five could start fresh. A world newborn.

CHAPTER 2

The noonday sun was almost directly overhead. A cavalry officer, followed by a trooper with a bugle, rode slowly to a high point of ground. Below, a thin line of mounted troopers, extending east and west out of sight, held their carbines pointed skyward.

Silence enveloped the land. The quiet was eerie, an unnatural stillness, broken only by the stamping hooves of horses and the chuffing hiss of locomotives. On the small knoll the army officer stared at his pocket watch, and in the distance, hushed and waiting, over fifty thousand homesteaders stared at the knoll. The Oklahoma Land Rush was about to begin.

Tilghman and Sutton were seated in the first passenger coach on the lead train. They watched through the windows as men on swift ponies and those aboard wagons struggled to hold their horses in check. Tilghman knew that the horseback riders, at the beginning of the race, would outdistance the train. But the Guthrie townsite was twenty miles south, and no horse could outrun a train over that distance. He was confident of winning the race.

Overnight the news circulated that added trains had been laid on at the southern boundary of the Unassigned Lands. Yet Tilghman was unconcerned, for the jump-off point was the South Canadian River, closer to the Oklahoma City townsite than to Guthrie. That news, along with thousands more arriving at the northern boundary during the night, widely increased the air of tension and excitement. There were now over one hundred thousand poised for the land rush.

The troublesome thing to Tilghman was not the number of people. Instead, he was bothered by those who refused to play by the rules. These men were being called Sooners, since they crossed the line too soon. Despite the soldiers' vigilance, they had sneaked over the border under cover of darkness, planning to hide until the run started and then lay claim to the choice lands. Cavalry patrols had flushed hundreds of them out of hiding, but word spread that there were several times that number who had escaped detection. This left the law-abiding homesteaders in an ugly mood.

All along the line people were gripped by the fear that there wouldn't be enough good land to go around. As noon approached, and the tension became pervasive, their mood turned to one of near hysteria. Since early morning the Santa Fe had moved four additional trains into position, fifteen now one behind the other, loaded with still more land-hungry settlers.

The men on horseback were reasonably certain they could outdistance the trains in the short run. But those in wagons and buckboards (by far the greater number) knew they would arrive too late for a chance at the most desirable claims. Tempers flared, fistfights broke out, and as the minutes ticked away fully fifty thousand people jostled and shoved for a better spot along the starting line.

On the knoll, the cavalry officer stared intently at his pocket watch. As the hands of the watch merged, precisely at high noon, he dropped an upraised arm. The trooper beside him put the bugle to his mouth and blew a single piercing blast. On signal, the cavalrymen below discharged their carbines into the air, but the gunfire was smothered beneath a thunderous human roar. The troopers scattered to avoid the onrushing stampede.

Horses reared and whips cracked, men dug savagely with their spurs, and in a sudden dust-choked wedge, a wave of humanity surged across the starting line. At first it seemed a mad scramble, as the earth trembled and trains gained headway. But within moments the race was decided for choice claims to the immediate south of the border.

Out of the blinding dust cloud emerged the swiftest horses, spurred into a wild-eyed gallop. Behind them, strung out and gaining speed, came the trains. Scattered across the countryside, quickly losing ground, wagons and buckboards, and even one solitary soul on a high-wheeled bicycle, brought up the rear. America's first great land rush was under way at last.

From the lead train, Tilghman watched as the horsemen broke clear and sped off into the distance. Not far away he saw two wagons collide and upend, spilling people and household goods across the prairie. He and Sutton exchanged an amused look as the adventurous soul on the bicycle quickly fell behind, obscured in a whirling cloud of dust. Then, as the train gathered speed, smoke and soot from the engine drifted through the open window. They sat back in their seats.

"Judas Priest!" Sutton hooted. "Never saw anything that could hold a candle to that. We could've sold tickets!"

Tilghman smiled. "Hell, that's just the start. The real fun's yet to come"—he nodded out the window—"when they butt heads with the Sooners."

"Yeah, I suppose you're right. There's liable to be some knock-down-drag-out brawls before this day's over."

"Fisticuffs would be the least of it, Fred. There's people out there willing to kill for a choice piece of land."

Sutton looked somber. "You think we'll run into trouble at Guthrie?"

"All depends," Tilghman allowed. "We'll see if anybody's on the ground when we get there. Or leastways, the piece of ground we want."

Every townsite claimant was entitled to stake out two lots. Between them, Tilghman and Sutton planned to stake claim to four lots. One of those, the choice lot, would be devoted to their joint enterprise. They intended to open the first sports-betting emporium in Oklahoma Territory.

In recent years, a cottage industry had sprung up around sports betting. Horse races, such as the Kentucky Derby, and championship prize fights had become national in scope with the advent of the telegraph. The results, transmitted from coast to coast by wire, enabled bettors to wager on a multitude of sports events. Sutton, along with other saloonkeepers in Dodge City, had provided an informal service for his customers. In Guthrie, he and Tilghman meant to corner the market with an across-the-board sports book. They envisioned it as becoming a veritable money tree.

"Mr. Tilghman?"

A man of distinguished bearing stood in the aisle beside their seats. He was perhaps fifty, with a mane of silver hair, and dressed in finely tailored clothes. He smiled pleasantly.

"William Tilghman?" he inquired. "Formerly the marshal of Dodge City?"

"Guilty on all counts," Tilghman said, climbing to his feet. "What can I do for you?"

"Allow me to introduce myself. Colonel Daniel F. Dyer, formerly adjutant to General Sherman and late of Kansas City. I dabble in real estate and other ventures."

Tilghman accepted his handshake. "You aim to settle in Guthrie, Colonel?"

"Indeed," Dyer affirmed. "A burgeoning new land

with unlimited opportunity for investment. Of course, the magnitude of such opportunity attracts the undesirable element as well."

"Likely draw them like flies to honey."

"Mr. Tilghman, I am a man of some wealth and political influence. I intend to play an instrumental role in making Guthrie the capital of Oklahoma Territory. I would like to enlist your aid in furthering that goal."

Tilghman appeared puzzled. "Politics aren't my game, Colonel."

"Quite so," Dyer agreed. "Yet you are a law officer of the first order, Mr. Tilghman. And Guthrie, as the territorial capital, must set an example for law and order."

"Sounds like you're offering me a job."

"All in good time, when we have established a city government. But, yes, Mr. Tilghman, I would be honored to propose your name for chief of police."

"Sorry," Tilghman said amiably. "I quit law work when I left Dodge. Business is my game now."

"Is it?" Dyer said with a dubious expression. "Last night, I observed your rout of those two unsavory characters. From all appearances, you've hardly lost your taste for law enforcement."

"Chalk it up to old habits, Colonel. I'll have to wean myself off that one."

"No need for a hasty decision, Mr. Tilghman. Think it over at your leisure. We'll talk again."

Tilghman grinned. "Talk won't change things, Colonel. I've got other irons in the fire."

"Nonetheless, you are admirably suited to the law, Mr. Tilghman. Give it some thought and we'll talk in Guthrie."

Dyer strolled off down the aisle. Tilghman resumed his seat and traded a look with Sutton. After a quick glance over his shoulder, Sutton shook his head.

"There's a gent not accustomed to taking 'no' for an answer."

"Guess he'll just have to learn. Like I told him, I'm done with law work."

Sutton silently wondered if that were the case. Some habits were harder to break than others.

Shortly before two that afternoon, Tilghman and Sutton stepped off the train at the Guthrie townsite. Neither of them had ever traveled this far into Indian lands, and they took a moment to get their bearings. What they saw hardly had the look of the future capital of Oklahoma Territory.

Before them stretched a rolling plain, bordered in the distance by stunted knolls. The Santa Fe tracks curved off to the southwest, roughly paralleled on the west by Cottonwood Creek. East of the tracks, directly across from a meandering bend in the stream, was a small depot flanked by a section house and a water tank. Several hundred yards east of the depot was an even smaller structure, the federal land office. The rest was empty land.

Three buildings and a water tank constituted the town of Guthrie.

Tilghman and Sutton skirted the depot, headed on beeline for the land office. There were now only minutes to spare, for hundreds of men were pouring off the train and running in the same direction. Reason dictated that the center of town would be located near the land office, and it was here that Tilghman meant to stake their lots. But as he hurried forward several men were already erecting a tent catty-cornered from the land office.

Tilghman immediately tagged them as Sooners. Yet there were other lots and he was satisfied to let latecomers argue the matter. He paced off twenty steps due north of the land office and an equal distance east of the tent. There he drove his stake, with his initials carved in bold letters at the top. Then, moving quickly, he repeated the process, hammering a second stake into an adjacent lot.

Sutton, meanwhile, was scurrying around what would logically represent an opposite corner. He jabbed two stakes in the ground on lots side by side, and not a minute too soon. The landscape all of a sudden sprouted horsemen and a bedlam of humanity emptying off of trains. Where moments before there had been a tranquil prairie the earth was now covered with a frenzied swarm of men, racing mindlessly to plant their stakes in what seemed the choicest spot.

Disputes erupted immediately as men attempted to claim the same lots, and within minutes a dozen slugfests were in progress. But no one came anywhere near the corner north of the land office, or the corner directly opposite. Tilghman stood between his stakes, hand on his pistol, and Sutton adopted a similar posture across the way. The message was clear, and however desperate for land, other men heeded it.

By nightfall Guthrie was a city of tents. Still, rather than sanity restored, pandemonium continued to reign. The Santa Fe station agent quit his post to stake a claim, and a southbound train collided head-on with a northbound from Oklahoma City. Cavalry troopers battled mobs of claim jumpers, who found their dirty work easier done in the dark. Saloons conducted a thriving business from planks resting across barrels, and bordello tents began servicing customers who apparently had a highly attuned sense of direction. Torches lit the night on what gave every appearance of a demented anthill.

Tilghman and Sutton maintained their vigil on opposite corners. They watched as land speculation flourished, rising to a fever pitch in the glow of blazing torches. Hundreds of men had staked claims for no other purpose than to sell them to the highest bidder, and many lots were resold on the hour. Speculators moved swiftly from location to location, dickering and swapping as the future shape of the city took form.

There were no sanitation facilities and no law enforcement. Unfouled drinking water was in short supply, and the stench of a garbage dump slowly settled over the land. By late that night scores of drunken men lay where they had fallen, brought down by the effects of cheap pop-skull whiskey. Yet there were better than ten thousand delirious souls squatted on their claims, and drunk or sober, they were in an exultant mood. They had themselves a town.

Tilghman thought it the greatest circus ever to hit the plains.

CHAPTER 3

There were never enough hours in the day. Tilghman had four projects in various states of completion, and his workday generally stretched from sunrise to well after dark. He often felt like a juggler with one too many balls in the air.

The intersection of Oklahoma Avenue and Second Street, just as he'd surmised that first day, had become the hub of downtown Guthrie. City Hall was taking shape on the southeast corner, and opposite that the post office was under construction. He and Sutton, their claims duly filed, owned the other two corners.

A sawmill as well as a brick kiln were now in operation on the outskirts of town. To meet building demand, the Santa Fe continued to haul in carloads of finished lumber and fixtures from Kansas. Along with the supplies a regiment of carpenters, bricklayers, and stonemasons had arrived in Guthrie. Their services, in the boomtown growth, went to the highest bidder. Others joined a long waiting list.

Tilghman's bankroll, though not inexhaustible, was larger than most. The funds from the sale of his Kansas ranch allowed him to purchase a carload of lumber and secure the services of a half dozen carpenters. On his lots, the sports book (dubbed the Turf Exchange) and a

mercantile store, already rented, were nearing completion. Across the way, Sutton was building the Alpha Saloon and a storefront leased to a hardware dealer.

Some blocks north of downtown Tilghman had
bought a lot from the original claimant. There, with yet
another crew of carpenters, he was building a frame
house. A modest affair, the house would have five
rooms with a roofed porch. Tired of bunking in a tent,
he had already ordered furniture, including a cushy bed,
for delivery from Kansas. Sutton, who preferred to be
closer to his work, was building living quarters over the
saloon.

Hustling back and forth between projects, Tilghman
rarely had a moment to spare. Yet his dawn-to-dark
workday seemed somehow normal amidst the hectic
sawing and hammering along every street. By the close
of the second week a small miracle of sorts had taken
place on the once-barren prairie. The tent city had virtually disappeared, and from this humble beginning, a
town had emerged. Guthrie took on a solid look of permanence and bustling industry.

Saloons and gambling dens were everywhere in evidence, as well as several sporting houses. The most
spectacular of the lot was the Reaves Brothers Casino,
where it was advertised men could find honest games
and fine whiskey. The sporting life, particularly at the
start, was the economic mainstay of any boomtown. But
Guthrie was gearing itself to become the center of commerce for the entire territory.

Under the sure hands of carpenters and stonemasons,
some fifty buildings were in various stages of construction. Among them were three banks, two newspapers,
three hotels, and several office buildings. While the activity was noteworthy in itself, what distinguished Guthrie from other towns was its leaders and their vision of
the future. The structures they erected were being built
to last, at least a third constructed of brick and stone.

Their common goal was to make Guthrie the frontrunner in the fledgling territory.

Tilghman was no less enterprising. His latest project had to do with the field south of town where the local elections had been held. The land was owned by a homesteader, who was an enterprising man himself. Originally, like other homesteaders, his plan had been to farm the land. But with the explosive growth of the town, he saw greater opportunity on the horizon. One day soon, Guthrie would spread beyond the townsite, and his land bordered the town limits. He figured he was sitting on a fortune in future town lots.

Though of a similar opinion, Tilghman's experience as a horse trader gave him an edge. The first step had been to convince the homesteader that his bonanza in town lots was at least a year down the road. With that accomplished, he'd persuaded the man that leasing the field near town would be more profitable than planting it in crops. After that, they got down to serious dickering over the price. The homesteader was wily, but no match for a seasoned horse trader. In the end, Tilghman got a one-year lease for three hundred dollars.

The lease enabled Tilghman to move ahead with a certain moneymaker. Horse racing in the west was, if anything, more wildly followed than in the east. Western races were smaller, usually of a regional nature, but widely attended, something of a festive event. Entry fees from horse owners made for large purses, and the betting was always heavy. So Tilghman, playing the game at both ends, intended to collect on a double hit. He would operate a racetrack and book the bets at the Turf Exchange.

Today, standing at the edge of town, he watched as workmen put the finishing touches on the racetrack. A crew of graders had leveled the field and then laid out an oval track a half mile around. At the southern side of the field a stable had been built large enough to house ten horses. The stable and the railing around the track were now in the process of being whitewashed. The overall visual effect was one of a professional operation.

Tilghman thought of it as a license to print money. The first race, advertised with posters around town, would be held Saturday, only three days away. His cut from the entry fees would be substantial, and weekly races would ensure a tidy profit. The Turf Exchange, though in the final stages of construction, was the only full-fledged sports book in Guthrie. There, eager for entertainment and generally enthused about horse racing, the townspeople would wager large sums. Westerners, who were inveterate gamblers, would bet on anything, especially a favorite horse. The races would do a landslide business.

Eleven horses had already been entered in the Saturday race. Some of them he'd seen working out on the track, and he wasn't overly impressed. His own string of four horses arrived today on the noon train from Kansas, still under the care of Neal Brown. He planned to run a leggy chestnut gelding in the race, and he thought the prospects of winning were far better than average. All that remained was for he and Sutton to calculate odds on the horses entered. He planned to post the board late that afternoon.

On his way to the train station, Tilghman passed through the heart of the business district. Citizen's National, the first bank to open its doors, would ultimately dominate the downtown area. Three stories high with a massive cupola, it was being constructed of native stone. Already the ground floor was completed, and as offices on the second and third floors were finished they would be leased to professional men and business concerns. Lawyers and physicians, arriving daily, were competing for office space.

Around the corner, the Palace Hotel presented an equally imposing sight. Four stories high, with polished granite columns at the entrance, it was intended to be a plush affair. The rooms were spacious, with all the latest conveniences, suitable to attract a select clientele. Other hotels were being built, but everyone agreed that the Palace was indeed palatial. Big and elegant, and with just the right touch of class.

Tilghman, as he passed by, was reminded that Guthrie's leading citizen occupied one of the ground-floor rooms. George W. Steele, formerly of Indiana, had been selected as the first governor of Oklahoma Territory. In the Organic Act, passed by Congress, the new territory comprised all Indian lands west of the Five Civilized Tribes, once those lands were opened to settlement. The territory was divided into seven counties, with lawmaking powers vested in a legislature to be elected by the people. The office of governor had been filled by presidential appointment.

Some thought Governor Steele was a tool of the railroads, a friend to robber barons. Others were equally firm in their belief that the new governor was a man of integrity. Tilghman, who preferred to judge a man on performance, thought Steele was handling the job pretty well. Elections were to be held shortly, and a sitting legislature would soon address the business of territorial government. Everyone, regardless of political persuasion, was jubilant that Guthrie had been designated the territorial capital. Confident of greater days ahead, the city council set aside four square blocks at the end of Oklahoma Avenue for the future capitol grounds.

At the Santa Fe depot, Tilghman got a pleasant surprise. The noon train was on time, and Neal Brown hopped off the steps of the caboose. Brown was short and wiry, with a quick smile and an uncanny way with horses. He waved, motioning toward the last boxcar on the freight train. His mouth split in a grin.

"By God!" he said, pumping Tilghman's arm. "Thought you never was gonna send for me."

The telegraph lines were now operating out of Guthrie. Two days before Tilghman had wired instructions for shipping the horses. "Good to see you," he said as they shook hands. "How was the trip?"

"Smooth as butter," Brown assured him. "Think the horses slept all the way."

"Glad to hear they're rested and full of vinegar. Big Red's scheduled for a race on Saturday."

The reference to the long-legged chestnut caught Brown short. "Gawdalmighty, Bill," he said, somewhat amazed. "That's pretty quick, ain't it?"

"Quick enough," Tilghman informed him. "The racetrack's all but done, and no need to dally around. You can start working Big Red this afternoon."

"You just move right along, don't you?"

"Timing worked out perfect, Neal. There's a prize fight set for Saturday, heavyweight championship. The bout's scheduled to start right after the race. We're bound to draw a big crowd."

"Goddamn," Brown said in mild awe. "Told me you aimed to make your fortune down here. Guess you wasn't kiddin'."

Tilghman smiled. "Never kid about money, Neal. Let's get those horses unloaded."

Brown began barking orders at the train crew. A ramp was rolled into place and the boxcar door thrown open. Big Red was the first in the string to set hoof on Oklahoma Territory.

The Turf Exchange was mobbed Saturday morning. The doors opened at eight o'clock and Tilghman and Sutton worked the betting cages straight through until noon. Guthrie had again led the way, staging the first sporting events in the territory, and people treated it like a civic celebration. Hardly a man in town failed to wager a bet.

Saloons and gambling dives also took bets. But just as Tilghman had foreseen, the public flocked to what was considered a legitimate sports book operation. To such a degree, in fact, that Tilghman and Sutton had deposited over thirty thousand dollars in wagers at the Citizen's National Bank. A nightly tally of the betting slips indicated that the wagers were roughly split between the prize fight and the horse race. At noon, with bettors still waiting in line, they were forced to close the doors. Their bankroll, taken with the odds, would cover no more wagers.

Post time at the track was scheduled for two that afternoon. An hour before some fifteen thousand spectators were mobbed around the track railing. On trains, by buggy and horseback, people had traveled from across the Territory to witness a double-barrelled sports extravaganza. Cafes and saloons also had struck pay dirt, and half the crowd was ossified on spirits by post time. The police force, led by the newly appointed town marshal, finally called it quits. There was no way to control such a large crowd.

The race went off shortly after two o'clock. Big Red, with Neal Brown aboard, surged across the starting line and took an early lead. Half a length behind was a roan stallion, imported for the event by a rancher outside of Oklahoma City. The rest of the pack, never really in the race, were strung out some distance behind. Big Red set the pace, but by the far turn the roan was edging closer. In the homestretch, the roan's rider applied the quirt and the stallion made it a neck-and-neck race. Valiant to the end, with Brown urging him on, Big Red matched the roan stride for stride. At the finish line, the roan at last gained half a step and won it by a nose. The crowd, hoarse from shouting, roared approval for both horses. Talk of a future rematch instantly swept the track.

An hour later, in a field west of the track, the prize fight got under way. Paddy O'Shea, the heavyweight champion of Kansas, was matched against Davy Dolan, a pugilist from St. Louis. The match was bare-knuckle, conducted under Marquis of Queensberry Rules: no hitting when a man was down. The crowd, raucous with excitement by now, surrounded an earthen ring of posts and ropes in the center of the field. At the opening bell, O'Shea proceeded to give the contender a lesson in the gentlemanly art of boxing. By the twenty-third round, Dolan looked like a man who had been savaged by wildcats. O'Shea charitably put him down and out with a clubbing right to the jaw.

The crowd went wild as O'Shea strutted around the ring. Tilghman and Sutton, who were standing near one of the corner posts, were only slightly less restrained. Laughing, pounding one another on the back, they exchanged mutual congratulations. Neal Brown, who had only just finished tending Big Red, found them moments after the fight ended. Consternation swept his face when they grabbed him, still laughing, and heartily shook his hand.

"What the hell you two lookin' so happy about? Our horse lost!"

"Who cares?" Sutton crowed. "Won or lost, it's all the same!"

"You gone nuts?" Brown demanded. "Won or lost ain't the same a'tall."

"Yeah, it is," Tilghman said. "Leastway if you're running the right kind of business."

"You're gonna have to spell that out for me, Bill."

Tilghman pulled him aside and told him. No matter who won or who lost—horses, baseball, or pugs—the oddsmaker had it covered both ways. The Turf Exchange, Tilghman revealed with a low chuckle, was the biggest winner of all.

"We cleared better than ten thousand dollars for the day!"

CHAPTER 4

Late Monday morning Tilghman and Sutton finished the accounting. Sutton was the bookkeeper of the partnership, and by his calculation they had netted closer to twelve thousand dollars. Their jubilance had abated none at all, and even more, they were of one mind. The Turf Exchange was indeed a license to print money.

Tilghman began laying out plans for the next race. He wanted to build bleachers on the south side of the track, in front of the finish line. People would pay top dollar for seats with a view, and the admission charge would further increase profits. As well, he wanted to install vendors' booths around the track, where spectators could purchase drafts of keg beer to quell their thirst. The money to be made, in his view, was there for the taking. Several thousand people could drink a lot of beer.

"Mr. Tilghman?"

A young boy stood in the doorway. Tilghman moved to the betting window at the counter. "I'm Tilghman," he said. "What can I do for you, sonny?"

The boy stepped into the room. "Marshal Grimes wants to see you over at his office. He told me to fetch you."

"I don't suppose he told you what it's about?"

"No sir, he didn't. Just said to bring you along."

Sutton turned from the ledger on his desk. "We haven't got any business with a federal marshal. Last I heard, it's no crime to take bets."

"We'll find out quick enough." Tilghman nodded to the youngster. "What's your name, sprout?"

"Tommy Brewster," the boy replied with a gap-toothed grin. "I run messages for folks over at the territory capitol."

"Well, lead the way, Mr. Brewster. I'm right behind you."

Tilghman followed the boy out the door. On the way across town, he reviewed what he'd heard of the newly appointed U.S. Marshal. Formerly from Nebraska, Grimes had made the land rush and claimed a homestead near the townsite of Kingfisher. Word had it that he had served two terms as a sheriff in Nebraska and had an enviable record for his hardline attitude toward outlaws. The way the grapevine told it, he'd sent a good many bad men to the gallows. President Harrison, at Governor Steele's urging, had appointed him United States Marshal only last week.

Until a capitol building was constructed, all territorial and federal offices were housed in the Herriott Building, located at the corner of Division and Harrison. Tilghman followed the boy to the second floor, still new with the smell of fresh lumber. There the boy left him at a door with a newly painted placard denoting UNITED STATES MARSHAL, OKLAHOMA TERRITORY. He rapped on the door.

"Door's open," a voice called out. "C'mon in."

Tilghman entered a room that had the look of a monk's cell. There was one desk, a battered veteran of better days, and three wooden chairs. A file cabinet flanked the desk, and a Winchester rifle was propped in one corner. A man he took to be Grimes was seated behind the desk, and a man unknown to him occupied one of the chairs. Chris Madsen, a deputy marshal he'd met around town, moved forward to greet him.

Short and barrel-chested, Madsen's name was known across the frontier. A soldier of fortune, Danish by birth, he had fought under Emperor Louis Napoleon in the Franco-Prussian War and later served in the French Foreign Legion. Emigrating to America in 1876, he had joined the army and distinguished himself in the wars with the Plains Tribes. Last year, he'd resigned from the army and accepted appointment as a deputy marshal working Indian Territory. His reputation was hard but fair, and deadly with a gun.

"Bill," Madsen said amiably, "good to see you. I'd like you to meet our federal marshal, Walt Grimes."

"Mr. Tilghman." Grimes rose, offering his hand across the desk. "Pleasure to make your acquaintance."

"Mutual," Tilghman said. "Congratulations on your appointment."

"Consolation might be more in order. Seems I've walked into a hornet's nest."

"How's that?"

"The Dalton boys," Grimes said tersely. "They're shooting up the territory."

"Who are the Dalton boys?"

"Hell, I jumped the gun. Before we get to that, I want you to meet one of our deputies. This here's Heck Thomas."

The man in the chair stood and shook Tilghman's hand. He was a lean six-footer, with steel-gray eyes and hard features. A slight smile touched one corner of his mouth.

"Bill Tilghman," he said. "Late of Dodge City and thereabouts. Your reputation travels."

"Not near as far as yours," Tilghman replied. "Pleased to meet you."

Tilghman's remark was hardly an overstatement. Heck Thomas was a renowned mankiller, one of the foremost lawmen in the West. A Georgian, he had served as a policeman in Atlanta before migrating to Texas. There, he had operated as a private detective prior to appointment as a deputy U.S. marshal. Later, he'd served under Judge Isaac Parker, the hanging judge, headquartered at Fort Smith but trailing outlaws who sought refuge in Indian Territory. He was reputed to have killed six men.

"Have a seat," Grimes said. "Let me tell you about the Daltons."

Tilghman reluctantly took a chair. He sensed that this was something more than a social visit. Thomas resumed his seat and Madsen moved to a window, staring outside. Grimes waved his hand as though batting at flies.

"There's four Daltons, all brothers. Crazy bastards decided to turn desperado, the whole bunch."

Grimes went on with a thumbnail sketch of an entire family turned outlaw. Former cowhands, three of the brothers had at one time served as deputy U.S. marshals. But Bob Dalton was fired for taking bribes, and the other two, Emmett and Grat, resigned amidst rumors that they were rustling cattle on the side. Afterward, fancying himself another Jesse James, Bob formed a gang that included Emmett, Grat, and the fourth brother, Will, along with a pack of some eight cutthroats. The outlaw band, like other predatory gangs, operated out of Indian Territory.

"Helluva note," Grimes concluded. "I'm one week on the job and they've robbed two trains. Hit the Santa Fe up in the Cherokee Outlet and the Katy express down in the Creek Nation. Then they're off and gone, like a goddamn puff of smoke."

"Where to?"

"Where else?" Grimes said hotly. "The Nations."

Any peace officer, even those who served in Dodge City, had heard tales about the Nations. But Tilghman had always thought them overblown, half hot air and half truth. He listened attentively as Grimes described the strangest circumstances ever faced by men sworn to uphold the law.

With wider settlement of the frontier, a new pattern of lawlessness began to emerge on the plains. The era of the lone bandit faded in obscurity; outlaws began to run in packs. Bank holdups and train robberies were boldly planned and executed, somewhat like military campaigns. The scene of the raids often resembled a battleground, strewn with the dead and dying.

Local peace officers found themselves unable to contend with the lightning strikes. Instead, the war evolved more and more into a grisly contest between the gangs and the federal marshals. But it was a game of hide-and-seek in which the outlaws enjoyed a sometimes insurmountable advantage. A deadly game that was unique in the annals of law enforcement.

Gangs made wild forays into Kansas and Missouri and Oklahoma Territory, terrorized the settlements, and then retreated into the Nations. There they found virtual immunity from the law, and perhaps the oddest sanctuary in the history of crime. Though each of the Five Civilized Tribes had its own sovereign government, their authority extended only to Indian citizens. White men were untouchable, exempt from all prosecution except that of a federal court.

Yet there were no extradition laws governing the Nations. Federal marshals had to pursue and capture the wanted men, and return them to white jurisdiction. In time the country became infested with hundreds of fugitives, and the problem was compounded by the Indians themselves. They had little use for white man's law; the marshals were looked upon as intruders in the Nations. All too often the red men connived with the outlaws, offering them asylum.

For the marshals, the chore of ferreting out lawbreakers became a herculean task. Adding yet another obstacle, even the terrain itself favored the outlaws. A man could lose himself in the mountains or along wooded river bottoms, and in some areas there were vast caves where an entire gang could hole up in relative comfort. The tribal Light Horse Police refused all assistance, and the gangs usually chose to fight rather than face a hangman's rope. It was no job for the faint of heart.

"There you have it," Grimes concluded. "The Daltons are running wild and their example just breeds more gangs. We need the help of experienced lawmen. Men like yourself."

Tilghman arched one eyebrow. "Are you offering me a job?"

"Hear him out," Madsen interjected. "I told the marshal how you'd made your mark in Kansas. We think you're the right man for the job."

"Chris makes a good point," Grimes added. "You proved yourself in Dodge City, and that's high recommendation. You're the kind of man we want."

"I appreciate the—"

"Let me finish," Grimes cut him off. "I've been authorized to recruit sixteen deputy marshals to police the territory. Chris and Heck are the first to sign on, and you'd be the third. That's pretty select company, Mr. Tilghman."

"Another day, another time," Tilghman said, "I'd be honored to serve with these men. But I've put law work behind me, marshal. I'm a businessman, now."

"So I hear," Grimes said shortly. "To be frank about it, that has me stumped. You're one of the best peace officers ever to pin on a badge. Why quit now?"

"Let's write it off to personal business and leave it there."

"Goddammit, Tilghman, this *is* personal business. You settled here, and men like you have a responsibility to make the territory safe for everyone. Where's your public spirit?"

Tilghman stood. "I generally don't overlook insults. In your case, I'll make an exception." He nodded to Madsen and Thomas. "See you gents around."

"Hold on!" Grimes said crossly. "I'm just trying to—"

Tilghman turned, ignoring him, and walked to the door. Heck Thomas rose from his chair and hurried into the hallway. He caught Tilghman at the landing to the stairs.

"Don't take it personal," he said amiably. "What with the Daltons and all, Grimes has a load on his shoulders. He's under a lot of pressure."

Tilghman shrugged. "A badge doesn't excuse bad manners. He ought not to push so hard."

"I tend to get riled on things like that myself. 'Course, he's right when he says that some men have more responsibility than others."

"Way I see it," Tilghman said, "I've done my duty more than most. I won't lose any sleep over it."

Thomas searched for a convincing argument. Over his years as a lawman he had learned a little about life and a great deal about death. He had few illusions left intact, and instead of thirty-nine, he felt fifty going on a hundred. These days, he saw people not as he wished them to be but simply as they were. He understood Tilghman.

In the Nations, even among other peace officers, Thomas had seen his share of hardcases. Yet there was nothing loud or swaggering about Tilghman, nothing of the toughnut. Instead, he seemed possessed of a strange inner calm, the quiet certainty more menacing than a bald-faced threat. Thomas respected a man of cool judgment and nervy quickness in tight situations. Those were the traits he wanted in men who rode beside him. The traits he saw in Tilghman.

"Funny thing," he said now. "Seems like I've been

wearin' a badge all my natural born life. Hard to remember a time when I wasn't."

"Same here," Tilghman admitted. "What with scouting for the army, and law work, it seemed like every day
led to another fight. I never had time for anything else."

"Maybe there's a reason," Thomas said. "Some men
are good at it and some men aren't. I suspect you and
me are two of a kind."

Tilghman wondered about that. For the past several
years, Thomas had served as a marshal under Judge
Parker. Until the Oklahoma Land Rush, Parker's court
in Fort Smith had had sole jurisdiction over the Nations.
Parker's administration of justice had been punctuated
repeatedly by the dull thud of a gallows trap. Almost
seventy men had been hanged, but in the process sixty-
five marshals had lost their lives tracking outlaws across
the Nations. The job was dirty and dangerous, and Heck
Thomas had survived because he was a highly skilled
killer of men. Though he was equally skilled, Tilghman
wanted something more from life. He thought he'd
found it in Guthrie.

"Yeah, I reckon we're alike," he agreed now. "But
some men burn out faster than others. Figure I've run
the course."

Thomas eyed him with a shrewd smile. "You know,
it's curious how being a lawdog gets in a man's blood.
I'd wager you're not shed of it yet."

"Would you?" Tilghman liked his easy humor, his
open nature. "Well, Heck, that's one bet you're bound
to lose. I've hung up my badge—for good."

"You wouldn't take offense if I brought it up now and
again, would you? Just by way of testin' the water."

"You've got a streak of stubborn, don't you?"

"Damnedest thing." Thomas laughed. "I got the same
notion about you."

They parted with a warm handshake. Tilghman went
down the stairs and disappeared into the street. Thomas

stood there for a long moment, turning the conversation over in his head. Then he chuckled softly, nodding to himself.

Bill Tilghman was going to make a hell of a marshal.

CHAPTER 5

The day was bright as brass, without a cloud in the sky. A gentle breeze drifted in from the south, and huge white butterflies floated lazily on warm updrafts of air. High overhead a hawk hung suspended in the sky, a speck of feathers caught against the blaze of a noonday sun.

Tilghman shaded his eyes against the glare, watching the hawk. He was mounted on a dun mare, one of his string quartered in Guthrie. The mare cropped grass where they had paused on a knoll overlooking a wooded stream. The hawk floated away and his gaze swept out across the land. There was something familiar about it, a distant memory.

The valley was located in the Sac and Fox tribal reservation, some forty miles southeast of Guthrie. He'd departed town yesterday afternoon, camping overnight on the trail, and pushed on steadily through the morning. The purpose of his trip was to inspect the horse herds of the Sac and Fox, famed throughout Indian Territory for their high-bred stock. Swift ponies with the endurance of plains horses would add to the bloodline of his racing stable.

The land before him stretched onward in gently rolling prairies and wide valleys. Like a latticework of water, the Deep Fork of the North Canadian fed the tributaries of Dry Creek, Bell Cow, Quapaw, and the Kickapoo. The streams were bordered on either side by trees, and an occasional timbered woodland stood stark against the sunlit plains. The earth seemed to sway with wave upon wave of lush tall grass.

The morning's ride had convinced Tilghman that the reservation was a wildlife paradise. While the buffalo herds were now gone, there was still an abundance of game. Great flocks of turkey swarmed over the woodlands; at dusk the timber along the creeks was loaded with roosting birds. Deer were plentiful, and grouse and plover were everywhere in the tall grass. Fat, lazy fish crowded the streams and river shallows, eager to take a hook baited with grasshopper. It was a land where no man need go hungry.

Summoned from long ago, Tilghman suddenly realized why the land appeared so familiar. From his boyhood on the farm in Kansas, he remembered these same rolling prairies and waves of grass. In his youth, he had hunted the woodlands and fields, and fished the creeks. He recalled returning home at sundown with his game bag stuffed full, and the savory smells in the kitchen as his mother cooked what he'd harvested from the wild. Those were good memories, fond memories, long ago of another life. Oddly, looking out from atop the knoll, he felt as though he'd somehow come home.

Tilghman shook it off, gently nudged the mare with his boot heels. His immediate destination was the reservation agency, where he intended to talk with the Indian agent. But as he rode across the prairie, unbidden thoughts intruded on the business at hand. Perhaps it was stumbling over old memories, made vivid in his mind's eye by the haunting familiarity of the land. Whatever the source, unbidden or not, he was forced to admit something he'd avoided until now. There was a restlessness within him, some inner spark of discontent with the way things were. He felt as though he'd taken a wrong turn in the road.

All of which left him thoroughly confused. A month ago, after that first horse race, he had thought of himself as a man with the world on a downhill slide. Everything had fallen into place just as he'd planned, one piece dovetailing with the other in rapid order. Even now, the Turf Exchange and the racetrack were coining money faster than he and Sutton could count. He owned several properties, his business concerns were a resounding success, and he was on a first-name basis with the civic leaders of Guthrie, including the governor. So he had to wonder about this nagging sense of discontent. No ready answer presented itself, and that bothered him even more. He was a man who'd always known himself.

A short while later he rode into the agency compound. Headquarters was a whitewashed frame house with a shaded porch out front. The agent, Joseph Monroe, was a spare man with spectacles and a talkative nature. He invited Tilghman inside, where one part of the parlor served as an office. There, once they were seated, he waved off into the countryside.

"What brings you to the reservation, Mr. Tilghman?"

"Horses," Tilghman remarked. "I hear the Sac and Fox breed good stock. I'm interested in buying."

"Well then," Monroe said jovially, "you've come to the right place. No tribe raises finer horses than the Sac and Fox."

"How would you suggest I go about it?"

"Oh, there's a certain protocol to these things. You'll have to deal with the chief, at least at first. His name is Moses Keokuk."

"Moses?" Tilghman said quizzically. "Where'd he get a name like that?"

"Fairly common," Monroe noted. "The original agent here was a missionary. He liked Biblical names!"

"So did Moses lead the Sac and Fox to the Promised Land?"

"Well put, indeed, Mr. Tilghman. And not far from the fact, I might add. The Sac and Fox are the most influential tribe on the reservation."

"How many are there?" Tilghman said. "I only heard about the Sac and Fox because of their horses."

Monroe warmed to his favorite subject, the diverse nature of his wards. He explained that the reservation was home to several tribes, each relocated from distant parts of the country. The Sac and Fox, still nomadic in their ways, roamed the reservation with their horse herds. The Iowas, who followed the white man's road, were now farmers with thousands of acres under cultivation. The Shawnee-Potawatomi were middle of the road, still in transition to becoming white Indians. Other than sharing a reservation, the tribes had little in common.

A good listener, Tilghman discerned that Monroe had little in common with those who ran the Bureau of Indian Affairs. The agent went on to relate that Washington was devouring Indian lands piecemeal. In their latest move, the bureaucrats had secured agreements by which members of the three tribes were each allotted one hundred sixty acres in severalty. The remainder of their lands, something over a million acres, had been ceded to the government. Thus another land rush, opening the land to settlers in early September, had been put in place. The reservation, for all practical purposes, was even now part of Oklahoma Territory.

To underscore the point, Monroe wryly observed that the Secretary of the Interior had already divided the reservation into two counties. One was named Lincoln, and in a twist of bureaucratic humor, the other was to be called Potawatomi. Federal surveyors had recently designated their boundaries and selected the county seat townsites. Washington, in a fit of noblesse oblige, had left it to the territorial legislature to provide for local government of the new counties. Which, in Monroe's opinion, would allow Governor Steele to award plum positions through patronage.

"All neat and tidy," he said with mild sarcasm. "Another instance of politics as usual."

"Way it sounds," Tilghman commented, "you'll soon be out of a job."

"Well, perhaps it's a blessing in disguise. Working for the Great White Father sorely tests a man's conscience. I intend to join the land rush and stake a claim."

"A homestead?"

"Hardly," Monroe said with a gruff chortle. "I'm no farmer, Mr. Tilghman. The townsite for the seat of Lincoln County will be called Chandler. I plan to stake out a town lot."

"Good idea," Tilghman said. "What business have you got in mind?"

Monroe laughed. "I think I'll open a saloon. Hard times or not, people always have money for liquor. I'll probably wind up a rich man."

"Never saw a saloonkeeper yet who went to the poorhouse."

Monroe appreciated a man with a sense of humor. He decided to personally escort Tilghman and introduce him to the Sac and Fox chief. Otherwise, given the tribe's nomadic wanderings, Tilghman might never find them. They went out to the corral to saddle Monroe's horse.

Toward midafternoon, they found the tribe camped on Bell Cow Creek. Tilghman was again struck with a sense of familiarity about the spot. A grove of trees bordered a bend in the creek and the surrounding prairie was a natural grazeland. There was an eerie similarity to the family farm site of his boyhood.

Moses Keokuk, chief of the Sac and Fox, was something of a surprise. A commanding figure, grown heavy with age, he spoke his own brand of broken English. His angular features and hawklike nose were offset by the humorous cast of his eyes. He looked like a red-skinned pirate who enjoyed his work.

Monroe performed the introductions. He explained that Tilghman was interested in horses and had ridden a long way to look at the Sac and Fox herds. Tilghman seemed uncertain as to how he should address the tribal leader, and there was an awkward moment. Then Moses Keokuk gave him a sly smile.

"We talk trade. Mebbe you call me Moses. Mebbe you call me Chief. We see."

"Sounds fair," Tilghman said, warning himself that the man was shrewder than he pretended. "I've heard the Sac and Fox raise fast horses."

"Plenty fast," the chief said proudly. "Wanna eat dust, try to outrun our ponies."

"Well, that's good to know. What I'm looking for is a couple of stallions."

Moses Keokuk grunted. "Gonna breed 'em to that mare you ridin'?"

"I might," Tilghman said. "Then again, I might just race them. Either way, they've got to be fast."

"Told you, we ain't got no horses ain't fast. Stallions, mares, all the same."

"You suppose I could have a look at some?"

"Do lots better," the chief said. "Let you see 'em run."

Moses Keokuk was as good as his word. Several stallions were selected from scattered herds grazing at different points on the prairie. Lean, young horse herders bounded aboard the stallions and rode them at top speed. Any questions about stamina were resolved, and the rumors were indeed true. Sac and Fox horses were fast.

Tilghman settled on only one stallion, a sorrel stud that seemed like the wind in motion. Moses Keokuk, adopting the stony-faced manner of a poker player, proved to be a haggler of the first order. In the end, certain that they would do business again, Tilghman decided not to dicker too hard. He allowed the chief to extract a price that was high, but still short of robbery. They solemnly shook hands on the deal.

By then it was nearing sundown, and Monroe invited Tilghman to stay the night. The agent's wife, a pleasant woman and a passable cook, laid out all the fixings for supper. Afterward, seated in rockers on the porch, Tilghman listened while Monroe stoked a pipe and told blistering tales about the Bureau of Indian Affairs. The stories dealt with a bureaucracy that operated on the principle of incompetence mixed with corruption. If nothing else, the evening convinced Tilghman that Monroe would make a good saloonkeeper. The man was too honest for government work.

Early next morning Tilghman rode out leading the sorrel stallion. The impressions of yesterday came over him again as he retraced his route across the reservation. The rolling prairies rekindled old memories, some better than others. He was realist enough to admit that part of his discontent was deeply personal. Though he'd never discussed it with anyone, he still mourned the loss of his wife. His fresh start, the excitement of Oklahoma Territory, was a poor substitute for the woman who had graced his life. His grief was hidden, but not gone.

Yet, however great his personal loss, there was more to the overriding sense of restlessness. The Turf Exchange and the racetrack, all the money in the bank, had failed to slake some inner need. Seemingly, he had the world by the tail, but in the midst of all he'd accomplished, something was missing. He felt as though he had wandered astray, somehow lost his way, and try as he might, he couldn't regain his sense of direction. He was searching for something and it was elusive. Hard to identify, or put into words.

Late that morning, as he approached the Deep Fork of the North Canadian, he was reminded of Bell Cow Creek. The lay of the land, the rushing stream and the grove of trees, all triggered a feeling that had come over him just yesterday. A spooky feeling, one that defied logic, but nonetheless real. A sense that he'd come home.

So maybe he wasn't lost. Instead, he told himself as he forded the river, maybe he had found the path after all. A path that could end his search. One thought triggered another and then another as he rode toward Guthrie.

CHAPTER 6

By midsummer the frontier boomtown was gone.

In its place was a city unlike any imagined by the original settlers. Guthrie was now a thriving metropolis, the population swelled to more than twelve thousand. A waterworks and pumping station were under construction, and along with it, a rudimentary sewerage system. Tracks were laid on Oklahoma Avenue and a horse-drawn streetcar began servicing one of the town's main thoroughfares.

A group of private investors had obtained the license for a generating plant. By early next fall they would provide streetlights at major intersections, and the wonder of electric illumination in offices and business concerns in the downtown area. Their plans, though considered overly ambitious by some, were to extend this remarkably efficient service to every home in town. The coal-oil lamp, astounding as it seemed, would soon become a thing of the past.

Near the Santa Fe railyards at the west end of Cleveland Avenue, another investor had built a warehouse and organized Guthrie's first wholesale grocery company. Directly across the street still another go-getter had established the town's largest lumberyard, buying in trainload lots, and outselling all other competitors combined. Mayor Dyer, by now a pillar of the community, had been instrumental in bringing all these improvements to the city.

But the mayor, for all his civic virtue, was a strong advocate of the free enterprise system. After sampling the water at a mineral well southwest of town, he bought the land, organized a bottling plant, and began selling Mineral Wells Elixir Water throughout the territory. Then, exploiting his scheme to the fullest, he built a bathhouse near downtown, piped the water in from the well, and charged outrageous prices for people to luxuriate in the warmth of a mineral bath. Nothing with the smell of profit escaped attention.

An accelerated rate of growth, stimulated by supply and demand, attracted investment at a dizzying pace. City Hall had approved the blueprints for a flour mill, two creameries, a distillery, and a bookbinding factory. The newspaper reported as well that approval was forthcoming for a wholesale meat company, a gristmill, and a cotton gin. By next summer, when the first full year of crops were harvested, the homesteaders would lack for nothing. To quench their thirst, Pabst was designing a brewing plant large enough to service the entire territory.

Growth was evident as well in the professions and retail establishments. A city directory listed fourteen doctors and thirty-six lawyers, half a dozen mercantiles, twenty-three cafes, and four drugstores. The public servants who prepared the directory were nothing if not discreet, and unlisted were eighteen saloons, five gambling dives, and several flourishing whorehouses. Still, in its own unobtrusive way, the sporting crowd did quite well in Guthrie.

For all that, Tilghman watched the surge of growth with mixed emotions. The Turf Exchange, with results relayed directly from the telegraph office, was now booking bets on horse races, prize fights, and baseball games from all across the country. The racetrack was mobbed every Saturday afternoon, and now drew horse owners from as far as Missouri and Texas. To run the whole operation required a payroll of twelve employees.

By some accounts, Tilghman and Sutton were two of the wealthiest men in town. But Tilghman rarely looked at his bank balance, and he'd turned down countless investment opportunities, including Mayor Dyer's mineral-water bonanza. For the most part, his days were spent at the track with Neal Brown, training horses, talking bloodlines, and planning the breeding program for their stock. He took greater pleasure in speculating on the foals sired by the Sac and Fox stallion than he did in the daily receipts from the Turf Exchange. His spark for business grew dimmer by the day.

The final blow occurred toward the end of June. The Guthrie *Statesman* reported that the wondrous invention of Alexander Graham Bell was coming to the territorial capital. The telephone, grown quite sophisticated since its invention in 1876, had spread rapidly to cities throughout America. According to the *Statesman*, plans were under way to provide Guthrie with telephone service by the fall of 1890. The age of science had overtaken the frontier.

Tilghman saw it in another light entirely. The frontier he'd known, from buffalo hunting to the cowtowns to the land rush, was swiftly vanishing. The telephone, rather than a modern convenience, represented the death knell of a way of life. To him, the jangle of a telephone bell was a sound he was never meant to hear. He didn't want to be there when it arrived in Guthrie.

On the Fourth of July, he made his decision. By a small quirk of nature, the fourth was also his birthday, and he thought it an auspicious time to put his life in order. The town celebrated the holiday with a parade and fireworks, and the Turf Exchange pulled down the largest single daily gross since the doors opened. A spectator of sorts, Tilghman celebrated his thirty-sixth birthday by stepping across a line he'd skirted for the last month. He decided to sell out.

The next morning he discussed his plans with Neal Brown. The reaction he got was much as he'd expected. Brown was more comfortable with horses than he was with people. Apart from a Saturday night on the town, he much preferred wide open spaces and working with horses. His years on the plains had left him with a general distaste for towns and an ingrained distrust of townspeople. Guthrie, with its mushrooming growth and hurly-burly of people, was for him the worst of all worlds. He'd stayed on only out of loyalty to Tilghman.

Early that afternoon Tilghman entered the Alpha Saloon. The interior was pleasantly cool, despite sunlight streaming through the front windows. A long mahogany bar occupied one wall, behind it a large mirror flanked by the ubiquitous nude paintings popular in Western saloons. Opposite the bar were faro and twenty-one layouts, with poker tables toward the rear. A four-man poker game was under way at one of the tables, and Fred Sutton, finishing a breakfast of ham and eggs, was seated at a nearby table. Tilghman took a chair across from him.

"Afternoon," he said. "Or by the looks of your plate, it's still morning."

"Late night." Sutton waved his fork around the room. "We had a crowd in here till the wee hours. Wish the Fourth of July came more often."

"Older I get, the less I like it. Just adds another year to my calendar."

"Damn!" Sutton dropped his fork and extended his hand. "What with the crowds and everything, I forgot to wish you happy birthday. All the best, Bill."

"Thanks." Tilghman shook hands, then nodded toward the nearby poker table. "Those boys been at it all night?"

The four men were hunched over their cards. One of them, attired in a checked suit and derby hat, had at his elbow stacks of gold coins and a large stack of greenbacks. The other three, scowling at their cards, were clearly losers.

"Some fools are born losers," Sutton scoffed. "The big winner's a tinhorn who passed himself off as a notions drummer. He's plucking the other three."

"Honest game, or is he a cardsharp?"

"Way it appears, he's just got 'em outclassed. 'Course, I've been fooled before. Some are slicker than others with a deck of cards."

Tilghman lost interest. "Want to talk to you," he said. "Are you satisfied with our take from the Turf Exchange?"

"Satisfied!" Sutton said, a bite of ham speared on his fork. "Christ, it's like a license to steal. We own the mint."

"How'd you like to own it all?"

"I don't follow you."

"Simple," Tilghman said. "I'm thinking of selling out my half. Thought I'd offer it to you first."

"Sell out?" Sutton said, astounded. "Why would you do a damnfool thing like that?"

"Fred, I'm wore out on the city life. Guthrie got too big, too fast for my tastes. I'm thinking of moving on."

"Where would you go? What would you do?"

"Figured to raise horses," Tilghman said. "There's another Land Rush toward the end of September. I've got a spot picked out on the Sac and Fox reservation."

"I'll be dipped." Sutton shook his head. "You're just a sackful of surprises."

"Hell, Fred, I wasn't cut out to be a businessman. All a pipe dream, and no sense kiddin' myself any longer. I see that now."

"Sort of sudden, isn't it? You never gave a clue."

Tilghman thought of it another way. He kept his own

counsel, rarely seeking the advice of others. Still, in looking back, there had been nothing sudden about his decision. A great deal of weighing and deliberation had taken place over the past month. The idea of telephones in Guthrie had merely been the last straw.

"Sudden or not," he said, "I aim to sell out. You interested?"

Sutton took a swig of coffee. He set the mug back on the table, his features unreadable. "What've you got in mind?"

Tilghman sensed that the mood between them had changed. Friendship was one thing, business was another. Sutton would attempt to drive a hard bargain.

"Fred, I'm not one to haggle. So I'll make you a fair deal."

"Go ahead."

"Twenty thousand cash," Tilghman said, "plus thirty percent of profits for six months. After that, I retain ten percent interest."

Sutton frowned. "Sounds pretty steep to me, Bill."

"I've thought on it, and that's my only deal."

"Are you saying, take it or leave it?"

"Yeah, I reckon so," Tilghman told him. "Lots of people would jump at the deal. I'd rather sell to you."

Sutton was silent a moment. "What about the racetrack? You plan to unload that, too?"

"Ten thousand cash buys the lease, the stables, the whole works."

"Throw in your house and we'll shake on it."

"Nope," Tilghman said slowly. "The house will fetch a good price on its own. We're talking the track and the sports book."

"Goddamn," Sutton grumbled. "Anybody says you're not a businessman, he's loco. You squeeze the turnip."

"One horse trade's like another, Fred. We got a deal?"

"Hell, why not! I'm partial to owning the whole she-bang anyhow. I'll have a lawyer draw up the papers."

"Sooner the better, so far as I'm concerned."

A snarled curse from the poker game filled the room. "You tinhorn sonovabitch! You're cheatin'."

"Am I?" the man in the derby hat replied. "How do you propose to prove it?"

"Don't have to prove it!" The accuser kicked back his chair and started around the table. "I'm just gonna beat the livin' shit out of you."

The gambler rose, pulling a bulldog pistol from his waistband. "Stop right there."

The other man shoved the table aside and lunged forward. At point-blank range, the pistol roared and the powder flash set his shirt afire below his breastbone. He staggered sideways, his eyes wide with shock. Then he dropped dead on the floor.

Tilghman stood, his reaction one of visceral instinct. He pulled his Colt and thumbed the hammer. "Drop that gun."

The gambler crouched, wheeling around, and brought the bulldog pistol to bear. Tilghman shot him in the chest, nicking the edge off the lapel on his coat. The impact drove him backwards, his feet tangled, and he collapsed onto the wreckage of the poker table. A trickle of blood leaked out of his mouth and his eyes rolled back in his head. He lay still.

"Jesus," Sutton mumbled hollowly. "Why'd you take a hand? Wasn't your fight."

The question, though phrased differently, was put to Tilghman several times over the course of the after-noon. Ed Kelly, the first lawman on the scene, was dumbfounded. He clearly thought it a mild form of in-sanity to take part in someone else's fight. There would be a coroner's inquest, with those who witnessed the double shooting required to testify. No one doubted that Tilghman would be cleared.

Heck Thomas arrived as the bodies were being carried out. When he posed the question, there was not a trace of surprise on his face as Tilghman explained that murder required a response. He felt confident that, with or without a badge, Tilghman would respond to any killing in exactly the same way. The traits that had made him an outstanding lawman were the traits that would permit him to do no less. To Thomas, it was a fundamental part of certain men's character.

Outside, they stood talking for awhile on the street. Thomas related that the Dalton gang had robbed yet another train, and vanished into the Nations. Tilghman, though he'd just killed a man, listened closely and asked questions that would have occurred only to a lawman. Still, despite his interest, he evidenced no sudden urge to pin on a badge. He meant to raise horses, not chase outlaws.

Upon parting, Thomas told himself that it was only a matter of time. Tilghman was one of that rare breed with no tolerance for those who stepped outside the law. He'd been born to wear a badge.

CHAPTER 7

The sun dipped lower, splashing great ripples of gold across the water. Overhead a hawk veered slowly into the wind and settled high on a cottonwood beside the stream. The bird sat perfectly still, a feathered sculpture, flecked through with a bronzed ebony in the deepening sunlight. Then it cocked its head in a fierce glare and looked down upon the men.

There were five of them, all lean and hard, weathered by wind and sun. Four were Sac and Fox tribesmen, their features like the burnt mahogany of ancient saddle leather. Tilghman watched as they wrestled a stout log onto their shoulders and jammed the butt end into a freshly dug hole. Small rocks and dirt were then tamped down solidly around the log until it stood anchored in the earth. This was the last in a rough circle of wooden pillars embedded in the flinty soil.

Tilghman had hired the men through Moses Keokuk, chief of the Sac and Fox. While they continued work on the corral, he slowly inspected the ranch compound. His homestead centered on a wide expanse of woodland, with cottonwoods along Bell Cow Creek and a grove of live oaks stretching westward for a quarter mile. Bordering the shoreline was a natural clearing, with a rocky ford and a stunted hill to the north, which would protect it from the winter blast of a plains blizzard. The terrain rolled away from the creek in virgin grassland.

Not quite three weeks past, in early September, Tilghman and Neal Brown had joined twenty thousand homesteaders in the land rush. Tilghman had claimed one hundred sixty acres along Bell Cow Creek, three miles northwest of the Chandler townsite. Farther west along the creek, Brown had staked a homestead abutting Tilghman's land. Their combined holdings provided over three hundred acres of natural pasture for raising horses.

The ensuing weeks had been a time of sweat and labor. Tilghman drove himself and the tribesmen at a furious pace, working from dawn to dusk, seven days a week. At the outset, he had informed them that two buildings must be erected, a main house and a stable for twenty horses. They felled trees, snaked logs to the clearing, and worked without respite under his relentless urging. The buildings were completed, including planked floors and a stone fireplace in the house, in less than three weeks.

Now, as dusk settled over the clearing, they stood back and marveled at the fruit of their labors. Set off away from the creek, shaded by tall cottonwoods, was a sturdy, shake-roofed log house. It had five rooms with windows overlooking the stream and an oak door with iron fittings. Across the clearing, set flush with the terrain, was the stable, also constructed of logs. Half the stalls were filled with brood mares, most of them topped by the Sac and Fox stallion and ready to foal in late spring. The stallion, by now named Steeldust, stood at his stall door watching the men.

The corral sat squarely in the middle of the clearing, a short distance from the stream. The cross posts were springy young logs, designed to absorb punishment from milling horses without snapping. There, in time to come, young horses would be gently educated in the ways of man and saddle. For the moment, the corral would serve as exercise ground and breeding pen for the stock. The tribesmen, all experienced horse herders, daily took the stock to graze on the prairie bordering the creek.

Moses Keokuk rode into the compound as the men stood admiring their handiwork. He was astride a prancing black stallion with fiery eyes and a flowing mane. As he reined to a halt, one of the tribesmen came forward to hold his horse. He stepped down from the saddle, grinning at Tilghman.

"Heap lotta work," he said, waving around the compound. "When you gonna stop?"

Tilghman smiled. "We ought to finish by tomorrow. Just odds and ends left to be done."

"You white men all the time work. Got no time for play."

"Well hell, Moses, only chiefs have time to loaf. The rest of us have to bust our humps."

Over the past several weeks Tilghman and Keokuk had become great friends. They were honorable men, steadfast in manner, with similar views on life. Of equal significance, they shared a fondness for sweeping plains and fast horses. By now, they enjoyed the bantering relationship of men who respected one another.

"Brown the same," Keokuk said, shaking his head. "Just come from his place. Work my men mighty hard."

"Good wages, though," Tilghman remarked. "Gives your boys hard money in their pockets. They like that when they go to town."

"Old days was lots better. Never needed money."

Tilghman understood the sentiment. With the land rush, the nomadic life of the Sac and Fox had ended. Tribal members were each awarded one hundred sixty acres, the same as their new white neighbors. But farming was foreign to their nature, and they hadn't yet taken to the white man's road. They still counted their wealth in horses.

For all that, Moses Keokuk had urged his followers to take work where it could be found. The reservation was gone, and with it the monthly food allotments. Tilghman had put four men on the payroll, and Neal Brown, who was building a small cabin on his claim, had hired two Sac and Fox. The old days were no more, but cash money gave them an independence of sorts. Their trade was welcome at the stores in Chandler.

"How 'bout tonight?" Keokuk asked. "You gonna go to town?"

"Wouldn't miss it," Tilghman said. "Figures to be quite a shindig. What about you?"

"Sure, I go." Keokuk gave him a sly grin. "Mabbe see white man not all work."

"Moses, I just suspect you will."

Three days ago elections had been held for town and county offices. To honor the occasion, the leaders of Lincoln County had organized a celebration. Everyone from miles around would attend, and there were certain to be large crowds. Chandler, as the county seat, was now a hub of activity. And a great curiosity to the Sac and Fox.

Keokuk grunted, looking thoughtful. "So you still not be a law chief. How come you turn 'em down?"

Tilghman had been asked to run for county sheriff. Though the arguments were persuasive, presented by several influential townspeople, he had declined. "Told you before, Moses," he said now. "Horses are my business, not the law. I've got all I can handle here."

"You're funny man, Bill Tilghman. Big honor to be chief."

"I'll stick to raising horses. Let me get washed up and we'll ride into town together."

Tilghman walked toward the house. Moses Keokuk stared after him, considering. In his mind, the position of law chief was on a magnitude of the red man's war chief. An honor not to be dismissed lightly.

White men, even those he knew well, were still a mystery. Tilghman more so than most.

The town square was a tableau of thriving commerce. In only three weeks, shops and business establishments had been hammered together with wagonloads of lumber imported from Guthrie. People already referred to it as Courthouse Square, though a courthouse, planned as a stone edifice, was yet to be built. The town leaders meant for Chandler to make its mark on the map.

The boardwalks were crowded with people, and farm wagons lined the street. By nightfall, over a thousand homesteaders and townspeople were gathered for the celebration. One part of the square was devoted to a feast, where quartered beeves roasted over low fires. On the opposite side, where a band blasted out merry tunes, a large section of level ground served as a dance floor. The climax of the evening would be an elaborate display of fireworks.

Tilghman and Keokuk drew stares as they walked through the milling throngs. A white man in company with an Indian aroused curiosity in itself. But a former lawman, known to have declined the post of sheriff, and the chief of the Sac and Fox attracted attention wherever they went. Tilghman, all too aware of the attention, thought Neal Brown had made a wise decision. Never one for large crowds, Brown had elected to forego the celebration. He was content to spend the evening in his cabin on Bell Cow Creek.

Keokuk abruptly grunted a low chuckle. He took Tilghman's elbow, tugging him along. "See a man you oughta know. Pretty honest, for a white man."

"Who's that?"

"Amos Stratton," Keokuk said. "There, with the girl."

Up ahead, Tilghman saw a man in his late forties attired in a dark suit and hat. But his attention was drawn to the girl and stayed there. He couldn't take his eyes off her.

Keokuk performed the introductions. Stratton and his daughter, Zoe, had made the land run and staked a claim on Quapaw Creek. Like Tilghman, Stratton fancied horses and had bought several head of breeding stock from the Sac and Fox. Tilghman listened, nodding in all the right places, occasionally offering a comment. His attention was fixed on the girl.

Zoe Stratton appeared to be in her early twenties, perhaps younger. She was tall and statuesque, with a rounded figure and a tiny waist. She had extraordinary green eyes, exquisite features, and a cloud of auburn hair worn in the upswept fashion. She carried herself erect and proud, and when she smiled Tilghman was mesmerized. He thought her the loveliest woman he'd ever seen.

After some moments of conversation, Stratton excused himself and strolled off into the crowd with his daughter. Tilghman considered the brief interlude all too short, and reluctantly turned away. As he fell in beside Keokuk, he found Heck Thomas approaching them. He introduced Keokuk, who seemed drawn now by the savory aroma of the roasting beef. Announcing that he was hungry, the chief walked off toward the fire spits.

Thomas smiled. "Looks like you made yourself a friend, there."

"Good one, too," Tilghman acknowledged. "Him and his men have been a big help in getting the ranch started."

"Sounds like you've got things well in hand."

"No complaints so far. What brings you to Chandler, Heck?"

"Same old thing," Thomas said. "Trailin' the Dalton boys."

"Thought you would've caught them by now."

"Yeah, me too."

Thomas appeared somber. He went on to relate that the Dalton Gang had robbed two trains within the last month. One was on the Santa Fe line, and the other was an express car on the Katy line. In the latter holdup, the express car guard resisted and had been killed. After each robbery, the gang had vanished into the Nations.

"Got a tip," Thomas concluded. "Word's around that some of the gang was sighted north of here."

"In Oklahoma Territory?" Tilghman said quizzically. "Why wouldn't they stay holed up in the Nations?"

"Damn good question." Thomas frowned, clearly troubled. "These boys are runnin' us ragged, Bill. We're always a day late and a dollar short."

"I remember the feeling, Heck."

"Last week Jim Masterson signed on as a marshal. But hell, he's only one man, and we're still spread thin. We need somebody that knows the ropes."

Tilghman stared at him. "Why do I get the notion you're here to see me?"

"Saw through it, huh?" Thomas shrugged, lifting his hands. "You're too good a lawman to sit this one out, Bill. Forget duty and obligation and all that. I came here personal to ask your help."

Tilghman was silent for a long moment. He still felt a strong reluctance to again become involved in law work. Yet he found it difficult to refuse a personal appeal from a man he respected. One who had now become his friend.

"Let's say I signed on," he said. "You understand it wouldn't be permanent?"

"Any way you want it," Thomas quickly agreed. "Just stick with me till we clean out this bunch."

"I'll need a week to get things squared away at the ranch. Then we'll call it official."

"Goddamn, I knew you wouldn't turn me down! We're gonna nail those bastards, Bill. Mark my word!"

"So far as I'm concerned, the sooner the better."

Tilghman's attention was distracted. Through the crowd, he saw Amos Stratton and his daughter watching couples swirl around the earthen dance floor. He nodded to Thomas, leading the way, and cleared a path through the spectators. Halting beside the Strattons, he tipped his hat to the girl.

"Miss Stratton," he said, smiling. "I'd count it an honor if you'd like to dance."

Amos Stratton gave him a sour look. But the girl graced him with a radiant smile and accepted his hand. He led her onto the dance floor, holding her at a respectful distance, and caught the beat of the music. They glided off into the throng of dancers.

Heck Thomas watched them with a broad smile. His toe tapped in time to the music and he mentally patted himself on the back. By his reckoning, the ride to Chandler had been worth every mile.

He'd landed his man.

CHAPTER 8

Trees along Red Rock Creek clattered in a bright and nimble wind. The tawny grasslands bordering the stream were littered with drifts of scarlet and gold. There was a frosty nip in the air, and at night, streamers of ice had begun to form along the banks. To those who could read the sign, it was a portent of a long winter.

Early in November Tilghman and Thomas forded Red Rock Creek. They were south of Nowata, a backcountry crossroads located deep in the Cherokee Nation. Their trail had led from Oklahoma Territory to the Kansas border, and then into the hinterlands of Indian Territory. They were tracking Tom Yantis, a member of the Wild Bunch.

In late September, Tilghman had taken the oath in Guthrie and pinned on the badge of a deputy U.S. marshal. He'd done so with lingering reservations, partly due to his reluctance to be away from the ranch. A new aspect, and perhaps a larger part, was his reluctance to be away from Zoe Stratton. After the election day celebration in Chandler, they had begun keeping company on an informal basis. Nothing serious but nonetheless a budding relationship, one he intended to pursue.

Then, hardly a week after he'd been sworn in, the Dalton Gang had staged a daring raid. Bob Dalton and his band of renegades had attempted to rob two banks simultaneously in Coffeyville, Kansas. Their plan went awry from the beginning, and armed townspeople blocked any hope of escape. When the gunfire ended eight men—four citizens and four bandits—lay dead in the street. Three of the Dalton brothers, Bob, Emmett, and Grat, were among the dead.

The Dalton Gang had been wiped out on the streets of Coffeyville. Only two of the outlaws had escaped, a blooded killer named Bill Doolin and the last of the brothers, Will Dalton. For a week or so, federal marshals thought their major problem had been eliminated. Tilghman had signed on to help rid the territory of the Daltons, and for all practical purposes, the Dalton Gang had ceased to exist. His thoughts turned to the ranch, and Zoe, and he began planning a tactful way to resign his commission. Once again, thanks to the citizens of Coffeyville, he could put aside the badge.

But then, as though risen from the ashes, Bill Doolin took up the mantle. Within a week of the Coffeyville massacre he had formed a gang of his own, and apparently devoted considerable time and thought to making fools of the lawmen who chased him. From the little known of Doolin, he had worked as a cowhand in the Cherokee Outlet until a drunken spree resulted in a shootout with lawmen. When the smoke cleared, Doolin was still standing, miraculously unscathed, and two peace officers were dead. A killer with a price on his head, he'd taken what seemed the logical step. He joined the Dalton Gang.

From all appearances, he had learned well riding with the Daltons. His first move in forming a gang was to appoint Will Dalton as his second in command. Then, according to the grapevine, he had recruited a band of misfits and killers far worse than the Dalton Brothers. Among those he'd enlisted were Red Buck Waightman, Tulsa Jack Blake, Dynamite Dick Clifton, and Cimarron

Tom Yantis. Their nicknames, like badges of dishonor, tagged them one and all as renegades. Under Doolin's leadership, they began terrorizing the territory.

Tilghman, as well as Thomas and the other marshals, was taken by surprise. Doolin moved quickly, forging a gang while on the run, and proved to be far craftier than any of the Daltons. Less than a fortnight after the Coffeyville massacre, he and his gang robbed the Missouri-Pacific express on its passage through Indian Territory. After the holdup, Doolin adopted a new tactic, scattering his band to the winds throughout the Nations. The federal marshals were left with too many trails and too few clues. The chase ended hardly before it had begun.

U.S. Marshal Grimes then adopted a new tactic of his own. He summoned Tilghman and Thomas to Guthrie, and assigned them full-time to the Doolin Gang. By then the newspapers, always alert to a catchy headline, had dubbed this latest band of outlaws the "Wild Bunch." No sooner were the Daltons wiped out than the Wild Bunch appeared, and Grimes was under immense pressure from the governor to bring them down. Given the circumstances, Tilghman saw no diplomatic way to turn in his badge. The ranch, and Zoe, would have to wait.

With Heck Thomas, he began scouring every known outlaw haunt in the Nations. Then, during the last week in October, the gang struck again. Crossing the border into southwestern Kansas, Doolin and his men robbed the bank in Spearville. The Ford County sheriff pursued the band as they fled southeast and crossed the line into Oklahoma Territory. There his jurisdiction ended and pursuit became a matter for the federal marshals. But the robbers scattered once more, taking refuge in the Nations. Organized pursuit ended at that point.

Tilghman and Thomas, still operating on their own, began searching for leads. Over the years, working as a marshal out of Fort Smith, Thomas had developed informants throughout the Nations. For the most part, they were Indian farmers who believed that lawlessness, whether red or white, ill-served the Five Civilized Tribes. Their information came from a backwoods grapevine that was part fact and part rumor, and often unreliable. Fearing for their lives, few red men told the whole truth where white outlaws were concerned. Even fewer risked being identified as the source.

Late that afternoon a farmer outside Nowata had taken the risk. Unlike most Cherokees, his resentment of white men was not wholesale. Some he trusted and some he didn't, and Heck Thomas had long ago earned his confidence. The rumor he'd heard placed Tom Yantis at the home of a farmer on Red Rock Creek. Word had it that Yantis paid a steep price for refuge and the farmer's silence. But only yesterday, at the general store in Nowata, the farmer had displayed newfound wealth. When asked about his sudden prosperity, he'd been unable to resist a brag. He had a generous friend, one of the notorious Wild Bunch. Cimarron Tom Yantis.

Shortly before sundown, Tilghman and Thomas made camp along the creek. Though they both wore mackinaws, the night promised to be cold, and they selected a sheltered spot in a grove of trees. After tethering their horses, Tilghman began dressing a rabbit he'd shot along the trail. Thomas gathered wood, built a fire, and soon had a coffeepot perking. They traveled light, but there was always room for a small pot and a bag of coffee beans in their saddlebags. That was one luxury neither of them were willing to forego on a manhunt.

By dusk, they were seated around the fire with steaming cups of coffee. Their saddles served as comfortable backrests, and they watched as the rabbit roasted on a spit made of green tree limbs. There was now an easy familiarity between them, borne of long days and nights on trail. Neither of them was given to small talk, nor were they bothered by silence. Any conversation generally centered on their work.

"Funny," Thomas said in a musing tone. "You bust your ass chasing all over creation and getting nowhere. Then you ask a simple question and presto! You're on the right track."

Tilghman sipped coffee, warming his hands on the metal cup. "Guess it all depends on who's being asked the question. Not many Cherokees would give a straight answer."

"Cherokees, Choctaws, they're all the same. I must've spent a year in the Nations before anybody would talk to me. They just don't cotton to white men—lawmen especially."

"How'd you finally get on their good side? The ones that give you leads?"

"Wasn't easy," Thomas allowed. "Took time to get 'em to trust me. 'Course, there's damn few that give a hoot in hell about lawbreakers. Most figure it's just white man's business."

"Understandable," Tilghman said. "Leastways if you look at it from their standpoint. Whites aren't known for giving Indians a square deal."

"Christ, tell me about it! After all these years, there's still not more than a handful that'll part with information."

"Well, we got it today, Heck. I reckon that's what counts."

According to their source, the farm they sought was another three or four miles upstream. They planned to camp overnight and be on the trail before first light. Years of experience had taught them that dark nights were a dangerous time to confront men with guns. Dawn was the better time, when men's heads were fuzzed with sleep. That was their plan for tomorrow.

"Liable to be fireworks," Thomas said grimly. "Yantis

has a reputation as a hardcase. I doubt he'll go peace-able."

"Let's hope otherwise," Tilghman replied. "Dead men don't tell tales."

"You talkin' about Doolin?"

Tilghman nodded. "We need to take Yantis alive. He likely knows where Doolin's holed up."

Thomas snorted. "But will the scutter talk, or even surrender? I'd say he's more likely to fight."

There was no arguing the point. Despite the efforts of federal marshals, Oklahoma Territory remained a spawning ground for outlaws. The men who rode the owlhoot refused to acknowledge either the rights of the people or the might of the law. Over the line, in Indian Territory, the deadly game of hide-and-seek raged on unabated. The marshals held their own, generally killing more than they captured since the wanted men seldom surrendered without a fight. Yet there were scores of fledgling badmen waiting to fill the boots of every out-law killed. Across the blackjack-studded hills of the Nations there was no end in sight.

"All the same," Tilghman said now, "Doolin's the prize catch. Let's try to take Yantis alive."

"No harm in tryin'," Thomas conceded. "Just don't get yourself killed in the bargain. Or me either."

On that note they fell silent. The rabbit, already split down the backbone, was removed from the spit. Fairly tender, dripping with succulent juices, the meat satisfied their hunger. After a final cup of coffee, the fire was built up against the chill night's wind. Then, their thoughts on tomorrow, they crawled into their bedrolls.

No more was said about Tom Yantis.

A faint streak of silver touched the eastern sky. The cabin stood in a clearing with a ramshackle shed and a corral off to one side. Beyond, in a large field, withered corn stalks bent beneath the morning frost. A tendril of smoke drifted skyward from the cabin chimney.

The lawmen waited in a stand of trees along the creek. Their horses were securely tied in a similar grove some hundred yards downstream. On foot, they had made their way along the north bank and taken a position opposite the front door of the cabin. They waited now for full dawn.

Tilghman carried a Winchester .44–.40 saddle carbine with a shell in the chamber. Thomas was armed with a 10-gauge double-barrel shotgun loaded with buckshot. Though both men packed pistols, experience dictated that a long-gun served better in the event of trouble. Given a choice, no man resorted to a pistol in a gunfight.

The sky slowly paled into full light. Neither of them spoke, for their plan was already in place. Thomas stepped clear of the trees, his shotgun extended, and advanced toward the cabin. Tilghman skirted the clearing, moving toward the shed, to cover the rear of the cabin. Three horses stood hip-shot in the corral, eyeing him warily as he approached. One of them suddenly snorted, and the other two took alarm. Hooves clattering on the frozen ground, they bolted to the opposite side of the corral.

The noise was like a drumbeat in the still air. From inside the cabin someone yelled, and the sound of feet on plank floors was plainly heard. Tilghman ducked behind the shed, thumbed the hammer on his carbine. Out front, Thomas threw the shotgun to his shoulder.

"Tom Yantis!" he shouted. "Federal marshals. Give yourself up!"

The back door burst open. A man in long johns and mule-eared boots rushed outside. He was carrying a cocked pistol in one hand and his pants in the other. As he turned toward the corral, he spotted Tilghman and abruptly stopped. His eyes were wide with fear.

"Hold it!" Tilghman ordered. "Drop the gun!"

Yantis reacted as though galvanized by the command. He snapped off a shot which thunked into boards of the shed. Thomas stepped around the corner of the house as Tilghman brought his Winchester to bear. The crack of the carbine mingled with the roar of the shotgun.

Struck from the front and the side, Yantis stumbled away in a nerveless dance. His long johns went red with blood and the pistol dropped from his hand. Then, arms flailing, he pitched to the ground.

Thomas advanced slowly, covering the rear door with his shotgun. He saw the Cherokee farmer dart a look through the open door, then slam it shut. Tilghman walked forward and knelt beside the fallen outlaw. He was amazed to find Yantis conscious, still alive.

"Tom," he said urgently. "Can you hear me?"

"Sonovabitch, you done killed me."

"Where's Doolin, Tom? Go out with a clear conscience. Tell me where to find Doolin."

Yantis smiled. "Go to hell."

Wet bubbles frothed his mouth with blood. The smile slipped, then vanished, and his eyes went blank. One boot wiggled in a spasm of death.

Thomas came closer. "What'd he say, Bill?"

"Told me to go to hell."

"Stupid bastard! Dumb as a goddamn rock. They all are!"

"Yeah, but he went out like a man, Heck. Leastways according to his lights."

"What d'you mean?"

"He died with his boots on."

Tilghman climbed to his feet. He stared down at the body, thoughtful a moment. Then he turned, headed back toward the creek. His features were solemn.

So much for taking Tom Yantis alive.

CHAPTER 9

The sky was dull as pewter. Tilghman studied the western horizon, where roiling clouds screened a late afternoon sun. There was a crisp smell in the air, and with Christmas only two days away, he wondered when it would snow. He hoped it would hold off until after tonight.

The Methodist Church in Chandler was holding a tree-decorating party. There would be food and fruit punch and carols to launch the Christmas season in proper style. Zoe had invited him to escort her to the party, even though he was a backslider where church was concerned. She jokingly threatened to bring him back into the fold.

Tilghman was still somewhat astounded by his own behavior. As he drove a buckboard toward the Stratton ranch, he calculated that he'd known Zoe not quite three months. In that time, he'd turned from a mature, sober-minded man to a moonstruck schoolboy. Or at least, in private moments, that's how he sometimes thought of himself. A man addled by a bewitching young woman.

Up ahead, in the deepening twilight, he saw the glow of lamps from the Stratton house. The ranch was situated along the banks of Quapaw Creek, with a sprawling log house overlooking the stream. To the rear of the house, there was a log barn with a corral attached to one side. The barn had stalls for ten horses and a milch cow, with cleared ground to the north for further expansion. There was a solid look of permanence about the place.

Outside the house, Tilghman reined his team to a halt. He stepped down, snapping a lead rope onto one horse's bridle, and left the team tied to a hitch rack. The air was sharp and brittle, and as he walked toward the house, it occurred to him that there was little question of a white Christmas. He crossed the porch and rapped lightly on the door. From inside, he heard the sound of footsteps.

Amos Stratton opened the door. "Good evening, Bill." He motioned inside. "Come in out of the cold."

"Evening, Amos." Tilghman stepped through the door, removing his hat. "Looks like we'll get snow before long."

"I would judge tomorrow at the latest."

Stratton led him into the parlor. By now they were on a first-name basis, though Tilghman was never comfortable in the man's presence. There was a forced cordiality between them, and he sensed that Stratton somehow disapproved of him. Nothing spoken, but nonetheless there.

A stack of logs blazed in the fireplace. Tilghman shrugged out of his greatcoat and hooked it on a coatrack beside the door. As he entered the parlor, Stratton waved to a sofa.

"Have a seat," he said. "Zoe will be along directly. She's still getting ready."

"Fire feels good tonight."

"Yes, you'll have a cold ride into town."

Tilghman took a seat on the sofa. Stratton dropped into an easy chair and began loading a pipe. Watching him, Tilghman thought he had the look of a lonely man.

Zoe's mother had died several years ago, and Stratton, who owned a farm in Missouri at the time, had taken it hard. Later, after selling the farm, he'd decided to join the Land Rush and homestead land in Oklahoma Territory. From his manner, he had yet to escape the ghosts of his past.

Stratton struck a match, lighting his pipe. He puffed a wad of smoke and tossed the match into the fireplace. "How're things?" he said distantly. "Your horses making out all right?"

"Ask me come spring," Tilghman said. "I'm hoping Steeldust sired some fast-steppers."

"Never understood what interests you about racehorses."

"Lots of money to be made with racing. Not bragging, but I did pretty good with that operation over in Guthrie."

"Saddle stock," Stratton announced. "There's always a market for saddle horses. Good business, solid and dependable."

"That why you got into it?"

"Farmed most of my life and little to show for it. Horses look to me to have a brighter future. Saddle horses, anyhow."

"Yeah, you're right," Tilghman agreed. "I see racing as a sideline with big potential. The other part of my breeding is for ranch stock, good cow ponies. That's steady business."

A silence fell between them. Stratton stared off into the fire, puffing his pipe. Tilghman got the impression that the other man was trying to pick an argument. But to what purpose, or for what reason, was unclear. At length, Stratton looked around.

"What's new with the Wild Bunch?"

"Not a whole lot," Tilghman admitted. "Seems like they've gone to ground."

"You think they've quit the territory?"

"Doolin's not the type to quit and run. Not from what I've heard, anyway. I tend to doubt we've seen the last of him."

Stratton grunted. "So why's he laying low?"

"One guess is as good as another. I reckon only Doolin knows the answer."

For all their determination, the federal marshals had been singularly unsuccessful in running Doolin to earth. The gangleader and his Wild Bunch seemingly had vanished into thin air. Nearly two months had passed with no robberies, and no reported sightings of Doolin or his men. Nor were the informants of Heck Thomas able to turn up a lead in the Nations. Despite rewards now totaling ten thousand dollars, there was nothing but silence. No one knew anything.

Tilghman suspected that it was somehow tied to the death of Tom Yantis. The killing might well have convinced Doolin and his gang to take a breather. Or for that matter, what with the cold and snow, the Wild Bunch might simply have taken the winter off. They had money in their pockets from the last bank holdup, and they could easily have decided on a holiday. For all anyone knew, they were in New Orleans or St. Louis having the time of their lives. After their money ran out and the manhunt subsided, they could return to work. There was always another train to rob.

In the meantime, Tilghman had kept himself occupied with the ranch and the routine tedium of a lawman. While liquor was legal in the territory, its sale was restricted to white men. Federal law made it a felony to sell alcoholic spirits of any variety to an Indian. The prohibition made for a brisk business in Oklahoma Territory, particularly along the borders of the Creek and Seminole nations. Over the past month Tilghman had arrested eight whiskey peddlers and confiscated their wares. All of them had been treated to a swift trial, and convicted.

Still, Tilghman had little interest in apprehending backwoods whiskey smugglers. He was convinced Doolin would resurface, and he stayed on because he'd given his word to Heck Thomas. Beyond that, he saw a pattern of lawlessness developing in Oklahoma Territory. Before the land runs, Texas ranchers had leased great tracts of grazeland from various tribes. But with settlement, farms had displaced the cattle spreads, and hundreds of cowhands were thrown out of work. Left to idle in saloons and contemplate the menace of railroads and sodbusters, many felt they had been dealt a low blow. They righted this seeming injustice by turning to an occupation with short working hours and incomparable wages. They became outlaws.

Just in the past week, working with the county sheriff, Tilghman had caught three former cowhands turned horse thieves. Given different circumstances, or bolder spirits, they could have easily robbed a bank. One crime led to another, and in the end, any man who rode the owlhoot was capable of killing to avoid a stretch in prison. The more he thought about it, the more Tilghman realized that it wasn't altogether his word to Heck Thomas that kept him on the job. Though he wouldn't admit it to anyone, he'd grudgingly come to accept what Neal Brown and other friends had told him for many years. He had the calling to be a lawman.

Stratton's voice intruded on his woolgathering. "Zoe tells me you've been married before."

"Yeah, I was," Tilghman said without inflection. "My wife died last year. Influenza."

"Sorry to hear it." Stratton stared at him, puffing on his pipe. "You looking to get married again?"

Tilghman shrugged it off. "I haven't given it much thought."

"High time, then," Stratton said in a hard voice. "A man your age ought not to toy with the affections of a young girl."

"A man my age?"

"Zoe tells me you're thirty-six. She's barely twenty, and the way I figure, that's a sight of difference. Aren't you a little old for her?"

Tilghman saw where the argument lay now. By all appearances, he and Stratton were separated in age by not more than ten years. Stratton clearly thought of him as an older man, someone in his own generation. Far too old for his daughter.

"I'm younger than I look," Tilghman said in an off-hand manner. "And I don't have any wrong intentions toward Zoe. You can rest easy on that score."

"Never said otherwise," Stratton muttered. "What I'm saying is, she hasn't so much as looked at another man since you came on the scene. Don't you think she deserves a man her own age?"

"I think that's for Zoe to decide. She's free to see whoever she wants."

"Not as long as you're around," Stratton said harshly. "She's got stardust in her eyes. Any fool can see that."

"Look, I'm not trying—"

"Good evening." Zoe suddenly swept through the entrance to the parlor. "Did I interrupt something?"

"No, no," Stratton said hurriedly. He rose, moving to the fireplace, and knocked the dottle from his pipe. "We were just debating the merits of racehorses versus saddle stock."

She looked at Tilghman. "Believe it or not," she said brightly, "I'm finally ready. Shall we go?"

"You bet." Tilghman walked to the door, gathering his hat and greatcoat. "Nice talking with you, Amos."

"You too, Bill," Stratton said amiably. "We'll have to do it again."

Zoe kissed her father good night while Tilghman shrugged into his coat. He helped her into a long cape with a fur-trimmed hood and they went through the door. Outside, he got her settled in the backboard and draped a woolen blanket over her lap for added warmth. Then he unhitched the horses and climbed into the driver's seat. He popped the reins.

"Well now," he said, glancing at her. "You're looking mighty pretty tonight."

She sniffed. "Don't try to pretty-please me, Bill Tilghman. What were you and father talking about?"

"Like he told you—"

"Honestly! You must think I'm a little scatterbrain. I want to know what you were arguing about—right now!"

Tilghman was tempted to kiss her. She was full of spirit and spunk, and he could imagine her eyes flashing green in the dark night. There was a vibrancy about her so compelling that he felt captivated all over again. He chuckled softly.

"You want the truth?"

"Yes, I do! And with no soft-soap, Mr. Tilghman."

"You won't tell him I told, will you?"

"Cross my heart," she said pertly. "So what did he say?"

"Well, in a nutshell—" Tilghman watched her out of the corner of his eye. "Your pa thinks I'm too old for you."

"Does he indeed?" she said in a exasperated tone. "And what did you say?"

"I told him I'm younger than I look."

"Of course you are!"

Tilghman suppressed a smile. "And that I have no improper intentions toward you."

"You didn't!" Her eyes danced with merriment. "You actually said that to him?"

"Seemed like the right thing at the time. What with you being so young and innocent, and all."

"Oh, fudge!" She dug him in the ribs with her elbow. "You're teasing me, aren't you?"

"Who, me?" Tilghman said with mock concern. "You think I'm one to step out of line?"

"Nooo," she said slowly. "But sometimes I wish you'd try—just a little."

"I'll be switched. I think you mean that."

"I never say anything I don't mean. You should know that by now."

"In that case," Tilghman prompted her, "what are you going to tell your pa?"

"I'm going to tell him to mind his own business. I'll decide who's too old and who isn't."

"So where does that leave me?"

"Just exactly where you belong."

She scooted closer, throwing the blanket over his lap as well. She put her arm through his, hugging him, and nestled her head against his shoulder. Then, closer still, she uttered a low, throaty laugh.

"Doesn't that feel about right?"

Tilghman smiled. "I think it's Christmas already."

The cold forgotten, they drove toward town.

CHAPTER 10

The corner of Harrison and Second was the liveliest spot in Guthrie. Chambers for the territorial legislature occupied the upper story of the International Building, which was located on the southeast corner. Across the street was the Palace Hotel, where the politicians made their home away from home when the legislature was in session.

The Reaves Brothers Casino, fanciest sporting emporium in the territory, stood three stories high on the northwest corner. Directly opposite was the Blue Bell Saloon, a most democratic bucket of gore catering to anyone with the price of a drink. A hangout for the town's rougher element, it was known by such aphorisms as the Slaughterhouse and the Butcher Shop.

On any given night the intersection was a beehive of activity. The hotel was elegantly posh, the casino was an orderly temple of vice, and the saloon was a riotous circus of mayhem. Businessmen and gamblers, hardcases and politicians, whores and barflies came there in a sweaty pursuit of the fast life.

Tilghman dismounted outside the hotel early that evening. A groom took his horse to a stable around the corner and he entered the hotel with his warbag. After registering, he went to his room and sponged off trail dust in the washbasin. Then, downstairs again, he treated himself to a steak dinner in the dining room. By eight o'clock he was headed uptown.

A few minutes later he knocked on the door of Heck Thomas's home. When Thomas opened the door, his face creased with surprise. "Bill!" he said, grinning. "Where'd you come from?"

"Just rode in," Tilghman said. "Took a room down at the Palace."

"Well, don't stand there." Thomas turned, shouting to his wife, "Hey, Dottie, look who's here."

Dorothy Thomas was a plain woman with an engaging manner. She greeted Tilghman warmly and served coffee after the men were seated in the parlor. Then, aware that Tilghman's visit was business rather than social, she excused herself. Thomas drained his coffee cup.

"I take it you're here for the big powwow tomorrow?" Tilghman nodded. "Got my invite yesterday."

"Helluva note," Thomas observed. "Just tied a can to Grimes's tail. He deserved better."

"That's politics, Heck. One day here, the next day gone."

Tilghman's remark went to the heart of the matter. The new year had gotten off to an unsettling start when President Benjamin Harrison reaffirmed the old adage that politics does indeed make for strange bedfellows. He opened 1890 with sweeping changes in the political hierarchy of Oklahoma Territory. The changes were the result of widespread criticism about what the newspapers termed the "anarchy of outlawism." Factions in Congress declared it a national disgrace.

Until statehood was granted, a territory was at the mercy of the federal government. The president, by the stroke of a pen, could alter virtually any aspect of territorial affairs. Which was precisely what President Harrison had done shortly after the first of the year. In one surgical stroke, after weighing the counsel of his advisors, he removed the Republicans and replaced them with Democrats.

Heading the list was Governor George Steele. He was unceremoniously dumped, and overnight, William Renfrow, a banker from the town of Norman, was sworn in as the new governor. Political wags were quick to note that he had been responsible for naming a street in the territorial capital after President Harrison. Apart from the governor, the shakeup extended to the territorial supreme court as well as district courts throughout Oklahoma. Over twenty political appointees fell before the axe.

For Tilghman, the general upheaval had only passing interest. He studiously avoided the political arena, and he held most politicians in low regard. Yet the U.S. marshal, who had served with distinction, had ultimately won his respect. Unlike most appointees, who saw themselves as administrators, Walt Grimes had often accompanied his deputies into the field, and traded shots with outlaws. Still, despite his efforts to establish law and order, he belonged to the wrong political party. He'd been swept out with the other Republicans.

The man who replaced him was Evett Nix, a staunch Democrat. Though he had no law enforcement experience, Nix was a prominent figure in Guthrie political circles. A former Kentuckian, he had joined the first land rush, and was a partner in the town's leading wholesale grocery concern. Quoted widely in the newspapers, he had vowed to rid Oklahoma Territory of its outlaw element. Upon appointment as U.S. marshal, he had requested authorization for a hundred deputies, five times the number currently serving. If nothing else, his brash demands kept his name in the headlines.

On January 8, the day after Nix's appointment, Tilghman received a tersely worded summons. He was to report to the marshal's office in Guthrie on the morning of January 10. The message gave no reason as to the purpose of the summons, or Nix's intentions. But Tilghman, figuring it was politics as usual, had a hunch his commission would be revoked. What surprised him most was that he found the thought curiously unsettling, not at all to his liking. He'd somehow experienced a turnaround during his months on the trail with Heck Thomas. He wanted to stay on as a deputy.

Tilghman departed the afternoon before the meeting. There was no train service between Chandler and Guthrie, though the stagecoach line made twice-daily stops. Still, he had no fondness for crowded coaches, and the inevitable conversations that developed with other passengers. He decided to travel on horseback, which gave him time to further ponder the situation. The ranch, as was customary during his absences on law business, was left under the care of Neal Brown. As he rode out, it occurred to him that his old friend was more essential than ever to the operation. Except for Brown, he could never have signed on as a marshal.

Outside Chandler, on the road to Guthrie, he'd been struck by a thought that kindled mixed emotions. Should he be dismissed as a deputy, that would allow him far more time to spend with Zoe. Since Christmas, he had seen her at every opportunity, and she clearly welcomed his company. Whatever she'd said to her father, Amos Stratton had never again raised the subject of their age difference. Yet, however much he wanted to be with her, he was uneasy with the idea of no more law work. The months spent tracking Doolin and the Wild Bunch had reawakened his taste for challenge. His life was somehow fuller as a lawman.

All in all, it required a fine balancing act. The ranch, and Zoe, and working as a lawman, kept him hopping like a one-legged man in a footrace. But he'd somehow come to the point that he wanted it all, the ranch and Zoe and the badge. Of course, as he pondered it now, the thought occurred that he might no longer have a problem. Evett Nix, the new U.S. marshal, might solve it for him. He could lose his badge tomorrow.

"For all we know," Thomas said, as though reading his mind, "we could be out of a job ourselves."

"Have you talked to Nix?"

"Not to speak of," Thomas replied. "Went by the office the day he took over. We shook hands and danced around the mulberry bush. He told me to sit tight until the meeting tomorrow."

"That's it?" Tilghman said. "No clue about what he intends?"

"Whatever it is, he wasn't talkin'."

"How'd you size him up?"

Thomas frowned. "Way I figure it, he's a crossbreed. Half go-get-'em businessman and half politician. Likeable enough, but a quick, no-nonsense way about him."

"What's the word around town?" Tilghman asked. "Does he aim to use the marshal's office as a stepping-stone to something bigger?"

"Haven't heard anything, but it wouldn't come as no shock. He's like fleas on a dog with the bigwig Democrats."

Tilghman knuckled his mustache. "So we're betwixt and between until tomorrow. Nothing to go on."

"Looks that way," Thomas grumped. "Just a cog in the wheel."

"What about Chris Madsen? Hear anything about him?"

"Yeah, he rode in late this afternoon. Sat where you're sittin' and asked the same questions. I had no more answers then than I do now."

Tilghman caught the concern in his voice. "What will you do if Nix turns us out to pasture?"

Thomas suddenly laughed. "Bill, I've been a lawdog most of my life. Never yet had a problem finding another badge."

"All the same, we started out to catch Doolin. I hate to leave a job undone."

"You've shore swung around, haven't you?"

"How's that?"

Thomas grinned. "Hell's bells, I had to twist your arm to sign you on. Now, you're worried it won't last. Go ahead and tell me I'm wrong."

"You're a bad influence," Tilghman said with a slow smile. "Knew it the day I met you."

"Howsomever, we're alike in one way, my friend."

"What way is that?"

"We feel naked without a badge—don't we?"

Their eyes locked in a moment of silent communion. Then, slowly, Tilghman nodded.

The following morning, at eight o'clock sharp, Thomas, Madsen, and Tilghman trooped into the U.S. marshal's office. To their amazement, they were the only ones there. None of the other deputies had been summoned.

Evett Nix was a stocky man, on the sundown side of forty. His manner was brusque and businesslike, his eyes penetrating and shrewd. He greeted them with a perfunctory handshake and asked them to be seated. Then, wasting no time, he went straight to the point.

"First things first," he said. "All the deputies on the roster still have a job. That includes you three."

A sense of tension seemed to melt from the room. He waited a moment, allowing them to absorb the news, then went on. "Walt Grimes lost his job for two reasons, gentlemen. One, which amounts to bad luck, he was a Republican. And second, which was a matter of poor timing, he failed to bring Bill Doolin to justice."

Again, he paused, awaiting a reaction. When none of the men spoke, he continued. "One day, I may lose this job because I'm a Democrat. But, gentlemen—" He stopped, looked each of them directly in the eye. "I assure you I will not be turned out because of some half-assed desperado. *Bill Doolin will be caught.*"

Nix let the words hang in the air. He had been standing during the entire speech, and now he took a seat behind his desk. He steepled his fingers into a church, staring at them.

"Mr. Thomas. Mr. Tilghman. In your opinion, why is Doolin still on the loose?"

Thomas and Tilghman exchanged a look. After a moment, Tilghman took the lead. "You'll recollect that Jesse James was betrayed and killed, but never caught. That's because he adopted the tactics of Quantrill, the Civil War guerrilla. Doolin operates the same way."

"Hit and run," Thomas added. "Then scatter and go to ground. Like Bill says, he's real slippery."

"I agree," Nix said, surprising them. "So we're going to increase the heat on Doolin. As of today"—he nodded pointedly to Chris Madsen—"you three are assigned to the Wild Bunch."

Tilghman looked uncomfortable. "Are we being transferred?"

"No," Nix said. "You'll stay in Chandler. Mr. Madsen remains in El Reno. And Mr. Thomas here in Guthrie. But starting now, you forget whiskey smugglers and other small-timers. Your efforts will be solely directed to Bill Doolin."

"Amen to that," Thomas said approvingly. "Do we work separately or as a team?"

"Do whatever the situation demands. Just get the job done quickly. Understood?"

Without waiting for a response, he looked at Tilghman. "An unsigned letter arrived the day I took office. Are you familiar with the town of Ingalls?"

"Never been there," Tilghman said. "It's about a half day's ride north of Chandler."

"According to the letter, Doolin has a hideout somewhere around Ingalls. I want you to scout it out on the quiet. Any questions?"

There were no questions. Nix shook their hands and the three lawmen walked to the door. In the hallway, Tilghman looked first at Madsen and then at Thomas. His expression was quizzical.

"What do you think, Heck?"

"Boys, I think we've got ourselves a marshal. Hooray and hallelujah."

CHAPTER 11

Three days later Tilghman rode into Ingalls. He wore rough range clothing and he was posing as a horse trader. The name he'd adopted was Jack Curry.

Tilghman had given considerable thought to the assignment. He was working on the premise that the information received in the anonymous letter was correct. If so, then Doolin was hiding out in the vicinity of Ingalls, betrayed by someone for reasons as yet unknown. Outlaws were oftentimes brought down by betrayal rather than good detective work.

Still, the letter itself was just a starting point. To pinpoint the location of Doolin's hideout would require detective work. So Tilghman had decided to operate undercover, adopting a disguise. In small towns, particularly one harboring a fugitive, any stranger was suspect. But horse traders, who commonly traveled the backcountry, were less suspect than most. Jack Curry might get someone to talk.

Ingalls was about what Tilghman had expected. The main street was less than a quarter mile long, with frame structures wedged together in a small business district. There were the usual shops and stores, with a saloon situated across from a two-story hotel. At the far end of the street, a livery stable was separated from the other buildings. Houses were randomly scattered across the land surrounding the business district. From all appearances, the population was less than four hundred people.

Tilghman tried to think like the man he hunted. From Doolin's standpoint, there was a certain warped logic in choosing Ingalls as a hideout. The town was located close to the Kansas border, and Doolin could easily stop off there after raids across the state line. Moreover, Guthrie was only a half day's ride to the west; no one would expect the Wild Bunch leader to hole up so near the territorial capital. With the rest of the gang scattered throughout the Nations, Ingalls was the last place anyone would look for Doolin. In many ways, it was a perfect hideout.

Tilghman reined to a halt outside the saloon. A recent snowfall had melted off, and the street was thick with mud. As he stepped down from the saddle, he was aware of the scrutiny of people along the boardwalks. Word spread quickly in a small town, and he warned himself not to overplay his hand. One misstep, particularly among people friendly to Doolin, and he would be pegged as a lawman. He took his time, acting the casual traveler, and loosened the cinch to give his horse a breather. Then, stamping mud from his boots, he entered the saloon.

The interior was bathed in sunlight from the front windows. Along one wall was the bar, and tables and chairs were arranged along the opposite wall. Halfway down the bar, in the middle of the room, a large potbellied stove glowed with heat. A lone customer stood with one foot hooked over the brass rail, staring into a whiskey glass. The barkeep, sporting a handlebar mustache, was wiping down the counter. His expression was neutral.

"Help you?"

"Gimme a beer," Tilghman said. "Little early for the hard stuff."

"Says you," the customer retorted in a slurred voice. "Ain't never no bad time for a drink."

"No offense, mister. Just makin' conversation."

Tilghman removed his mackinaw and draped it over the counter. The bartender filled a schooner from the tap, then walked back and placed it in front of Tilghman. Leaning closer, he cut his eyes at the other customer. He spoke in a muffled voice.

"Don't pay him no mind. He's got a snootful."

"Likes his liquor, does he?"

"Every town's got a barfly. He's ours."

"Know what you mean," Tilghman said. "In my business, I see lots of towns. They're all the same."

"What line you in?"

"Horse trader." Tilghman stuck out his hand. "Name's Jack Curry."

"Joe Harmon." The barkeep accepted his handshake. "You from hereabouts?"

"Here, there, and everywhere. I buy stock for the army."

"Army payin' good these days?"

"Top dollar." Tilghman sipped beer, wiped foam off his mustache. "Government buys the best for its soldier boys."

Harmon nodded. "That what brings you to Ingalls?"

"Heard there were some good size ranches around these parts. Thought I'd have a looksee."

"Yeah, there's some with horses."

"Anybody special?" Tilghman inquired. "I'm lookin' for top-notch stock."

Harmon considered a moment. "You might try the Dunn brothers. Got a spread out on Council Creek."

"Yeah, you do that," the barfly crowed, chortling a drunken laugh. "Careful of their visitor, though. He don't cotton to strangers."

"What visitor's that?"

"Why, the big man hisself—"

"Close your trap!" Harmon thundered. "Or somebody'll close it for you."

"Hell, Joe, I ain't tellin' tales outta school. Everybody in town knows."

"You heard me, you stupid son-of-a-bitch. Button your lip!"

"Aww, for chrissakes."

The man wobbled away with his whiskey glass, dropping into a chair at one of the tables. Harmon stared at him angrily, then let out a long sigh. He shook his head, glancing at Tilghman.

"Pay him no mind. Just a drunk runnin' off at the mouth."

"None of my business," Tilghman said pleasantly. "Sounded like hot air to me."

"Bastard's full of it, all right."

"Let's get back to horses. You were tellin' me about—what'd you say—the Dunn brothers?"

Harmon appeared troubled. He wrestled with it a moment, then shrugged. "Bee and George, they're brothers. Always got horses for sale. Ask for either one."

Tilghman got directions while he finished his beer. After paying for the drink, he gathered his mackinaw and headed for the door. The barkeep's display of temper convinced him that he'd struck a nerve. Even more so from the barfly's slip of the tongue. The Dunn brothers were hiding someone.

Outside, Tilghman surveyed the street. Across the way he saw a barber shop, and decided to probe a bit further. A few minutes later he was seated in the barber's chair, once again relating his business as a horse trader. The barber was a loquacious man who admired the sound of his own voice. His shop, just as Tilghman had suspected, was a clearing house for the town's gossip.

"Yessir," the barber said, snipping away with his scissors. "The Dunn boys pride themselves on their horses. You ought to do right well."

"Guess they made the run like everybody else?"

"Ummm." The scissors stopped, and the barber's voice dropped to a confidential tone. "Don't tell 'em I told you, but they were Sooners. Got themselves the best piece of land on Council Creek."

"Mum's the word with me," Tilghman promised. "Curious you mention it, though. I heard something over in the saloon that's hard to believe."

"Oh, what's that?"

"Well, there was this drunk—"

"Lon Anderson, a first-rate boozehound!"

"Never caught his name," Tilghman went on. "Anyway, he says the Dunns are hidin' that outlaw, Bill Doolin. Damn hard to believe."

The barber glanced around the empty shop, as though he might be overheard. "Not exactly a secret," he said softly. "Everyone in town has known about it for months."

"You're joshin' me!"

"No, it's the truth. Way I hear it, Doolin's sweet on Edith Ellsworth. The postmaster's daughter."

Tilghman looked worried. "Maybe I ought not to pay a call on the Dunns. I'd sure hate to run across Bill Doolin in the flesh."

"Well—" the barber started snipping again. "So I'm told, he's not there now. Took off a couple of days ago."

"By golly, for an outlaw, he's got damn few secrets. Seems a mite strange."

"The Ellsworth girl tells her friends, and they tell their friends, and word gets around. Not many secrets in a small town."

"And nobody's turned him into the law?"

The scissors stopped. "I wouldn't risk my life against him and his Wild Bunch. Would you?"

"Nosiree," Tilghman said, wagging his head. "Let him rob all the banks and trains he wants. Live and let live, that's my motto."

"Exactly right, Mr. Curry. Why borrow trouble?"

Early that afternoon Tilghman reined to a halt on Council Creek. He was two miles southeast of Ingalls, and ahead, beyond a bend in the stream, lay the Dunn brothers' ranch. Dismounting, he took a folding telescope from his saddlebags and left his horse tied in a grove of trees. He walked forward, taking cover in the treeline.

Extending the spyglass, he slowly studied the ranch compound. The main house was a log and frame structure, situated at the bottom of a low knoll. A short distance away was a large corral with some thirty head of horses standing hip-shot in the corral. East of the house a storm cellar had been dug in the hillside and roofed with heavy timber. Smoke funneled from the house chimney, indicating it was occupied. But no one was in sight.

After a thorough inspection, he collapsed the spyglass. Based on the barber's information, he hadn't expected to spot Bill Doolin. Still, he'd wanted to scout the lay of the land, perhaps have a word with the Dunns about horses. But now, having seen it, he decided there was no point in pushing his luck. Better to return another day, when he was certain that the gangleader was there. The idea was to capture Doolin, not put him on guard.

On the way back to town, Tilghman sorted through the pieces. There was no reason to disbelieve a talkative drunk or a gossipy barber. In fact, from their reactions as well as their words, there was good reason to believe they were telling the truth. All of which would explain where Doolin had spent the winter months, and why. Even outlaws had a personal life, and everything indicated that Doolin was serious about the Ellsworth girl. The masterstroke was that no one would have looked for Doolin so close to Guthrie. He'd fooled them all.

Yet one piece of the puzzle was still to be found. The letter to the U.S. marshal left no doubt that someone had a score to settle with Doolin. A grudge so strong, in fact, that someone had betrayed him to the authorities. Whoever it was preferred to remain anonymous rather than risk death. But the letter had been postmarked from Ingalls. . . .

Tilghman played a hunch. Earlier that day, he'd noticed a post office sign hanging over the door outside the general store. A bitter wind blew in from the north as he dismounted before the store and looped the reins around a hitch rack. Inside, a woman waited while a man behind the counter made change for her purchases. She was the only customer in the store.

A cage at the rear fronted a space that served as the post office. Tilghman walked to the cage window and halted, leaning on the counter. The storekeeper was in his early forties, a heavyset man with thinning hair and wire spectacles hooked over the bridge of his nose. When the woman departed with her parcels, he turned and moved toward the rear. He nodded to Tilghman.

"Afternoon."

"Howdy," Tilghman said. "Got anything general delivery for Jack Curry?"

The storekeeper glanced at a rack of mailboxes on the wall. "Sorry," he said. "Nothing for general delivery at all."

"Too bad." Tilghman looked at him through the cage. "You the postmaster?"

"John Ellsworth," the man said, nodding. "I take it you're Mr. Curry."

"That's me," Tilghman said. "Just got to town today, and you know—I heard the darnedest thing."

"What might that be?"

"Heard your daughter's keeping steady company with Bill Doolin."

Ellsworth's face blanched. His jowls rippled as he shook his head. "You heard wrong, Mr. Curry."

"Think not," Tilghman corrected him. "Not after that letter you sent to the U.S. marshal."

Ellsworth blinked, his features suddenly gone pasty. "I don't know what you're talking about."

The startled reaction was all Tilghman needed. He now had the answer as to who had written the letter. A respectable storekeeper, trying to protect his daughter, had silently betrayed an outlaw. He nodded to Ellsworth, then walked toward the door.

"Give my regards to Doolin next time he calls on your daughter."

CHAPTER 12

The plains of western Kansas were blanketed with light snow. Overnight the skies had cleared and a warm morning sun was slowly melting the snowfall. Wet and glistening, a ribbon of steel, the Santa Fe tracks stretched onward to the horizon.

The California Express hurtled through the town of Cimarron. Coupled to the rear of the engine and the tender were an express car and five passenger coaches. As the locomotive sped past the small depot, the engineer tooted his whistle. The train's final destination was Los Angeles.

A mile west of town, on a dogleg curve, a tree had been felled across the tracks. The engineer set the brakes, wheels grinding on steel rails, and the train jarred to a screeching halt. The sudden jolt caught the passengers unawares, and there was a moment of pandemonium in the coaches. Luggage went flying from the overhead racks as women screamed and men cursed.

Then, suddenly, a collective hush fell over the coaches. From under the bridge where trees bordered the river, a gang of riders burst out of the woods. Four men rode directly to the express car, pouring a volley of shots through the door. Another man, his pistol drawn, jumped from his horse to the steps of the locomotive.

The engineer and his fireman dutifully raised their hands.

The three remaining gang members, spurring their horses hard, charged up and down the track bed. Their pistols were cocked and pointed at the passengers, who stared open-mouthed through the coach windows. No shots were fired, but their menacing attitude and tough appearance made the message all too clear. Anyone who resisted or attempted to flee the train would be killed.

The threat made eminent good sense to the passengers. Like most railroads, the Santa Fe was not revered by the public. For thirty years, Eastern Robber Barons had plundered the West on land grants and freight rates. A holdup, according to common wisdom, was a matter between the railroad and the bandits. Only a fool would risk his life to thwart a robbery. And there were no fools aboard today.

From the coaches, the passengers had a ringside seat. They watched as the four men outside the express car demonstrated their no-nonsense approach to train robbery. One of the riders produced a stick of dynamite and held the fuse only inches away from the tip of a lighted cigar. Another rider, whose commanding presence pegged him as the gangleader, gigged his horse onto the road bed. His voice raised in a shout, he informed the express guards that they had a choice.

"Open the door or get blown to kingdom come!"

The guards, much like the passengers, were unwilling to die for the Santa Fe. The door quickly slid open and they tossed their pistols onto the ground. Three of the robbers dismounted and clambered inside the express car. The leader, positioned outside the car, directed the operation from aboard his horse. His tone had the ring of authority, brusque and demanding. His attitude was that of a man accustomed to being obeyed.

From start to finish, the holdup took less than five

minutes. The robbers inside the express car emerged
with mail sacks stuffed full of cash and mounted their
horses. On signal from their leader, the gang raked the
length of the train with a barrage of gunfire. The shots
were purposely placed high, but windows shattered and
wall panels splintered. As bullets ripped through the
coaches, everyone dove for the floor and prudently
stayed there. A moment later the thud of hoofbeats
drummed the earth.

Bill Doolin led his gang down the embankment at the
edge of the bridge. They disappeared into the trees and
rode single file along the river. To their rear, they heard
the train get under way and commence backing toward
the town of Cimarron. Within the hour word of the
holdup would spread across Kansas by telegraph. But
for now, there was no pursuit and they'd looted the train
without taking casualty. Their excitement erupted as
they turned south toward the state line.

"Gawddamn!" Dynamite Dick Clifton whooped. "We
pulled it off slicker 'n greased owlshit!"

"Bet your sweet ass!" Tulsa Jack Blake howled. "How
much you think we got, Bill?"

"Enough," Doolin said shortly. "Quit yellin' and keep
your mind on business. We're not out of the woods yet."

"Aw hell, Bill," Blake protested. "Don't be a spoil-
sport. We done good."

"There's time to celebrate when we cross the line.
You boys keep a sharp lookout."

Doolin set a faster pace. He understood their need to
let off steam, but his mind was fixed on eluding pursuit.
He found it impossible to unwind until they crossed the
border, split the loot, and scattered. His tireless vigilance, mixed with a healthy respect for lawmen, was the
reason he'd never been caught. Unlike most outlaws,
who viewed their profession with a degree of fatalism,
he had no intention of dying with his boots on. That was
for suckers and superstitious dimdots.

Apart from brutish courage, the men he rode with had contributed little to the gang's unblemished record. They were vengeful and reckless, superb haters, but not a mental wizard in the bunch. To a man, they gloried in their nicknames—Bitter Creek, Tulsa Jack, Dynamite Dick—devoting considerable thought to the selection of a *nom de guerre*. That was their mark in life, the prize sought by emotionally stunted men. A badge of distinction in a world that had branded them outcasts.

It took a strong man, someone with brains and nerve, to hold them in line. Doolin imposed his will by force when necessary, but more often through cunning and a steel-trap mind. There was nothing striking about his appearance, for he was lean and of average height, his skin seared by years of wind and sun. Yet he was hard and ruthless, deadly when provoked, with a certain genius for channeling the hate of others to his own ends. His manner was like that of a crafty savage.

When he'd organized the Wild Bunch, he had started with a band of congenital misfits. With leadership and discipline, he had converted them into a fierce, tightly-knit gang, and never for a moment had he let them forget that it was his savvy which kept them alive. Every job was planned in detail, and the holdups were staged with a military sense of precision. Anyone who got in the way was dispatched with businesslike efficiency, and the raids were characterized by the gang seemingly vanishing in a cloud of dust. His men looked upon him with the awe of stupefied boys watching a magician.

Today, as on other raids, Doolin's attention centered on the next step in the plan. Telegraph wires were singing and pursuit by Kansas lawmen was certain. The immediate goal was to cross the line into Oklahoma Territory, where Kansas jurisdiction ended. Even then, sheriffs and federal marshals throughout the territory would have been alerted by telegraph. But once the loot was split, and the gang scattered, the odds improved

greatly. There would be eight trails to follow instead of
one, and the law hadn't yet proved equal to the task.
Still, he relied on caution as much as guile, for there
were no old, bold outlaws. A man survived on the
owlhoot by taking nothing for granted.

He led his men toward the border.

Late the next day Doolin rode into Ingalls. He was accompanied by Jack Blake and Dick Clifton, who stared
suspiciously at passersby on the street. Outside the hotel
the men assisted him off his horse and he hobbled inside on one foot. The desk clerk nodded to them with a
sallow smile.

"Afternoon, gentlemen."

"I want a room," Doolin ordered. "Give me one on
the ground floor."

"Yessir," the clerk said. "How long will you be staying
with us?"

"Till I'm ready to leave. Let's have a key."

Doolin signed the register as John Smith and took the
key from the clerk. Then he turned to his men. "Jack,
go find the local sawbones and send him over here. After that, get the girl I told you about and bring her
along. Got it straight?"

"Sure thing, Bill."

Blake hurried out the door. Doolin, one arm around
Clifton's shoulders, limped off down the hallway. Once
inside the room he tossed his hat aside and flopped
down on the bed. A dark stain, crusted with blood, covered the arch of his left boot. He pulled a jackknife
from his pocket and flicked open the blade. He handed
it to Clifton.

"Let's get that boot cut off, Dick. Hurts like a bastard, so take it easy."

While he watched Clifton work on the boot, Doolin
silently cursed poor timing and bad luck. Yesterday, as
the gang crossed into Oklahoma Territory, they'd been

intercepted by the Beaver County sheriff and a posse. A running gunfight ensued, and a stray bullet had hit Doolin in the foot. None of the other men were wounded, though over a hundred shots had been exchanged. Finally, under cover of darkness, they had escaped the posse.

Doolin had made an on-the-spot decision. With the alarm sounded, every lawman in the territory would be on the scout. There was safety in numbers, and he'd chosen to keep the gang together. The nearest hideout was the Dunn brothers' ranch, and he had led his men eastward through the night. Some of the men already knew about the Dunn brothers, and he saw nothing to lose by taking them there. He had to get them out of sight as fast as possible.

Bee and George Dunn were of another mind. Hiding Doolin was one thing, but harboring the entire gang was a far riskier matter. Harsh words were exchanged, and the Dunns had finally agreed after being given a full share in the loot from the holdup. Doolin had left Will Dalton in charge, and departed for town with Blake and Clifton. The law knew nothing of the Dunns or his visits to Ingalls, so there was little chance of being caught out. All the more so since the townspeople could have long ago betrayed him. His affair with the Ellsworth girl was hardly a secret.

The doctor arrived first. After examining Doolin's foot, he found that the bullet was embedded on the inside of the arch. He gave Doolin a dose of laudanum to kill the pain, and then began laying out instruments. While Clifton held Doolin's foot steady, the doctor went to work with a scalpel. Doolin gritted his teeth, clutching the bedposts, his forehead beaded with sweat. At last, with the incision completed, the doctor extracted the slug with a pair of forceps. He dropped it into a johnnypot at the side of the bed.

Edith Ellsworth arrived just as the doctor finished

stitching the wound. The laudanum had taken effect, and Doolin seemed to have recovered his composure. He ordered Clifton to pay the doctor and wait in the lobby with Blake until he sent for them. The doctor promised to return in the morning and change the dressings he'd applied on Doolin's foot. Then, nodding to the girl, he followed Clifton out of the room.

The girl was nothing if not brave. She had long ago accepted the fact that the man she loved was an outlaw. He explained the events of the last twenty-four hours, and she listened without tears. She was short, somewhat plump, by no means the prettiest girl in town. But he'd treated her like a lady and often declared his intention to make an honest woman of her. There was never any question in her mind that she would stand beside him. Wounded, he needed her more than ever.

"Don't worry," Doolin said, holding her close. "I'll be as good as new before you know it."

She was silent a moment. The outlaw life frightened her, though she'd never voiced her fears before. Still, given the situation, she thought it was worth a try. She wanted a live husband.

"Bill," she said softly. "Did you mean it, all those times you told me we'd get married?"

"Why sure, I meant it." Doolin was somewhat taken aback by the question. "Why'd you bring that up now?"

"Would you quit?" she asked, beseeching him. "Would you marry me and leave this life? Start over somewhere?"

"Honey, I always intended to quit. Just as soon as I build us a stake."

"What good's a stake if you're dead? You always said the law wouldn't get you. Now, here you are shot and hurt and the law—"

"Won't happen," Doolin interrupted. "The law's not gonna get me. Don't fret yourself about it."

Tears welled up in her eyes. "I waited to tell you till I

was sure. . . ." She wiped away tears, took a deep breath. "Bill, I'm in a family way. I want a father for our baby. And I want a husband—a live husband!—not a memory."

"Godalmighty." Doolin stared at her with a foolish grin. "I'm gonna be a daddy?"

"Yes, I'm almost two months along."

"Then it's high time we got married. You go round up a preacher. Bring your ma and pa along, too."

She looked stunned. "You mean now—here?"

"Nothing else," Doolin said, laughing. "Today's our weddin' day!"

"And you'll quit?" she pressed him. "We'll go away?"

"Honey, I've got a plan, had one all along. I've been buildin' us a nest egg, a real stake."

"Bill—"

Doolin stopped her, cupped her face in his hand. "Just gimme a little time. That's all I'm askin'. Then we're headed for California."

"California?"

"Told you I had a plan. We'll leave all this behind. Build ourselves a good life out there."

She searched his eyes. "You really mean it?"

"Honest to God," Doolin promised. "You got my word on it."

"Oh, God, Bill, don't let me down."

"Honey, we're as good as on our way."

A preacher married them in a private ceremony that evening. By nightfall everyone in town knew that the Ellsworth girl and Bill Doolin were man and wife. Their wedding night was for her one of joy and lingering anguish.

She prayed he would keep his word.

CHAPTER 13

Tilghman rode into Guthrie the following afternoon. Yesterday, upon his return from Ingalls, he'd stopped off at the ranch and then spent the evening with Zoe. Had he located Doolin, he would have ridden straight through to the capital. But with Doolin gone, there was no rush to deliver his report. Today seemed soon enough.

On Division Street, he left his horse at a stable, then walked over to the Herriott Building. Upstairs, the hallway was crowded with people rushing in and out of the governor's suite. So much activity was unusual, but he didn't pause to inquire the reason. He made his way to the marshal's office and pushed through the door. Heck Thomas turned from the window with a startled look.

"Bill!" he said loudly. "Goddamn, am I glad to see you."

"What's all the excitement at the governor's office?"

"Oh, that," Thomas said dismissively. "The president's just authorized opening the Cherokee Strip. There's gonna be another land rush."

Tilghman was impressed. The Strip included the former Cherokee Outlet as well as parts of the Pawnee and Tonkawa reservations. In total, the president's proclamation opened some eight million acres to settlement.

By far the largest land rush to date, it would add more than nine thousand square miles to Oklahoma Territory.

"That's some news," Tilghman said. "Ought to draw lots of people."

"Liable to be a stampede," Thomas told him. "There's talk it'll pull a couple of hundred thousand settlers into the territory."

"Have they set a date for the opening?"

"Looks to be May fifteenth. The governor called Nix down to his office to start planning. They want federal marshals to police the townsites."

"Any idea when Nix will be back? I've got word on Doolin."

Thomas gave him a strange look. "What kind of word?"

"I scouted things out," Tilghman said. "That letter was right on the money. Doolin holes up there at a horse ranch on a regular basis. Got himself a girl in Ingalls, too."

"When were you in Ingalls?"

"Day before yesterday. Stopped by Chandler and rode on here."

"I'll be damned," Thomas mumbled. "You haven't heard about the holdup, have you?"

"Holdup?" Tilghman said, amazed. "Doolin pulled another job?"

Thomas quickly recounted details of the Santa Fe robbery in Kansas. He went on to relate the gun battle between the Wild Bunch and the Beaver County posse. He ended with Doolin's escape.

"But that's old news," he hurried on. "This morning we got the latest, and you're not gonna believe it. Doolin's holed up in a hotel in Ingalls."

"Hotel?" Tilghman said skeptically. "Why would he come out in the open like that? Where'd you get this story?"

"From a preacher." Thomas grinned, shaking his

head. "Old bird was hot under the collar, too. Rode all night to get here."

"What's a preacher got to do with Bill Doolin?"

The preacher, according to Thomas, had been struck by a sudden fit of conscience. After the wedding ceremony, he'd become incensed that a decent girl would marry an outlaw. All the worse, he speculated that it was a shotgun wedding, the girl in a family way. He also reported that Doolin had been wounded in the foot.

"To cork it," Thomas concluded, "Doolin brought the whole gang into town to celebrate his weddin'. I tell you that preacher was plenty pissed."

Tilghman took a moment to digest what he'd heard. His forehead wrinkled in thought. "Doolin's no dummy. He won't stick around Ingalls too long. He knows the word will leak out."

"Exact same thing I told Nix. We've got to hit Doolin tomorrow. Next day might be too late."

"Does he agree?"

"We got in an argument," Thomas said flatly. "He wants to send an army up there, and I'm against it. Too many men just get in one another's way. A couple of good ones, maybe three, that's all we need."

"We'd never get Madsen here from El Reno in time."

"There's always you and me, Bill. I'm not one for big posses and lead flyin' every whichaway. Just the two of us, we'd figure a way to nail Doolin."

"How'd you leave it with Nix?"

"We were still at it hot and heavy when the governor sent for him."

The office door opened. Evett Nix entered, his expression harried as he walked to his desk. He took a seat, nodding at Tilghman. "Has Heck filled you in?"

"We both did the honors," Tilghman said. "I just got back from Ingalls, so it wasn't a surprise. Doolin's been hiding out there off and on for months."

"Which means our outraged parson was on the mark.

We have an opportunity to rid the territory of Doolin once and for all."

"Looks that way."

Nix's gaze shifted to Thomas. "Have you changed your mind?"

"Nope," Thomas said, his eyes narrowed. "You send a crowd and there'll be hell to pay. Seen it happen time and again."

"Heck, I know your opinion of me as a lawman. But good judgment dictates that two or three men have no chance against a gang that large. I won't risk it."

"Heck's right," Tilghman interceded. "The larger the posse, the greater the risk of failure. Let the two of us handle it and the odds improve on getting Doolin. He's the main target, more so than his gang."

"I disagree," Nix said. "I want Doolin *and* his gang. Now, I stepped out of the meeting with the governor to settle this matter, and it's settled. Let's leave it at that."

Thomas scowled. "You're fixin' to get some men killed to no good end."

"Enough!" Nix said sharply. "We have local officers who carry standby federal commissions. Get them together and do your job."

Nix rose, rapidly crossing the room. He paused at the door, looking back. "Heck, despite any differences, you're our most experienced marshal. You'll be in charge."

"Christ!" Thomas snorted when the door closed. "What d'you think of them apples?"

"Well, Heck," Tilghman said, "I think he just put the bee on you."

"Guess he did, 'cause I sure as hell feel stung."

The sky was heavy with clouds, and beneath it the earth was cold and still. Trees along the creek swayed in the wind, bare branches crackling like the bones of old skeletons. A flock of crows fluttered against the sky, then wheeled and vanished beyond the treeline.

There were nine men in the posse, bent low as they crept forward in single file. The creek bank covered their movements, and the rush of water deadened the sound of their footsteps. A mile or so downstream where the creek angled southeast, they had left their horses hidden in a stand of trees. Stealthily, as though stalking game, they had spent the last hour working their way up the rocky stream.

Ahead, the bank sloped off sharply, and Council Creek swung westward in a lazy curve. Beyond the bend, hardly more than a stone's throw away, stood a squalid collection of buildings. Heck Thomas held up his hand and the men halted, flattening themselves against the creek bank. Except for Thomas, who carried a double-barrel shotgun, every man in the party was armed with a Winchester. A sense of suppressed violence, something unseen but menacing, hung over the ramshackle town.

Tilghman scrambled forward on his hands and knees. He stopped beside Thomas, who nodded and jerked his thumb toward the town. They removed their hats, still hunched low, and slowly eased themselves to eye level at the top of the bank. Their weapons held at the ready, they subjected the huddled buildings to an intense, door-to-door scrutiny. For a time, with the squinted gaze of veteran scouts, they absorbed every detail.

Ingalls under an overcast sky was little more than a backwoods eyesore. The single street, rutted and dusted with snow, petered out into a faint wagon road on either side of town. Nearest to the creek was a blacksmith shop, beside that a mercantile emporium, and farther along the dulled windows of the two-story hotel. Across the street was a seedy-looking saloon, flanked on one side by a cafe and on the other by a general store. Beyond, a short distance upstreet, was the livery stable.

Heck Thomas whistled softly between his teeth, motioned toward the town. Everyone already had their instructions, and as they scrambled over the creek bank, the lawmen split into two groups. Tilghman headed for the cafe, trailed by three men, and Thomas led the others on a direct line to the smithy. Taking one building at a time, they were to work both sides of the street, one party covering the other, until they flushed the gang. A metallic snick broke the stillness as one man after another eased back the hammer on his Winchester.

Then, too quick to fathom, their plan came unraveled. The door of the cafe opened, and a man accompanied by a young boy emerged onto the street. A moment later Bitter Creek Newcomb stepped through the door of the saloon, a bottle in hand, and started across to the hotel. On the instant he spotted Thomas, then his eyes flicked past the man and boy to Tilghman. His reaction was one of sheer reflex, without regard for the consequences. He jerked his pistol and fired.

Tilghman's shouted warning to the man and boy melded with the gunshot. The marshals behind him and those across the street shouldered their rifles in unison. The first sharp crack blended into a rolling tattoo, and Newcomb was struck in the left arm, dropping his bottle. Caught in the crossfire, the man outside the cafe went down like a puppet with his strings gone haywire. Beside him, jolted back by the impact of a slug, the boy dropped onto the boardwalk. Newcomb took off running for the stable.

Suddenly the street came alive with sizzling lead. Someone fired from an upstairs room in the hotel, and the front of the saloon appeared wreathed in a wall of flame as men opened fire through the door and windows. The marshal behind Tilghman grunted, clutching at his stomach, and dropped to the ground. Tilghman hefted his rifle and levered four shots into the upper floor window of the hotel. Glass shattered and a moment later Arkansas Tom Daugherty toppled over the windowsill. His rifle clattered to the boardwalk below.

From across the street, Thomas let go with his shotgun. Tilghman was aware that the other officers had concentrated their fire on the saloon, and he swung his rifle in that direction. Another lawman went down, a dark splotch blossoming on his coat, but the remaining Winchesters hammered out a withering barrage. The saloon windows disintegrated in a maelstrom of glass, and the building jounced as heavy slugs shredded the front wall. A third marshal swayed and crumpled to the earth.

Doolin suddenly leaped through the saloon door, followed by Clifton and Raidler. They sprinted toward the stable, where Newcomb was popping off shots at the lawmen. Tilghman fired simultaneously with the roar of Thomas's shotgun, and the four remaining officers loosed another volley. Clifton staggered, then righted himself, as slugs pocked the walls of the general store. He darted into the stable on the heels of Doolin and Raidler.

There was a momentary lull in the gunfire. Then, as though prearranged, Will Dalton, Jack Blake, and Red Buck Waightman rushed out of the saloon. Doolin and the men in the stable covered their retreat, emptying their pistols rapid fire at the marshals. The officers returned fire, Thomas fumbling to reload his shotgun, and Tilghman winging Blake in the arm. The three outlaws, dodging and twisting through a hornets' nest of lead, raced past the store and ducked into the stable.

An eerie stillness settled over the street. The marshals waited, staring over their sights at the stable. But the outlaws, unaccountably and all too abruptly, had ceased fire. Then, as Thomas cautiously motioned the officers forward, the screech of rusty door hinges broke the stillness. Doolin and his men, mounted on their horses, suddenly burst through a rear door of the stable and pounded across the countryside. They disappeared into a stark timberline at the north edge of town.

"Goddammit!" Thomas roared, hurling his shotgun to the ground. "The bastards already had their horses saddled. We let 'em get away."

Tilghman crossed the street. "Why should that surprise you, Heck? Doolin's smart and he always thinks ahead. He was fixed to run if anything happened."

"Would you look at this?" Thomas stormed, gesturing wildly around the street. "Holy Jesus Christ!"

The man and the small boy lay dead outside the cafe. Nearby, one of the marshals in Tilghman's group stared sightlessly at the overcast sky. Opposite them, in front of the blacksmith's shop, two other lawmen were sprawled on the ground. The smell of blood was ripe in the cool, still air.

Along the street, townspeople slowly emerged from the shops and stores. The blacksmith walked forward, knelt beside the fallen marshals, and shook his head. A woman outside the cafe gently cradled the dead boy in her arms.

"A goddamn bloodbath!" Thomas raged, shaking his fist at the hotel. "All for that."

Arkansas Tom Daugherty, arms dangling, hung from the hotel window.

PART TWO

CHAPTER 14

"Never saw a horse so proud of himself."

Neal Brown laughed. "Figures he's cock-o'-the-walk around here."

"Guess that's not far from the truth."

Tilghman led the sorrel stallion from the stable to the corral. The weather was brisk even though a bright noonday sun stood at its zenith in a cloudless sky. The stud was frisky, impatient to be turned loose. He snorted, frosty puffs of air steaming from his nostrils.

Brown swung open the corral gate. Tilghman led Steeldust into the enclosure and unsnapped the lead rope. The stallion raced away, crossing the corral in a few strides, then swerved away an instant before colliding with the fence. Snorting frost, heels kicked high in the air, he circled the corral. His eyes were fierce with freedom.

Tilghman stepped outside as Brown latched the gate. They stood, shaking their heads with amusement, watching the sorrel stud cavort around the corral. Brown took out the makings, spilling tobacco into a paper, and rolled himself a cigarette. He struck a match on his thumbnail.

"Tell you what's a fact," he said, puffing smoke. "That critter almost makes me wish I was a horse."

Tilghman smiled. "Yeah, he leads a pretty cushy life."

"Cushy!" Brown hooted. "All he can eat, not a lick of work, and all the mares he can service. I'd trade places with him any day of the week."

"I suspect lots of folks would, Neal."

Tilghman was in a rare good mood. A month had passed since the murderous shootout at Ingalls. At first, the press had lambasted U.S. Marshal Evett Nix and the deputies involved for the debacle. Innocent citizens gunned down, one of them a nine-year-old boy, and three lawmen killed. On the other side of the ledger, only one outlaw had been slain and the Wild Bunch had escaped. Headlines denounced it as a tragic disaster.

Republicans, widely quoted in the newspapers, demanded Nix's resignation. Neither Heck Thomas nor Tilghman offered any comment. In private, they reminded Nix that they had been opposed to such a large raid from the outset. In public, they quietly accepted the brunt of the blame, refusing to make Nix the scapegoat. Thomas, as leader of the raid, was vilified in the press.

Tilghman, the memory raw in his mind, had relived the bloody fight again and again. Fragmented in time, those moments were so brutalizing that the smallest detail would remain vivid all the rest of his days. Awake and in his dreams, he saw again the man and the boy step from the cafe only to be chopped down in a hail of gunfire. He wondered what would have happened if they had taken longer with their meal, remained in the cafe. At the very least, he ruminated, they would still be alive.

For the other part, though, nothing would have changed. He often reflected that fate, or perhaps simple bad luck, had brought Bitter Creek Newcomb through the door of the saloon at that particular moment in time. Given another minute, the marshals would have gained the element of surprise, trapping the gang in the saloon. But they'd lost the edge, and with it their composure, their ability to shoot straight in a moment of stress. Over and over in his mind he saw the outlaws retreating along the boardwalk toward the stable. He was still astounded that the other marshals, their guns blazing, had hit nothing.

In times past, from talking with Civil War veterans, he'd heard that most of the shots fired in battle never hit the mark. Still, looking back on Ingalls, there was no accounting for the marshals' inaccuracy at such short range. After all, the Wild Bunch had killed three lawmen, and probably fired fewer shots. The whole affair reminded him of the cardinal rule for survival in a gunfight: Speed's fine but accuracy is final. He took small consolation in the fact that he had killed Arkansas Tom Daugherty. The score was still three to one.

To make matters worse, Doolin and the Wild Bunch had again pulled their vanishing act. Following Ingalls, every lawman in Oklahoma Territory and the surrounding states had been put on alert. The rewards had been increased to five thousand dollars on Doolin and two thousand on every member of the gang. But there had been no sightings, no reports, absolutely nothing on where the gang had gone to ground. There was a rumor that they had crossed the Red River, taking refuge in Texas. Yet federal marshals and local lawmen in Texas had been unable to verify the story one way or another. The Wild Bunch, as a practical matter, had again disappeared.

Only one thing was known for certain. The doctor in Ingalls had confirmed that he'd treated Doolin for a gunshot wound to the foot. The wound, as near as Tilghman could piece it together, had been suffered in the running gunfight with the Beaver County posse, two days before the raid on Ingalls. Edith Doolin, the outlaw's new bride, refused to confirm or deny any part of the story. Yet the wound, to some small degree, explained the month-long absence of the Wild Bunch. Doolin would stick to cover until his foot was healed.

"Consarn it," Brown grumbled. "You got to where you just drift off, don't you?"

Tilghman realized he'd been staring into space. "Only now and then," he said lightly. "What'd I miss?"

"I asked you when we was gonna buy some more mares. We got land enough for a herd four or five times this size."

"Well, I thought we might hold off till spring. I'd like to take a look at brood stock up in Missouri, or down south. Maybe improve our bloodlines."

"Time's a-wastin'," Brown said. "Why wait till spring?"

"Unfinished business," Tilghman replied. "You know I can't leave."

"You're talkin' about Doolin and his bunch, aren't you?"

"Who else?"

Brown took a final drag on his cigarette. He dropped the butt and ground it underfoot. "So you're stuck here," he said. "I'm a pretty fair judge of horseflesh. Why don't I go?"

"You're stuck, too," Tilghman said. "I wouldn't trust anybody else to run the place."

The Sac and Fox tribesmen were reliable workhands. Under Brown's supervision, they cleaned out the stables, fed and watered the stock, and saw to it that the horses were exercised regularly. But Tilghman was wary of entrusting the brood mares, or Steeldust, to outsiders. He relied solely on Neal Brown.

"Helluva note," Brown said, kicking at a clod of dirt. "We're markin' time till Doolin pops up again. Somebody oughta shoot the bastard."

"Somebody will," Tilghman observed. "His kind always gets it, sooner or later."

"Trouble is, sooner's already past. We're workin' now on later."

Tilghman caught the disgruntled tone in his voice. Off and on, they'd had similar conversations several times over the last few months. Brown never stated it openly, but his opinion on the matter was hardly in question. All the more so since the vitriolic newspaper articles and editorials following the Ingalls shootout. He thought the job of federal marshal was a thankless task, often drawing criticism but seldom praise. Horses, in his view, were of far greater consequence than outlaws.

Before Tilghman could reply, a buggy rolled into the compound. Zoe waved gaily, gently hauling back on the reins, and brought her team to a halt. Tilghman walked forward as she scooted across the seat. He assisted her down from the buggy.

"Welcome surprise," he said, grinning. "What brings you over this way?"

"Oh, just passing by," she said, smiling past him at Brown. "Hello, Neal."

"Howdy, ma'am." Brown touched the brim of his hat, shy and curiously tongue-tied in the presence of a pretty woman. "Bill, I'd better check on things down at the stables. Nice seein' you, Miss Zoe."

"Nice seeing you too, Neal."

Brown bobbed his head and walked off. Zoe stared after him a moment. "After all this time, he still runs whenever he sees me. Am I that forbidding?"

"You're a woman," Tilghman said simply. "And Neal's not exactly a ladies' man. He's lots more comfortable with horses."

"And you?" She looked at him, amused. "Are you a ladies' man?"

"Common knowledge that I hold the title in Lincoln County. 'Course, I limit my attentions to one lady."

"How gallant of you, Mr. Tilghman."

"Believe me, it's my pleasure."

She laughed, touching his arm. Then, a startled look in her eyes, her gaze went past him. On the opposite side of the fence, Steeldust charged toward them, suddenly pulled up short, and whinnied a shrill blast of greeting. He was barrel-chested, standing fifteen hands high, his hide glistening in the sun. He watched them, pawing the earth as though he spurned it and longed to fly.

Tilghman smiled. "I think Steeldust likes you, too."

Zoe nodded, her gaze abstracted. The stallion came on at a prancing walk, moving with the pride of power and lordship. Always protective of his mares, who returned his whinny from the stables, he halted a few paces short of the fence. Then he stood, nostrils flared, like a statue bronzed by the sun. He tested the wind, staring directly at Zoe.

The stallion fascinated her. Whenever he came this close, she always felt a curious sensation in her loins. Oddly enough, Tilghman and Steeldust were somehow intertwined in her thoughts. On occasion, when she looked at Tilghman, a fleeting image of the stallion flashed through her mind. The feeling she experienced made her skin tingle and left a sweet aftertaste in her mouth. Almost as though she'd bitten into a moist peach.

"Goodness," she said softly. "He's a handsome brute, isn't he?"

"King of the mountain." Tilghman chuckled. "Thinks he owns everything between here and St. Louis."

"You certainly made a good choice. Father says you bought the best the Sac and Fox had to offer."

"I reckon we'll find out come spring. His foals will tell the tale."

Tilghman's breeding program centered on Steeldust. The stud had the spirit of his noble ancestors, the Barbs, the forerunners of all Indian horses. From generation upon generation of battling to survive on the plains, an almost supernatural endurance had been passed along to Steeldust. From this fusion with his Kansas mares, Tilghman hoped to breed colts and fillies with the speed for racetracks.

The brood mares he'd bought from the Sac and Fox were another matter entirely. By culling them, continually breeding up, he planned to breed the ultimate range horse. With Steeldust as the original sire, the offspring would have the stamina and catlike agility necessary for working cattle. Some would fall short of the mark, but with the sorrel stallion's blood, he nonetheless thought they would have great value. He planned to sell them to the army, or horse dealers, for saddle mounts.

"So?" Tilghman said as Steeldust turned and loped across the corral. "What brings you over our way?"

Zoe rolled her eyes. "Don't tell me you've forgotten!"

"Forgotten what?"

"The dance in town tonight. Have I lost a day somewhere? This is Saturday, isn't it?"

"Let me think." Tilghman feigned confusion. "No, by golly, you're right. Today's definitely Saturday."

"See!" she teased. "You needed reminding after all."

"Then it's good you dropped by. I'll make it a point to be at your place on time."

"Actually," she paused, gave him a minxish look, "I came by to invite you to Sunday dinner."

Tilghman cocked one eyebrow. "You could've done that tonight."

"Yes, but this gave me an excuse to see you."

"I get the feeling there's something missing here. What's the rest of the story?"

"Well," she said coyly, "as long as you're coming for Sunday dinner—"

"Now I get it," Tilghman broke in, wagging his head. "Why not make a day of it and escort you to church, too. That the idea?"

"How gracious of you to ask. I accept."

"Accept, my foot! You tricked me into it."

"A little religion never hurt anyone, especially you. God loves a heathen."

"Heathen!" Tilghman appeared wounded. "I'm as good a Christian as the next man."

She patted him on the cheek. "Then I'm sure you'll enjoy tomorrow's sermon. See you tonight."

When she drove off, Tilghman turned back to the corral. He stood watching Steeldust, wondering at the ways of women. A few moments later Brown walked up from the stables.

"You're a goner," he said ruefully. "That little lady's got the look in her eye."

"You think so, Neal?"

"I'd bet on it and give you good odds."

Tilghman smiled. "No bet."

Steeldust pawed the ground, fierce eyes fixed on the stables. His nose to the wind, he scented his mares.

CHAPTER 15

The men rode into town in three groups. Doolin and Dick Clifton entered by the farm road from the south. Charley Pierce, Jack Blake, and Red Buck Waightman appeared on the road north of town. Bill Raidler and Little Dick West rode along a sidestreet from a westerly direction.

Located in the southwest corner of Missouri, the town was aptly named Southwest City. A farm community with a population of less than a thousand, it lay some five miles east of the border with the Cherokee Nation. Hardly a center of commerce, it was nonetheless a thriving hamlet built on the trade of the area's farmers.

Southwest City, like most farm towns, was bisected by a main thoroughfare. The business district, small but prosperous, consisted of four stores, a saloon and a blacksmith shop, and one bank. There were few people about and little activity on a Monday afternoon. Typically the slowest time of the week, it accounted in part for the seven strangers. Their business was better conducted without crowds.

A week past, Doolin had assigned Jack Blake to scout the town. Blake had returned with a crudely sketched map after stopping for a drink in the saloon. He reported that the bank was manned by only the president and two tellers. Law enforcement consisted of the town marshal, who operated without regular deputies and rarely patrolled the streets. The townspeople, apart from shopping and the usual errands, were seldom about on weekdays. All in all, Southwest City looked like easy pickings.

Doolin had selected the farm town for just that reason. He needed a simple job, and one that would give his men a decent payday. After the Ingalls shootout, he'd been roundly criticized by Will Dalton for poor leadership. Dalton blamed him for keeping the gang in Ingalls too long, creating a situation that fairly begged for a raid by the law. The argument became heated, with Doolin prepared to kill in order to hold the Wild Bunch together. Dalton wisely avoided a showdown, for he was no match for Doolin with a gun. Instead, he'd quit the gang and taken off on his own.

The others had elected to stick with Doolin. He had persuaded them to scatter throughout the Nations and stay in deep cover until he felt it was safe to resume operations. When the heat died down, he'd promised them, there would be more and bigger paydays. With money in their pockets from the last robbery, the men had kept out of sight for the past four months, all of them still somewhat spooked by the close call at Ingalls. But finally, short on money and tired of hiding out, they seemed on the verge of splitting apart. Doolin had no choice but to plan another raid.

From a personal standpoint, Doolin was no better off than his men. He was nearly broke, and his foot wound had healed poorly, leaving him with a pronounced limp. Even worse, his wife was with child, and given the circumstances, there was no way for them to be together. Every few weeks he'd managed to sneak into Ingalls, always under cover of darkness, and visit her for a night. But she was afraid and dispirited, and constantly badgering him to quit the outlaw life. For that he needed a stake, and he'd decided to resume operations with a job that offered quick escape into the Nations. Southwest City appeared to fit the bill.

The men held their horses to a walk. Travelers converging from different directions, they proceeded toward the center of town. Outside the bank Doolin and Clifton wheeled to the right and halted before the hitch rack. Upstreet, the three men approaching from the north stopped in front of a mercantile store. Down from the bank, Raidler and West reined in on the same side of the street.

There was a military precision to their movements, smooth and coordinated, somehow practiced. The riders on either side of the bank dismounted and took positions to cover the street in both directions. Some checked their saddle rigging, others dusted themselves off, and to a man their eyes checked nearby buildings. Doolin paused a moment and subjected the whole of the business district to a slow, careful scrutiny. Then, followed by Clifton, he turned and entered the bank.

Inside the door, Doolin quickly scanned the room. The cashier's window was to the rear, and beyond that the vault door, which was open. To his immediate left, seated behind a desk, the bank president was engaged in conversation with a man dressed as a farmer. One teller stood at the cashier's window while the other worked on a set of books.

"This is a holdup!" Doolin announced. "Keep quiet and you won't get hurt."

There was an instant of leaden silence. At the desk, the president stared at him with disbelief, and the farmer swiveled around in his chair. The cashier froze, watching him intently, and the other teller paused with his pen dipped in an inkwell. Clifton positioned himself to cover everyone in the room.

"Don't nobody get stupid," he said jovially. "Hell, gents, it's only money."

Doolin walked to the cashier's window. He casually wagged the snout of his pistol, nodding to the teller. "Forget your cash drawer. Empty the vault and be quick about it."

"What'll I put it in?"

From inside his coat, Doolin pulled out two neatly folded gunnysacks with draw strings. He pushed them across the counter, motioning with his gun, and the teller turned toward the vault. The other teller suddenly dropped his pen and jerked open the drawer of his desk. He stood, panic written across his face, a pistol in his hand.

"No!" Doolin thundered. "Drop it!"

From the door, Clifton sighted and fired. The slug punched through the teller's head and tore out the back of his skull. A halo of bone and brain matter misted the air, and he stood there a moment, dead on his feet. Then he pitched headlong onto the floor.

"Goddammit!" Doolin shouted. "I had him covered. Why'd you shoot?"

Clifton shrugged. "Bastard shouldn't've pulled a gun."

"Well, you damn sure put the town on notice." Doolin turned to the teller at the vault. "Get them sacks loaded. Muy goddamn pronto!"

A roar of gunfire, several shots in rapid succession, suddenly sounded from outside. Clifton glanced through the front window and saw gang members popping shots at merchants who had appeared in doorways along the street. Across the way the town marshal emerged from his office, pistol in hand, and started along the boardwalk. Another volley erupted and his right leg buckled under the impact of a slug. He went down on his rump.

"Hop to it!" Clifton yelled. "We got trouble."

The teller shoved the loaded sacks across the counter. Doolin grabbed them, backing to the door, and tossed one to Clifton. The gunfire swelled in intensity as they rushed outside and moved toward the hitch rack. On either side of them, the men posted as guards were trading shots with merchants up and down the street. Their horses were wall-eyed with fright as they bounded into the saddle.

A rifle ball opened a bloody gash on Clifton's forehead. He whirled his horse and fired, dropping the owner of the mercantile store. Across the street, the town marshal rose unsteadily to his feet and triggered three quick shots. One of the slugs sizzled past Doolin's ear and he wheeled about, fighting to control his horse, and ripped off two shots in return. The lawman staggered backward, crashing into the wall of a building. He slumped to the boardwalk.

All along the street storekeepers were firing from windows and doorways. The other gang members hastily mounted, their pistols barking flame in a steady roar. Upstreet a merchant pitched forward in his doorway, and in the opposite direction, the blacksmith tumbled to the ground. Then, with Doolin in the lead, the gang reined their horses around and spurred for the south edge of town. Behind them, the townspeople peppered their retreat with a barrage of lead.

The Wild Bunch thundered west toward Indian Territory.

Will Dalton and Jim Wallace dismounted in the alley beside the bank. A few moments later Asa and Tim Knight entered the alley from the opposite direction. After they dismounted, Tim Knight took the reins of the other two men's horses. Dalton and Wallace walked toward the street.

The town of Longview was the center of trade for farmers and several large logging operations. Located in northeastern Texas, it was some eighty miles south of the Red River, the boundary between the Lone Star State and the Choctaw Nation. A prosperous community, Longview was the county seat, with a stone courthouse dominating the town square.

The First National, the largest bank in town, was located on the north side of the square. Dalton had selected the bank as the first full-fledged job for his newly formed gang. After splitting with Doolin, he had joined forces with Wallace, a small-time bandit who operated out of the Chickasaw Nation. Wallace had in turn introduced him to the Knight brothers, former loggers turned outlaw who were originally from Longview. Their tales of a vault stuffed with mountains of cash had sold Dalton on the First National. He meant to eclipse the record of the Wild Bunch with a single holdup.

Dalton led the way into the bank. He covered the door, his pistol drawn, and commanded everyone to lie on the floor. Wallace collared the bank president, put a gun to his head, and forced him to unlock the vault. The shelves lining the walls, just as the Knight brothers had promised, were stacked with piles of cash. At first overawed, Wallace quickly located the shelves with bills of larger denominations. He produced cloth sacks from inside his coat and ordered the president to get busy.

"Whooee!" he yelled out to Dalton. "We're gonna be rich. Filthy rich!"

"Tell me about it later," Dalton said sternly. "Get them sacks filled and let's get out of here."

Only a few minutes were required to complete the job. Wallace came out of the vault, struggling with two heavy sacks thrown over his shoulder, and moved to the front of the room. Dalton glanced through the door window, watchful a moment as townspeople went about their business on the courthouse square. Then, turning back, he fixed those in the bank with a menacing scowl.

"Stay put and don't get brave! Anybody comes out this door will get his head blowed off."

Dalton stepped through the door, followed by Wallace. On the street, passersby spotted their drawn guns and immediately ran for cover. By a fluke of timing, in that same moment, Town Marshal George Muckley and his deputy, Wally Stevens, emerged from the courthouse. Their attention drawn by the commotion, they saw the two men hurrying from the bank and the Knight brothers holding four horses in the alley. The Knight brothers, who had fled Longview after a string of petty robberies, were known to them on sight. On the instant, they realized the bank was being robbed.

The lawmen pulled their guns and opened fire. Muckley, hoping to spook the horses and prevent escape, let off three quick shots at the Knight brothers. One of the slugs caught Asa Knight in the chest and he fell spread-eagled in the alley. Deputy Stevens trained his fire on the two men scurrying along the boardwalk outside the bank. A bullet shattered the bank's plate-glass window in an explosion of jagged shards.

Dalton and Wallace, firing as they ran, reached the entrance to the alley. Their shots were wild and for the most part pocked harmlessly into the front of the stone courthouse. But a wayward ball drilled the marshal through the bowels and he folded at the waist, then keeled over. Stevens dropped to one knee, stone chips flying all around him, and emptied his gun. A townsman passing the courthouse was caught in the crossfire and took a slug through the lungs. He toppled to the ground.

In the alley, Tim Knight fought to control the horses as he knelt to check on his brother. His face blanched with rage as he saw the sightless eyes and realized Asa was dead. He climbed to his feet, the horses' reins clutched tightly in one fist, and winged a shot at Stevens on the courthouse steps. The deputy shucked spent car-

tridges and reloaded as a merchant opened fire with a
rifle from the corner. Upstreet, in the opposite direction, a saloonkeeper armed with a sawed-off shotgun
joined the fight.

Buckshot and lead whistling about their ears, Dalton
and Wallace returned the fire. Wallace's snap-shot
singed the merchant's coatsleeve and drove him back
into his store. Dalton halted, took deliberate aim, and
loosed a round to silence the shotgun. The saloonkeeper staggered backwards, arms windmilling, then
dropped the scattergun and crashed to the boardwalk.
Still leading the way, Dalton darted into the alley.

Tim Knight was already mounted. Holding the reins,
he waited while Dalton and Wallace scrambled aboard
their horses. Encumbered with the money sacks, the two
men were forced to holster their pistols as they reined
away. Knight covered their retreat, emptying his gun
across the courthouse square. The three men spurred
toward the end of the alley.

Deputy Stevens, his gun reloaded, got off one last
shot. Then, as the outlaws disappeared, he stared
around at the carnage with a stunned expression. The
marshal lay dead at his feet, and the townsman caught
in the crossfire was knotted in a grotesque heap. Across
the street on the boardwalk, the saloonkeeper lay pud-
dled in blood.

The courthouse square looked like a slaughterhouse.

CHAPTER 16

OUTLAW GANGS ROB TWO BANKS IN THREE DAYS
THE WILD BUNCH STRIKES MISSOURI AND TEXAS

The headline in the Guthrie *Statesman* covered the width of the front page. The dateline was May 22, 1890, and fully half the page was devoted to coverage of the robberies. In separate articles, the newspaper reported on the May 19 holdup in Missouri and the May 21 raid in Texas. An editorial by the publisher, enclosed in a black border, rendered a blistering attack on the U.S. marshal.

Evett Nix slammed the paper onto his desk. Lined up before him were Tilghman, Heck Thomas, and Chris Madsen. Upon news of the first robbery, he had recalled the three deputy marshals from their assignments in the Cherokee Strip. The telegraph report on the second holdup had arrived even as they rode into Guthrie late last night. Today, facing him across the desk, they waited for Nix's tirade to subside.

None of the deputies responded as he paused to take a breath. Nor were they expected to respond, for Nix was clearly not finished with his harangue. He scooped the newspaper off the desk, balled it into a wad, and hurled it across the room. His features were mottled with anger.

"What happened?" he demanded. "Why were we caught flat-footed? Why weren't you men on the case?"

"Maybe you forgot," Thomas said with intended irony. "You sent us to play po-licemen in the Cherokee Strip. We were just a tad out of touch."

Tilghman thought it a telling remark. In the four months since the Ingalls shootout, federal lawmen had been assigned to police the Cherokee Strip land rush, which brought over two hundred thousand settlers pouring into the Territory. During all that time, not a single lead had been uncovered as to the whereabouts of the gang. There was widespread speculation, particularly in the newspapers, that the Wild Bunch had quit Oklahoma Territory altogether. The federal marshals, Tilghman more so than most, were not wholly persuaded by the argument. Doolin's wife, rumored to be with child, still lived in Ingalls, and showed no signs of leaving. That alone indicated Doolin had not gone far.

Over the last four months Tilghman had occasionally slipped out of the Cherokee Strip to scout Ingalls and the Dunn brothers' ranch. His attempts to interrogate Doolin's wife and her storekeeper father had proved to be an exercise in futility. Their attitude was polite but distant, and both of them denied any knowledge of Doolin's whereabouts. The townspeople, fearing reprisals from men quick to kill, were even less willing to discuss the Wild Bunch. As a practical matter, Doolin and his gang seemed to have disappeared off the face of the earth. The federal marshals were stymied, their search seemingly at a dead end. Until today.

"Excuses, nothing but excuses!" Nix thundered now. "You're supposed to keep your ear to the ground. How could you not get wind of something this big?"

"Why would we?" Tilghman said, tired of being bullied. "You want a fortune teller, get yourself another crew. None of us have a crystal ball."

"Bill's right," Madsen chimed in. "We had our hands full with the land rush and claim jumpers. You're the one that pulled us off the Wild Bunch."

"That's not true!" Nix said hotly. "The governor wanted federal marshals assigned to the Strip."

"Then blame him," Thomas said with an edge to his voice. "We're not gonna be your whipping-boys, Mr. Nix. That's the end of that story."

Nix stared at them in baffled fury. They were united, obviously unfazed by his harsh manner, and on the verge of telling him to go to hell. What with the newspaper articles and censure from Washington, he could hardly afford to risk losing his top three deputies. He decided to switch tactics.

"Let's all cool down," he said, dropping into his chair. "Nothing to be gained in arguing amongst ourselves. You gentlemen have a seat."

The deputies took chairs ranged before his desk. He massaged his forehead, got a grip on himself. "Tell me this," he said in a calmer tone. "Where have Doolin and his gang been all this time? Why have they suddenly reappeared . . . after four months?"

"Wrong question," Tilghman corrected him. "How could they pull two holdups in three days—over three hundred miles apart?"

"They couldn't," Thomas said simply. "Horses don't have wings."

Madsen nodded sagely. "Doolin was identified in the Missouri job. So the one in Texas had to be somebody else."

"Yes and no," Nix said quickly. "I received a wire this morning from the U.S. marshal in Texas."

From the clutter on his desk, Nix showed them a two-page telegraph message. The gist of it, he related, was that a posse comprised of Longview citizens and federal marshals had tracked the outlaws to the border of Indian Territory and west along the Red River. There the trail had petered out, lost in the Chickasaw Nation.

"Here's the corker," he concluded. "The town deputy in Longview positively identified Will Dalton. Recognized him from those wanted posters we circulated months ago."

"Holy Christ," Thomas said softly. "You mean to say Doolin's operatin' two gangs now?"

"Sounds odd," Tilghman observed, shaking his head. "Will Dalton was the runt of the litter, and no wizard. Doolin wouldn't trust him to pull a job on his own."

"You betcha not," Madsen agreed. "Doolin's the brains of that outfit. He'd never let Dalton branch off."

Thomas clucked to himself. "Whole thing's fishy as hell. There were seven men in the Missouri raid and four in Texas. Where'd all these gawddamn desperadoes come from?"

"Oh, I forgot," Nix broke in, waving the telegram. "The other men in the Longview robbery were identified as well. Asa Knight was killed, and his brother, Tim, got away. The last one is a known friend of theirs, Jim Wallace."

"Kiss my rusty butt!" Thomas said, astounded. "The Knights and Wallace are wanted men, known throughout the Chickasaw Nation. Wallace has a brother down there—lemme think—Houston Wallace, that's his name."

"Down there?" Tilghman repeated with a questioning look. "You mean the Chickasaw Nation?"

"Yeah," Thomas said. "Near as I recollect, it's somewheres around Ardmore. Heard he married a Chickasaw woman, turned farmer."

Nix appeared surprised. "Are you saying he owns land in the Nations?"

"Long as he stays married."

Thomas briefly expounded on his remark. The Chickasaw Nation, like all the Five Civilized Tribes, was virtually an independent republic. Unlike the western Plains Tribes, the Nations had never accepted annuities or financial assistance from Washington. Thus they had maintained their independence as well as their own courts and legal system. By law, white men were not allowed to own land or property in the Nations except through intermarriage. Their Indian wives, in effect, controlled the purse strings. Divorce could reduce a man to a pauper.

"That raises a legal question," Nix said when he concluded. "Let's presume Wallace provides a hideout for his brother and Dalton. That makes him an accomplice to robbery and murder."

"So?" Thomas replied. "What's the question?"

"Well, as you've said, he's married to an Indian woman. Does that make him a Chickasaw citizen and immune to federal law? Or do we still have jurisdiction?"

"The courts ruled on that a long time ago. He's white, and married or not, we've got first dibs."

"Do you know Wallace?" Tilghman asked. "Was he ever on the owlhoot?"

"Not that I heard," Thomas said. " 'Course, it makes sense he'd let his brother hide out there. For all we know, that's where Dalton's been holed up the past four months."

Madsen grunted sourly. "That would explain how he got tied in with the Knight brothers and Jim Wallace."

"Maybe," Tilghman said. "But it still doesn't explain why he pulled a job without Doolin."

"Neither here nor there," Nix informed them. "The attorney general wants results, and an end to these damnedable newspaper articles. Right now, Dalton is the only lead we have."

Thomas raised an eyebrow. "Dalton's a small-fry

compared to Doolin. Are we gonna let Washington politicians tell us how to do our job?"

"Indeed we are," Nix said sharply. "Not to mention the fact that three men were killed in the Longview robbery. That makes Dalton a prime target."

"Makes good headlines, too," Thomas said with a caustic smile. "Assuming we catch him."

Nix tossed another telegram across the desk. "Forget catching him, gentlemen. Those are your marching orders."

The deputies scanned the telegram. The message was terse and pointed, an official directive without equivocation. It was, in effect, a death sentence from the United States Attorney General.

I have reached the conclusion that the only good outlaw is a dead one and I order you to employ extraordinary measures in resolving this problem. You are directed to instruct your deputies to bring the Wild Bunch in dead.

"Judas Priest!" Thomas muttered. "It's open season on outlaws."

"I don't like it," Tilghman said quietly. "That makes us judge, jury, and executioner—hired guns."

"Think about it, Bill." Thomas looked dour. "None of the bastards ever surrender peaceable. They always put up a fight."

"Heck's right there," Madsen added. "They're like a pack of rabid dogs. I say better them than us."

Tilghman still appeared doubtful. Before it could go any further, Nix took the lead. "Orders are orders, and we have ours. I want you gentlemen to locate Will Dalton."

The three lawmen stared at him without expression.

Though couched in subtle terms, there was no ambiguity in his directive. Nor was he allowing them a choice.

Will Dalton was to be found and killed.

Four days were required to locate the farm of Houston Wallace. By horseback, it took three days for the lawmen to reach the heart of Chickasaw country. Another day was spent in clandestine meetings between Heck Thomas and informants he had developed over the years. Finally, by early afternoon on the fourth day, they had a solid lead. The farm was situated south of Ardmore, on Elk Creek.

The need to move quickly was all too apparent. The Chickasaws, like tribesmen throughout the Nations, were openly defiant of federal marshals. Word would spread rapidly that they were in the area, clearly there in search of white outlaws. Will Dalton and his men, if they were hiding on the Wallace farm, would be warned no later than tomorrow. There could be no delay in staging the raid.

Tilghman was elected to scout the farm. Based on their information, the Wallace place was a mile or so west off the wagon road leading south from Ardmore. He left Madsen and Thomas with their horses in a grove of trees not far from the road. A rutted trail bordered the creek, and he cautiously made his way upstream. Late that afternoon, rounding a gentle curve in the stream, he suddenly stopped and ghosted into the woods. He had found their quarry.

The farmhouse was a crude log affair, on the north bank of the creek. A buck deer hung from the limb of a tree, and an Indian woman was busy skinning the carcass. Four men were seated outside the house, basking in the late afternoon sunshine. A jug of whiskey passed from man to man, and their laughter carried across the clearing. From wanted dodgers, Tilghman recognized one of the men as Will Dalton. There was a family resemblance between two of the men, probably Houston and Jim Wallace. The fourth man he took to be Tim Knight.

An hour later, downstream again, he briefed Madsen and Thomas. Sundown was close at hand, and from Tilghman's description, the gang was lazing around, swigging whiskey, waiting on a supper of venison steaks. Tilghman sketched a map in the dirt, and from the layout, there was no way to circle the house without being spotted. After weighing tactics, they decided to advance on line through the woods and take positions east of the house. That would allow them to cover the corral, which was off to the rear of the house, in case any of the outlaws made a break for their horses. Thomas was elected to issue a single warning, demanding surrender. Anyone who resisted was fair game.

By dusk, they were positioned in the treeline beside the clearing. There was still adequate light to see and sight, and each of them carried a Winchester carbine. Tilghman was nearest the creek with Thomas off to his right, and Madsen several paces farther north. To their front, the three outlaws and Houston Wallace were still seated outside the house. A lamp glowed inside, and through a window, they could see the woman working over a wood cookstove. Thomas raised his voice in sharp command.

"Federal marshals! Surrender or be killed!"

Dalton scrambled off the ground, clawing at his holster. Knight and Jim Wallace were only a beat behind, their pistols clearing leather. The lawmen's carbines, like rolling thunder, cracked in swift unison. Knight and Wallace went down as though struck by the fist of God. Dalton stumbled sideways, still trying to raise his pistol, and Tilghman shot him again. Driven backward, he sagged to the ground.

Houston Wallace, a farmer with no wish to die, stood with his hands overhead. He stared down at the body of his brother as if unable to comprehend the terrible suddenness of death. The lawmen moved out of the treeline, their carbines held at the ready, and crossed the clearing. Wallace's wife, hovering inside the doorway, watched them with a hand pressed to her mouth. She fully expected them to kill her husband.

Tilghman kept Wallace covered while Madsen and Thomas checked the bodies. A quick search of the house turned up two burlap bags, stuffed with the loot from the Longview bank robbery. Then, in an unusually kind voice, Thomas subjected the farmer to a skilled interrogation. Wallace told him everything.

Will Dalton, as they'd suspected, had used the farm as a hideout. The story of his split with Doolin, brought out under close questioning, revealed that he had quit the Wild Bunch several months ago. Afterward, he'd returned to the farm and eventually formed his own gang with Jim Wallace and the Knight brothers, who frequented the Chickasaw Nation. The time since had been spent in planning the Longview holdup.

The woman, still convinced they would kill him, watched fearfully as Madsen stood guard over her husband. Tilghman and Thomas walked off a short distance, to confer in private. Thomas glanced back at the farmer, who now seemed unable to look at the bodies. He wagged his head.

"Hard thing," he murmured. "Seeing your brother shot down like that."

"Always knew it," Tilghman said with a slow grin. "You're just an ole softy at heart."

Thomas was embarrassed. "Hell, Bill, you know what'll happen if we take him back. Gawddamn Nix will have him hung for accomplice to murder."

"You know what I think?"

"What?"

"Three dead men will get Nix all the headlines he wants. Let's leave it at that."

"And if Nix don't like it, to hell with him!"

Thomas issued a stern warning to the farmer about the wages of crime. Then, pressing the advantage, he converted him into an informant. The woman, still watchful, uttered a silent prayer of thanks to the white man's god. Ten minutes later, as darkness fell, the marshals walked off to gather their horses.

They left Houston Wallace to bury the fallen outlaws.

CHAPTER 17

Word preceded them by telegraph on the shootout. Three days later, when they rode into Guthrie, their names were the talk of the territory. People stopped to cheer them on the street outside the Herriott Building.

Upstairs, they found Evett Nix in a wildly euphoric mood. Newspapers throughout the territory lauded the marshal and his deputies, where only a week before they had been vilified. There was particular praise on the death of Will Dalton, generally accepted as second-in-command of the Wild Bunch. The Guthrie *Statesman* recommended the same fate for every member of the gang.

Nix hurriedly arranged a press conference. His stated purpose was to provide the newspaper with a first-hand account from the men who had brought down a notorious outlaw. Unstated, though clearly understood, was an attempt to gain political mileage for himself from the exploits of Thomas, Tilghman, and Madsen. The reporter from the *Statesman*, usually one of their harshest critics, was today their enthusiastic supporter. All the more so since the interview represented a scoop on other newspapers.

"Tell me this," he said, pencil poised over his notepad. "Which one of you actually killed Will Dalton?"

Thomas and Madsen looked at Tilghman. After a moment, he offered a casual shrug. "What with all the shooting, things were pretty confused. Just say we all had a hand in it."

The reporter scribbled furiously. "The last of the Dalton brothers. The outlaw family that spawned Bill Doolin and the Wild Bunch. Killed by—" He paused, momentarily stumped. "I need a name for you three. Something with a ring to it."

"Excellent idea," Nix prompted him. "They're our top three deputies, guardians of law and order."

"That's it!" the reporter said, wide-eyed with a sudden fit of inspiration. "The Three Guardsmen! France had the Three Musketeers. We have the Three Guardsmen."

Nix beamed. "A fitting analogy. For a fact, they do guard Oklahoma Territory."

"The public will love it." The reporter appeared overjoyed with himself. "Now, let me ask you gentlemen—" he stopped, looking from man to man. "Having rid the territory of Dalton, what are your plans for Doolin and the rest of the Wild Bunch?"

"You can quote me directly," Nix said, desperate to insert his own name into the interview. "We are hot on the trail of Bill Doolin and his gang. Results will be forthcoming shortly."

"That's the headline! Three Guardsmen Hot On The Trail! What a story!"

On that high note, Nix tactfully ended the interview. Grinning broadly, he ushered the reporter to the door and saw him off with a warm handshake. Then, turning back into the room, his grin melted away. He took a seat behind his desk.

"Reporters," he said with mild disgust. "One day your friend, the next your nemesis."

Thomas snorted. "We'll play hell livin' down that tag he hung on us. The Three Guardsmen! Jesus Christ."

"Don't worry about it," Madsen said jokingly. "Tomorrow it will be old news."

"Speaking of which," Nix interjected, "I still wish you'd arrested that farmer. I just can't believe he knew nothing of Doolin's whereabouts."

"Done told you," Thomas said crossly. "I grilled him six ways to Sunday. He would've spilled it if he knew."

"Nonetheless, what Chris said is true. We need a new headline for tomorrow. One with Doolin's name in it."

"Fat chance," Tilghman remarked. "We're not even close to being hot on the trail. Maybe you should've told that reporter the truth. There is no trail."

"I've been thinking about that," Nix said. "What about that ranch outside Ingalls? Where Doolin holed up before?"

"The Dunn brothers," Tilghman noted. "What about them?"

"I think we should raid the place. Who knows, Doolin could be there right now. At the very least, we might uncover a lead through the Dunns."

"Bad move," Tilghman said. "Doolin's nowhere near Ingalls or that ranch."

"Oh?" Nix sounded dubious. "What makes you so certain?"

"By now, Doolin knows we know he married that girl. He'll steer clear of her—and the Dunn ranch—until he's ready to move her somewhere else."

"You believe Doolin will move his wife?"

"Has to," Tilghman affirmed. "Otherwise they'll never be together."

Nix considered a moment. "Then perhaps we should put surveillance on his wife."

"Town that small, Doolin would get wind of it. His wife and the Dunn ranch are our only solid leads. Touch either one and we tip our hand to Doolin."

"So what are you suggesting?"

"Wait and see," Tilghman said. "Somebody in Ingalls

—the preacher, the doctor, maybe the girl's dad—will let us know when Doolin shows up again. Until then, we sit tight."

"Sit tight?" Nix repeated testily. "Are you saying we do nothing?"

"We wait for Doolin to make a mistake. Often as not, that's what ends a manhunt—the other fellow gets careless."

"Bill's got a point," Madsen broke in. "Any move on the girl, or the Dunns, would cause Doolin to back off. We just have to wait it out."

"All right," Nix said reluctantly. "But let's have it understood, I won't wait too long. I want results."

"So do we," Thomas told him. "Don't you worry, we'll keep our ears open."

Their meeting ended on that note. Nix wasn't pleased, but he saw little choice in the matter. A good leader, he reminded himself, listened to the advice of his men. Yet he was uncomfortable with the outcome.

He needed Bill Doolin. Dead.

Tilghman rode straight through to Chandler. He arrived late that night, weary from ten hard days in the saddle. Too tired to eat, he had a cup of coffee with Neal Brown, relating only the bare details of the manhunt. Then, unable to resist sleep any longer, he went to bed.

The next morning, feeling rested, he was up early. He ate a large breakfast of bacon and eggs, sourdough biscuits, and strong black coffee. Afterward, he and Brown spent the morning going over the books and discussing ranch matters. Following the noon meal, he retired to a tub of hot water and soaked away the layers of grime accumulated on the trail. He then stropped his straight razor, gave himself a close shave, and splashed on a touch of bay rum lotion. He felt like a new man.

Late that afternoon he emerged from the house. He was attired in a blue serge suit, a starchy white shirt cinched at the collar with a tie, and his Sunday hat. As he stepped off the porch, Neal Brown walked up from the corral. Brown gave him a slow once-over.

"You headed for church on a weekday?"

"Nope," Tilghman said. "Tonight's Zoe's birthday party. Promised her I wouldn't miss it."

Brown sniffed the air. "You shore smell sweet. Sorta like a petunia."

"You ought to try it yourself sometime."

"Take a bath ever' time it rains. Reckon that's enough."

"Anybody downwind wouldn't doubt it."

"Sorry state of affairs," Brown grumped. "That little lady's got you turned inside out."

"Neal, you've got no idea."

A short while later Tilghman drove off in the buckboard. He often thought that Brown was right, that he was addled by a younger woman. Though their birthdays were only a month apart, he and Zoe were separated by a span of years. She was now twenty-one, and come July 4 he would be thirty-seven. Still, for him, the years seemed to have fallen away. He felt like a kid again.

Not long after dark he arrived at the Stratton place. The buggies and buckboards of neighbors were parked outside, and the house was ablaze with lights. Gaily colored Chinese lanterns had been strung between the roof and nearby trees, and the crowd had spilled out onto the yard. Zoe saw him step down from the buckboard, and she excused herself from her guests. She hurried toward him.

"You're here!" she said, her eyes radiant. "Somehow I knew you would make it."

"Told you I would," Tilghman said, taking her hands. "How could I miss your birthday?"

"When did you return?"

"Late last night."

"Everyone's heard," she paused, searching his eyes. "About Dalton, I mean. Was it bad?"

"Time for that later," Tilghman said, smiling at her. "I thought you invited me to a party."

"Yes, of course, you're right. Come and say hello to everyone."

She led him to the guests congregated under the Chinese lanterns. The women smiled, watching him with curious expressions, and the men shook his hand, greeting him warmly. Several offered their congratulations, alluding to Dalton, and waited expectantly for details. But Zoe warded them off, pulling him through the crowd toward the house. Her father came through the front door.

"Look who's here," she said, leading Tilghman onto the porch. "He got in just last night."

"Bill." Amos Stratton extended his hand. "Glad you could make the party."

"Glad to be here, Amos. Looks like everyone in the county turned out."

"That reminds me," Stratton said. "Zoe, you'd better check the punch bowl. It's just about empty."

"Oh, fudge!" She squeezed Tilghman's hand. "Don't run off. I'll be right back."

She hurried into the house. Stratton was silent a moment, then cleared his throat. "Your name's been in the papers the last couple of days. Way it sounds, Dalton put up a stiff fight."

"Nothing out of the ordinary," Tilghman said. "Like most, he didn't know when to quit."

"Zoe worries about you something terrible. She'd never say so, but it's a fact."

"Not all that much to worry about. I look after myself pretty close."

"You must," Stratton said amiably. "Or maybe you carry a lucky charm?"

"Never tried that," Tilghman said with a good-humored smile. "I always figured a man makes his own luck."

"I suspect that's so in your line of work."

"Daddy!" Zoe came out the doorway. "No talk of work tonight. This is a party!"

"Whatever you say, honey. It's your night."

She kissed her father on the cheek. Then, hooking her arm through Tilghman's, she turned back into the yard. Smiling, nodding to her guests, she led him under the Chinese lanterns, leaving the crowd behind. They paused beneath a tree.

"I know it's shameless," she said gaily. "But I don't want to share you with anyone tonight."

"Same here," Tilghman said. "Fact is, I was wondering how I could get you alone."

"Were you really?"

"Well, you see, I've been thinking about your birthday present. So I went by a shop over in Guthrie yesterday."

"You got me a present?"

Tilghman took a small box from his coat pocket. He snapped open the lid and the light from the lanterns sparkled off a diamond set in a slim gold band. Her mouth ovaled in a silent gasp and she stared at it as though bewitched. She finally looked up.

"Bill—"

"No, let me talk. You're everything a man could want in a wife and . . . well, if you'll have me, I'm, proposing marriage."

"Yes."

"What?"

"I said 'yes.' I'll marry you."

"You will?"

"Of course I will. Just tell me one thing . . . do you love me?"

"So much it hurts like a toothache."

Though hardly poetic, the sentiment was there. By now, she knew he was a man rarely given to a display of emotion. Still, once they were married, she could change that easily enough. She held out her hand.

"Put the ring on, Bill."

Tilghman slipped the ring on her finger. The sparkle in her eyes was no less than that of the lantern light off the diamond. She kissed him soundly on the lips.

"I do love you, Bill," she murmured. "So very much."

Tilghman enfolded her in a great hug. Across the yard there was a buzz of conversation. Then the crowd went silent, staring at them. She stepped out of his embrace, took his arm. She nodded to the watchful crowd.

"Shall we?"

"Shall we what?"

"Announce our engagement."

Tilghman grinned and led her toward the house.

CHAPTER 18

Tilghman still felt slightly dazed. The party had ended with another round of handshakes and warm congratulations from all their neighbors. Even Amos Stratton had pumped his arm, welcoming him into the family. Then Zoe had seen him off with a long, lingering kiss.

A full moon bathed the landscape in a spectral glow. He was humming to himself, filled with a sense of well-being for the moment and the future. Though he'd hoped to be married sooner, Zoe had insisted on an engagement period of six months. She wanted everything done in the proper manner, and she needed time to plan the wedding. The way he'd felt tonight he could refuse her nothing. He told himself six months wasn't long to wait.

The buoyant mood suddenly evaporated. As the buckboard rolled into the compound, he spotted two horses hitched outside the corral. A moment later two men rose from where they were seated in shadows at the front of the house. When they stepped into the moonlight, he saw that it was Heck Thomas and Chris Madsen. He brought the buckboard to a halt, swearing softly under his breath. He knew without asking that it was bad news.

"Look who's here," he said, stepping down from the buckboard. "Where'd you come from?"

"Guthrie," Thomas replied. "We've got trouble, Bill."

"Figured that when I saw you. What's the problem?"

"A warrant's out on the Dunn brothers."

"On what charge?"

"Horse stealing."

Thomas quickly related the details. The sheriff of Payne County had obtained a warrant against the Dunns on charges of horse stealing. There was evidence that the brothers bought rustled stock from horse thieves and later resold it after altering the brands. Evett Nix had learned of the charges only that afternoon, and he'd moved quickly to forestall the Dunns' arrest. In effect, he had made a deal with the Payne County sheriff.

"We bought some time," Thomas concluded. "The sheriff will hold off till we finish our investigation. But if we don't move on the Dunns, he will."

"What's his hurry?" Tilghman asked.

"Longer he waits, the more horses get stole. He wants the Dunns behind bars."

Tilghman was thoughtful a moment. Some months ago, when he'd posed as horse trader in Ingalls, he recalled the saloonkeeper mentioning that the Dunns had horses for sale. He saw now that their ranch was actually a way station for rustled stock. As well, it explained their connection to Doolin and the Wild Bunch. Thieves were drawn to thieves.

"Birds of a feather," he said at length. "The Dunns probably met Doolin through the horse thieves. All that crowd knows one another."

"Likely so," Thomas agreed. "We're gonna find out pretty damn quick. Nix wants us to raid the Dunns."

Madsen chuckled. "Told us to tell you it's a direct order. He figured you'd object."

"Nothing's changed," Tilghman said. "All we'll do is tip our hand to Doolin."

"Orders are orders," Madsen said. "Besides, if we don't, the sheriff will. Might as well be our play."

"You've got a point there, Chris."

Thomas held his pocket watch to the moonlight. "Quarter till eleven," he said, glancing at Tilghman. "You reckon we could hit the Dunns by sunrise?"

"Yeah, I suppose so." Tilghman's gaze went past him to the house. "You boys seen Neal Brown?"

"Gave us short shrift," Madsen said in a bemused tone. "Wouldn't say where you were, and told us to wait for you outside. Not the friendly sort, is he?"

"Neal figures I'm in the wrong line of work."

Thomas eyed him closer. "Where you been, anyway? Never saw you in duds like that."

"Well, Heck, you might say I dressed for the occasion. I popped the question tonight, and she said yes."

"You're gonna get married?"

"C'mon, I'll tell you about it while I change clothes."

Tilghman led them into the house. They pumped him with questions and laughingly joshed about the bliss of wedded life. The commotion awakened Brown, who grumpily went to make a pot of coffee. Then, figuring it might be a long time between meals, they all trooped into the kitchen. A short while later everyone sat down to a hurriedly prepared breakfast.

They toasted his engagement with flapjacks drowned in sorghum.

The moon heeled over to the west. The lawmen were some twenty miles north of Chandler, their horses held to a steady trot. All around them, the plains were awash in moonglow, the terrain clearly visible. Their thoughts were on the job ahead.

On the ride north, Tilghman had described the layout of the Dunn ranch. The main compound, he told Mad-

sen and Thomas, was situated on Council Creek southeast of Ingalls. The house was set back off the creek,
with a low knoll to the rear. To the west was a large
corral, and east of the house was a roofed storm cellar.
He recalled a stovepipe protruding from the storm cellar, and they all agreed that visiting outlaws were probably quartered there. After some discussion on tactics,
they had agreed on a plan. Their raid would be staged
from three directions.

Some miles south of Council Creek, the lawmen suddenly reined to a halt. Ahead, like an illusory phantom,
a rider materialized out of the moonlit night. Without a
word being spoken, they spread out, hands resting on
the butts of their pistols. The rider slowed to a walk,
then halted a few yards away. There was a moment of
tense silence.

"Howdy," Tilghman finally said. "You gave us a
start."

"You like to scared the pee outta me, too."

The voice startled them even more. They peered
closer, squinting in the moonlight, and saw that the
rider was a girl. She was dressed in men's clothing, pants
stuffed in her boot tops, a vest over her shirt, and a
weather-beaten hat. She looked to be no more than sixteen or seventeen.

"I'll be switched!" Thomas said, amazed. "Your folks
know you're out so late, missy?"

The girl stiffened. "Don't see as how that's any of
your business."

Her voice was tough, high-pitched but oddly hard.
Staring at her, Tilghman suddenly realized that she was
armed. The stock of a Winchester protruded from her
saddle scabbard and a holstered pistol was strapped
around her waist. He casually motioned off into the
night.

"You live around here?"

"What's your name, Nosey Ike? You gents ask a lotta questions."

Tilghman shifted in the saddle, and a flash of moonlight glinted off his badge. "We're just surprised to see a girl out here by herself. Where you headed?"

The girl hesitated, staring at their badges. Then, hauling the reins about, she gigged her horse. "Don't nobody follow me!" she yelled. "You'll git yourself shot."

She pounded off toward the east. Somewhat stunned, the lawmen were speechless, watching her disappear at a gallop across the plains. Finally, the first to recover, Thomas found his voice.

"What the hell do you make of that?"

"You got me," Tilghman said. "Did you see the hardware she was packin'?"

"A real spitfire," Madsen said in wonderment. "Maybe she's the daughter of some rancher around here."

"Well, boys," Thomas allowed, "whoever she was, she's gone now. Guess we'll never know."

Tilghman studied the sky. "Couple of hours till first light. Let's move out."

They rode toward Council Creek.

A shaft of golden sunlight touched the horizon. The lawmen, their horses hidden, were secreted in stands of trees around the Dunn ranch. Sunrise was their prearranged signal, and they started forward.

Tilghman approached from the creek, Winchester in hand, and headed toward the house. Thomas, carrying a shotgun, moved on a direct line to the storm cellar, the sun at his back. To the north, Madsen came down the knoll, with a line of fire to the rear of the house as well as the storm cellar. They moved quickly, every sense alert.

A hand signal between Tilghman and Thomas kicked off the raid. One pounded on the front door of the

house and the other rattled the stovepipe on the roof of
the storm cellar. In loud voices, they identified themselves as federal marshals and ordered everyone outside. Tilghman waited at the side of the house, his
carbine trained on the door. Thomas, standing on top of
the storm cellar, covered the entrance with his shotgun.

"Hold your fire!" someone yelled from inside the
house. "We're comin' out."

From the storm cellar, as though echoing in a cave, a
voice cried out. "For chrissakes, don't shoot! We're not
gonna fight!"

The door of the house creaked open. Hands raised,
two men in filthy long johns and their women in night-
dresses stepped outside. At the storm cellar, three men
in hastily buttoned pants, their boots forgotten, moved
into the daylight. While Tilghman and Thomas kept
them covered, Madsen quickly searched the house.
Then, crossing the yard, he cautiously inspected the
storm cellar. He waved an all clear signal.

The men at the house identified themselves as the
Dunn brothers, Bee and George. From the storm cellar,
his features wreathed in disgust, Thomas called out,
"These boys are a sorry lot of two-bit horse thieves. I
arrested one of them before. Know the other two on
sight."

Tilghman interrogated the Dunn brothers. Thomas
poked the man he'd arrested in the belly with his shotgun. The man blanched, his knees wobbly, and began
answering questions. Some while later, they herded everyone together in the yard of the house. The lawmen
walked off a short distance.

"You first," Thomas said, nodding to Tilghman.
"What'd you find out?"

"Nothing much," Tilghman admitted. "The Dunns
say they never saw your horse thieves until last night.
Claim they just gave them a place to sleep."

"One part jibes," Madsen said. "I took a good look

around that storm cellar. There's eight bunks and a wood stove. Stinks like a wolf den."

Thomas gave them a dour look. "That knothead I questioned spilled his guts. You remember the girl we ran across last night?"

"Yeah?" Tilghman said. "What about her?"

"She goes by the handle of Cattle Annie. Her and another girl—calls herself Little Breeches—run together. Sounds so dumb it's got to be true."

"So?"

"Turns out they're friends of the Wild Bunch. Cattle Annie damn near killed her horse to beat us here. Guess who she brought a warnin' to?"

"You serious?" Tilghman said. "Doolin was here?"

Thomas nodded. "Bastard rode out before dawn."

CHAPTER 19

The lawmen were in a quandary. Doolin's trail was still fresh, less than two hours old, and they needed to start tracking. Yet they weren't sure they'd heard the full story. Or the entire truth.

After a hurried conference, they decided to have another talk with the horse thieves. Then, depending on what was learned, they might question the Dunns further. Their thought was that the Dunns, hoping to avoid prison and thereby save their ranch, would admit nothing. The horse thieves, with less to lose, would be more cooperative. They simply wanted to stay out of jail.

The Dunn women were ordered to brew coffee. While they were inside, Madsen kept their husbands under guard in front of the house. Tilghman and Thomas marched the three horse thieves back to the dugout storm cellar. Thomas adopted the role of the tough but sympathetic lawman, explaining that he was merely following orders. The man in charge, he told them, wasn't satisfied with their story. He then gave the stage to Tilghman.

Tilghman was no slouch as an actor himself. Over the years he had played out the same routine with such consummate performers as Bat Masterson and Wyatt Earp. He stuck his thumbs in his gun belt, the Winchester in the crook of his arm, and squinted at the thieves with a fierce glare. His voice was lowered to a harsh rasp.

"Horse stealing," he said bluntly, "carries a sentence of five to ten years. I figure you boys deserve the maximum."

The three men looked stricken. Tilghman allowed a moment of silence to underscore the message. Then, his voice cold and threatening, he went on. "This is your last chance," he said. "Tell me the truth and we might cut a deal. Lie to me and I'll put you away for ten years. I guaran-goddamn-tee it."

The thieves tripped over one another to save themselves. As the story unfolded, one then the other rushed to provide missing details. Doolin had ridden in late last night, after visiting his wife in Ingalls. An hour or so later Cattle Annie had rapped on the door of the storm cellar and called Doolin outside. Within minutes, Doolin had collected his gear, saddled his horse, and galloped off with the girl. One of the men, who had stepped outside to relieve himself, saw them ride southeast along the creek.

Probing further, Tilghman discovered that the thieves felt they'd been betrayed. Doolin or the girl could have warned them that lawmen were headed for the Dunn ranch. Yet they were left in the lurch, probably in the hope that they would engage the marshals in a long, time-consuming gun battle. To their way of thinking, Doolin had been willing to sacrifice them in order to cover his own escape. Had they put up a fight, the plan would have worked without a hitch.

Tilghman intended to wait until full sunrise before he started tracking. He checked the horizon, saw that he still had a few minutes, and prodded the men to talk about Cattle Annie. The girl's real name, they told him, was Annie McDougal. Her partner, known as Little Breeches, was Jennie Midkiff. Word had it that they were runaways, formerly from somewhere in Ohio. They rustled a few cattle, whored for members of the Wild Bunch, and looked upon Doolin as their idol. Their hideout was a mile or so north of where Council Creek fed into the Cimarron.

The Dunn brothers, the thieves hastened to add, were known to everyone on the owlhoot. For a price, they provided Doolin with a refuge from the law. Their regular business was operating in stolen horses and occasionally rustled cattle. The Dunns never tried to gouge, always paying a fair price for good stock. George, who was an artist with a running iron, skillfully altered the brands. Bee was the thinker of the family and attended to business matters. The stolen horses were sold to a network of crooked livestock dealers.

"Here's the deal," Tilghman told the thieves when they finished talking. "We'll tell the judge you boys were a big help with information on the Wild Bunch. I think he'll agree to probation."

"Probation?" one of them parrotted with disbelief. "You mean he'll turn us loose?"

"Yeah, probably, on the condition that you go straight. Steal another horse and you're on your way to prison."

Tilghman turned, exchanging an amused look with Thomas, and walked back to the house. He took Madsen aside, quickly explained the situation, and secured agreement to go along with a plan he'd hatched over the past few minutes. Then, while Madsen went to retrieve their horses, he moved back to the Dunns. He addressed his remarks to Bee.

"Those boys," he said, nodding toward the storm cellar, "are headed for jail in Guthrie. You and your brother are working on borrowed time."

Dunn was a short man with a potbelly and beady eyes. His brow furrowed with skepticism. "Why aren't you arrestin' us too?"

"Simple," Tilghman informed him. "You gents will

keep your mouths buttoned about today. When Doolin asks, you'll tell him nobody spilled the beans about him being here. Just say we were after horse thieves."

"And if we don't?"

"Then I'll personally escort you to federal prison."

Dunn frowned. "What makes you think Doolin will buy that story?"

"You'll convince him," Tilghman said with a hard grin. "That's what I meant about borrowed time. Either way, if you don't convince him, you lose. He'll kill you or I'll put you in prison."

"Cold one, aren't you?" Dunn said. "I'll bet you piss ice water."

"Let me down and you'll find out."

Some ten minutes later Madsen rode south with the horse thieves. The men were mounted, hands manacled behind their backs, their horses hitched to a rope attached to Madsen's saddlehorn. The Dunn brothers watched silently from the house.

Tilghman and Thomas rode southeast along Council Creek. The tracks, churned earth of horses at a gallop, were simple to follow. Downstream a ways, Thomas finally broke the silence. His expression was somber.

"Why'd you let the Dunns off the hook?"

"Hedged our bet," Tilghman said. "We've lost nothing in the bargain if we catch Doolin. But if we don't catch him, then maybe he'll still believe the Dunns' place is a safe hideout. Down the road, that might be our ace in the hole."

"Jesus," Thomas said in an admiring tone. "You're a lot more devious than I gave you credit for."

"Learned it all watching you, Heck."

"Hell, don't lay it off on me. Nix is gonna have kittens when he hears about this."

"Let him," Tilghman said easily. "Last few months, we've got a better handle on Mr. Nix. When the three of us stick together, he folds like a house of cards."

"By God!" Thomas said with a sudden grin. "Never thought of it that way, but you're right. We do have his number."

"Well, look here." Tilghman reined to a halt, studying the tracks. "Doolin and the girl parted company. She went on downstream, probably headed for her place. He took off on a beeline for the Nations."

"How do you know him from her?"

"I got their tracks separated out back at Dunn's corral."

Thomas decided to keep quiet, and let him sort it out. Tilghman's experience as an army scout made him the most skilled tracker of all the marshals. His experience as a peace officer had taught him an equally important lesson, perhaps a cardinal rule. He'd learned long ago that a wilderness manhunt requires patience.

For that reason, like any seasoned tracker, he had awaited full sunrise before trying to cut sign. On hard ground the correct sun angle made the difference between seeing a print or missing it entirely. The tracker stationed himself so that the trail would appear directly between his position and the sun. In early morning, with the sun at a low angle, he worked westward of the trail. The easterly sunlight then cast shadows across the hoofprints of a horse.

A tracker seldom saw an entire hoofprint unless the ground was quite soft. On hardened terrain the tracker looked for flat spots, scuff marks, and disturbed vegetation. Of all sign, flat spots were the most revealing. Only hooves or footprints, something usually related to man, would leave flat spots. Small creatures might leave faint scuff marks or disturb pebbles. But a flat spot, unnatural to nature, was always made by a hooved animal or a man. A shod horse made the sign even simpler to read.

Tilghman kept the sun between himself and the hoofprints. The trail angled across the plains, the direction east by southeast. He looked for the change of color caused when the dry surface of the earth is disturbed to expose a moister, lower surface. Heat increased the rate at which tracks age, and the sun had been out now for more than a hour. The under-surface of the prints, he noted, was almost restored to the normal color of the ground. All the sign indicated that Doolin was slightly more than two hours ahead.

The tracks took on an irregular zigzag pattern through streams and timbered woods. Whenever possible, Doolin chose rocky terrain or ground baked hard by the summer sun. He clearly suspected he was being pursued, and he'd resorted to evasive tactics. Yet his general direction never deviated, even though he had elected to take a winding route. He was headed for a sanctuary somewhere in the Nations.

By midday, the lawmen had covered better than ten miles. A good part of the time Tilghman was forced to dismount and conduct the search on foot. At several points, particularly on hard ground, the hoofprints simply disappeared. He then had to rely on pebbles and twigs dislodged as horse and rider had passed that way. The direction in which the ground was disturbed, invisible except to a veteran tracker, indicated the line of travel. Slowly, sometimes step by step, he clung to the trail.

Shortly after noonday Tilghman located a troubling sign. Upon crossing the Cimarron, he discovered that Doolin had stopped to watch his backtrail. The spot was located at a bend in the river where a stand of trees bordered the shoreline. Hidden behind the trees, Doolin had dismounted and waited, with an open field of fire across the width of the Cimarron. From there, with a lever-action rifle, he could have ended the chase. Or at the very least, discouraged further pursuit.

On foot, Tilghman inspected the spot. Farther into the trees he found where Doolin had tied his horse sometime before midday. The prints were deep and clear, the ground thoroughly scuffled, indicating a wait of close to an hour. Nearer the river bank, screened by the treeline, he saw where Doolin had selected a vantage point with a field of fire covering the stream and the opposite shoreline. Imprints of his boots were recorded in the soft earth beneath the trees.

"Doolin's tricky," Tilghman said. "Glad we didn't ford the river an hour ago."

Thomas was still mounted. He'd halted on the river bank and watched the search from a distance. "Hope you're jokin'," he replied. "The bastard was gonna bushwhack us?"

"Way I figure it, he would've waited till we were in the middle of the river. Then he'd have cut loose."

"And us stuck out there like sitting ducks. No place to run, no place to take cover."

"Heck, I just suspect we would've been dead ducks. Wouldn't have taken more than two shots."

"Goddammit!" Thomas exploded. "If he tried it here, he's liable to try it somewheres up ahead. We're gonna have to keep a sharp lookout."

"No argument there." Tilghman walked back to his horse, stepped into the saddle. "Maybe he didn't get us, but he sure as hell slowed us down. Told you he was tricky."

"What I wouldn't give to get that sonovabitch in my sights."

"Count your lucky stars, Heck. An hour ago he would've had us in his sights."

Tilghman led the way. He started at the tree where Doolin had tied his horse and began tracking from there. Yet another element, the prospect of an ambush, had entered into the chase. They both kept a wary eye on the terrain ahead as they moved off through the woods. The hunters, in no small sense, had now become the hunted.

Late that afternoon, Tilghman reined to an abrupt

halt. Before him lay a wide stretch of rocky terrain bordering the Cimarron. Not far ahead he spotted sign where Doolin had crossed the river onto soft ground along the opposite bank. A short distance beyond that point the sun had baked the upper shoreline as hard as brick. There, as though Doolin's horse had taken wings, the tracks disappeared.

By sundown, Tilghman had walked the ground a mile in each direction on both sides of the river. There were no tracks, no upturned pebbles, no disturbed vegetation. Finally, with a grudging sense of admiration, he ended the search. Doolin had once again outfoxed them.

CHAPTER 20

The moon stood like a mallow globe in a starlit sky. Where they'd lost the trail, they made camp along the banks of the Cimarron. Their horses were hobbled, grazing on a nearby patch of grass. The swift rush of water was the only sound in the night.

Their supper consisted of hardtack, jerky, and thick black coffee. Seated around the fire, they stared into the flames, their mood at a low ebb. The chase, ending in yet another stalemate, had left them withdrawn and thoughtful. Neither of them had spoken in a long while.

Thomas cracked a twig, tossed it into the fire. He rubbed his whiskery jaw, suddenly restless with the silence, and finally broached the subject that had them both disturbed. "How you reckon he ditched us?"

"Wish I knew," Tilghman said dully. "Just a guess, but he might've doubled back on that hard ground and taken to the river. He could stick to the shallows a long ways downstream."

"We could ride both banks in the mornin'. Might just turn up some sign."

"I'd seriously doubt it. Doolin's slicker than I thought."

"You mean the way he gave us the slip?"

Tilghman knuckled his mustache. "Wherever he

learned it, he knows every trick in the bag. Probably took lessons from his Indian friends."

"I hear you right," Thomas observed, "you're sayin' we lost him."

"Heck, he's long gone into the Nations by now. We're playing a busted flush."

"Sorry bastard's got more lives than a cat."

"I've been sittin' here studying on that. Appears to me there's only two ways we'll catch him. One's by pure accident, the right place at the right time. The other's through his wife."

"You got a point," Thomas agreed. "He's sure enough been bit by the love bug."

"No doubt about it," Tilghman said. "For a smart man, he takes lots of risks to be with that girl. Ingalls ought to be the one spot he avoids at any cost."

"Which is just where he was last night. Before he rode out to the Dunns' place."

"Well, I imagine the girl being in a family way has a lot to do with it. Doolin strikes me as a man who takes his obligations pretty serious."

"Life's funny," Thomas said without mirth. "Here's a goddamn robber and killer with all the conscience of a scorpion. But he's true blue to his woman. What a joke."

Tilghman chuckled. "You're startin' to sound like a philosopher."

"A plumb pissed-off philosopher. I thought for sure we had him this time."

"The accident went against us this time, Heck. Bad luck in spades when we stumbled across that girl."

"Cattle Annie?"

"Miss Annie McDougal, every outlaw's sweetheart. Except for her, we would've caught Doolin sound asleep."

Thomas grunted. "Somebody ought to pull her drawers down and spank her butt."

"That's a dandy idea." Tilghman suddenly grinned, nodding to himself. "Why go back to Guthrie empty-handed?"

"You talkin' about arresting the girl?"

"Don't see any reason why not. We've got her on obstruction of justice and aiding a fugitive. All federal charges, too."

"By God!" Thomas's mood brightened. "I like it."

"Another thing," Tilghman added. "Lock her up and she won't be giving Doolin the tip-off anymore. Starts to sound better all the time."

"What about her pardner, Little Breeches? Wonder how the hell she got that name?"

"However she got it, she's in thick with Doolin too. We'll arrest her on the same charges."

Thomas took the small, galvanized coffeepot from the edge of the fire. He poured himself a cup, his expression abruptly solemn. "You know we're gonna get razzed for bringin' in girls instead of Doolin. Christ, I can hear it now."

"You forget," Tilghman advised him. "Annie was carrying a pistol and a rifle. Threatened to blow our heads off, as I remember."

"You really think they'd fight?"

"I think we'd be smart to approach it that way. A gun doesn't care who pulls the trigger."

"Yeah, you're right," Thomas said thoughtfully. "That could be downright embarrassin'!"

"What?"

"Gettin' yourself shot by a girl."

Tilghman started laughing, and a moment later Thomas joined in, struck by such a preposterous notion. But later, as they lay in their bedrolls, Thomas stared soberly at the star-studded sky. He hoped Tilghman was wrong, that they wouldn't fight. He'd never before killed a woman. Or even worse, a girl.

Tomorrow, he told himself, wasn't the time to start.

* * *

Late the next afternoon, west along the Cimarron, they sighted Council Creek. They turned northwest where the tributary emptied into the river, sticking to the shoreline. Their information, squeezed from the horse thieves at the Dunns' ranch, was that the girls had a hideout a mile or so upstream. Half a mile farther on they dismounted, leading their horses.

A short while later the wind shifted and they caught the scent of woodsmoke. Up ahead, through trees crowding the creek bank, they saw the outlines of a small cabin. As they approached nearer, it became apparent that the cabin was a crude one-room affair thrown together with logs, a stovepipe sticking out of the roof. On the wind, they heard the sound of girlish laughter.

Tilghman motioned a halt at the edge of the treeline. Beyond was a clearing, the cabin set back a short distance from the creek. At the far corner of the cabin, hitched to a metal ring in the wall, two horses stood hipshot and saddled in the heat. The door was open, and through it, they saw shadowed movement as one of the girls moved across the cabin. The sound of voices was followed by another burst of laughter.

The lawmen left their horses in the trees. Then, circling through the woods, they approached the cabin from the rear. Their pistols drawn, they flattened themselves against the wall and moved to the front of the cabin. As they stepped around the corner, one of the horses at the opposite end awoke with a start and snorted in alarm. Swiftly now, afraid the girls had been alerted, they hurried along the front wall of the cabin. But even as the horses reared back in fright, there was still another round of laughter from inside. They jumped through the open door.

"Hold it!" Tilghman ordered. "Federal marshals."

The girls froze, their laughter stilled. Little Breeches,

a tiny waif of no more than fifteen, was stretched out on a bunk bed. On the opposite side of the room, Cattle Annie stood silhouetted before an open window. They were both dressed in men's clothing, holstered pistols strapped around their slim hips. For an instant, thunderstruck, they stared with their mouths ajar.

"Easy now," Thomas said in a loud voice. "Don't try anything foolish."

Cattle Annie dived through the open window like a dog through a hoop. Tilghman turned back toward the door as Little Breeches leaped off the bed. Thomas crossed the cabin in three swift strides and caught her wrists as she pulled her pistol. He bore down, squeezing hard, and the gun dropped from her hand. Holstering his pistol, he smiled down on her.

"Now I know why they call you Little Breeches."

She slugged him in the balls. His mouth ovaled in a whoosh of air and he bent double, clutching at his groin. The girl loosed a shrill screech and attacked him with the ferocity of a wildcat, clawing and scratching as he hopped around with fire in his crotch. Her nails raked his face from forehead to chin.

After several moments, battered and savaged by her assault, Thomas was finally able to draw a full breath. He warded her off with one arm, still clutching his groin with the other hand, and she kicked him in the shins. Howling with pain, he grabbed her by the hair and lifted her off the floor. The girl screamed like a banshee, flailing and thrashing while he held her at arm's length. His face was ribboned with purple welts and bloody slashes.

Outside the cabin, Cattle Annie bounded onto her horse like a circus acrobat. She wheeled away at a lope as Tilghman came through the door. He jerked the reins loose on the other horse, vaulting into the saddle, and took off after her. A beaten path behind the cabin tunneled through the woods and emerged onto an open prairie. The girl whipped her horse into a headlong gallop.

Tilghman was perhaps ten yards behind when he cleared the treeline. The girl looked over her shoulder, her features contorted, screaming obscenities that were lost on the rush of wind. Then, as he booted his horse and closed the distance, her eyes went round with panic. She pulled her pistol, turning in the saddle, and fired three quick shots at Tilghman. The slugs whizzed past him with an angry snarl.

Hauling back on the reins, Tilghman brought his horse to a skidding halt. He grabbed the stock of a Winchester carbine, jerking it from the scabbard as he stepped out of the saddle. A quick glance confirmed that it was much like his own carbine and he levered a shell into the chamber. The butt snugged into his shoulder, he caught the sights and drew a bead on the girl's horse. When he fired, the horse went down forelegs first, dead even as it struck the ground. The girl was hurled out of the saddle like a cannonball.

Tilghman led his mount to where Cattle Annie lay sprawled on the prairie. The jolt had rattled her senses and sapped her will to fight. He took her pistol, then unbuckled her pants belt and pulled it loose. She moaned, her eyes fluttering, as he cinched her wrists together with the belt. Before she could resist, he hefted her off the ground and dumped her over the saddle. She began cursing as he mounted behind her and rode back toward the creek.

Thomas was waiting outside the cabin. Little Breeches was seated on the ground, her wrists bound with rope and a bandanna stuffed in her mouth. Her eyes welled up with tears as Tilghman reined to a halt and dropped Cattle Annie at her feet. He stepped out of the saddle, eyeing the latticework of scratches across Thomas's face. Tilghman's mouth lifted in a crooked grin.

"Looks like you got the worst of it, Heck."

"No laughin' matter," Thomas said sourly. "She's mean as tiger spit and twice as deadly. I've fought men no tougher'n her."

"You lousy bastards!" Cattle Annie shrieked. "Take that gag outta Jennie's mouth. She's just a kid!"

"Some kid," Tilghman commented dryly. "Quit yellin' or I'll gag you. We've had enough nonsense for one day."

She fell to her knees beside Little Breeches. Thomas studied them a moment, then looked at Tilghman. "What was all that shootin'?"

"Annie tried to stop my clock. I brought her horse down with a saddle gun."

"Jesus Crucified Christ! We're never gonna live this down."

"Think not?"

"Know not," Thomas grumped. "You tradin' lead with a slip of a girl. And me cut up like I'd tangled with a grizzle bear." He gingerly touched a bloody gash on his jaw. "Wish't I'd never let you talk me into it."

"Whoa now," Tilghman said with a wry smile. "I seem to recollect it was your idea."

"Whoever thought it up," Thomas retorted indignantly, "it was a pea-brain notion. Here on out, I'm not chasin' any more girls."

"Way you look, I don't blame you, Heck."

"Don't you start on me! I'm warnin' you."

A short time later they rode out of the clearing. The girls were mounted double on Little Breeches's horse, hands now secured behind their backs. Tilghman took the lead and Thomas brought up the rear, nursing his wounds with a kerchief dipped in creek water. Little Breeches, whose gag had been removed, taunted him in a shrill voice.

"Hey, you big sissy! Hurt bad, are you?"

"Close your trap or I'll close it for you."

"Yeah!" Cattle Annie chimed in. "Way you jumped us, you're nothin' but cowards. Let's try it fair and square."

"Awww, for chrissakes," Thomas moaned. "It's never gonna end."

The Guthrie *Statesman* ran a front-page story two days later. A banner headline confirmed Heck Thomas's worst fears.

STALWART MARSHALS APPREHEND DESPERADOES
CATTLE ANNIE AND LITTLE BREECHES NABBED

CHAPTER 21

A fortnight later the girls were still in the news. After being lodged in the Guthrie jail, Cattle Annie and Little Breeches had escaped. There was lax security for women prisoners, and they had managed to outwit the night guard. The newspaper, with caustic humor, played it as farce.

Sheriff's deputies recaptured the girls the following day. From that point, justice moved swiftly for the young runaways. They were brought to trial and rapidly convicted on testimony by the three horse thieves captured at Dunns' ranch. The judge, though lenient, passed sentences the same day.

Annie McDougal and Jennie Midkiff, being underage, were not sentenced to prison. Instead, they were committed to a reform school in Massachusetts for two years. The girls, who considered themselves full-fledged outlaws, took it as a personal insult. A day later, on Tilghman's recommendation, the horse thieves were sentenced to five years' probation. They were admonished to follow the straight and narrow.

To Evett Nix's dismay, he was again lambasted in the press. As U.S. marshal, according to the newspapers, he was hell on underage girls but no significant threat to the Wild Bunch. Doolin and his gang had vanished in yet another puff of smoke, leaving no trace as to their whereabouts. They were generally thought to be hiding out in the Nations, but no one had a clue. Once again, they'd gone to ground.

Tilghman returned home following the court proceeding. Nix had ordered him, as well as Madsen and Thomas, to redouble their efforts. Still, without a tip from an informant, or another holdup by the Wild Bunch, the trail was cold. On the ride to Chandler, Tilghman had pondered the matter at some length. Thomas and Madsen would work their informants, and hope for a break. He decided to take more direct action.

On his first morning at home, Neal Brown brought him up to date on ranch operations. The mares had foaled a week past, dropping four colts and six fillies. An inspection of the stables confirmed that all were doing well under the care of the Sac and Fox hands. The offspring were frisky, their legs sturdy, and all clearly had the conformation of their sire, Steeldust. The breeding program was off to a rousing start.

Tilghman was immensely gratified with the results. For the first stage, he thought the crop of colts and fillies held great promise for the future. When time permitted, he still intended to expand the bloodlines with another stallion and other thoroughbred mares. But for the moment, with his duties as a lawman, he was content with the progress thus far. Steeldust had performed admirably as a stud, and there was reason to be pleased.

At the noon meal, Brown finally ran out of talk about horses. He looked up from his plate with mock solemnity. "Those girls you arrested?" he said, waving a fork. "From the newspapers, sounded like you had your hands full."

"Yeah, couple of real hardcases." Tilghman played along, aware that he was being ribbed. "First time I ever traded shots with a female."

"So what happens to them now?"

"Tried, convicted, and sentenced. They're on their way to reform school."

"No joke?" Brown asked idly. "Well, I guess reform school's the right place for pint-sized desperadoes. Evett Nix must've been tickled you brought 'em in."

"After a fashion," Tilghman said, laughing. " 'Course, I think he would've preferred Doolin."

"What the hell," Brown said in a bantering tone. "You got your man—uh, girl. That's what counts."

"Too bad you weren't with me, Neal. Things might have gone better."

"Think so, do you?"

"Yeah, I do," Tilghman said, nodding. "Fact is, I wanted to ask your help on another matter."

Brown squinted at him. "You talkin' about law work?"

"Not anything all that risky. I just need someone to cover my back."

"Cover your back where?"

Tilghman sipped his coffee. "Thought I'd scout the Dunn ranch again. It's been two weeks since that last raid, and who knows? Doolin might figure we wouldn't look there so soon."

"Why me?" Brown said crossly. "I ain't no lawdog."

"Well, you might say it's a secret mission. I halfway forgot to clear it with Nix. Thought I'd have a looksee on my own."

"Just a looksee?" Brown scoffed. "What if we stumble acrost Doolin and his bunch?"

"Doubtful," Tilghman replied. "I had in mind a quick scout, in and out. Figured you wouldn't object to lending a hand."

"You get my ass shot and I won't never forgive you."

"Appreciate the assist, Neal. Knew I could count on you."

"Yeah, sure," Brown said gruffly. "Just a prize sucker, that's me."

"You're an upstanding citizen, always were."

"Tell me that when the shootin' starts."

Early that evening Tilghman called on Zoe. She hadn't expected him, unaware that he had returned to Chandler. But she pulled him into the house, insisting that he stay for supper. He gladly accepted.

"Just potluck," she said, walking him into the parlor. "Nothing special, I'm afraid."

"Beggars can't be choosers," Tilghman said. "Don't put yourself to any trouble."

"I'm so happy to see you I could skip supper. Who needs food?"

She squeezed his arm as they entered the parlor. Amos Stratton smiled and rose from his easy chair, extending his hand. After a moment, Zoe excused herself and hurried off to the kitchen. Stratton motioned him to a chair.

"When'd you get back, Bill?"

"Late last night. Rode in from Guthrie."

Stratton struck a match, lit his pipe. "We read about you in the newspaper. Those two little girls must've been a sorry pair."

"Sad thing," Tilghman observed. "They got mixed in with a bad lot."

Stratton now took an interest in his work. Their conversation, rather than stiff and formal, had become a casual exchange between friends. Tilghman was treated more as a family member, his calls a welcome occasion. Their talks often ranged over a wide variety of subjects.

"Speakin' of news," Stratton said, nudging a crumpled newspaper at the foot of his chair. "You heard the latest on the statehood movement?"

"Heard it yesterday," Tilghman acknowledged. "There's talk of little else in Guthrie."

"Yeah, I'd bet they're beatin' the drum over there. Big things are in the works."

"Guess it depends on whose ox gets gored."

"Same as always," Stratton said easily. "The Indian's got to make way for progress."

"There's a difference here, Amos. We're talking about the Five Civilized Tribes."

Tilghman's remark went to the heart of a wide-ranging debate. The battle for statehood had been joined, and at stake was twenty million acres of land in the Nations. The debate, by now a matter of national interest, raged in the halls of Congress as well as the White House itself. No one doubted that the future of both Oklahoma Territory and Indian Territory would be played out along the banks of the Potomac. There, in the political arena, the issue of statehood would be decided.

The key to the debate was that the Nations possessed almost all of the mineral wealth to be found in both territories. Coal mines had begun operating on tribal lands as early as 1871, when the Katy railroad first laid tracks through the Nations. The largest of these mines was located in the Choctaw Nation, and for the most part had remained under strict tribal control. But with the rapid growth of Oklahoma Territory, and a steadily increasing demand for coal as fuel, the situation had changed. White entrepreneurs, as well as government, now coveted the red man's natural wealth.

"Indians are Indians," Stratton said. "I never bought that stuff about the Five Civilized Tribes. Don't appear all that civilized to me."

"You've never been there," Tilghman observed. "They have towns and schools, and laws and courts. Their system of government's even patterned on ours."

"Maybe so, but they've had that land for fifty years. What've they done with it?"

Zoe called them to supper. At the table, the conversation resumed with the give and take of a friendly debate. Tilghman's view of the Nations, a subject they'd never discussed, was a pleasant surprise for Zoe. She found herself nodding with his defense of the Five Civilized Tribes.

The power brokers, Tilghman commented, had decided that Oklahoma Territory and Indian Territory should be joined as one state. Indian leaders, on the other hand, had lodged fiery protests against single statehood. They feared, and rightly so, that Oklahomans would monopolize government and politics, and the rule of law. As the Plains Tribes had been dispossessed of their lands, it now appeared that similar tactics were to be used against the Five Civilized Tribes. There was an odor of conspiracy involving white money barons and the federal government.

The Indians, Tilghman went on, were right in their suspicions. Joint statehood would be impossible until all Indian lands had been allotted in severalty and the tribal governments abolished. Quick to respond to pressure from Congress, the president had appointed a commission and ordered that negotiations commence with the Five Civilized Tribes. The purpose was to extinguish tribal title to their lands, and Indian leaders were aligned in their determination to resist. The last battle was about to be joined.

"I don't get it," Stratton said, puzzled. "Everybody in the Nations sides with outlaws and works against federal marshals. Why would you take up for them?"

Tilghman helped himself to a second serving of beef stew. "Question of what's right," he said. "Fifty years ago we took their homelands in the South and forced them to move out here. Not right to rob them again."

"The same could be said of the Plains Tribes. We took their land."

"Yeah, but there's a difference. The Plains Tribes were nomads, lived off the buffalo. The people in the Nations operate businesses and run farms. They adopted our way of life."

Stratton sopped stew gravy with a hunk of bread. He chewed thoughtfully a moment. "No offense, Bill," he said finally. "But you and me wouldn't have land except for broken treaties. What changed your mind about the Nations?"

"Hard to say," Tilghman admitted. "What seemed fair yesterday doesn't seem so fair today. Maybe we ought to stop breaking treaties."

"Sounds like wishful thinkin' to me. Would you return your land to the Sac and Fox?"

"Too late now to turn back the clock. But we've got a chance to do the right thing in the Nations. We owe those people more than a hundred sixty acres."

Congress had directed that a roll be taken of every man, woman, and child in Indian Territory. Clearly, this was a preparatory step to allotment of lands in severalty, one hundred sixty acres to a family. Yet the rolls being taken were also a death knell for a way of life. It was the first step in the dissolution of the Five Civilized Tribes.

Amos Stratton saw it as progress. To his way of thinking, at least ten million acres would be opened to white settlement in Indian Territory. But for Tilghman it had slowly become a symbol of all that was wrong between the white man and the red man. He had pioneered the opening of Oklahoma Territory, and he was proud of what had been achieved. Still, in retrospect, he saw that it could have been handled in a more equitable manner. He thought the Five Civilized Tribes deserved better.

After supper, Zoe shooed her father back into the parlor. Then, once the table was cleared, she and Tilghman walked down to the creek. The summer sky was ablaze with stars, and they paused beneath the dappled shadows of a tree. She took his face in her hands, kissed him softly on the mouth. Her eyes shone in the starlight.

"You're a good man," she said in a dreamy voice. "I'm so proud of you."

Tilghman was taken aback. "What makes you say that?"

"Because I saw a different side of you tonight. You believe right is right—even for Indians."

"Took a while," Tilghman confessed. "Working over in the Nations opened my eyes. They've got reason not to trust whites. We don't keep our word."

"That's why it bothers you," she said, staring at him. "You do keep your word."

"Watch out," Tilghman said with a roguish smile. "You're liable to give me a swelled head."

"No fear of that."

"You think not, huh?"

Her voice was husky. "Hold me, Bill. Hold me tight."

Tilghman enfolded her in his arms. She stood quietly in his embrace a moment, and then looked up, her mouth moist and inviting. He kissed her beneath the dappled starlight.

The katydids along the creek went silent.

CHAPTER 22

Tilghman and Neal Brown rode north the following night. The plains glimmered beneath bright starlight and a cloudless sky. A soft breeze whispered through the rolling sea of grass.

By now, the trail was a familiar one to Tilghman. His previous scouts to Ingalls and the Dunn ranch had left a map of the landscape imprinted in his mind. He timed their departure to put them on Council Creek shortly before dawn. He planned to be in position by sunrise.

Brown was in a grumpy mood. He'd arranged for the Sac and Fox workhands to look after the stock while they were gone. One day would suffice for the trip, and he had told them he would return by the next evening. But that was based on the assumption that he and Tilghman would encounter no problems. His sour mood indicated that he wasn't sold on the argument. To him, outlaws were always a problem.

"No end to it," he muttered as they rode along. "Doolin or somebody else, there's gonna be robbers and such till hell freezes over. You'll never catch 'em all."

Tilghman nodded agreeably. "Never said I would, Neal. Doolin's the one I'm after."

"Who you kiddin'?" Brown said with a short laugh.

"Once't you catch Doolin there'll be another one, and then another one. You've got the tin badge disease."

"Well, lucky for you, it's not contagious."

"Bet your life it ain't! I'll stick to horses any ole day. You oughta do the same."

Tilghman couldn't argue the point. As a practical matter, there was a greater future in horses than in outlaws. But the challenge of capturing Doolin was one he'd been unable to resist. Even with Doolin caught, he wasn't entirely sure that he would ever quit as a lawman. So he had to consider that Brown was right, after all. Perhaps he had contracted the tin badge disease.

"Hard to quit," he said now. "Thought I'd put it behind me when we left Kansas. Guess that's not the case."

"No guesswork about it," Brown said gloomily. "You'd lots rather be off chasin' desperadoes. Don't see nobody twistin' your arm."

"You got me there, Neal."

"What's Miss Zoe say about all this? She don't worry about you gettin' yourself killed?"

"She never says one way or another. I reckon she figures she got the badge in the bargain."

"Damn poor bargain." Brown rubbed the bridge of his nose. "You must've sold her a bill of goods."

"Maybe she's just not a worrywart . . . like some people I could name."

"Think that's what I am, do you?"

"Never thought otherwise."

Brown mumbled something under his breath. He let the matter drop, reminded all over again that it was probably a lost cause. They rode in silence toward Council Creek.

Sunrise found them positioned in the treeline east of the Dunn ranch. Below, apart from some thirty horses in the corral, there was no sign of movement across the compound. Armed with Winchesters, they settled down to wait.

Tilghman had no immediate plan of action. He intended to watch and react as developments unfolded. Should Doolin appear, then he would play the situation as the moment dictated. If Doolin failed to appear, then he would pull back and await another day. Like most manhunts, it was all a roll of the dice.

A short while after sunrise smoke began billowing from the chimney on the house. Some moments later Bee Dunn stepped through the doorway, followed by his brother, George. They paused in the yard, talking briefly, then Bee ambled off toward the dugout storm cellar. George yawned, stretching his arms to loosen his shoulders, and walked to a haystack near the corral. He began forking hay to the horses.

Bee gave three sharp knocks on the door of the storm cellar. Then he pulled the door open, moved inside, and closed it behind him. The walls of the dugout deadened any sound, and there was no way to tell if anyone else was inside. After a few moments, tendrils of smoke drifted from the stovepipe on top of the roof. Someone had clearly stoked the fire in the stove.

Tilghman waited, his gaze fixed on the door. Several minutes passed, and Bee Dunn still hadn't emerged from the dugout. Across the way, George Dunn finished forking hay to the horses and walked back to the house. A stillness settled over the compound.

Brown jerked his chin at the dugout. "What d'you make of that?"

"Somebody's in there," Tilghman said. "Otherwise he wouldn't have knocked, or started a fire."

"Why would anybody build a fire in the summertime?"

"Way it appears, he just woke somebody up. They're fixing morning coffee."

Brown grunted. "You think it's Doolin?"

"Maybe," Tilghman said. "Then again, maybe it's another crew of horse thieves. Hard to tell."

"So what's our next move?"

Tilghman considered a moment. Dunn had been inside for some time, and showed no signs of coming out. By now, it was clear that he was talking with someone in the dugout. Whether to wait and see what happened, or force the issue seemed to Tilghman a tossup. He decided to act rather than react.

"Here's how we work it," he said. "I want you to stay here and give me cover. I'll see who's in that dugout."

Brown gave him a bewildered look. "You're gonna go down there?"

"That's the general idea."

"Gawddamn, Bill, you're liable to get yourself shot. Wouldn't it be safer to wait and see who comes out?"

"Not much," Tilghman said. "I think I'd rather flush them out."

"Crucified Christ." Brown's voice sounded parched. "What'll I do if something goes wrong?"

"Keep one eye peeled on the house. Anybody comes out with a gun, let loose in a hurry."

"You want me to kill him?"

"Whatever it takes to stop him. I'm liable to be too busy to handle it myself."

"Gawdalmighty," Brown said with a bleak expression. "Knew I wasn't cut out to be a lawdog."

Tilghman handed over his Winchester. "That'll save you from having to reload. Shoots a hair to the right."

"Sounds like you're plannin' on fighting a war."

"Just figure to have a looksee, Neal."

"Do me a favor next time."

"What's that?"

"Don't ask me along."

Tilghman moved clear of the treeline. He crossed the open ground on a direct line to the dugout. He pulled his pistol as he halted before the door. For a moment, he waited, listening, but there was no sound from inside. He rapped on the door three times.

A beat of silence slipped past. Then, deadened by the sod wall, a voice called out. "Who's there?"

"Federal marshal," Tilghman said. "Come on out, Bee."

There was no reply for several moments. "Door's unlatched," Dunn finally yelled back. "C'mon in."

Tilghman debated briefly with himself. Then, standing to one side of the door, he flung it open. Sunlight flooded the inside of the dugout, which resembled a barracks. Four double bunks lined either side of the room, with blankets draped over the front for privacy. There was no way to tell if the bunks were occupied, someone hidden behind the draped blankets.

Dunn stood at the far end of the room. Beside him, on a small wood stove, a coffeepot began to belch steam. The dugout was a rainbow of odors, stale sweat mixed with dried earth and the aroma of coffee. Tilghman took one step inside the door, halting at the edge of the first bunk. He kept his pistol trained on the rancher.

"Expecting company, Bee?"

"No, I'm not," Dunn said hastily. "Always come down here for coffee in the mornin'. Old lady raises hell if I get her up too early."

Tilghman motioned with the pistol. "Eight bunks and a stove, all the comforts of home. You running a hotel?"

"Well, you know, people stop over and want a bed. I try to oblige."

"Yeah, I recollect you're the obliging sort. Last time I was here, you had three horse thieves holed up."

Dunn shifted from foot to foot. "Told you I never saw those boys before. Just let 'em stay the night."

Tilghman noted that he appeared agitated. His voice was an octave too high and a muscle ticced along his jawline. He seemed unable to stand still.

"How about today?" Tilghman waggled the snout of his pistol. "Anybody in those bunks?"

A slight rustling noise sounded as someone shifted in the farthest bunk. On two of the bunks closer to the door, the draped blankets moved as though touched from behind. Dunn's eyes went wide with fright.

"Nobody's here," he said in a shaky voice. "Told you, I'm just makin' coffee."

Tilghman sensed that he'd stepped into a vipers' den. There were at least three men, probably more, hidden behind the draped blankets. He was outnumbered and outgunned, and the wrong word now would be his last. He was reminded that discretion often proved the better part of valor.

"I'm after three bank robbers," he lied casually. "Got a posse of ten men waitin' in the woods. Any strangers come through here last night?"

Dunn's mouth twitched. "Nobody come through here."

"You're real sure about that, Bee?"

"Plumb certain."

Dunn stole a furtive glance at the bunks. For a moment, the silence in the dugout was like breathing suspended. Tilghman knew then his bluff had worked; the men in the bunks believed he had a posse outside. They were convinced for now that their only chance was if he left the dugout alive. He decided not to press his luck.

"We're headed north," he said, underscoring his bluff. "Do yourself a favor and keep your nose clean. Get my drift?"

"Don't worry, marshal." Dunn bobbed his head. "I'm not lookin' for trouble."

"Then I guess we understand one another. See you around, Bee."

Tilghman took a step backwards through the entrance. He purposely slammed the door shut, a signal to everyone inside that he was gone. Holstering his pistol, he turned from the dugout and walked toward the trees. All the way across the open ground he felt as though he was lugging an anvil on his shoulders. Yet he forced himself to maintain a brisk, unconcerned pace.

Brown waited behind a large live oak. He kept his carbine trained on the compound until Tilghman was well within the treeline. Then, a Winchester in either hand, he retreated deeper into the woods. He let out a huge sigh of relief.

"What happened?" he said nervously. "I started to think you was a goner."

"So did I," Tilghman replied. "I think Doolin and some of his men are in that dugout."

"How'd you get out alive?"

"They thought I had an ace in the hole."

"Ace in the hole?" Brown looked rattled. "What the hell you talkin' about?"

"I'll tell you about it later. Let's see what they do now."

Tilghman retrieved his carbine and motioned Brown to follow. Crouched low, they moved forward to a patch of shadows just inside the treeline. There they went belly down on the ground, hidden from sight. Quiet and still, careful not to betray their position, they waited.

A long half hour passed in silence. Then with a screech of hinges, the door of the dugout swung open. Bee Dunn moved into the sunlight, blinking against the glare. He shaded his eyes with one hand and slowly examined the woods on all sides. Finally, satisfied that no one waited in ambush, he turned back toward the door. His voice was muffled.

Red Buck Waightman emerged from the dugout. He was followed by Doolin, and then, one at a time, the rest of the Wild Bunch. They stood ganged together, eyes shaded against the sunlight, searching the woods. Dunn's woman appeared in the doorway of the house and her call to breakfast sounded across the compound.

On signal from Doolin, the men trooped toward the house.

Tilghman shouldered his Winchester. He caught the sights and drew a bead on Doolin's back. A touch on the trigger, one shot, and the leader of the Wild Bunch would be dead. The urge to fire and end it here was almost overwhelming. But he found himself unable to squeeze off the shot. He was no assassin.

Doolin and his men entered the house. Tilghman lowered the hammer on his carbine and rose to his feet. Brown gave him a strange look. "Where you headed?"

"Guthrie," Tilghman said. "We're coming back with more men."

He walked off toward their horses.

CHAPTER 23

"Are you serious? You had him in your sights?"

"That's about the size of it."

Evett Nix stared at him with a flabbergasted expression. Tilghman was seated before the desk and Heck Thomas stood at the window. There was a moment of strained silence.

"For God's sake!" Nix snapped. "Why didn't you shoot him?"

Tilghman's gaze was steady. "I'm no bushwhacker."

"We're not discussing some gentlemanly code of honor. We're talking about a cold-blooded killer!"

"Speak for yourself. I don't shoot men in the back."

"Those were your orders," Nix said indignantly. "Bring them back dead, which is to say, kill them. Who are you to decide the right or wrong of it?"

"I've already told you," Tilghman said levelly. "I won't kill a man without fair warning."

Tilghman had briefed them on his scout of the Dunn ranch. He'd spared no details, nor had he spared himself. The tense moments in the dugout, as well as the chance to kill Doolin, had been recounted at length. He had offered no excuses.

"Now that I think of it," Nix said, "who authorized

you to go off on your own? You didn't clear that with me."

"The man on the spot has to make his own decisions. I played a hunch."

"Let's get this straight," Nix ticked off points on his fingers. "You went to the Dunn ranch without authorization. You placed yourself in jeopardy by acting on your own. You disobeyed a direct order to shoot Doolin on sight. Does that about cover it?"

Tilghman waggled one hand. "I reckon you hit the high points."

"Careful with your tone of voice, Mr. Tilghman. I will not tolerate insubordination."

"Try a civil tone of voice yourself. You want respect, then give it."

Nix swelled up like a toad. "Don't push me too hard. I hired you and I can fire you."

"Tell you what," Tilghman said bluntly. "Anytime you want my badge, all you have to do is ask."

"Hold on!" Thomas broke in, turning from the window. "Just back off before things get out of hand. That goes for both of you."

"Indeed?" Nix said stiffly. "Are you issuing the orders around here now?"

"Not orders," Thomas said with restraint. "I'm talkin' common, ordinary horse sense. We'll get nowhere fightin' amongst ourselves." He paused, looking from one to the other. "Let's stick to fixin' Doolin's little red wagon."

Nix took a deep breath, collected himself. "All right," he said. "What's to be done now that Doolin has escaped?"

"Who said he'd escaped?" Tilghman asked. "Odds are he's still at the Dunn place."

"Really?" Nix said with skepticism. "After your surprise visit, I hardly think he'd hang around."

"Well, first off, he doesn't know we know he uses the

Dunn place as a hideout. So there's no reason for him to run."

"Prudence would dictate otherwise. But go on with what you were saying."

Tilghman ignored the interruption. "Doolin probably brought the gang together to pull another job. Depending on his timetable, they might still be there. Or they might come back there after pulling the job."

"You got a point," Thomas said thoughtfully. "Leastways where Doolin's concerned. He'd likely want to see his wife again."

"So?" Nix prompted. "What are you suggesting?"

"Another raid," Thomas said. "Bill and me could make it up there by late tonight. I vote we hit them first thing tomorrow mornin'."

Nix regarded him a moment. "We don't have time to get Madsen here from El Reno. But on the other hand, two against eight make for poor odds. I think we should deputize some of the local officers."

"Count me out," Thomas said bitterly. "We'd more 'n likely wind up with another bloodbath like Ingalls. I want no part of it."

"Heck's right," Tilghman cut in. "You'll recollect we told you the same thing before the raid on Ingalls. Let the two of us handle it."

"Suppose I do?" Nix said pointedly. "And suppose you have another crack at Doolin? Will you kill him?"

Tilghman held his gaze. "Any man deserves a warning, and that includes Doolin. But if he resists, I'll get the first shot."

Nix sounded weary. "You have a way of making your own rules. I'd think orders would mean more to a lawman."

"Guess that all depends on the orders. Even a lawman's got to live with himself."

"So it appears." Nix summoned a tight smile. "Gentlemen, I wish you good hunting. Bring me Bill Doolin —dead."

Outside the office, Tilghman and Thomas made their way down the stairs. On the street they paused to watch a horse-drawn trolleycar clang past. The sight seemed curiously at odds with their backcountry pursuit of outlaws.

"You're a hard one," Thomas said with amusement. "Thought you were gonna give Nix a heart attack."

"Him and his orders," Tilghman said heavily. "I'd wager he's yet to kill his first man. Doubt he's got the stomach for it."

"Most don't," Thomas allowed. "Sounds easy till you're set to pull the trigger. Guess that's why there's fellers like us."

Tilghman considered a moment. "Tell me the truth, Heck," he said finally. "Would you have back-shot Doolin?"

"I'd have been sorely tempted."

"Yeah, but would you have done it?"

"Probably not," Thomas admitted. "Like you said, a man's got to live with himself. I wouldn't be partial to that kind of dream."

Tilghman looked surprised. "You dream about the men you've killed?"

"Only on bad nights. How about you?"

"Once a month or so. Nothing regular."

Thomas laughed. "We ought not let Nix hear us talkin' this way. He'd figure we'd lost our nerve."

"Guess he would," Tilghman said, grinning. " 'Course, for a brave soul like him, what's another dead man?"

"Ink on paper, my friend. A nice, big headline."

An hour later they rode out of Guthrie. The trail, once again, led toward Council Creek.

* * *

Before dawn they moved into position. Thomas was hidden in the treeline by the creek and Tilghman was directly opposite the dugout. They settled down to await sunrise.

Their plan was simple. From their positions, they were afforded an interlocking field of fire on the storm cellar. When the gang emerged for breakfast, Tilghman would order them to surrender. At the first sign of a fight, both lawmen would open fire on Doolin. The gang, with their leader dead, would almost certainly scatter and run.

Tilghman briefly had considered the same plan yesterday morning. Yet he had discarded it just as quickly because of Neal Brown. His friend could have provided covering fire, but Brown lacked the experience for a pitched gun battle. Today, should the gang fight rather than run, Tilghman was confident that Thomas would hold his own. Hidden in the treeline, firing on men in the open, there was no question of the outcome.

Shortly after sunrise George Dunn stepped through the door of the house. He walked directly to the corral and forked hay to the milling horses. Then, his morning chore completed, he returned to the house and disappeared inside. There was no sign of Bee Dunn, even though smoke funneled from the chimney. Nor was there anything to indicate that the bunkhouse in the dugout was occupied. The stovepipe on the roof stood as further proof. No smoke appeared.

Tilghman waited until full sunrise. Finally, troubled that their plan had gone awry, he circled back through the trees to the creek. He found Thomas leaning against a tree, watching the house. They exchanged an unsettled look.

"What d'you think?" Thomas said. "Anybody in that dugout?"

"Doesn't look that way," Tilghman said. "By now,

they'd be up and making coffee. Not a trace of smoke from the stovepipe."

"Maybe they rode out to pull a job. Could've left yesterday after you were here."

"I've got an inkling that's the case."

"We could wait," Thomas suggested. "Like you said, they might come back this way."

"Yeah, they might." Tilghman stared at the house a moment. "What say we have a talk with the Dunns?"

"Any particular reason?"

"They'll likely know Doolin's plans. Leastways they'll know more than we do."

"That'll tip our hand," Thomas said. "Dunn will figure we're keepin' a watch on his place."

"Things have changed," Tilghman observed. "After yesterday, we've got solid proof he was harboring fugitives. I'd say it's time to convert him."

"Turn him into an informant?"

"You're reading my mind, Heck."

Ten minutes later they rode into the compound. Outside the corral, they dismounted and hitched their horses. Bee Dunn appeared in the doorway of the house, his expression unreadable. He spoke to someone over his shoulder, then walked toward the corral. His brother took a position at the door, stationed to act as a watchdog.

Dunn halted before the lawmen. "You gents are gettin' to be regulars."

"Listen close, Bee." Tilghman nodded toward the house. "George looks like he might have a rifle hidden behind that door. If he tries anything, you're a dead man."

Dunn motioned his brother into the house. When the door closed, he turned back to Tilghman. "Satisfied?"

"For now," Tilghman said. "That dugout appears to be empty. Where's Doolin?"

"How would I know?"

"Don't dance me around, Bee. I stayed behind yesterday and waited to see what happened. You treated Doolin and his boys to breakfast."

Dunn gave him a sharp, sudden look. "I'll be gawddamned! You didn't have no posse up in the woods. You were by yourself, weren't you?"

"Maybe, maybe not," Tilghman said. "Either way, I'm eyewitness to the fact that you're harboring fugitives. You've been caught out, Bee."

"So what d'you want from me?"

"Let's take first things first. Where's Doolin?"

"Gone," Dunn answered in a monotone. "You spooked him with all that talk of a posse. Him and his boys went back to the Nations."

Tilghman appraised him. "Were they planning a holdup?"

"I'm not privy to Doolin's plans. He keeps such to himself."

"Where does he hide out in the Nations?"

"Dunno," Dunn said stonily. "Never asked him."

"You think we're stupid?" Thomas demanded, poking him in the chest with a thorny finger. "You'd better come up with some answers, pronto! Otherwise you're up shit creek."

"What's that supposed to mean?"

Tilghman riveted him with a look. "By law, you're an accomplice after the fact to murder, robbery, and conspiracy to commit criminal acts. How'd you like to take a short drop on a hangman's rope?"

"Jesus Christ, I never killed nobody!"

"You're still guilty under the law. A judge and jury would convict you in a minute."

"What if they would?" Dunn sounded unnerved. "Why haven't you arrested me?"

"Here's the deal." Tilghman's eyes were like nail heads. "We'll drop all charges against you, even for horse stealing. In exchange, you feed us information on

Doolin and his gang. Their whereabouts, their plans—
anything you know."

"You expect me to inform on Bill Doolin?"

"Get the wax outta your ears," Thomas warned. "You
waltz us around and we'll put your ass smack-dab on the
gallows. You hear me?"

"Yeah," Dunn said dully. "I hear you."

"So let's try again," Tilghman said. "Where's Doolin
hole up in the Nations?"

"Swear to God I don't know. I'm tellin' you the
truth."

"You ever lie to me and I'll personally put the rope
around your neck."

Dunn's expression became one of bitter resignation.
"You done convinced me, awright? I got the message."

Tilghman quickly laid out the ground rules. He explained the location of his ranch outside Chandler as
well as the marshal's office in Guthrie. Dunn was to get
word to him whenever there was information on Doolin.
He underscored the urgency should Doolin return to
the Dunns' ranch.

"One last thing," he concluded. "Your brother's as
guilty as you are. Any slipups and you'll both swing."

"Don't worry about George," Dunn said weakly. "He
does whatever I tell him."

"We'll expect to hear from you, Bee—real soon."

The lawmen mounted and rode toward the creek.
Dunn stared after them a moment, his pudgy face
wreathed with disgust. His mind whirled at what he'd
done.

He was now the Judas goat for the certain execution
of Bill Doolin.

CHAPTER 24

Late that afternoon Tilghman and Thomas rode into Guthrie. On the street, they hitched their horses and then trudged into the Herriott Building. Neither of them relished the thought of delivering their report.

Evett Nix greeted them with an expectant look. But as Tilghman related the details of the raid, his expression changed. His eyes hooded and his mouth set in a razored line. Finally, unable to suppress his anger, he slapped the top of his desk with the flat of his hand. His voice was tense.

"You say Doolin and his gang were gone. Gone *where*?"

"The Nations," Tilghman told him. "They pulled out yesterday morning."

Nix glared at him. "After you failed to shoot Doolin —despite your orders."

"We've already covered that ground."

"And you assured me Doolin would be caught. But now, he's escaped again. For the umpteenth time!"

Tilghman hadn't slept for almost two days. His features were drawn, and he was in no mood to be bullyragged. He shifted in his chair, his temper frayed, on the verge of replying in kind. Thomas swiftly interrupted.

"You're overlooking something," he said to Nix. "Doolin and his boys were plannin' on pulling a holdup somewheres. Bill's visit there yesterday gave them cold feet. Except for that, the newspapers would be hawkin' another robbery."

"Thank God for small favors," Nix scoffed. "The fact remains that the Wild Bunch has once again slipped through the net. Why are you sitting here telling me this? Why aren't you on their trail?"

"Waste of time," Thomas said. "They're scattered all over the Nations by now."

"So you intend to twiddle your thumbs and wait for them to commit yet another robbery. Is that it?"

"Well, no, not just exactly. We've got ourselves a new informant."

Nix looked at them speculatively. "Do you indeed? And who might that be?"

"Bee Dunn," Tilghman replied. "We made a deal with him. All charges will be dropped against him and his brother. Horse stealing. Harboring a fugitive—"

"What?"

"—accomplice to murder. The whole works."

"Are you addled?" Nix said, flaring. "You can't just willy-nilly drop such charges."

"In exchange," Tilghman went on, ignoring the outburst, "Dunn will tip us the next time Doolin shows at his place. Or let us know anything he learns about Doolin's plans."

"You had no authority to make that kind of deal. Good God, you've given the man virtual immunity!"

"Arresting Dunn wouldn't have gained us anything."

"On the contrary," Nix said irritably. "His arrest would have shown that we're capable of putting away Doolin's cohorts. The newspapers would have loved it."

"I'm not interested in headlines," Tilghman said. "With Dunn, we've got a real chance at Doolin. I'll settle for that."

"What makes you think Dunn will keep his word?"

"No fear of that," Thomas said with a sardonic half-smile. "Unless he squeals on Doolin, the charges don't get dropped. He'll hold up his end."

Nix scowled. "You place a good deal of faith in a horse thief."

"I put my faith in him being a coward. He's more afraid of a hangman's noose than he is of Doolin."

"Even so—" Nix paused, his gaze shifting to Tilghman. "I have no authority to authorize this deal. You may have misled Dunn."

Tilghman stared at him. "U.S. marshals make deals all the time."

"Perhaps," Nix said curtly. "But this one requires the approval of the governor and the U.S. attorney general. Otherwise there could be serious repercussions."

"How so?"

"Because it involves Bill Doolin and the Wild Bunch. I won't take that responsibility on myself."

"Even if it means catching Doolin?"

"And if you don't?" Nix let the question hang a moment. "Then it would put me out on a limb, wouldn't it? Had you thought of that?"

"What the hell," Tilghman said, motioning to include Thomas. "We put our necks on the line every time we ride out. Thought you knew, that's part of being a lawman."

"Don't presume to lecture me," Nix said furiously. "You'll overstep yourself once too often."

"Look here," Thomas broke in before it could go any further. "What we're talking about is the fastest way to catch Doolin. Am I right?"

When they both nodded, he looked at Nix. "You say you need approval," he noted. "But all that takes is for you to endorse the deal we made with Dunn. Do that and we're in business."

"You expect me to sell the idea, is that it?"

"Yeah, I do," Thomas said breezily. "Leastways if you expect us to catch Doolin."

A vein stood out on Nix's forehead. "You're quite a pair," he said in a tight voice. "What I'm hearing sounds vaguely like extortion."

Thomas waved it off. "We're just trying to do our job. Why take it personal?"

Nix glowered at them a moment. "All right," he said, rising from his chair. "For what it's worth, I'll have a word with the governor. Wait here."

Neither of them spoke as he crossed the room. When the door closed, Tilghman shook his head. "Turned out to be just another gutless wonder. He should've stuck to the grocery business."

"Hell, Bill," Thomas said without rancor, "all politicians are the same. Let somebody else make the decision in case it goes sour. That way your butt's covered."

"Guess that's my problem," Tilghman observed. "I was never much good at politics. Too slick a game for me."

"Trouble is, you expect everybody to be on the up and up. Politics is like cardsharps being elected to office. You gotta allow for dealing from the bottom."

"Tell you the truth, I'm startin' to wonder if it's worth it. There's better ways to spend your life."

"Name one," Thomas said, grinning. "You and me, we're two of a kind, Bill. We'll be old and feeble when we lay down the badge."

"Don't bet on it," Tilghman said. "One more go-round with Nix might be the last. All he wants are the headlines."

"I've heard of worse bargains. For him to get what he wants, we get what we want."

"You talking about Doolin?"

"Only in passing," Thomas said. "Nix and his crowd, they're after higher office, runnin' things. We're simpler, the way we look at it. All we want is law and order."

"Maybe we're not simpler," Tilghman said, unable to resist smiling. "Maybe we're outright simpletons. We do the work and they get the glory."

"When the history books get written, things don't always work out that way. Lemme ask you a question."

"Shoot."

"Who killed Billy the Kid?"

"Pat Garrett," Tilghman said. "So what?"

"When Garrett shot the Kid"—Thomas gave him a sly, sideways glance—"who was governor of New Mexico Territory?"

"I haven't got the least notion."

Thomas grinned. "I rest my case."

"Pretty funny," Tilghman said, his smile wider. "Guess that means one of us will have to kill Doolin."

"Don't worry about it, Bill. One of us will."

A short while later Nix came through the door. He walked to his desk and sat down in the swivel chair. His expression was curiously benign.

"The governor bought it," he said in a cheery voice. "In fact, he thought it was a top-notch idea. We have his full endorsement."

Neither Tilghman nor Thomas missed the use of "we" in his statement. Clearly, with the governor's endorsement, Nix was now a staunch advocate of the plan. Thomas managed to keep a straight face.

"So what d'you think?" he asked. "Will the attorney general approve the deal with Dunn?"

"No question of it," Nix said genially. "I'll draft a telegraph message that includes the governor's endorsement. We should have approval from Washington by tomorrow."

Nix was still beaming when they went out the door. On the street, they paused as passersby hurried along the sidewalk. Then, unable to restrain himself, Thomas burst out laughing.

"Whatta world!" he said. "Before long, Nix will think we hung the moon."

"All the same," Tilghman said with some amusement, "he's still a gutless wonder."

"You clean forgot what I told you."

"What's that?"

"You know—" Thomas hesitated, grinning. "Who shot Billy the Kid?"

"One thing's for certain, Heck."

"Yeah?"

"It damn sure wasn't Evett Nix."

Tilghman called on Zoe the following evening. After riding in from Guthrie, he'd managed a full night's sleep, and he once again felt rested. Yet, for all that, his good humor seemed somehow forced. He was still thinking of the encounter with Nix.

Following supper, Zoe banished her father to the parlor and his newspaper. She led Tilghman outside, and they seated themselves in the porch swing. A breeze off the prairie had displaced the day's heat shortly after nightfall. Off toward the creek, fireflies blinked dots of light in the dark.

For a while, lulled by the motion of the swing, they talked of his upcoming birthday and her plans to hold a party. Yet, beneath the surface, she sensed that he was not himself tonight. By now, she could detect the slightest shift in his mood, particularly when he was troubled by something he was trying to hide. She knew, despite his pleasant manner, that his mind was worlds away. He was brooding on something.

"All right," she said, squeezing his arm, "tell me all about it."

"All about what?"

"You're not fooling me for an instant. I can almost hear the wheels grinding. What's bothering you?"

"Nothing much," Tilghman said, avoiding a direct answer. "Besides, I'd rather spend our time together talking about us. Why spoil it talking about business?"

"Because we should share things," she persisted. "The good as well as the bad. Are you talking about ranch business or law business?"

"Won't give up, huh?"

"Oh, for goodness sakes! Anything that involves you involves me. You should know that by now."

Tilghman was silent a moment. Then, aware that she wouldn't be put off, he finally told her. His voice quiet with anger, he related the encounters over the past few days with Evett Nix. His words were filled with loathing.

"Hate to admit it," he concluded, "but I'm about at the end of my rope. Nix looks at Doolin as just another feather in his cap. He's a politician, pure and simple."

"He sounds perfectly terrible," she said. "But on the other hand, he is the U.S. marshal. How do you get around that?"

"Short of quitting, there's no way around it. I'm stuck with him."

She often experienced a whipsaw of emotions about his job as a lawman. She was constantly frightened for his safety, terrified that he would ride out one day and never return. Yet his devotion to the law, his inner conviction that right should prevail, was all too apparent. She had long since reconciled herself to the fact that he would not be the same man without a badge. Nor would she attempt to change him.

"You know what I think?" she said with a disarming smile. "You hate taking orders from a man you don't respect. You feel like you've compromised yourself."

"How'd you know that?" Tilghman said, slightly astounded. "You a mind reader, or something?"

"No," she said softly. "But I know you."

"Well, you hit the nail on the head. Half the time, I feel like kicking myself for not turning in my badge."

"And yet, turning in your badge isn't the answer, is it? You take great pride in being a lawman."

Tilghman nodded. "Not bragging, but I'm good at it. Sort of comes natural."

"Then you shouldn't quit," she said confidently. "People always say you have to take the bitter with the sweet. Nothing's ever perfect."

"Evett Nix is a bitter pill, all right. One that I find damn hard to swallow."

"Perhaps that isn't the answer, either."

"How do you mean?"

"Well—" She hesitated, searching for the right words. "Where you're concerned, I'm hardly impartial. But you're a resourceful man, the most determined man I've ever met. I just suspect you'll find a way to deal with Mr. Nix."

Tilghman put his arm around her. He held her close and she snuggled into the hollow of his shoulder. He stared off into the dark for a time, thinking about what she'd said. Then, finally, he chuckled and hugged her tighter.

"You know, I just suspect you're right. One way or another, I'll deal with Nix."

CHAPTER 25

A fortnight slipped past with no word on the Wild Bunch. Then, as though contemptuous of the law, they struck in the heart of Oklahoma Territory. On a dark night, late in July, the gang robbed a train outside the town of Dover. They got away with over twenty thousand dollars from the express-car safe.

News of the holdup went out on the telegraph before midnight. Tilghman, who was in Guthrie at the time, was awakened shortly afterward in his hotel room. Less than an hour later, he and Thomas met with Evett Nix to map out a strategy. There was no train between Guthrie and Dover, and they had no choice but to travel by horseback. By two o'clock, they rode west into the night.

Dover was a small town north of the Cimarron River, located some thirty miles northwest of Guthrie. El Reno, where Chris Madsen was posted, was some sixty miles south of where the robbery had occurred. The Rock Island railroad had service from there northward, and Nix ordered him by telegraph to commandeer a train. He was to meet Tilghman and Thomas in Dover.

An hour or so after sunrise Madsen's train pulled into the station. Tilghman and Thomas, sipping coffee provided by the stationmaster, were standing on the depot platform. They waited while Madsen unloaded his horse from a boxcar behind the locomotive. The three men had about them a sense of grim determination, as well as quickened excitement. The Wild Bunch, missing since the raid on Dunn's ranch, had at last surfaced. This time, they meant to run the gang to earth.

Once they were mounted, they rode south along the railroad tracks. Some three miles outside town a trestled bridge spanned the Cimarron. At the northern end of the bridge, the bandits had felled a tree to halt the train. Following the robbery, a posse had been hastily organized by the Dover town marshal. Working by torchlight, they had attempted to uncover the gang's trail, and finally abandoned the search. Their horses had churned the earth on both sides of the tracks.

"Helluva note," Thomas muttered, staring down at the jumbled hoofprints. "Had good intentions, but they sure left a pretty mess. How're we gonna find the trail?"

Tilghman studied the terrain a moment. On the opposite side of the bridge were rolling hills, studded with trees. To their immediate east, bordering the river, the land was flatter, less wooded. He shaded his eyes against the sun.

"You and Chris stay here," he said. "I want to have a look at that flat ground."

"Figure they're headed for the Nations?"

"So far they've run true to form. I'll just have a look-see."

Ten minutes later Tilghman cut sign a hundred yards downstream. By the tracks, he knew there were eight riders moving at a fast clip. The trail generally followed the river, and the direction was due east. He estimated that the gang was now some seven hours ahead.

Turning in the saddle, he motioned Madsen and Thomas forward. When they joined him, he pointed out the tracks. "Sign's easy to follow," he said. "Trouble is, they're too far ahead."

"Have to stop somewheres," Thomas said. "They'd kill their horses tryin' to make a direct run for the Nations."

"Who knows?" Madsen ventured. "Maybe they've split up and Doolin headed for Dunn's place. Think it's worth a try?"

"Tend to doubt it," Tilghman told him. "Doolin's likely to stay clear of there after pullin' a job. I'd say he's headed for the Nations."

Madsen shifted in his saddle. "So what do we do now? Got any ideas?"

"If I was them," Tilghman said, "I'd swing south of Guthrie. The land's less settled down that way."

"Yeah, but where?" Thomas said with a quizzical frown. "You're talkin' about a lot of land."

"Heck, you were right about them having to rest their horses. You know where the river makes a wide horseshoe bend, about halfway between here and Guthrie?"

"Sure do," Thomas said, nodding. "There's a good ford there, too."

"That's what, maybe fifteen miles?" Tilghman remarked. "Hard as they're pushing their horses, that'd be a good rest stop. Ford the river there and that puts them south of Guthrie."

"So what's your plan?"

"We cut overland and catch them at the ford. I figure they'd rest up for four, maybe five hours."

"Sounds good to me," Thomas said. "How about you, Chris?"

Madsen shrugged. "One guess is as good as another. Let's go find out."

They crossed the river over the railroad bridge. Then, with the sun in their faces, they turned cross-country toward the distant ford. They held their horses to a steady trot.

* * *

A hot noonday sun scorched the land. The lawmen topped a low knoll on the south side of the Cimarron. Their horses were lathered with sweat, their shirts soaked. Before them, the river arced in a broad horse-shoe bend.

Tilghman suddenly yanked back on the reins, brought his horse to a dust-smothered halt. Thomas and Madsen were only a beat behind, but still too late. Below, on the south side of the ford, they spotted men and horses in a grove of trees. Even as they reined to a stop, they saw that the men were in the midst of saddling their horses.

A shout of alarm went up from the trees. One of the outlaws pulled his pistol and winged three shots toward the knoll. The distance was perhaps fifty yards and the shots went wild. The other men, fighting to control their horses, scurried for cover behind the trees. The marshals bailed out of their saddles, grabbing Winchesters as they stepped down. They swatted their horses on the rump, turning them to the back side of the knoll.

The dull boom of rifles sounded from the distant trees. Slugs kicked up dirt along the crest of the knoll, forcing the lawmen onto the reverse slope. They went belly down on the ground and snaked their way back to the crest. Warily, after removing their hats, they edged their Winchesters over the top of the knoll. Madsen saw one of the outlaws still struggling with a spooked horse along the border of the treeline. He sighted quickly, allowing for the downward angle, and fired. The man staggered sideways, then dropped on the river bank.

Tilghman and Thomas waited for targets of opportunity. Whenever a gang member eased from behind a tree to fire, they peppered him with lead. Madsen joined them, turning his fire on the grove, and they hammered out a volley of shots. Bark flew off trees and slugs zinged through the woods, but none of the outlaws were hit. The return fire, with the odds now seven to three, kept the lawmen ducking as bullets raked the knoll. For every man they fired on, other men fired on them, and the snarl of slugs was constant. Their accuracy was thrown off as they were forced to sight and fire in an instant.

Yet they held the high ground. Despite the odds, it slowly became apparent that the lawmen had the advantage. Doolin was a shrewd tactician, and he gradually realized that his position was untenable. To charge the marshals over the open ground would have been tantamount to suicide. But as the gun battle raged, it was clear that his men would be picked off one at a time. Though they were behind trees, they had to expose themselves to get off a shot. The marshals, with only their heads exposed, offered much smaller targets. Time worked in their favor.

A shouted command brought all gunfire from the trees to an abrupt stop. Then, in the next instant, men were darting through the grove toward their horses. The marshals suddenly realized that the gang had been ordered to break off the fight and fall back in retreat. Without thought, they assumed solid kneeling positions on the knoll and began firing at the outlaws. A horse went down, thrashing and kicking, as they levered a barrage of shots. The rider screamed a curse, blood spurting from his hand, and scrambled aboard behind one of the other men. A second horse faltered, clearly wounded, but managed to regain its stride. The outlaws pounded east along the river at a hard gallop.

The marshals quickly collected their horses. They mounted, Winchesters laid across their saddles, and rode down to the grove. As they approached, the wounded horse kicked one last time and went slack in death. The downed outlaw lay sprawled on his back at the river's edge, a rosette of blood spread across his shirt. The lawmen reined to a halt, staring down at the body. Thomas finally broke the silence.

"Tulsa Jack Blake," he said. "You drilled him dead center, Chris."

Madsen nodded. "Wish to Christ it was Doolin."

"Look on the bright side," Thomas said. "None of us got hit, and it's a puredee wonder. I could've sworn we had a mile or so to go when we came over that rise."

"Luck was with us," Madsen agreed. "The way we stumbled onto them, they should've shot our lights out."

Tilghman was staring off downstream. "We'll play hell catching them," he said, as though thinking aloud. "They're mounted on fresh horses and ours are pretty well spent. Doolin's the one that lucked out."

Thomas looked at him. "Are you sayin' we break off the chase?"

"Not by a damnsight," Tilghman said levelly. "But we'll have to take it slow and easy. Otherwise our horses won't last."

Madsen shoved his carbine into the scabbard. "Way I see it," he said, "they're slowed down, too. One horse carrying double and another wounded. Maybe we've still got a chance."

"Hope you're right," Tilghman said. "We're long overdue a decent break."

After watering their horses, they rode out from the grove. Tilghman took the lead, following the tracks along the river bank. He thought their chances were slim, unless Doolin made a mistake. But even that seemed a remote likelihood.

So far the Wild Bunch had gotten all the breaks.

The trail looped south from the Cimarron. The outlaws were moving at a fast pace, and their course was plain to read. They would skirt Guthrie and make a run for the Nations.

The land was sparsely settled, scattered farms located along creeks. There were no towns on the line of march, and thus no way to telegraph ahead and alert the authorities. Doolin, ever the tactician, had once again selected an escape route that hampered pursuit. Hour by hour, forced to conserve the strength of their horses, the three lawmen fell farther behind.

Toward mid-afternoon Tilghman signaled a halt. Ahead, on the opposite side of a creek, the horse they'd wounded earlier lay dead. Dismounting, he searched the area on foot, and found a grisly trophy. He held up a man's forefinger crusted with blood.

"We winged somebody," he called out. "Looks like it was almost shot off and he finished the job with a knife."

"Better than nothin'," Thomas said. "Leastways we've drawn blood."

Tilghman pointed to the dead horse. "There's two of them riding double now. That'll slow them down."

"Let's pick up the pace," Madsen said. "Maybe we'll get lucky."

They rode on at a sedate trot. The trail led straight as a string on an easterly course. Tilghman had no trouble cutting sign, for the gang was still pushing their mounts. Yet two of the horses, the ones carrying double, were lagging behind the others. That meant four of the outlaws were slowly losing ground, and Tilghman was encouraged. He thought perhaps Madsen was right, after all. Maybe their luck had changed.

Late that afternoon the trail led them across a plowed field to a farmhouse. As they rode into the yard, they saw a woman and a small girl crouched over a body on the ground. The body was that of a man in bib overalls, and the woman was wailing hysterically. The girl stood sucking on her thumb, her eyes blank with shock. Flies buzzed around a splotch of blood on the farmer's overalls.

Thomas managed to separate the woman from her husband. The girl trailed along, eyes still round, as he led the woman into the house. Tilghman and Madsen inspected the body, and saw that the farmer had been shot at point-blank range. Mixed with the blood on his overalls were scorch marks from the muzzle blast of a pistol. They gently hefted the body and carried it to the front porch of the house. Inside, they heard the woman trying to talk between choked sobs.

A short while later Thomas emerged onto the porch. His features were grim. "Got most of the story," he said. "The gang rode in here and took the only two horses this man had. He went runnin' out to the barn and tried to stop them. From her description, the one that shot him was Red Buck Waightman."

"Sonovabitch," Madsen cursed in a low growl. "I'd like to get him in my sights."

"Yeah," Tilghman said, his expression wooden. "Only you'd have to beat me to him."

Thomas stared down at the farmer. "We're gonna have to bury him for the woman. She's out of her mind with grief."

"What about the gang?" Madsen said. "We've still got a couple of hours of daylight left."

"Lost cause for now." Tilghman's toneless voice underscored the words. "They're all mounted and they've got fresh horses. We'd never get close."

"Bill's right," Thomas said, shaking his head. "Sometimes things just don't work out. Today wasn't our day."

They dug a grave beneath a tree near the house. Shortly before sundown, with the farmer wrapped in a blanket, they gathered under the shadows of the tree. The woman sobbed while the girl stood clutching her legs, and Tilghman read a passage from the family Bible. Madsen and Thomas lowered the shrouded body into the hole.

Dusk fell as they began shoveling earth onto Homer Godfrey.

CHAPTER 26

The next morning they followed the trail into the Creek Nation. They felt obligated to continue the manhunt as long as there was sign to follow. All the more so since the outlaws had wantonly killed an innocent man. Still, none of them held out any great hope of cornering the Wild Bunch.

The trail ended shortly after they crossed into the Creek Nation. Tilghman found the spot where the outlaws had halted, presumably to split the loot from the train robbery. Like leaves scattered by the wind, the gang then split off in different directions. From past experience, the marshals knew there was nothing to be gained by further pursuit into the Nations. The manhunt ended where the tracks were obliterated on a heavily traveled wagon road.

The lawmen were less than a day's ride from Tilghman's ranch. Thomas decided to stay the night and then continue on to Guthrie. Though they had killed one of the gang, he was in no rush to deliver their report to Evett Nix. Madsen was determined to push on to El Reno, even though it meant spending a night on the trail. They parted at a crossroads southeast of Chandler.

Tilghman and Thomas arrived at the ranch shortly before sundown. As they rode into the compound, they saw a strange horse tied outside the corral. Neal Brown hurried from the house as they dismounted and began hitching their horses. His features were troubled.

"Wondered if you'd show up," he said by way of greeting. "There's a feller waitin' inside to see you."

Tilghman nodded. "Who is it?"

"Don't know," Brown said. "Wouldn't give me his name. But he's nervous as a whore in church."

"Why'd you let him in the house?"

"Told me it was official business. I figgered he was somebody from the marshal's office, in Guthrie."

Tilghman and Thomas exchanged a look. They followed Brown back to the house and filed through the door. George Dunn was seated in the parlor, nervously running the brim of his hat through his hands. He jumped to his feet as they entered the room. His expression was a mixture of relief and worry. Tilghman turned to Brown.

"Do me a favor, Neal. Would you unsaddle our horses? Give them some grain?"

Brown appeared offended. "Hell, I know when I'm not wanted. All you had to do was say so."

"Nothing personal," Tilghman said. "I'll explain it later."

"Don't even wanna know. Keep your damn secrets."

Brown stormed out of the house. When the door closed, Tilghman turned back to Dunn. The parlor lamps were lighted, and in the cider glow the man's features seemed pasty. He continued to twirl his hat by the brim.

"Let's have it," Tilghman said. "What brings you here?"

Dunn's throat worked. "Bee sent me to fetch you. Pierce and Newcomb are at our place."

"What about Doolin?"

"Just them two. They showed up a little after noontime."

Tilghman's look betrayed nothing. Out of the corner of his eye, he saw that Thomas's features were set in a skeptical frown. In the past, none of the gang members had stopped at Dunn's ranch except when accompanied by Doolin. The presence of Charley Pierce and Bitter Creek Newcomb—by themselves—seemed oddly out of character.

"That's a new one," Tilghman said absently. "They just turned up unannounced—without Doolin?"

"Never done it before," Dunn said in a raspy voice. "Bee thinks Doolin don't know nothin' about it. He's worried sick."

"Why would they come there alone?"

"Told us that was the last place you'd look. Figure you're still off chasin' around the Nations."

Tilghman watched him. "Bee could've brought word himself. Why'd he send you?"

"Lots safer," Dunn said earnestly. "Them boys never pay me no mind. They won't miss me."

"Where's Bee now?"

"Took 'em into Ingalls to get some poon-tang. Woman just outside town runs her own little cathouse. Just her and her daughter."

"Will they spend the night?" Thomas broke in. "Or will they come back to your place?"

"They'll come back," Dunn said. "Bee just went along to introduce 'em. This woman don't generally take in strangers. Too dangerous."

"How long you reckon they'll be there?"

"Till their peckers go limp," Dunn said with a quirky smile. "Them boys was on the rut somethin' fierce."

"So they'll be back tonight?" Tilghman asked, staring at him. "You're sure about that?"

"Don't see no reason why not. They said they was gonna stick around a couple of days, maybe more."

"And they'll sleep in the dugout?"

"Have to," Dunn said. "No place for 'em in the house."

"Here's what you do," Tilghman said in a reassuring tone. "Tell Bee we'll hit the dugout at sunrise. Take 'em by surprise."

"One last thing," Dunn said. "Bee don't want our names brought into it. You gotta make 'em think it was one of your regular raids. Just outhouse luck."

"You and Bee have held up your end of the deal. We'll keep you out of it."

Tilghman showed him to the door. Framed in the glow of lamplight, he stood there until Dunn rode out of the yard. Then he turned back into the parlor.

"Sounds all wrong," Thomas said as he closed the door. "Why would Pierce and Newcomb double back and hide out there? They'd already lost us in the Nations."

"Monkey see, monkey do," Tilghman pointed out. "Doolin's pulled the same trick before, and it worked. So they figure it'll work for them."

"Then they damn sure take the prize for dumb."

"Heck, nobody ever accused them of being bright. Doolin's the brains of that outfit."

Thomas was skeptical. "Still stinks to high heaven. I don't like it."

"Why?" Tilghman pressed him. "You think it's a trap of some sort?"

"Anything's possible with that bunch. They're all snakes, the Dunns included."

"In that case, George Dunn's a smooth liar. I got the feeling he was telling the truth."

"What if he wasn't?" Thomas persisted. "We're liable to have a reception committee when we walk in there."

"Only if we get there at sunrise."

"That's what you told him, wasn't it?"

"I was lying," Tilghman said with a wintry smile.

"We're leaving right now, on fresh horses. That'll put us there not long after midnight."

"I'll be a sonovabitch!" Thomas marveled. "That's why you asked him how long they'd be at the cathouse. You aim to lay a trap of our own."

"Good night for it, too. We'll have a full moon."

"Like I've said before, you've got a devious mind. I'm glad we're on the same side."

Outside they met Brown walking toward the porch. He waved back at the corral. "Got your horses unsaddled and grained."

"Give us a hand," Tilghman said, moving past him. "We need a couple of fast horses out of the work stock."

"Where the hell you headed now? You just got here."

"No rest for the weary, Neal. We're off again."

"Just knew it!" Brown trotted along beside them. "That jasper without a name brought you some hot news. What is it, another holdup?"

"Not exactly," Thomas said with a faint smile. "More like a surprise party."

"Party?" Brown sounded bewildered. "For who?"

"A couple of gents without invitations."

"That don't make no sense."

Thomas laughed. "They're liable to think so, too."

Brown watched them ride out a few minutes later. He turned from the corral, walking back toward the house, still at a loss. He told himself all over again that lawmen were a strange breed.

And pure hell on horses!

The moon heeled over to the west. A glow like spun silver sparkled off the waters of Council Creek. The house was dark and the horses in the corral stood immobile, statues bronzed in sleep. Somewhere in the distance an owl hooted a mournful cry.

Tilghman checked the angle of the moon. He calculated the time at somewhere around three o'clock. His position was north of the trail that led into town. Across from him, Thomas was hidden in the trees closer to the creek. They had been waiting since shortly after midnight.

Their horses were tied deep in the woods. They had approached on foot, and taken their time inspecting the compound. There was no way to tell if Charley Pierce and Bitter Creek Newcomb were already asleep in the dugout. But based on what George Dunn had told them, that was doubtful. The outlaws apparently intended a long night of celebration.

The plan, like most good plans, was flexible. Tilghman and Thomas had agreed to wait in the woods, operating on the premise that the outlaws would make a late night of it. Barring that, they could only assume that the wanted men were already in the dugout. In that event, they would await sunrise and keep on waiting. The outlaws would have to emerge from the dugout at some point, however long it took. Either way, the trail or the dugout, the result would be the same.

"Whooeee!" a voice crowed from farther down the trail. "Flushed the birds outta that little 'uns nest!"

"Charley, I still say the mama was a better lay. A broke horse is always the best ride."

"Hell, you must be gettin' old. That young 'un was just too much for you."

"That'll be the day! How come she squealed when I forked her? You tell me that."

Pierce and Newcomb rode around the bend in the creek. Still some thirty yards away, they were visible in the shaft of moonlight that lit the trail. By the tone of their voices, they had consumed copious amounts of whiskey while frolicking at the local cathouse. Their horses came on at a slow walk.

Tilghman waited until the distance had closed to ten yards. The Winchester at his shoulder, he laid the sights on Newcomb, who rode on the north side of the trail.

Across the way, he caught movement as Thomas edged from behind a tree and sighted on Pierce. His shouted command split the night.

"Federal marshals! Raise your hands!"

The outlaws reined up sharply. Pierce went for his gun while trying to wheel his horse around in the trail. Thomas fired, working the lever on his carbine, and touched off another shot. The slugs caught Pierce in the throat and the head, blowing out the back of his skull. He pitched sideways onto the trail.

The fiery muzzle blasts spooked Newcomb's horse. Instead of turning away, the crazed animal bolted straight up the trail toward Tilghman. Newcomb managed to get off one shot, which buzzed harmlessly through the woods. Tilghman fired as the range closed to five yards, and drilled the outlaw through the chest. The impact drove Newcomb backwards out of the saddle and dropped him on the ground. His horse pounded past on a beeline for the corral.

The reverberations of the gunshots slowly faded along the creek. Tilghman and Thomas moved from the trees, their carbines still cocked, and walked forward on the trail. In the moonlight, the bodies of Pierce and Newcomb lay twisted in death. Thomas grunted sharply under his breath.

"Good riddance," he said. "Gone to hell just in time for breakfast."

Tilghman nodded. "Homer Godfrey ought to rest a little easier now."

"His wife won't be happy till Red Buck Waightman's dead and buried."

"None of us will, Heck. We'd all like the honors on him."

They turned and walked toward the compound. A match flared and the glow of a lamp lighted the house. As they moved through the yard, Bee Dunn opened the front door. He stood framed against a spill of light from inside.

"I heard shots," he called out. "Did you get 'em?"

"The party's over," Thomas said with cold irony. "Your visitors got their candles snuffed."

"You just remember, I kept my part of the bargain."

"We'll remember," Tilghman said, halting outside the door. "We need to borrow a wagon and team."

"What for?"

"What d'you think?" Thomas growled. "We're gonna cart 'em back to Guthrie."

Dunn looked puzzled. "Why would you do that?"

"Our orders were to bring 'em in dead. We aim to please."

Tilghman restrained a laugh. Under normal circumstances, he wasn't much for gallows humor. But he thought it fitting in this instance.

Evett Nix was about to see his first dead outlaw.

CHAPTER 27

The crowds began gathering along Division Street. Thomas drove the wagon bearing the dead men, with his horse hitched to the rear. Tilghman rode alongside the wagon, somewhat amazed as more and more people flocked around them. By the time they reached the center of town, young boys were running ahead to spread the word.

Outside the Herriott Building, Thomas brought the wagon to a halt. Stores emptied along the street and the crush of people grew steadily larger. Tilghman dismounted, leaving Thomas with their grisly cargo, and entered the building. Upstairs, he moved along the hallway to the marshal's office. He found Nix seated behind his desk.

"Afternoon," he said. "We've got a present for you downstairs."

"A present?" Nix said, staring at him. "What are you talking about?"

"Charley Pierce and Bitter Creek Newcomb. We caught up with them early this morning."

"Are they alive?"

"Nope," Tilghman said simply. "Dead as doornails."

Nix was stunned. "You brought them here?"

"Got them outside in a wagon. Left Heck to guard the remains."

"Are they . . . presentable?"

Tilghman smiled. "The townfolks seem to think so. Quite a crowd out there."

"I—" Nix hesitated, clearly taken aback. "I got a telegram from Madsen just a few minutes ago. He told me about Jack Blake."

"And the two outside make three. You want to have a look?"

Nix seemed to shrink back in his chair. Then, as though struck by a sudden inspiration, he sat upright. "You know," he said, nodding rapidly to himself. "We might get some newspaper coverage out of this."

Tilghman feigned a concerned look. "I'd say the reporters better hurry. What with the warm weather, our boys are startin' to get a little ripe."

"Ripe?"

"Not all that good on a sensitive nose. They'd bear looking after by an undertaker."

Nix blanched. "Perhaps you should take them on to the funeral parlor."

"What about the reporters?" Tilghman fought back a smile. "Thought you were interested in the newspapers."

"Yes, of course, you're right. We need to issue a statement."

Tilghman led the way. When they emerged from the building, a mob of some five hundred people jammed the street. The press, drawn by the excitement of the crowd, was already hard at work. A camera platform, jerry-rigged with boxes from nearby stores, had been positioned at the rear of the wagon. The outlaws, arms neatly folded across their chests, were being photographed for posterity.

Nix seemed momentarily nonplussed by the enormity of the event. For his part, Tilghman was reminded that people had a ghoulish, altogether morbid fascination with the spectacle of death. He'd witnessed a similar reaction at public hangings, when mobs ganged around to watch a man step off into eternity. There was often a festive air to such occasions.

Tilghman shouldered a path through the crowd. Nix had no choice but to follow along and mount the wagon seat with an assist from Thomas. His Adam's apple bobbed when he stared down at the dead men and got a whiff of the rank odor. For a moment, his features colored and the taste of bile gagged his throat. But then, ever the politician, he collected himself and looked straight into the camera. The flash pan exploded, capturing his pose as a brave defender of the law.

Hastily avoiding another look onto the wagon bed, Nix climbed down to the street. He was followed by Thomas, who cast a sly wink at Tilghman. A reporter from the Guthrie *Statesman* appeared from the throng of people massed about the wagon. His eyes were wild with fervor and he held a pencil poised over a notepad. He nodded to Nix.

"A great day for the law, Mr. Nix. Would you care to comment?"

"Indeed I would," Nix said staunchly. "In the past four days, three of the Wild Bunch have been killed. You may quote me as saying that we now have this murderous gang on the run."

"Three?" the reporter queried. "I only see two in the wagon."

"Tulsa Jack Blake was slain in a vicious gun battle four days ago. I might add, that was only one day after the train robbery outside Dover."

"Who was responsible for tracking down these desperadoes?"

"Who else but the Three Guardsmen? Heck Thomas, Chris Madsen, and Bill Tilghman. The people of Oklahoma Territory owe them a large debt of gratitude."

"Marshal Thomas. Marshal Tilghman," the reporter said, pointing at the wagon. "Exactly where were these men killed?"

"Outside the town of Ingalls," Thomas replied. "We surprised them after a night of revelry at a house of ill repute."

"That's really something! A house of ill repute. How did you know they were there?"

Tilghman jumped in to cover the Dunn brothers. "We tracked them there," he improvised quickly. "Tried to give us the slip in the Nations, but we stuck to their trail. Led straight to the bordello."

"First rate!" The reporter jotted it all down. "Did they resist arrest?"

"Fired on us," Thomas said. "After we ordered their surrender. So we cut loose."

"Cut loose and cut them down. That's great, just great! Now, what about Bill Doolin? Anything new on him?"

Nix reclaimed the interview. "You may quote me directly," he said. "Doolin and his Wild Bunch are not long for this world. They will be brought to justice in the most forceful manner."

Later, after delivering the bodies to the undertaker, Tilghman and Thomas paused outside the funeral parlor. The crowds had drifted away, quickly losing interest after the spate of excitement downtown. Tilghman rubbed his whiskery jaw, silent a moment. Then he chuckled softly.

"Guess the tables were turned on us. Nix got himself plastered all over the newspapers."

"Who cares?" Thomas said with a broad grin. "Did you see his face when he got a gander at them dead boys? Tell you, Bill, it was worth haulin' them in here."

"I suppose so," Tilghman said agreeably. "Likely as not, he'll skip supper tonight."

"Hell, he might not eat for a week!"

"We ought to be ashamed of ourselves, Heck."

"I'd be lyin' if I said I was. How about you?"

"Well, for me personally—" Tilghman broke out laughing. "I wouldn't have missed it for all the tea in China."

"Goddamn!" Thomas crowed. "Better'n a circus, wasn't it?"

"Yeah, it was. Even without the elephants."

On Saturday, Tilghman took Zoe into Chandler. The town square was crowded with farmers and their families, and cowhands from ranches throughout the county. Saturday was the one day of the week that everyone came to town.

Apart from laying in supplies, the attraction centered on various forms of entertainment. Every Saturday afternoon horse races were held on a flat stretch of prairie outside the town limits. During warm weather months, following the races, a dance was held that evening on the town square. Local merchants, eager for business, supplied the orchestra.

Tribesmen from the various reservations always comprised a good part of the crowd. Like the white men, they brought their wives and children early every Saturday morning. The weekly trek to town was to them a peculiarly white ritual, but one they enjoyed. Their trade was welcomed by merchants, though there was widespread prejudice toward any Indian. Still, the array of goods in the stores, and most especially the horse racing, made the white man's patronizing manner more bearable. Inveterate gamblers, the race drew them like steel to a magnet.

Moses Keokuk never missed the races. The Sac and Fox chief generally arrived with a string of fleet ponies, and a willingness to wager his last dollar. His horses were admirably suited to the racetrack, a mile-long graded oval bordered by rails. Speed, coupled with endurance, usually decided a race, and his prize stock was renowned for stamina. He invariably left the races a richer man than when he'd arrived.

The largest purse, and the wildest betting, was reserved for the last race of the afternoon. The favorites in today's final outing were a roan stallion owned by Keokuk and Steeldust, Tilghman's sorrel stud. Tilghman and Zoe, along with Keokuk, stood behind the railing at the finish line, waiting for the race to start. The friendship of a lawman and a tame Indian was still thought to be somewhat odd, and drew criticism from some quarters. Yet no one, drunk or sober, voiced their opinion within Tilghman's hearing.

The field of eight horses got off to a clean start. Steeldust jumped out to an early lead, while Keokuk's roan was mixed with the pack. The horses held their positions until the turn for home, when the roan stallion attempted to close ground by going to the rail. The stratagem failed, for the roan was boxed in by Steeldust out front and another horse on the outside. The jockey, a young tribesman, then had no choice but to pull back and pass on the outside. In the homestretch, the roan swept past the other horse, gaining ground quickly if too late. Steeldust crossed the finish line a length ahead.

"Big fool!" Keokuk, thoroughly disgruntled, shook his fist at the young jockey. "Got me robbed by them . . . mules!"

Tilghman laughed, waving to Neal Brown who was up on Steeldust. Then, with Zoe hugging his arm, he turned to the chief. "You weren't robbed, Moses. The better horse won."

Keokuk rolled his eyes. "Your horse Sac and Fox horse. Never shoulda sold 'im to you!"

The chief stormed off in a huff. Zoe wagged her head at Tilghman. "Shame on you," she said, squeezing his arm with merriment. "You've spoiled his whole day."

"Fat chance," Tilghman said, grinning. "Moses probably covered himself with a bet on Steeldust. He's a cagey old fox."

"You mean he bet on his horse *and* yours?"

"Knowing Moses, I'd say he had himself covered six ways to Sunday."

The races over, they followed the crowd into town. There, in one of Chandler's better cafes, they had a leisurely supper. Shortly after dark, the Saturday evening dance began on the courthouse square. They joined throngs of people attracted by the fiddlers and the brass section of the orchestra. Farmers and cowhands, their women held closely, swept around the enclosure to a variety of rousing tunes. On the sidelines, fascinated by yet another of the white man's curious rituals, the Indians watched with vast amusement. Children, laughing and playing, darted through the crowds of onlookers.

Tilghman and Zoe left about ten o'clock. The drive to the Stratton ranch, and then back to his place, would put him home well after midnight. As the buckboard rolled out of town, she snuggled closer, gaily chattering on about their day together. But a mile or so farther on, when she began talking about wedding plans, Tilghman fell silent, listening but not responding. She slowly realized that she was talking to herself.

"Bill?" She searched his face intently. "What's wrong? You suddenly got very quiet."

Tilghman avoided her gaze. Smiling and cheerful until a moment ago, he now seemed wrapped in gloom. "Something's been bothering me," he said at length. "Started eating on me after we dropped those boys off at the funeral parlor in Guthrie. I don't rightly know how to tell you."

"Just tell me," she said promptly. "Whatever it is, you know I'll understand."

"Well—" Tilghman stared off into the distance, as though wrestling with some inner turmoil. Then, all in a

rush, he let it out. "I got to thinking we ought to postpone the wedding."

She sat back, startled. "Why on earth—" Her voice
failed her and she fought for control. "Have you
changed your mind, about marrying me?"

"Not for a minute," Tilghman said quickly. "I want to
marry you worse than before. That's the God's honest
truth."

"Then what's wrong?" she asked. "Something has to
have changed."

Tilghman looked away. "Zoe, I've got myself involved
in a war. The other night, when we shot it out with those
boys, I saw it for what it was." He hesitated, reluctant to
put it into words. "We'll have to kill every one of them.
They're not about to surrender."

She tilted her head. "And you don't want to leave me
a widow. Isn't that what you're thinking?"

"Yeah, in a way." Tilghman's tone softened. "I never
believed any man could kill me. Hell, I still don't. But
there's always . . ."

"Always a chance," she said, finishing the thought.
"Isn't that what you were going to say?"

"I'm just sayin' we ought to wait till this Doolin
thing's ended. For all I know, that could be tomorrow."

"But you believe it will be longer, much longer?"

"That's my hunch," Tilghman said in a thick voice.
"They'll fight to the last man."

She was suddenly caught in a crosscurrent of emotion. If she insisted, she had no doubt he would go
through with the wedding as planned. Still, he would be
worried for her sake, and in the midst of a gunfight, that
concern might rob him of the edge, cause him to make a
mistake. His mind needed to be on the deadly business
of survival, not on her.

For a moment, she toyed with the idea of an ultima-
tum. She could demand that he choose between her or
the law. But then, just as quickly, she set the thought

aside. She had no right to make such demands, to force a decision that they both might regret. Instead, she must somehow lessen his concern for her. Her role was to give him strength rather than an added burden.

"You're silly to worry," she said brightly, "but I think I have a solution."

"I'm open to anything that makes you happy."

"Suppose we leave our plans just as they are. But if you haven't caught Doolin by December, then we'll postpone the wedding till it's ended. I think that makes perfect sense."

"You're sure?" Tilghman said. "That's what you want?"

"Yes, on one condition."

"What's that?"

"Shoot first," she said fiercely. "Don't be noble about it."

Tilghman laughed and she snuggled again against his arm. Neither of them said anything more, for the decision had been made. A wedding was a wedding, whenever it happened.

They drove on into the night.

CHAPTER 28

Α week later there was still no word on the Wild Bunch. Doolin and his men were thought to be in the Nations, but little else was known. For all practical purposes, the manhunt was at an end.

Tilghman was hardly surprised. Newspapers across the territory had trumpeted the deaths of Blake, Pierce, and Newcomb. Three of the Wild Bunch hunted down and killed made for splashy headlines and a clearcut warning to the remainder of the gang. Their vaunted record of escaping without harm had been ended on a deadly note. Far from invincible, they were now at risk.

To Tilghman, the gang's reaction was almost predictable. Whatever else Doolin was, he was a man who coolly calculated the odds, and weighed the risks. With three men dead, he had wisely opted to lie low and let time work in his favor. In effect, he operated on the old military adage that it was sometimes better to give ground, and live to fight another day. There was every likelihood that the Wild Bunch would not strike again until they ran out of money.

On that assessment, Tilghman bided his time. He arrested a few backwoods whiskey smugglers, and late one night, he paid a secret visit to the Dunn brothers. But they, too, were in the dark, having seen nothing of

Doolin or his men. For the most part, Tilghman worked around the ranch and devoted his spare time to Zoe. Tomorrow, the last Saturday in July, they planned to attend the races in town and then the evening dance. Given an even break, Steeldust would bring home yet another purse.

But late that afternoon his plans abruptly took a wrong turn. He was seated on the porch thinking of tomorrow's race when Heck Thomas rode into the yard. His first thought was to get word to Zoe that their Saturday outing was now off. For even as Thomas stepped down from the saddle, he knew that the interlude had just ended. Their manhunt was about to resume.

"Helluva note," Thomas said, walking toward the porch. "I work my butt off and you've turned into a loafer. Don't hardly seem fair."

"Grab a chair." Tilghman motioned to a nearby rocker. "I take it you've come bearing glad tidings."

Thomas took a seat in the rocker. He removed his hat and wiped sweat from his forehead with a soiled kerchief. "Got a tip this morning," he said casually. "A headman of the Osage tribe had some government business in Guthrie. He brought word from Johnny Longbone."

"Who's Johnny Longbone?"

"One of my Osage friends. Off and on, he whispers things in my ear."

Tilghman nodded. "One of your informants."

"Johnny's more than that." Thomas set the rocker in motion. "Damn good scout when it strikes his fancy."

"So what did he whisper in your ear?"

"Bill Raidler."

Raidler was one of the five remaining gang members of the Wild Bunch. Tilghman shifted in his chair. "Let me guess," he said. "Raidler's somewhere in the Nations."

"Yep," Thomas affirmed. "A cabin on Five Mile

Creek, over in the Cherokee Nation. You familiar with that country?"

"I don't recollect having been there."

"Near as I recall, it's about a two-day ride northwest of here. We'll pick up Longbone and his cousin along the way. They've scouted for me before."

Tilghman looked at him. "The Osage know Cherokee country that well?"

"Like the back of their hand," Thomas said. "They've been dealin' with the Cherokee for fifty years. Longbone will get us there."

"What about Madsen?"

"Take too long to get him here from El Reno. Nix figured you and me could handle it."

Tilghman considered a moment. "There's no moon tonight. We'd best leave at daylight."

"Sounds reasonable," Thomas said, rocking back and forth. "What's for supper?"

Tilghman arranged for one of his workhands to carry word to Zoe. After supper, with Thomas and Neal Brown seated around the table, he started collecting his gear. They were still sipping coffee when he brought oily rags and a ramrod to the kitchen.

He began cleaning his Winchester.

Three days later they forded the Caney River shortly after sunrise. They were in the heart of the Cherokee Nation, a remote stretch of wilderness as yet unsettled. On the opposite shore Five Mile Creek emptied into the river.

Their scouts led the way. According to Johnny Longbone, the creek ended five miles farther on, at a backcountry crossroads called Talala. Somewhere ahead, perhaps two or three miles, a deserted cabin was situated along the creek. There they would find Bill Raidler.

Tilghman was impressed by their Osage scouts.

Johnny Longbone and his cousin, Tom Dog Eater, were
taller than most Indians he'd met. Their features were
angular and dusky red in color, with high cheekbones
and deep-set eyes. Though they spoke passable English,
they clearly descended from a long line of warriors.
They read the sign of wild things, and men, as if it were
written in a book.

On the trail, Thomas had explained that the Osage
were one of the fiercest tribes on the Southern Plains.
Long ago, they had roamed over what was now Kansas
and Missouri, until finally being resettled in Indian Territory. At one point, they had warred constantly on the
Cherokee, who were seen as intruders on Osage land.
The two tribes had been at peace for many years, but
not without lingering hostility. The Osage still looked
upon the Cherokee as unwelcome foreigners.

In years past, operating as a marshal out of Fort
Smith, Thomas had exploited this ancient rivalry. He'd
gone out of his way to befriend the Osage, though many
of them still had no use for federal lawmen. His most
stalwart converts were Longbone and Dog Eater, who
had assisted him on several manhunts into the Nations.
Their contempt for the Cherokee was aggravated by the
fact that tribes in the Nations were quick to grant refuge
to white outlaws. The hunt for Bill Raidler was a case in
point.

For all their ancient rivalry, a certain amount of trade
went on between the Osage and the Cherokee. Johnny
Longbone, who kept his ear to the backwoods grapevine, had picked up a rumor. A white man had bought
supplies at the trading post in Talala, and word was out
that he'd taken over an old cabin on Five Mile Creek.
Further inquiry, discreetly conducted by Osage traders
with business in Talala, had identified the man as Bill
Raidler. Longbone had then arranged for the message
delivered to Thomas.

A short distance ahead, Longbone now held up his

hand. He signaled for quiet, then motioned upstream, apparently alerted to a sound not heard by the marshals. The terrain was heavily wooded, and nothing was visible to their direct front. After a moment, Longbone and Dog Eater slid off their ponies, armed with worn Winchester repeaters. Tilghman and Thomas dismounted, pulling carbines from their saddle scabbards. Longbone stood listening to a distant sound, then waved them onto a line. They advanced through the trees.

Some fifty yards ahead the woods opened onto a small clearing beside the creek. A log cabin, with one side of the roof caved in, was centered in the clearing. As they emerged from the treeline, a man on horseback, until then hidden from view, appeared on the far side of the cabin. Unaware of their presence, he reined his horse toward a narrow trail that led upstream. Tilghman and Thomas moved out front of the Osage scouts, shouldering their rifles. Thomas bellowed a command.

"Federal marshals! Halt right there!"

The man glanced over his shoulder, and they saw the face of Bill Raidler. He hunched low in the saddle, raking his horse savagely with his spurs, and took off at a lope up the trail. The lawmen fired in unison, their shots clipping bark off trees on either side of Raidler. They worked the levers on their carbines, but by then Raidler had disappeared into the woods bordering the creek. The thud of hoofbeats faded rapidly in the distance.

"Goddamn the luck!" Thomas thundered. "Sonovabitch didn't even know we were here!"

"Never had a clue," Tilghman agreed. "Looked like he was headed for the trading post. I saw a gunnysack tied to his saddlehorn."

"Well, he's not all that far ahead. Let's get after him."

A few minutes later they rode upstream. But Raidler, schooled in the tactics of the Wild Bunch, proved to be elusive. A mile or so upstream, he crossed the creek, then swung wide through the woods and doubled back

to the Caney River. There he turned north along the
rocky stream.

The Osage scouts clung to his trail. By early evening,
as dusk fell, they were some twenty miles upriver. On a
rocky stretch of shoreline, where a small creek fed into
the Caney, the tracks abruptly vanished. Longbone and
Dog Eater, after studying the terrain, were of the same
opinion. Raidler had quit the ground and taken to the
water.

One way led upriver. The other led west along the
creek. Tilghman agreed with the scouts that either direction was a tossup. There was no alternative but to
separate and search in both directions. With dark approaching they camped on the river bank and settled it
with the toss of a coin. Thomas and Longbone would
continue north, along the Caney. Tilghman and Dog
Eater would take the creek.

The next morning they parted as dark turned to
dawn.

Tom Dog Eater taught Tilghman a new trick. Instead of
separating, and riding both banks, they stuck to the center of the creek. That way, wherever their man left the
water, they would not overrun the tracks. In single file,
their eyes sweeping north and south, they rode west.

Four miles upstream Dog Eater motioned a halt.
Along the south bank, he spotted scuff marks on an
outcropping at the water's edge. On ground beyond the
outcropping, he found horse tracks and the bootprints
of a man. There, as he pointed out to Tilghman, their
man had made a cold camp and watched his backtrail.
Anyone who had followed last night would now be
dead.

The trail led southwest toward Osage country. Tom
Dog Eater was no less surprised than Tilghman. As the
day progressed, their surprise turned to thoughtful deliberation. The tracks were on a line straight as a string,

never deviating, always headed southwest. Raidler was moving at a slow trot, with no idea that he'd been followed. He clearly had a destination in mind.

Tilghman and Dog Eater camped that night on the open prairie. The chase resumed at dawn and by noonday they were some forty miles from where they'd parted with Thomas. Toward midafternoon they topped a low rise and before them lay a great northward bend in the Arkansas River. A stand of woods wound a mile or so to the west along the shoreline, and to the east was a field of corn. Between the field and the trees, smoke spiraled from the chimney of a log farmhouse.

"I know this place," Dog Eater said in a guttural voice. "Man's name is Sam Moore."

"A white man?" Tilghman asked.

"Umm," Dog Eater grunted. "Married to Osage woman."

"Let's have a look."

The tracks led straight to the yard of the farmhouse. As they approached, Tilghman saw a stock pen beside the barn, but no sign of a saddlehorse. A man in rough work clothing moved from the barn into bright sunlight and stood waiting. They reined to a halt.

"Mr. Moore," Tilghman said bluntly, "I'm a U.S. deputy marshal."

Moore blinked, his features suddenly waxen. The reaction was all the tip-off Tilghman needed. "A man rode in here yesterday," he went on. "His name is Bill Raidler and he's wanted for murder. Hiding him makes you an accomplice to murder. You're under arrest."

Tilghman was bluffing. But the effect on Moore was immediate, and devastating. To avoid arrest, he agreed to cooperate, and began talking. He was providing Raidler with food and a place to sleep, and a stall for his horse, in exchange for payment. Yet Raidler was a wary man, and he stayed hidden deep in the woods during the day. He came to the house only at sundown, where he took his evening meal and spent the night. By sunrise, he was back in the woods.

Satisfied with the story, Tilghman ordered Moore to the house and told him to bolt the door. Then he and Dog Eater took their horses into the barn, treating them to grain and water. For the rest of the afternoon, hidden in the barn, they took turns peering through a crack in the logs on the west wall. Time weighed heavily, but the sun finally tilted over and began dropping westward. Toward sundown, Tilghman relieved Dog Eater and took his place at the spyhole.

Raidler came out of the woods shortly after dusk. He paused a moment, guardedly inspecting the layout, then headed for the house. From the barn, Tilghman watched until Raidler was closer to the house than to the woods. He wanted his man out in the open, with no place to take cover if a shootout developed. As Raidler neared the house, Tilghman cocked his Winchester, motioning Dog Eater to take a position off to one side. He stepped through the barn door.

"Raidler!" he commanded. "Get your hands up!"

In midstride, Raidler took off running for the house. He jerked his pistol, firing as he sprinted across the yard, and winged a shot toward the barn. Lamplight from the windows silhouetted him against the house, and Tilghman fired. The slug struck Raidler in the side, jarring him to a halt, and he swung around. He raised his pistol.

Tilghman shot him twice in the chest. Raidler collapsed at the knees, dropping his pistol, and pitched to the ground. He groaned, both hands clamped to his chest as Tilghman and Dog Eater hurried across the yard. His breathing was shallow, a trickle of blood leaking out of his mouth.

"Bastard," he mumbled, staring at Tilghman through a haze. "I think you've killt me."

Tilghman knelt beside him. "Get right with God, Raidler. Go out with a clean slate. Where's Doolin?"

"Stuff it up . . ."

His voice trailed off and his body went slack. Tilghman climbed to his feet, lowering the hammer on his carbine. He glanced around at Tom Dog Eater.

"Damn fool had to do it the hard way."

Dog Eater shrugged. "Only way some men know."

"Sure as hell seems like it."

Tilghman walked toward the house.

CHAPTER 29

The last week in August was sultry and humid. Late every afternoon thunderclouds rolled in from the west, threatening rain. But the hot weather held, with no rainfall for the month, and the plains slowly parched under the heat. People watched the thunderheads, fearful of the darkened skies, waiting for a tornado.

The air was stifling in Evett Nix's office. The windows were open but there was no hint of a breeze. For once, sacrificing dignity to comfort, Nix had discarded his suit jacket. He was in shirtsleeves, seated behind his desk, trying to cool himself with an oval-shaped hand fan. Before him, sweltering in the heat, were Tilghman, Thomas, and Madsen.

The marshals had been summoned to Guthrie only that day. They sat now, watching Nix fan himself, awaiting a tirade. In the month since Bill Raidler's death, there had been no word of Doolin or the Wild Bunch. Inquiries and investigation had led nowhere, and informants, as though struck dumb, had nothing to report. The lawmen fully expected to be dressed down in scathing terms.

Nix paused with the fan. He wiped a rivulet of sweat off his forehead and again set the fan in motion. Then, to their amazement, he smiled. "Wonders never cease," he said with curious good humor. "You'll be interested to know that I have been contacted by the distinguished attorney-at-law, Simon Warner. He's due here any moment."

The lawmen exchanged puzzled glances. "Don't get it," Thomas finally said. "What's this got to do with us?"

"Everything," Nix replied, enjoying himself. "Mr. Warner has formally advised me that he represents Bill Doolin."

There was a moment of stunned silence. The marshals stared at him like three owls suddenly blinded by a flare of light. Tilghman was the first to recover.

"Doolin's got a lawyer?" he said, as though the notion defied belief. "What's his game?"

"I just imagine Mr. Warner has all the particulars. We'll find out shortly."

"A deal," Madsen said in a tone of sudden discovery. "Doolin wants to make a deal of some sort."

"I suspect you're right," Nix acknowledged. "Which is precisely why I asked you gentlemen here today. You have spent how long chasing Doolin?"

"A year next month," Thomas said. "Seems like a helluva lot longer."

"No doubt," Nix agreed. "For that very reason, I felt you gentlemen should hear what Warner has to say for yourselves. I want your counsel before framing a response to whatever Doolin has in mind."

The lawmen were less surprised than skeptical. Nix was prone to issuing edicts rather than seeking advice. By now, they had him pegged as something of a gloryhound, perhaps more interested in political fortunes than in seeing justice done. A deal with Doolin might easily be his springboard to future public office. They were leery of being drawn into what smacked of personal intrigue.

Before anyone could reply, a knock sounded at the door. The man who entered was tall and beefy, with sharp eyes and a commanding bearing. He was attired in a well-tailored suit and a fashionable hat, and there was not a drop of perspiration on him. Nix performed the introductions and got him seated in a chair angled to face the three marshals. Their immediate impression, though unspoken, was uniformly shared. None of them trusted a man who didn't sweat.

"Well, now," Nix said, spreading his hands. "You certainly have our interest whetted, Mr. Warner. How did you come to represent such an infamous client?"

"Every man," Warner said in an imposing voice, "has the right of legal counsel. I was retained to act in that capacity on behalf of Mr. Doolin."

"So Doolin contacted you directly?"

"I believe that falls under the category of privileged information."

Nix studied him. "Are you also privileged as to the matter of Doolin's whereabouts?"

"Come now," Warner admonished him. "You know I'm not about to discuss such matters."

"Then let's move right along. Why are you here, Mr. Warner?"

"To bring an end to the bloodshed and violence. Bill Doolin wants to surrender."

"Does he?" Nix said blandly. "To be perfectly frank, I'm not surprised. After all, our marshals have dispatched four of his men in the last six weeks. Your client would be wise not to risk a similar fate."

"I agree," Warner remarked. "In fact, I've advised him to surrender at the earliest opportunity. Naturally, that would be contingent on certain conditions."

"Such as?"

"All murder charges waived—"

Warner paused for a reaction, and Nix said, "Go on."

"All robbery charges waived, except for one of your choice. Of course, my client would plead guilty to the one charge. For that, he would receive a maximum sen-

tence of ten years. With assurance of early parole for
good behavior."

"Anything else?"

"No, I believe not," Warner observed. "Except to say
the offer merits your serious consideration. God knows
the public would applaud an end to this matter."

Nix steepled his fingers. "What about the other members of the Wild Bunch?"

"I speak only for Mr. Doolin. However, with his surrender, I suspect the others would listen to reason."

"Would you excuse us?" Nix rose from his chair. "I
would like to discuss your offer with my marshals. Perhaps you could wait in the hall."

Warner appeared momentarily flustered. Then, with a
polite nod, he stood and crossed the room. Nix waited
until the door closed.

"Your opinion, gentlemen?" he said, nodding to the
three marshals. "Let's take it one at a time. Heck?"

"Horseshit," Thomas said sullenly. "I didn't work my
ass off just to see Doolin get a slap on the wrist."

"Chris?"

Madsen's face hardened. "The man's a cold-blooded
murderer. I say we kill him, or bring him in and hang
him. Anything less would be like selling our souls."

"Bill?"

"Seems pretty cut and dried," Tilghman told him.
"We're close, probably closer than we know. Otherwise
Doolin wouldn't be so hot to cut a deal. I vote with
Chris and Heck."

"Excellent!" Nix looked positively chipper. "Antici-
pating an offer of some nature, I took the liberty of
telegraphing the attorney general. In so many words, I
suggested that it would be a travesty of justice to dismiss
even a single charge. I'm delighted to report that he
concurred in full."

The lawmen stared at him with blank astonishment.
For all his grandstanding, they realized that they had

misjudged Evett Nix. Whatever his political maneuverings, he was, in the end, a man of some integrity. He would not barter honor.

Warner was brought back into the room. Nix made a point of not offering him a chair. "No deals," Nix said curtly. "Not now, not ever. Tell Doolin he has twenty-four hours to surrender. Barring that, we will hunt him down and kill him. Have I made myself clear?"

"Abundantly," Warner said. "You leave me no choice but to take this matter before the governor."

"Take it wherever you please and be damned! Good day, Mr. Warner."

When they were alone, Nix briskly rubbed his hands together. He looked invigorated, his eyes bright with newfound resolve. His face creased in a wide grin.

"Gentlemen, in the truest Biblical sense, I demand an eye for an eye. Go forth and do your duty."

The next evening Tilghman and Zoe came outside after supper. He was stuffed on pot roast and fresh garden vegetables and a huge chunk of chocolate cake. His belt felt one notch too tight as they seated themselves on the porch swing. He wondered if fat men were as jolly as they pretended.

Zoe saw through him like a gypsy fortune teller. Whenever he came for supper, he was normally talkative, and often related amusing anecdotes. But tonight, at the dinner table, he had been unusually quiet, as though mired in his own thoughts. She knew he was brooding on something, and that worried her. He was not the brooding sort.

After a few minutes of desultory conversation, she saw that his mind was still elsewhere. She decided on a direct approach. "Aren't you in a mood?" she said in a huffy voice. "I feel like you would rather be somewhere else."

"You know better than that," Tilghman said quietly. "Guess I'm just not good company tonight."

"Well, it's certainly not my cooking. You ate enough to founder a horse."

"Got a lot on my mind, that's all."

"Why not talk about it?" she insisted. "Keeping it bottled up inside doesn't solve anything. Unless it's a big dark secret, why not tell me?"

A jagged streak of lightning split the sky off to the west. Another bolt struck nearby and Tilghman was silent a moment, watching nature's fireworks. Then, halting at first, he told her about the meeting with Doolin's lawyer. He ended with Evett Nix's admonition to get the job done.

"I'm stumped," he said in a glum tone. "How can you get the job done when you've got no idea where to start? No leads, no rumors . . . nothing."

She sensed his bitter frustration. "What about Heck Thomas and Chris Madsen? Do they have any ideas?"

"We're all in the same fix. We've got to feeling like dunces. Doolin's fooled us at every turn."

"You shouldn't blame yourself. You've done everything humanly possible."

"Easy to say," Tilghman muttered. "Not so easy to admit you're downright baffled. It's like I hit a dead end."

"Look on the bright side," she said, catching his eye. "You've all but put the Wild Bunch out of business. Doesn't that count for something?"

"Doolin can always recruit more men. So long as he's on the loose, the Wild Bunch isn't finished."

"You've been a lawman for what, ten years? Have you ever failed to catch the man you were after?"

"Not until now."

"So there!" she said with a mischievous smile. "If you were betting on it, who would you bet on? Yourself or Doolin?"

Tilghman was forced to laugh. "Led me right into it, didn't you?"

"Let's just say my bet is on you."

A flash of lightning lit the distant sky. Tilghman put his arm around her and set the swing in motion. He told himself he was a lucky man.

She was so full of ginger it was catchy.

Late that night Tilghman rode into the ranch. A strange horse was hitched to the corral, and his every sense alerted. As he stepped out of the saddle, he saw the figure of a man on the porch. Bee Dunn moved into the yard.

"Howdy," he said, walking forward. "Wondered if you was ever comin' home."

"How long have you been here?"

"Couple of hours."

Tilghman nodded. "You met my partner, Neal Brown?"

"Crotchety, ain't he?" Dunn said. "Told me to park it on the porch and wait till you showed."

"Well, I'm here now. What's up?"

"Thought you oughta know," Dunn said stolidly. "You remember John Ellsworth? The father of Doolin's wife."

"I remember him."

"Ellsworth pulled out of town today. Way I hear it, he bought himself a new store over in Lawson. That's maybe fifteen miles northeast of Ingalls."

Tilghman sensed there was more. "And the girl?"

"Her and the baby went with him."

"She's already had the baby?"

"Just last week," Dunn said. "Doolin's got himself a boy."

Tilghman suddenly put it together. Doolin's offer to surrender was prompted by the birth of his child. A light prison sentence, rather than a hangman's rope, ultimately would have given him a normal family life. He wanted to live to see his son grow to manhood.

"Sort of sudden," Tilghman said now. "Ellsworth moving just after the baby was born."

"For a fact," Dunn affirmed. "Figured you'd wanna know right away."

"How'd you get wind of this?"

"Mary Pierce told my old woman in town today. She's the wife of Bob Pierce, runs the hotel. Come to think of it . . ."

Dunn hesitated, and Tilghman gave him a sharp look. "What is it?"

"Just occurred to me," Dunn said. "The Pierce woman and Edith Doolin got to be good friends. Lots of folks looked down on the girl for marryin' a wanted man. Mary Pierce sorta took her under wing."

"You think the Pierce woman ever met Doolin?"

"Hard to say." Dunn hawked up a wad of phlegm and spat it on the ground. "One thing's for sure, though."

"What's that?"

"Doolin won't be visitin' Ingalls any more. Not with his wife and kid over in Lawson."

Tilghman gave him a long level gaze. "Stranger things have happened, Bee. Doolin might figure your place is a safe hideout, now that his wife's moved on." He hesitated, stressing the point. "Leastways Doolin might figure the law figures that way."

Dunn grimaced. "So I'm not off the hook yet. That what your tellin' me?"

"You're off the hook when Doolin's caught. Or killed, whichever happens first."

"Like I told you one time, you must piss ice water."

"I appreciate you ridin' all this way, Bee. Keep up the good work."

"Do I have a choice?"

"Not one you'd like."

When Dunn rode out, Tilghman stood staring after

him for a moment. The information had improved his mood like a shot of elixir tonic. A new father, looking for a new lease on life, might yet make a mistake.

He thought he'd pay a quiet visit to Lawson.

CHAPTER 30

Tilghman rode into Lawson two days later. Located in Pawnee County, the town was situated some five miles south of the Arkansas River. The business district, which was fairly large, serviced the area's farmers. Shops and stores, as well as a bank and a newspaper, lined the main street.

Merchants were opening for business as Tilghman reined up before a cafe. He wore rough range clothes, and he was once again posing as Jack Curry, the horse trader. His principal concern was that he would be spotted by John Ellsworth, who knew him on sight. The storekeeper would almost certainly alert his daughter.

The cafe was all but empty. Like most small towns, people got an early start and were off to work before eight o'clock. Tilghman took a table by the window, where he had an unobstructed view of the street. A waitress, who greeted him pleasantly, bustled over with a coffeepot. He ordered a breakfast of ham and eggs.

Two nights before, following Dunn's visit, he had composed a letter to Evett Nix. He'd outlined that Doolin and the girl were now parents, and that the girl had accompanied her father to Lawson. His plan was to place the girl under surveillance, in the hope of uncovering a lead on Doolin's whereabouts. The next morning, before riding out, he had given the letter to Neal Brown. He instructed that the letter be placed in the express pouch on the noon stage.

The waitress returned with his breakfast. As Tilghman ate, he pondered the thing that concerned him most. He was convinced that Doolin's offer to surrender was directly tied to the recent birth of the baby. Yet there had been no robberies, no sign of the Wild Bunch, for six weeks. He considered the possibility that Doolin had disbanded the gang and quit Oklahoma Territory. That being the case, particularly after the offer to surrender had been rejected, Doolin might never return. Instead, in some clandestine fashion, he might try to secret his wife and child out of the territory. Which made the girl the last remaining lead to Doolin.

Still, given all that, it begged the question of why the girl had moved with her father to Lawson. If she was planning on fleeing, she could have just as easily done so from Ingalls. So maybe Doolin had some other scheme in mind. Or maybe he hadn't disbanded the Wild Bunch, after all. The possibilities were endless, and it made second-guessing Doolin an exercise in futility. The one certainty in the whole affair was the girl, and her baby, Doolin's son. She had to be located.

The waitress brought the check. Tilghman counted out money and gave her a generous tip. Local customers were usually far less generous, and by her smile, he saw that she was impressed. He thought she might be helpful.

"I'm just passing through," he said. "Where would a man mail a letter in Lawson?"

"Granby's—" She paused, correcting herself. "No, it's Ellsworth's store now. He just moved to town this week."

"Guess that makes him the new postmaster, too."

"Sure does," she said. "He even bought Ed Granby's house. Took over everything."

"Granby left town, did he?"

"Sold out lock, stock, and barrel. I heard he moved to Oklahoma City."

"That a fact?" Tilghman stood as though losing interest. "Well, I gotta be on my way. You serve a mighty fine breakfast."

"Come back and see us next time you're through."

"I'll do it."

Outside, Tilghman paused, inspecting the street. Half a block to the north, he saw a freshly painted sign over Ellsworth's store. He turned downstreet, entering a hardware store, and engaged the owner in conversation. By pretending he was passing through looking for Ed Granby, he got much the same story. But in the process, with a few offhand questions, he managed to learn the location of the Ellsworth house. He emerged from the store with a place to start.

The house was situated two streets to the west, on the south edge of town. Tilghman rode past, searching for a place where he could keep watch on the house and not be observed. He saw an older woman standing in the doorway holding a baby, as a girl in her early twenties walked to a wagon at the side of the house. Neither of them was looking his way, and he gigged his horse into a trot. Like John Ellsworth, they both knew him on sight.

The older woman was Ellsworth's wife. The girl, her daughter, was Edith Doolin. Last year, following the gun battle in Ingalls, Tilghman had met them both while questioning the family. He hadn't forgotten them, and given the circumstances, he doubted that they would have forgotten him. At the end of the block, he rounded the corner and slowed to a walk. Looking back, he saw the girl hike her skirts and climb into the wagon. She reined the horse into the street.

Tilghman watched as she turned in the opposite direction. After the older woman entered the house, he followed at a discreet distance. The girl drove to the business district, and he thought she was headed for her father's store. But she surprised him by turning right on Main Street, away from downtown. She drove south on the wagon road out of Lawson.

Tilghman trailed her by a half mile. Some distance south of town, he began to get a prickly sensation on the back of his neck. No more than a hunch, he nonetheless believed he knew her destination. He thought she was headed for Ingalls.

A noonday sun seared the land. Tilghman dismounted in the stand of woods north of town. A mile or so back, certain of her direction, he'd left the road and cut overland. He waited now for her to roll into Ingalls.

From his saddlebags, Tilghman pulled out a small telescope. He would have preferred to be closer, but his face was too well known by the townspeople. Whatever the purpose of her trip, he would have to watch from a safe distance. Any hint that she'd been followed would spoil the game.

Edith Doolin brought her wagon to a halt in front of the hotel. As she carefully stepped over the side, a woman hurried from the hotel and rushed across the boardwalk. She threw her arms around the girl, laughing with happiness, and hugged her tightly. Then, talking with great animation, they moved into the hotel entrance.

In the woods, the telescope extended, Tilghman watched them disappear through the door. There was no doubt in his mind that the woman was Mary Pierce, wife of the hotel owner. Why the girl had driven fifteen miles to see her, or to what purpose, was still a mystery. All the more so since the girl had moved from Ingalls to Lawson only three days ago. To return so soon had about it a sense of urgency. He settled down to wait.

Shortly after the noon hour a wagon rolled through town and stopped outside the store previously owned by

John Ellsworth. The driver hopped down, gathering the daily mail delivery of a postal bag and several packages, and entered the store. Within minutes, he returned to the wagon with the postal bag and a single package. As he drove out of town, Mary Pierce emerged from the hotel, waving to him as he went past. She hurried toward the store.

A few minutes later she stepped outside and rushed across the street. Through the telescope, Tilghman saw that she was holding a letter in her hand. He noted as well that her expression was curiously merry, and that the letter appeared to be unopened. She scurried along the boardwalk, skirts flying, and ran into the hotel. Somewhat puzzled, uncertain what it meant, Tilghman lowered the spyglass.

Not quite ten minutes later the Pierce woman and the girl came out of the hotel. Edith Doolin looked overcome with joy, somehow radiant. She was holding the letter clutched to her breast, laughing and talking as they stopped beside her wagon. Unexpectedly, she began crying, and pulled Mary Pierce into a fierce hug When they separated, the Pierce woman was crying as well, and the scene had the look of two friends caught up in a moment of final parting. The girl quickly mounted the wagon and backed into the street. She drove off with a last wave.

Tilghman collapsed the telescope. He stood there a moment, all uncertainty now erased. Mary Pierce was acting as a go-between, passing letters back and forth between Doolin and his wife. The girl had clearly returned to Ingalls because a letter she'd been expecting hadn't arrived. Still more telling was her outpouring of elation at what she'd read in the letter. Added to that was her tearful farewell from the Pierce woman.

To Tilghman, the girl's obvious joy was the most telling factor. He thought she wouldn't be returning to Ingalls any time soon, if ever. But he wondered if she might be planning another trip, a longer trip. A reunion.

He followed her back to Lawson.

There was yet another tearful farewell the following morning. John Ellsworth and his wife stood waving goodbye as their daughter pulled away from the house. Beside her, in a wicker basket padded with blankets, was her baby. All her worldly possessions were loaded in the back of the wagon.

Tilghman trailed her out of town. He expected her to travel east, toward the Nations. But instead, she turned onto the farm road leading north out of Lawson. The Kansas border lay some fifty miles to the north, and in a practical sense, that seemed an even more logical destination. From there, she could catch a train to anywhere.

Toward midmorning Edith Doolin forded the Arkansas River. She continued north across the plains, pausing occasionally to tend to her baby. Tilghman followed a mile behind, using the telescope to keep her in sight. He was forced to admire her spirit, for the trail was rough and no place for a woman to be traveling alone. Her bond with her husband was clearly equal to any hardship.

By noontime she was deep in Osage country. From a knoll, Tilghman watched as she brought the wagon to a halt outside a farmer's log house. The farmer and his wife, who were both Osage, greeted her as though they were old friends. Thoroughly puzzled, Tilghman watched as they assisted her from the wagon and carried the baby inside. At first, he thought she'd stopped for the night, to rest for the journey ahead. But then, as time passed, he became aware that no one had unhitched her horse from the wagon. He took up a lookout on the knoll.

Hardly an hour later, Edith Doolin emerged from the house. Her bonnet shielded her from the harsh sun, and the Osage man walked beside her, carrying the wicker basket. She climbed into the wagon, taking the basket from the farmer, and gently positioned it beside her on the seat. When she drove out, the farmer stood watching as she forded a creek near the house. She once again set a course almost due north.

Later that afternoon the wagon rolled into Pawhuska. A trading center for Osage farmers, the small village was some twenty miles south of the Kansas border. When the girl halted outside a store, Tilghman felt certain she meant to locate a place to spend the night. After a hard day's travel, there was little doubt that she and the baby needed a good night's rest. But as she stepped down from the wagon, a vagrant breeze whipped the bonnet back over her head. Tilghman almost dropped the telescope.

The face in the lens was not Edith Doolin. Angered, cursing himself roundly, Tilghman saw instead the Osage woman, the farmer's wife. He suddenly realized that he'd been duped by a simple, yet devilishly clever, masquerade. The Osage woman had changed into Edith Doolin's gingham dress, with the sunbonnet to hide her face, and driven out of the farm. The clincher was the baby basket, which Tilghman knew beyond doubt had been empty at the farm, and was empty now. He'd been gulled into following the wrong woman.

Thinking back, Tilghman ruefully admitted that he had been outfoxed. Doolin had expected his wife to be followed, and he'd devised a plan to throw off pursuit. The only question was how much the Osage farmer and his wife had been paid to take part in the masquerade. Tilghman felt outraged that he'd taken the bait, swallowed it whole. One last look at the Osage woman as she entered the store brought the taste of bile to his throat. He swung into the saddle and rode south.

Shortly after midnight Tilghman burst through the door of the farm house. His pistol cocked, he routed the

Osage farmer out of bed and marched him into the main room. He ordered the man to light a lamp, then rammed the snout of the pistol into his belly. The Osage stared at him with a stoic expression.

"Let's have it," Tilghman said coldly. "Where's the Doolin woman?"

"You won't kill me, white man. Your law forbids it."

"Don't push your luck, mister. I want some answers."

"No," the Osage said stolidly. "Find your own answers."

"You sorry bastard," Tilghman said, his eyes glinting. "You're helping an outlaw escape."

The Osage smiled. "Why don't you arrest me?"

Tilghman knew he'd lost. He wouldn't kill the man, and he couldn't stoop to a physical beating in order to extract information. Nor was there anything to be gained in arresting the farmer. Since he was Osage, the courts were reluctant to enforce federal law. The charges would simply be dropped.

The farmer was still smiling when he walked out the door. Tilghman was angry and baffled, and infuriated that he'd been played for a fool. He mounted his horse, reining away from the farm, wondering on his next move. Then, though the admission came hard, he saw that there was little choice. The place to begin was where he'd started.

He rode toward Lawson.

CHAPTER 31

Doolin reined to a halt. He sat for a moment, studying the grove of trees ahead. A warm September sun beat down on the prairie, and birds flitted from limb to limb within the trees. He saw no other sign of activity.

The grove was located in southern Kansas. Less than a year ago, while planning a raid, Doolin had scouted it as an emergency hideout. A natural spring, deep within the trees, provided clear water for man or horse. The thick stand of timber provided cover.

Off to one side of the spring there was a lush patch of grass. Doolin dismounted, unsaddling his horse, and carried the saddle to the spring. After watering the horse, he attached hobbles to its forelegs and left it to graze. He opened his bedroll and took out a frayed shirt, a tattered pair of trousers, and a rumpled jacket. From his saddlebags, he collected a worn pair of ankle-high brogans and a battered slouch hat. He began undressing.

The idea was to convert himself into a tramp. He removed his range clothing and boots, wrapping everything into a bundle with his gunbelt. Then he donned the bedraggled outfit, and stuffed his pistol into his waistband, hidden by the threadbare jacket. When he finished, he looked like a shabby, disreputable bum who lived off of handouts. There was no need to dirty his face, or wallow about to give himself a foul body odor. He had just ridden almost seven hundred miles.

The disguise completed, Doolin surveyed his new campsite. The spring was an out of the way spot, and there was little likelihood that his horse or his gear would be discovered by anyone. He made his way through the woods and emerged from the treeline with the sun directly overhead. Some two miles to the east was a town he'd once scouted, among others in the area, as suitable for a bank holdup. But he'd never gotten around to it, and looking back, that seemed a rare stroke of luck. He walked off with a pronounced limp.

The limp was not part of his disguise. Doolin's foot had never healed properly after he'd been wounded in the running gun battle with a posse. Some eight months had passed, and in that time, the added complication of rheumatism had developed in his foot. He found it painful to walk, every step sending fiery streaks shooting from his foot to his lower leg. The worn brogans he wore today further complicated the problem, but he had no choice in the matter. A tramp could hardly ride into town on a fine-looking horse.

Far ahead, he made out the irregular shape of buildings against the skyline. A small farm town, Burden was located in the southeastern quadrant of Kansas. The state line was some twenty miles to the south, and directly across it, the land of the Osage. As he trudged along on his game foot, Doolin was reminded that the town's proximity to the border was only one of the reasons he'd chosen it. The larger reason had to do with the matter of transportation. Burden was serviced by the railroad.

Doolin's plan was at once simple and devious. In the letter to his wife, delivered through Mary Pierce, he had instructed her to meet him in Burden the week of September 4. To throw off pursuit, he had made arrangements through Dick West with the Osage farm couple outside Pawhuska. Once he and Edith were reunited, they would then take passage by train to California, and a new life. Yet, even with the elaborate planning, he had to assume a disguise and proceed with caution. His picture was still plastered on wanted dodgers throughout Oklahoma Territory and the border states.

The thought reminded him that all his grand schemes had gone to hell in a hurry. He marked the Dover train robbery as the turning point, where luck seemingly ran out for the Wild Bunch. Since then, in only two months, federal marshals had killed Jack Blake, Charley Pierce, John Newcomb, and Bill Raidler. With four men dead and the law on their heels, he'd had no choice but to disband the gang. From there it was every man for himself, and the wise ones had departed the territory. What none of them knew was that he had departed it for good. His days on the owlhoot were at an end.

In town, Doolin hobbled along the main street. His money belt, with over three thousand in cash, was cinched beneath his shirt. But he warned himself, as he entered a mercantile, that he had to play the part of a tramp. The storekeeper gave him a leery eye when he came through the door and moved to the aisle with women's goods. Finally, he found what he wanted, an inexpensive shawl. He walked back to the front counter.

"How much?" he asked.

"Two dollars," the storekeeper said. "Hard cash."

Doolin pulled a handful of coins from his pocket. He slowly counted out the correct amount, as though parting with his life's savings. The storekeeper scooped up the money, fixed him with a curious look.

"What d'you want with a ladies' shawl?"

"It's a present," Doolin said with a diffident smile. "For somebody that done me a favor."

The storekeeper sniffed. "You ought to spend it on some duds for yourself."

"Maybe next time. Could you wrap that for me?"

Outside, Doolin continued on his way uptown. A block before the main intersection, he crossed the street and entered the Royal Hotel. Though hardly royal, the place was clean and the rooms were modestly priced. As he approached the desk, the room clerk caught a whiff of his clothes. He nodded politely.

"You have a Mrs. Barry stayin' here?"

"Why?" the clerk countered, wrinkling his nose in distaste. "What business is it of yours?"

Doolin held up the parcel, wrapped in brown paper and tied with twine. "Got a package for her."

"Just leave it with me. I'll see that she gets it."

"Wish I could, but I can't. Feller that hired me, he said to give it to her personal."

The clerk considered a moment. Then, with a heavy sigh, he consulted the registration ledger. "Mrs. Will Barry," he said in an officious tone. "Room two-oh-one."

"Much obliged."

Doolin crossed the lobby. He took the stairs to the second floor, checking room numbers as he walked along the hall. He hadn't seen his wife since before the baby was born, and his pulse quickened as he stopped outside 201. He rapped softly on the door.

"Yes?"

"Package for Mrs. Barry."

Footsteps sounded on creaky floorboards. A moment later Edith Doolin opened the door. "Who—" she faltered, recognition flooding her features. "Omigod!"

Doolin shushed her with a finger to his lips. He stepped into the room, nudging the door shut with his foot, and took her in his arms. She went up on tiptoe, her arms around his neck, and gave him a long, lingering kiss. Finally, short of breath, she broke the embrace. Tears welled up in her eyes.

"Oh, Bill," she said joyously. "You're here. You're really here."

"With bells on," Doolin said, grinning. "When'd you get in?"

"Yesterday. Yesterday afternoon. I've been waiting and waiting for you to knock on that door."

"Well, I'm here now."

She suddenly became aware of his clothes. "Why are you dressed like that?"

"Just being careful," Doolin said. "Folks don't give a bum a second glance. Here, I brought you something."

"For me!"

She took the package and swiftly unwrapped it. The shawl was clearly inexpensive, but she hugged it to her breast, kissing him again. "You always were a sweet man."

"Forget me," Doolin said. "I hear I've got a son. Let me see him."

"How on earth did you hear that?"

"Honey, there's no secrets on the owlhoot grapevine. News gets around."

She led him across the room. The baby was asleep on the bed, tiny arms and legs stretched out in repose. Doolin stared down, stock-still with awe, his features oddly gentle. Several moments passed in silence, and then he let out a slow breath. His mouth creased in a wide smile.

"You've done us proud, Edie. He's a fine boy."

"Poor little thing," she said, her eyes on the baby. "The trip up here just wore him to a frazzle."

"Any trouble?" Doolin said. "Everything go like we planned?"

"I did just what you told me in your letter. Traded horses and wagons with that Osage man, and came on here. Nobody tried to follow me."

"Somebody did," Doolin said with a bitter smile. "You can bet the law's been keepin' an eye on you."

"After all this time?" She looked downcast. "Wouldn't they have given up by now?"

"Not on your tintype! Why do you think I laid low so long?"

Doolin had no doubt that his life was at risk. After the death of Jack Blake, he had decided to put distance between himself and Oklahoma Territory. Along with Dick West, he'd crossed the plains on horseback and drifted into New Mexico Territory. There, under the names of Bill Hawkins and Dick Porter, they had found work as cowhands. The rancher who had hired them, Eugene Rhodes, suspected they were operating under aliases. But men were asked few questions in that part of the country.

The ranch was located in Socorro County, deep in the San Andres Mountains. A short distance from the border of Old Mexico, the area was widely known as "Outlaws' Paradise." Wanted men from across the West came there to hide out until their trails cooled down. At times, half the cowhands in the county were thought to be on the run. But they generally behaved themselves, and the ranchers found them to be a strong deterrent against cattle rustlers. The law usually turned a blind eye, and on those occasions when men were sought, nothing came of it. They skipped across the border into Old Mexico.

The third week in August, after mailing the letter to Mary Pierce, Doolin had headed for Kansas. Dick West had tagged along, drawn by the notion that the gang would be reformed in the Nations. Doolin gave him no reason to believe otherwise, for he'd confided in no one about his plans for California. Instead, he had sent West on ahead to deal with the Osage couple, who had assisted the Wild Bunch in the past. All he'd told West was that he wanted his wife and child out of Oklahoma Territory, away from the law. Then, his destination still a secret, he had proceeded to the spring outside Burden.

"Hey, I forgot to ask," he said now. "What'd you name the boy?"

Edith smiled. "I waited till we could talk about it. But I sort of like Bill, Junior."

"I dunno," Doolin said haltingly. "We'll have to change our names in California. Let's think about it on the train."

"When were you planning on leaving?"

"Since you're here, we ought to leave tomorrow. No sense takin' chances."

"I can't," she said, not looking at him. "This morning I had to go see a doctor. I started spotting . . . bleeding."

"Bleeding?" Doolin appeared confused. "You mean from—" He hesitated, clearly embarrassed. "From having the baby?"

She nodded. "The trip in that wagon must have jarred something. The doctor said I needed bed rest." She paused, her head lowered. "Otherwise it could turn into something serious."

"How serious?"

"He wants to keep an eye on me for a few days. But if it gets any worse, he said he might have to operate."

"That settles it," Doolin said forcefully. "You're not movin' till the doc gives you the go-ahead."

Tears suddenly spilled down her cheeks. "Oh God, Bill, what about the law? I'd sooner die than have them catch you now."

"Forget the law," Doolin said with grim assurance. "I've stayed a jump ahead of them so far. We'll manage somehow."

"Will you stay here, with me?"

Doolin paced across the room, thinking. She saw his limp, the wince of pain when he put weight on his foot. He stopped at the window, staring down at the street a moment. Then he turned back to her.

"Wouldn't do for us to be seen together. This place got a back door?"

"Yes," she said. "On the alley."

"Good." Doolin moved across the room. "I'll sneak in here every night to see how you're doing. Meantime, I'll stay at a camp I've got outside town."

Her shoulders squared. "I promise you it won't be long. I just won't let anything stop us from going to California."

"You get well, that's the important thing. Don't worry about nothing else."

"What about yourself? Your foot's worse, isn't it?"

"Comes and goes," Doolin told her. "Got a touch of rheumatism just now."

"You should see the doctor," she said. "We have to stay here anyway, so why not? He might be able to help."

"Damn thing hurts something fierce. Maybe that's not a bad idea."

"I'll tell him I met a poor soul on the street with a lame foot. He'll probably treat you for free."

Doolin laughed. "He'd believe that story. I stink like a garbage wagon."

She touched his arm. "You smell sweet as candy to me. I've missed you so much."

"Been a long time." Doolin got a funny look in his eyes. "Guess you're not up to any monkey business, are you?"

"Heaven knows, I wish I was. I can't keep my hands off you."

"Tell that sawbones to get you well quick."

"I will," she promised. "Until then, we'll just suffer together."

Doolin enfolded her into his arms. His gaze went past her to the baby, and a strange look came across his face. The full impact of it hit him abruptly, that he had a son, even more reason to live. He hugged her tighter, swore an oath to himself.

Come hell or high water, they would make it to California.

CHAPTER 32

The ride to Lawson required two days. Along the way, Tilghman had considered and discarded any number of ideas. None of them were workable, and he'd finally decided that he had no option in the matter. Nor did he have anything to lose by coming out in the open. The direct approach was the only approach.

Tilghman sighted Lawson at dusk. Given the circumstances, he had no great confidence that John Ellsworth would divulge anything. The storekeeper was, after all, the father of Edith Doolin, and grandfather to her son. Yet he remembered the anonymous letter betraying Doolin's whereabouts to the U.S. marshal. That was many months ago, and the situation had now changed, but it was worth a try. He had nowhere else to turn.

Upon reflection, Tilghman decided to speak with the storekeeper in private. He thought Ellsworth would be even more reluctant to talk in front of his wife. Often as not, the women of a family were more protective than the men, and less fearful of the law. Not quite a week ago, when he'd first located the house, he had seen the Ellsworth woman holding her grandchild. Some instinct told him that she would be as hostile as a grizzly sow defending her young. He decided to stay away from the house.

The town's main street was closing for the night. Tilghman dismounted outside the store and left his horse at the hitch rack. He came through the door just as Ellsworth started to trim the wick of a lamp suspended over the front counter. The storekeeper turned, on the verge of telling a late customer that he was closed. Then, unable to hide the reaction, he recognized Tilghman. His eyes narrowed in a guarded look.

"Evening," Tilghman said, closing the door. "I'd like to talk with you."

Ellsworth's mouth set in a line. "What do you want?"

"I followed your daughter when she left here. Lost her outside of Pawhuska."

"Why would you follow Edith?"

"Don't play dumb," Tilghman said evenly. "By now, she's met up with Doolin. I figure they're somewhere in Kansas."

Ellsworth's face went ashen. "That's got nothing to do with me."

"You don't sleep good at night, do you?"

"What's that supposed to mean?"

"Well, your daughter's married to a wanted man. Your grandson's got a killer for a father. I'd say you're worried sick."

"You're wrong." Ellsworth averted his gaze. "Nothing I can do about it."

Tilghman gave him a piercing look. "You could tell me where they are. It's only a matter of time till Doolin gets himself killed." He paused, letting the storekeeper think about it. "You want your daughter there when the shooting starts?"

"I—" Ellsworth suddenly appeared stricken. "I wish to God she'd listened to reason. But she's headstrong, takes after her mother. I don't know where they are, and that's the truth."

There was a moment of silence. Tilghman examined him, slowly accepted that his words were genuine. "Too bad," he said at last. "Any idea where Doolin's headed?"

"Edith might have told her mother. But her or her mother don't tell me anything. They know I don't approve."

"Wherever they go, your daughter's bound to write home. When she does, will you let me know where they are?"

Ellsworth stared out the window into the deepening twilight. Finally, with a resigned expression, he nodded. "When she writes, I'll get word to you. She'll never have a decent life with Bill Doolin."

"No life at all," Tilghman assured him. "Doolin's living on borrowed time."

They shook hands on it. But as Tilghman walked from the store, he was struck by a wayward thought. One that had to do with an exchange of letters, and old friends. A particular friend came immediately to mind.

He decided to have a talk with another postmaster.

Early the next morning Tilghman rode into Ingalls. He reined to a halt outside the general store and dismounted. Whether or not he was seen was of no particular concern. His dealings there would be of a confidential nature.

The store had just opened for business. A heavyset man, bald with sagging jowls, stood behind the counter. There were as yet no customers, and he looked around with an alert eagerness as Tilghman came through the door. He smiled pleasantly.

"Good morning."

"Mornin'," Tilghman said. "You the new owner?"

"I am," he replied, staring at Tilghman's badge. "Joshua Burnham's the name. How can I help you?"

"I'm Bill Tilghman. Deputy U.S. marshal. I need your assistance."

"Always glad to oblige the law."

"A lady in town," Tilghman said easily. "Mary Pierce, down at the hotel. I'm interested in her mail."

Burnham looked startled. "Her mail?"

"In particular, the letters she receives. I want to know where they're from."

"I don't think I can do that. Bob and Mary Pierce are friends of mine."

"You'll do it." Tilghman's voice was cold and clear. "Otherwise I'll charge you with obstruction of justice. The Pierce woman is involved in aiding and abetting criminals."

"I don't believe you! Mary Pierce is a fine woman."

"How would you like to spend five years in federal prison on her account?"

Burnham swallowed, his jowls quivering. "You're talking about Edith Doolin, aren't you? Everybody knows her and Mary are friends."

"Good guess," Tilghman said with a slight smile. "Look, I'm not interested in Mary Pierce. You cooperate, and nobody gets hurt —including her."

"You'd let her off, not press charges?"

"You've got my word on it."

Burnham thought about it a moment. Then, as though reconciled to the situation, he shrugged. "Mary's in bed with the croup, and Bob's tendin' her along with the hotel. Guess he didn't have time to come get the mail yesterday."

Tilghman felt his scalp tingle. "There's a letter for her?"

Burnham darted a look out the windows. After inspecting the street, he led the way back to the mail cage. He took a letter from one of the bins, weighing it with a last moment of deliberation. Finally, with a heavy sigh, he slid it across the counter.

Tilghman stared down at the envelope. The writing was in a delicate hand and it was addressed to Mary

Pierce. But his attention fixed on the return address. He burned it into memory.

MRS. WILL BARRY
ROYAL HOTEL
BURDEN, KANSAS

"You know," Burnham said, as though reading his mind, "it's against the law to open somebody else's mail."

Tilghman's smile darkened. "You just keep your part of the bargain. Not a word to Mary Pierce about me being here. Understood?"

"No need to worry about that."

"I'll hold you to it, Mr. Burnham."

Tilghman rode out of town calculating time and distance. He placed Burden, Kansas, some sixty miles southeast of Wichita, and perhaps thirty miles north of the state line. By horseback, he was at least four days away, and that seemed far too late. By train, he could be there tomorrow.

He rode west toward the Santa Fe depot at Perry.

The train pulled into Burden late the next afternoon. Tilghman stepped onto the platform with his warbag and walked to the end of the stationhouse. His badge was in his pocket, and his appearance was that of a grungy, bearded cowhand. He stood for a moment surveying the town.

The overnight trip had taken him north from Perry to Winfield, Kansas. There he had switched to the afternoon eastbound, which made several stops before arriving in Burden. He'd stalled his horse at a livery stable in Perry, and brought only the essentials he could cram into his warbag. He thought it would be a short stay.

Doolin and his wife were in Burden, or they were gone. Either way, Tilghman expected to be in town for no more than a day. On the train ride, he'd decided not to contact the local town marshal. His federal commission was good in Kansas, and the fewer who knew of his presence, the better. There were no secrets in small towns, and he was also unwilling to entrust his life to a lawman he'd never met. He preferred to handle it himself.

Uptown, Tilghman kept to the opposite side of the street from the Royal Hotel. A block beyond the main intersection, he checked into the town's only other hotel, and dumped his warbag. Then, outside again, he turned south as the sun dipped toward the horizon. He had no choice but to verify that Edith Doolin was still in Burden. Whether or not Doolin was staying with her at the hotel was a moot point. He had to take the risk of being seen.

The room clerk had a newspaper spread across the counter of the front desk. He glanced up as Tilghman entered the door, and an expression of distaste came over his face. His eyes were frosty.

"Help you?"

"Hope so," Tilghman said amiably. "Depends on whether we can make a deal."

The clerk frowned. "What kind of deal?"

"Information." Tilghman pulled a wad of greenbacks from his pocket. "I'm willing to pay."

"Information about what?"

"Somebody stayin' in the hotel."

The clerk quickly scanned the empty lobby. His voice lowered in a conspiratorial tone. "That kind of thing doesn't come cheap."

Tilghman peeled off several bills. He fanned them out on the counter. "Fifty dollars," he said. "For the information and your silence."

Fifty dollars represented almost a month's wages for the clerk. His eyes brightened with avarice. "What do you want to know?"

"You have a woman here by the name of Mrs. Will Barry?"

"She's in room two-oh-one."

Tilghman jerked a thumb upward. "On the second floor?"

The clerk nodded. "All the way up front. Faces the street."

"Anybody stayin' with her?"

"Just her and her baby."

"Anybody called on her?"

"No." The clerk paused, remembering. "A tramp delivered a package for her. Somebody hired him to bring it around."

Tilghman looked interested. "Describe this tramp."

"Worn-out clothes. About my height. Dark hair."

"Anything else?"

"Yeah," the clerk said, nodding. "Walked with a real bad limp. Must've hurt his foot somehow."

Tilghman pushed the bills across the counter. "Don't let me hear that you told anybody about our little talk. You'd regret it."

The cold look in his eyes unnerved the clerk. "No need for threats," he said. "I'll keep my mouth shut."

"See that you do."

Tilghman turned toward the door. Outside, he crossed the street and entered a saloon with a plate-glass window. He took a spot at the end of the bar, where he had a direct view of the hotel. Ordering a beer, he nursed it, mentally reviewing what he'd learned. He felt charged with energy.

For whatever reason, the Doolin woman was still in town. But it was the tramp, more than the woman, that kindled his interest. He recalled that Doolin had been shot in the left foot, and reports had it that the wound hadn't healed properly. Operating in disguise, Doolin might easily have passed himself off as a tramp. What he couldn't hide was the limp.

After supper at a nearby cafe, Tilghman returned to the saloon. There, with one eye on the hotel, he engaged several men in conversation. Casually, as though making small talk, he commented on the number of bums traveling the country these days. Other men picked up on the subject, and before long he learned that Burden had a new bum. The man had attracted attention because of his game leg, and the fact that he was rarely seen during the day. He was around mainly at night, and even then not for long. One moment he was on the street, and the next, he was gone.

Late that night, Tilghman walked back to his hotel. He was now fairly sure that the tramp was in fact Bill Doolin. The way it appeared, Doolin was camped somewhere outside town, out of sight. He apparently came into Burden only at night, probably to visit his wife. Which raised the question of how he got into her hotel room without being seen. Beyond that was the greater question of why they were still in town. What was holding them in Burden?

Tilghman got the answer in part the next day. Around midmorning he resumed his spot at the bar, keeping watch on the hotel. A short while later Edith Doolin emerged from the hotel, carrying her baby. He gave her a short lead, then followed as she proceeded uptown. At the main intersection, she turned east, and a block down the street, she entered a one-story frame house. He strolled past, and suddenly the last piece of the puzzle fell into place. A doctor's shingle hung on the wall beside the front door.

Downstreet, near a feed store, Tilghman waited beneath the shade of a tree. A half hour later, when Edith Doolin emerged from the doctor's office, he trailed her back to the hotel. All doubt had been erased as to why she and Doolin remained in town. Either she or her baby was ill, and required care by a physician. When care was no longer required, he felt certain they would depart Burden. Which left him with an immediate problem. He had to locate the tramp.

And positively identify him as Bill Doolin.

CHAPTER 33

The campfire smoldered, all but dead. Doolin sat with a cup of coffee, staring into the embers. Dark had fallen, and the glow of the coals lighted his features. His expression was one of troubled deliberation.

Four days had passed since he'd first made camp at the spring. Yet there had been little or no improvement in his wife's condition. The bleeding, though slight, showed no signs of stopping. The doctor had no cure, and seemingly, only the most basic of medical advice. She had to have bed rest.

Doolin was genuinely concerned. There had been many women in his life, from lusty young farm girls to cowtown whores. But Edith was the first one who had ever touched the core of emotion that lay buried deep within him. Touched him to such an extent that he had gladly married her, and been happier still when she gave him a son. He dreaded the thought that she might need an operation.

Along with the dread, there was anger. Doolin's plans for California, and a new life, were now at a standstill. Looking back, it was as though all the scheming to get her safely out of Oklahoma Territory had been for nothing. They were stranded in Kansas, and according to Dr. Bailey, the local sawbones, no idea when it might end.

Whether fate, or simple bad luck, it reaffirmed what he'd been brooding on for the past couple of days. Something always seemed to go wrong.

Mulling it over now, Doolin saw no ready solution. He was determined that he wouldn't leave without Edith and the baby, and yet the risk grew with each passing day. Sooner or later someone was bound to stumble across his camp in the grove and begin asking questions. For that matter, people in town were already curious about his strange comings and goings. He'd seen it in the faces of men he passed on the street, the regulars who frequented the saloon across from the hotel. Their curiosity would lead to idle speculation, and eventually, the kind of talk that spread. A bum who hung around too long just naturally drew attention.

Doolin tried to offset the risk by varying his schedule. He went into town after dark, and each night he'd made it a point to arrive at a different hour. Still, whether early or late, there was no way to avoid being seen. There were always people on the street, and by now, many of them had begun to recognize him on sight. He'd made only one trip during the day, to replenish food supplies for his camp. But that had been one too many times, and he grew warier each time he set out for town. Luck could be stretched just so far.

Tonight, some three hours after dark, Doolin prepared to leave. After checking that his horse was secured to the picket line, he doused the fire with water from the spring. Then he moved through the trees in what had become a nightly journey into his own personal hell. The two-mile hike into town was an exercise in torture every step of the way. His left foot felt as if thousands of barbed quills had been jabbed through nerves and flesh, and now pressed against bone. He hobbled off across the darkened prairie.

Three days ago, at his wife's insistence, Doolin had gone to see Dr. Bailey. Following a long and painful examination, the physician had told him what he already knew. The bullet wound had damaged nerves in his foot and brought on rheumatism, which was now in an advanced state. Apart from liniment, which provided fiery if temporary relief, there was little to be done. In passing, Dr. Bailey had suggested therapeutic treatment at one of the mineral bath resorts in Arkansas. The waters were famed for their soothing effect, though nothing offered a permanent cure. The best advice was simply to stay off the foot.

By the time he reached town, Doolin was acutely aware that these nightly walks were crippling him. He felt another round-trip might well reduce him to using a crutch. On the outskirts, he crossed the end of the street and limped toward the uptown area. He stayed on the boardwalks where shadows were the deepest in an effort to avoid being seen. Still, there were streetlamps at every corner, and no way to elude the light when he crossed an intersection. Tonight, with sparks shooting through his foot, he was unable to move through the lampglow as fast as usual.

A block from the hotel Doolin slowly scanned the street ahead. He normally turned right at the intersection and walked to the alley behind the hotel. But as he approached the streetlight, he saw a man step out of the saloon and pause on the boardwalk. Some visceral instinct set off a warning, and he moved into the shadows. He watched as the man stood at the edge of the boardwalk, staring up at the second story of the hotel. After a time, the man turned, and for an instant his features were framed in the spill of light from the saloon window. He slipped into the darkened doorway of a store next to the saloon.

Doolin's blood went cold. The face he'd seen in that instant was one he remembered from newspaper photographs in Oklahoma Territory. He recalled pictures of federal marshals, and suddenly he put a name to the face: Bill Tilghman. One of the much-ballyhooed Three Guardsmen. The marshals who had hounded the Wild Bunch and killed four of his men. Then, so abruptly that he took a sharp breath, he realized the full meaning of what he'd just seen. Tilghman was watching the window of his wife's hotel room.

For a moment Doolin was paralyzed with shock. His mind roared with sudden comprehension. Tilghman had somehow tracked him to Kansas. With startling clarity, he saw that all his slippery plans and clever maneuvering had been for nothing. The Osage farmer, the exchange of wagons, even the Osage woman's masquerade to throw off pursuit, had been an exercise in folly. Tilghman hadn't tracked him anywhere, let alone to Kansas. Instead, in a neat switch, Tilghman had turned the tables on him. His wife was being used as bait.

Doolin turned back downstreet. He moved from doorway to doorway, hugging the shadows, fearful that he might be spotted at any moment. Halfway along the block, he ducked into a narrow passageway between two buildings. A short distance ahead he emerged into the alley and reversed directions, again heading north. At the end of the alley, his hand on his pistol, he paused and inspected the corner on Main Street. There was no one in sight.

Wincing with every step, his foot on fire, Doolin scuttled across the street. He disappeared into the alley and moved through the dark, halting behind the hotel. At the back door, he pulled a jackknife from his pocket, and jimmied the blade between the door and the doorframe. There was a muted *click* as the tip of the blade sprung the bolt. He stepped into the hallway.

A rear stairway led to the second floor. Doolin paused at the top of the landing to check the hall. There was no one about and he moved to the end of the corridor. He rapped gently on the door.

From inside, he heard the creak of floorboards under

quick footsteps. Edith Doolin opened the door, a welcoming smile across her face. He shushed her, a finger to his lips, warning silence as he moved into the room. He closed and locked the door.

Her eyes were now wide with fright. Doolin quickly scanned the room, saw the baby asleep on the bed. A lamp glowed on the dresser, which was positioned near the window. He nodded to his wife.

"Don't ask questions. Put out the light."

She moved to obey. At the dresser, she cupped a hand behind the lamptop and expelled a sharp breath. The flame was extinguished, casting the room into darkness. A dim ray of light seeped through the window from distant streetlamps.

"Stay away from the window," Doolin ordered. "We're being watched."

Her mouth sagged. "Who is it?"

"A federal marshal from the territory. I spotted him on the street."

"Do you think he knows you're here?"

"Has to," Doolin said. "He wouldn't be watching your room otherwise."

"Oh, my God." Her voice trembled. "How did he find us?"

"Only one way that makes any sense. He must've trailed you from the time you left home."

"What are we going to do?"

"I dunno just yet."

Doolin crossed the room. He removed his hat, tossing it on the dresser, and edged into position beside the window. Slowly, careful not to disturb the curtains, he eased his head past the drape of the cloth. He stared across the street.

The doorway of the store next to the saloon was framed in darkness. For several moments, his eyes squinted, Doolin saw nothing. Then, as his vision adjusted to the dim light, he uttered a low grunt. He saw the faint outline of a man in the doorway.

"Bastard's still there," he said, turning from the window. "Wouldn't know it unless you were looking for him."

"Just one?" she asked softly. "Maybe he hasn't called in the town marshal."

"You might be right about that. He probably figures to take me himself."

She moved to a chair near the washstand. As though drained of energy, she sat down heavily. "I don't understand," she said. "Even if he followed me, how would he know you're here? How could he be certain?"

"He's not certain," Doolin told her. "But he's got no doubts you're here. Hell, he even knows what room you're in. He's just waitin' for me to show up."

"And if you don't show up?"

"Then he'll stick with you till hell freezes over. He knows you're the only link to me."

She lowered her head. In the darkness, Doolin heard a sniffle, and then a choked sob. He moved to her and knelt on the floor. He took her hands.

"Don't go teary-eyed on me."

"It's not that," she said miserably. "It's just so . . . unfair."

"What d'you mean?"

"I saw the doctor today. The spotting has stopped, Bill. We could have left for California tomorrow."

Doolin laughed ruefully. "Honey, you haven't got the picture. We're damn lucky we didn't try boardin' that train yesterday. Or any other day."

She looked at him. "Why do you say that?"

"Because our friend out there would've followed you to the train station. Sure as God made little green apples, he'd have waited for me to put in an appearance. Then it'd all be over."

"Over?"

"Yeah," Doolin muttered. "He would've collared me or killed me. Whichever come handiest."

"Sweet Jesus," she moaned. "Won't it ever end?"

Doolin rose to his feet. He began pacing the room like a trapped animal pacing a cage. His mind whirled, exploring and discarding ideas for a way out. There was no sense in sending her on to California, for Tilghman would just follow. Nor was there anything to be gained by leaving her here, hoping Tilghman would weary of his vigil and leave town. The last year had proved that Tilghman hung on like a bulldog.

For a moment he toyed with the idea of killing Tilghman. But that, too, posed a host of risks. The major one being that he might himself be killed. To leave behind a widow and a fatherless child was not an option. Not after he'd come this far, this close to a new life. Hard as it seemed, there was only one way to handle the situation.

"Hate to say it." Doolin stopped pacing, halted in front of her. "You're gonna have to go back to your folks."

She bolted from her chair. "What are you talking about?"

"Edie, I don't like it any better than you do. But we're gonna have to start all over again."

"Start where?"

"Here's the idea," Doolin explained. "Sell the wagon and horse for whatever you can get. I don't want you busted up again makin' that trip in a wagon. Then you and the boy take a train back to the territory."

"But why?" she demanded. "What does that accomplish?"

"That jaybird outside will follow you all the way back to Lawson. So we've got him off my trail and we've bought time to come up with a new plan. I'll think of something."

"You mean you'd stay here?"

"Nooo," Doolin said in a musing tone. "You know what that sawbones told me about the mineral springs over in Arkansas? I might give it a try. See if it'll help my foot."

"And then what?" she persisted. "How long do we wait?"

"Just till things cool down. Nobody'll think to look for me in Arkansas. Couple of weeks, and they'll get tired of watchin' you. Then we'll make our move."

"How will I know where to reach you?"

"I'll write you through Mary Pierce. Tell her I'll use the same name as before—Tom Wilson."

"Oh God, Bill." She slumped against him, tears flooding her eyes. "I can't bear to leave you after all this. I'm afraid I'll never see you again."

"What a way to talk." Doolin gently stroked her hair. "Have I ever let you down before?"

"No . . . never."

"Well, I won't now, either. Trust me a little longer, and you'll see. We're gonna get to California—the three of us."

She sniffed, tilted her head back. "You're proud of him, aren't you?"

"Proud as punch," Doolin assured her. "A man's naturally partial to havin' a son."

"We'll have more, won't we, Bill?"

"Have ourselves a blessed litter. You got my word."

She laid her head on his shoulder. Doolin wrapped her tighter in his arms, rocking back and forth in a snug embrace. He wanted nothing more than to take his wife and child and move on, put the past behind them. Yet, unbidden, her words of a moment ago echoed through his mind.

He too wondered where it would end.

CHAPTER 34

Tilghman was at a loss.

For three days he had tagged after Edith Doolin. Whenever she left the hotel, he had followed her around town. At night, from his lookout across the street, he'd kept watch on her room. Yet, in all that time, he had seen nothing to indicate that she was in touch with her husband. He began to wonder if Doolin somehow got messages to her.

Yesterday morning, to his surprise, the Doolin woman had not visited the doctor. The only reasonable conclusion was that she, or her baby, whichever had been ill, was now well. But it that were so, he had to ask himself why she continued to stay on in Burden. Which raised the greater question of why she'd ever come there in the first place.

Then, one surprise following another, the situation became even more murky. Yesterday afternoon Edith Doolin had emerged from the hotel with her baby and walked to a livery stable on the south edge of town. There, with a man who appeared to be the livery owner, she had inspected a wagon parked at the rear and a horse in the outside corral. The livery owner had then counted out a small stack of greenbacks.

Tilghman had no doubt that it was the horse and

wagon she'd used on the trip to Burden. He was no less certain that he had just witnessed her selling them to the livery owner. To confound matters even further, she had then spent the rest of the afternoon on a shopping spree. She'd bought herself and the baby some new clothes, as well as a matched pair of suitcases. On her last stop, at a novelty store, she had purchased what appeared to be souvenirs. All of the goods had been delivered to her hotel.

Last night, once more watching her room, Tilghman had felt thoroughly bewildered. The sale of the horse and wagon indicated that she planned to travel by train. By the same token, the purchase of clothes and suitcases, not to mention souvenirs, indicated a trip was in the offing. All that being true, the obvious question was where she was headed and when did she plan to leave? Perhaps more to the point, was she planning to meet Doolin at some distant destination?

None of it made sense. She could just have easily eluded pursuit in Oklahoma Territory, and caught a train from one of a dozen different locations. Instead, she had made an arduous trip by wagon through Osage country and then on to Kansas. To presume that she'd done all that simply to catch a train boggled the mind. Logic dictated that she had traveled to Kansas for one purpose only, to somehow connect with Doolin. But if that were the case, where the hell was he?

One thing troubled Tilghman even more. From the hotel clerk, and again with regulars in the saloon, he had confirmed that a tramp was hanging around town. To further his suspicions, he'd verified that the man had a pronounced limp and fit the general description of Doolin. The corker was that the tramp hadn't shown up in Burden until the day after Edith Doolin's arrival. All of that was coincidence compounding coincidence, and to Tilghman, any coincidence was suspect. He still believed that Doolin was camped out somewhere around Burden.

But now, his fourth day in town, Tilghman was no closer to the truth than before. A late morning sun filtered through the saloon window as he stood at the bar. Inwardly, though he had no notion of what it might be, he felt certain that something would happen today. Yesterday's shopping spree, and the suitcases, seemed to him too great a tip-off to ignore. Edith Doolin was headed somewhere, and he thought today was the day. Which merely brought him full circle in a looping enigma. Where the hell was Bill Doolin?

Through the window, Tilghman saw a man wearing a porter's cap enter the hotel. Looking closer, he saw Edith Doolin holding the baby in the lobby. A moment later, the porter came out the door, carrying her suitcases, and moved off in the direction of the train station. She followed a few paces behind, attired in one of the new outfits she'd bought yesterday. She looked like a woman who knew where she was going, and how to get there.

Tilghman trailed them by a half block. Some minutes later, they rounded the corner of the train station and disappeared down the platform. He stopped at the corner, looking around the edge of the building, and saw Edith Doolin enter the depot. The porter guarding her bags remained on the platform, surrounded by a crowd of people waiting on the train. Shortly she came through the door, nodding to the porter, the baby cradled in her left arm. In her right hand, she held a train ticket.

Off in the distance a whistle sounded. Tilghman glanced to the east and saw a passenger train perhaps a quarter of a mile away. Time was short, and he felt there was no choice but to risk being seen. He stepped around the corner, aware that the Doolin woman was looking downtrack at the approaching train, and strode rapidly along the platform. He scanned the faces of the crowd, assuring himself that Doolin was not among them. As the locomotive rolled into the station, he hurried through the waiting room door.

The ticket agent was a spare man with a receding hairline. He looked up with an expression of birdlike alertness, nodding pleasantly. Tilghman pulled out his badge.

"Federal marshal," he said. "I need some information."

"What can I do for you, marshal?"

"A woman with a baby just bought a ticket. What was her destination?"

"Wearing a blue dress, was she?"

"That's the one."

"Oklahoma Territory," the agent informed him. "Final destination the town of Perry."

For a moment Tilghman was too stunned to speak. "One last thing," he finally said. "Where does she change trains?"

"Winfield," the agent replied. "Southbound from there takes her to Perry."

"Much obliged."

Tilghman walked out of the depot. The passengers were in the process of boarding, and he saw the porter follow Edith Doolin onto the train. His head was still reeling from the fact that she was headed back to Oklahoma Territory. Her trip to Kansas made even less sense now. Something about the whole affair smelled.

Still, fishy or not, Tilghman had no choice but to follow her. There was always a chance that she would change tickets at Winfield, or meet Doolin at a stop somewhere along the line. His badge would guarantee him passage, and he delayed boarding until the last moment. He watched as the porter stepped off the train.

Then, oddly, Tilghman sensed that he was being watched. He glanced around the platform and saw no one but the stationmaster. His gaze swept the passenger coaches, and abruptly stopped at the one directly in front of the depot. Edith Doolin was seated at the window, the baby cuddled in her arms. She was staring at him with a strange smile.

When their eyes locked, she suddenly turned away. But in that instant, Tilghman saw that her smile was more on the order of a gloating smirk. The realization came over him that he'd been spotted, that she knew him. Perhaps not his name, but she had no doubt that he was a lawman. Her look, the sly smile, said it all. She knew he was following her.

Tilghman made a snap decision. Some inner voice told him that the Doolin woman was bait, meant to lure him away from Burden and out of Kansas. His instincts had never played him false, even in situations when his life was on the line. Whatever the source, these sudden hunches had never failed him, and another one came over him now. He felt an eerie certainty that Doolin was somewhere close at hand.

The thought was reinforced as the locomotive belched steam and got under way. Tilghman saw Edith Doolin's head snap around, staring at him as the passenger coach pulled away from the station. Her eyes were filled with a look of disbelief and desperation, the sudden awareness that he had no intention of boarding the train. As the coach gathered speed, her face became a mask of bewildered outrage. Her expression betrayed her, and he knew he was right. She'd tried to gull him.

The train rolled out of Burden, heading west. Tilghman watched until the last coach in the string was far down the tracks. Then he turned and walked back into the depot. The ticket agent gave him a curious look.

"Find the lady you were asking about?"

"More or less," Tilghman said. "Who do I see about sending a telegram?"

"You're looking at him," the agent said with a slow

smile. "Tickets, telegraph, sweep the floor. Jack of all trades."

He pushed a telegram form across the counter, along with a pen and inkwell. Tilghman considered a moment, composing the message in his head. Then he began writing.

Evett Nix
U.S. Marshal
Guthrie, Oklahoma Territory

Edith Doolin arrives Perry on Santa
Fe tomorrow. Have her followed to
determine final destination. Heck
Thomas knows her on sight.
Believe Doolin still in Kansas.
Will keep you advised.

                    Tilghman

Finished, Tilghman slid the form across the counter. The agent read through it quickly, silently mouthing the words. His eyes went round and he glanced up with a questioning look.

"Bill Doolin's here in Burden?"

"Let's understand each other," Tilghman said in a low voice. "You keep your lip buttoned, or I'll have to see you in an official capacity. You get my drift?"

"Bet I do," the agent said hastily. "Don't give it another thought, marshal. You can depend on me."

"How much do I owe you?"

Tilghman paid for the telegram and walked to the door. Outside, crossing the platform, his thoughts turned again to Doolin. How he'd been spotted, or when, seemed to him a moot point. Edith Doolin's sudden departure, her return to Oklahoma Territory, spoke for itself. He'd somehow given himself away, and the result was a change in Doolin's plans. Which left him with few options and no real choice. He had to turn up a fresh lead.

Headed uptown, Tilghman mentally reviewed the last few days. The Doolin woman had spoken with several people during her stay in Burden. A short list included the hotel clerk, the doctor, the livery stable owner, and clerks in various stores. However smart she thought she was, she might have dropped some telltale clue in conversation. So his first task was to talk with those who had spoken with her at any length. From the first day, he'd been curious about her visits to the doctor. He decided to start there.

Some ten minutes later a nurse ushered him into the physician's office. Phillip Bailey was in his fifties, with a mane of white hair and an open manner. Seated at an ancient roll-top desk, he motioned Tilghman to a nearby chair. His smile was inquisitive.

"What seems to be the problem today?"

"Nothing medical." Tilghman showed him the badge. "I'm a federal marshal. I'd like to ask about one of your patients."

"You don't say?" Bailey examined the badge, nodding. "Which patient would that be?"

"A woman staying at the Royal Hotel, Mrs. Will Barry. Or maybe her baby was the patient. I never really knew."

"Yes indeed, a fine young woman. And you're right, she was the patient rather than her baby. May I ask your interest in Mrs. Barry?"

"Just routine," Tilghman said evasively. "She got herself involved with some unsavory people."

"What a shame." Bailey appeared saddened by the news. "Well, in any event, she had complications resulting from childbirth. A few days' bed rest and she was fine. The problem took care of itself."

"Did she mention anything about herself? Where she

was headed, who she was traveling with? Anything of that sort?"

"No, not that I recall. She just said she was stopping over in Burden for a few days."

Tilghman looked at him. "So you only talked about her medical condition? Nothing else?"

"No, nothing—" Bailey hesitated, suddenly thoughtful. "Well, now that I think on it, there was one thing. She asked me to see some poor fellow she'd met on the street. A panhandler."

"A tramp?" Tilghman said quickly. "Dark hair, average height, with a lame foot?"

"Yes, that's the fellow. Told me he'd accidentally shot himself in the foot some time ago. Developed into a bad case of rheumatism."

"Are you still treating him?"

"I saw him only once. Four or five days ago, as I recall. Gave him a bottle of liniment to ease the pain."

"Have you seen him around town since then?"

"No, I haven't," Bailey said. "Perhaps he took my advice. I suggested one of the bath resorts, in Arkansas."

"Which one?" Tilghman asked. "Hot Springs or Eureka Springs?"

"Actually, I made no specific recommendation. I just mentioned that the waters would relieve his condition."

"Did he say anything about one over the other?"

"Not that I remember."

"What name did he give you?"

"Let me see." Bailey thumbed through an index file on his desk. "Yes, here it is. Thomas Wilson, male, advanced rheumatism of the left foot. No address, I'm afraid."

"Out of curiosity," Tilghman said, "how old would you say his gunshot wound was?"

"Less than a year." Bailey paused, his expression benign but his eyes inquisitive. "You seem to have taken quite an interest in Mr. Wilson. Has he committed a crime?"

"I'll know that when I find him, doctor. But if you're a betting man, bet the farm."

Tilghman left the office at a vigorous stride. The day was half gone and there was still a great deal to be accomplished. He had to buy a horse and a saddle, camping gear and a rifle, and then start a hunt too long delayed. For while he was days behind, there was one thing he knew with dead certainty.

Bill Doolin, alias Thomas Wilson, would never take the train to Arkansas.

CHAPTER 35

Tilghman began the manhunt on a central premise. He was convinced Doolin would not take the train from Kansas to Arkansas. For one thing, the Wild Bunch had staged several robberies in the area where Kansas and Arkansas abutted Indian Territory. For another, trains were often crowded, and the risk of being recognized was simply too great. Doolin's face was widely known from wanted posters and newspapers.

So the greater likelihood was that Doolin would travel by horseback. Tilghman tried to look at it through the other man's eyes whenever he conducted a lone manhunt. There were several routes by which a man might travel from Burden to the state line of Arkansas. But he thought Doolin would take the shortest route, while at the same time hugging the border of Indian Territory. That way, were he recognized, a short hop took him into the Nations.

One other factor entered into Tilghman's thinking. From the doctor in Burden, he knew that Doolin was suffering considerable pain from his foot. Should the pain worsen, Doolin might well seek medical attention along the way. That meant entering towns—where there were doctors—and running the risk of being recognized. Whether or not Doolin would stick with his tramp's disguise was a matter of conjecture. But if he needed a doctor, it made sense that he would look for one in a small town. The chances of being spotted by the law would then be reduced by a large degree.

All these things were weighed in the balance before Tilghman departed Burden. His approach to an investigation was to think it out, rather than conduct a harum-scarum search. Studying a map of Kansas, he found what seemed the perfect route for a man with Doolin's problems. In the southeastern corner of the state, there was a string of small towns along the border of Indian Territory. The towns would have doctors, with little law enforcement, and great strategic advantage. None of them were more than five miles from refuge in the Nations.

The wild card in all this revolved around Doolin's ultimate destination. There were two notable bath resorts in Arkansas, Eureka Springs and Hot Springs. Which one Doolin might choose was a matter of pure guesswork. After pondering on it, Tilghman saw that there was no way to pick one over the other. He might have to search both, and hope that Doolin continued to use the same alias. On the other hand, any investigation was equal parts deduction and good detective work, and getting the breaks. This time out, things might fall his way.

For three days Tilghman rode steadily eastward along the border. He stopped in one town after another, pausing only long enough to question the local doctor. Though they were cooperative, none of them had been consulted by a man with a lame foot. On the fourth morning, still confident that he was on the right track, he rode into the town of Chetopa. By now he had covered some eighty miles, and all the towns had begun to look alike. But he was no less determined than when he'd set out from Burden.

Tilghman discovered that there were two doctors in

Chetopa. He learned as well that they were father and son, Harold and John Millsap. The younger Millsap, who routinely made house calls across the countryside, was out of town. Dr. Harold Millsap, who no longer made house calls, was in the office. He was a frail man, on the sundown side of sixty, stooped and hard of hearing. He greeted Tilghman with a genial warning.

"You'll have to speak up. I'm damn near stone deaf. What ails you?"

"Nothing," Tilghman said loudly, taking a chair beside the physician's desk. "I'd like to ask you some questions."

"Questions?" Millsap boomed, shouting in order to hear himself. "What sort of questions?"

Tilghman pulled out his badge. "Federal marshal," he said. "I'm looking for a fugitive."

"A what?" Millsap asked sharply. "Consarn it, you'll have to speak louder."

"A fugitive," Tilghman bellowed. "A man with a game left foot. He's got rheumatism."

"Well, why didn't you say so? I treated a man like that a couple of days ago."

Tilghman sat straighter. "Had he been gunshot in the foot?"

"Yeah, a while back," Millsap acknowledged. "Nothing to be done for that. He'd run out of liniment and wanted more. I gave him another bottle."

"Did he ask you anything about the mineral baths over in Arkansas?"

"Told him it's the closest thing to a miracle. I've got a touch of arthritis in the spine. Go over there myself once or twice a year."

"Did you recommend any particular resort?"

"Told him to go where I go. The Davidson Hotel in Eureka Springs. Has the best waters in Arkansas."

Tilghman allowed himself a smile. "Do you think he'll follow your advice?"

"Why hell, yes," Millsap trumpeted. "He'd chew nails if he thought it'd help. He was hurting bad."

"Thanks." Tilghman stood. "You've put me on the right track, doctor."

"What'd he do, anyhow? Murder somebody?"

"That and a few other things."

Millsap cackled. "By golly, I knew it! Told me he'd shot himself in the foot. Didn't believe him for a minute."

Tilghman turned at the door. "Was he using the name Tom Wilson?"

"Now that you mention it, he was. Yessir, that was it. Tom Wilson."

"How was he dressed?"

"Looked more like a cowhand than he did a desperado. Smelled like he'd been on a horse for a while, too."

"Thanks again."

Outside, Tilghman felt like clicking his heels. His assessment of Doolin had proved to be on the mark. Avoiding trains, the outlaw had taken a route along the border. Two days ago, almost by happenstance, he'd stopped to see a doctor who had definite opinions about the bath resorts in Arkansas. There was little doubt that Doolin would be found in Eureka Springs.

Tilghman saw no reason to waste time. By switching from horseback to train, he could be in Eureka Springs sometime tomorrow. A half hour later, after a short dickering session, he sold his horse and saddle to a local livestock dealer. Then, at a mercantile store, he swapped his new rifle for a black suit and a parson's white, ringed collar. The merchant, knowing he'd got the best of the deal, even threw in a black, broad-brimmed hat.

For the past few days, Tilghman had dwelled at length on having been spotted in Burden. The obvious answer was Edith Doolin, who knew him on sight. But that set him to thinking about pictures of himself and other marshals that had appeared in newspapers. The more he wondered, the more it made sense that Doolin knew him on sight as well. So he'd decided to give himself whatever edge was possible when they finally met. He would assume the guise of a preacher.

From the store, with his bundle of clothes, Tilghman proceeded to the train station. A passenger train, headed eastbound, was scheduled into Chetopa in two hours. After purchasing a ticket, he composed a telegram, worded in cryptic language, to Evett Nix. The wire stated that business affairs required his presence in Eureka Springs, and he asked for an immediate reply regarding his last telegraph message. Less than an hour later, he was handed an equally cryptic telegram from Nix. The package, Nix informed him, had arrived as scheduled, and had been delivered to Lawson.

The meaning was clear. Edith Doolin had arrived by train in Perry, and Heck Thomas had trailed her to her parents' home in Lawson. Upon reading it, Tilghman suddenly realized that all the pieces had fallen into place. Eureka Springs was some fifty miles east of the border with the Cherokee Nation. From there, Doolin planned to take the healing waters and bide his time. Then, after a suitable interval, he would again spirit his wife and child out of Oklahoma Territory. All of which dovetailed with what Tilghman had suspected from the beginning. Doolin never intended to return to the territory, or the Wild Bunch.

Tilghman boarded the train shortly after one o'clock. He placed his bundle in the overhead rack, took a seat, and stared out the window. He was reminded of the adage that time and tide waits on no man.

He thought Bill Doolin had lived on borrowed time long enough. The tide finally had ebbed.

Eureka Springs was the oldest bath resort in Arkansas. Located in the Ozark Hills, the town was a place of twisting streets and houses that clung precariously to steep slopes. People came from across the country to luxuriate in the steaming sulfur waters.

Tilghman stepped off the train early the next morning. The porter had pressed his new suit and blacked his boots, and the white dog-collar of a minister encircled his neck. He carried his range clothes and gunbelt in a warbag, and his pistol was stuffed in the waistband of his trousers. He looked like a preacher in search of miracle waters.

The Davidson Hotel was located along the town's main street. A short walk from the train depot, the hotel was situated beneath rugged hills dotted with the yawning mouths of large caves. On the street, men tipped their hats and ladies nodded pleasantly as Tilghman strolled uptown. He played the role, smiling with benign good cheer, thinking that Zoe would be amused. At last, in a manner of speaking, he'd got religion.

Entering the hotel, Tilghman walked straight to the registration desk. The lobby was crowded and he scanned faces from beneath his broad-brimmed black hat. There was always the risk that he would stumble across Doolin and be spotted, despite his disguise. Still, the parson's outfit seemed to hold people's attention, and the risk was unavoidable. He had to verify that Doolin was staying at the hotel.

"Good morning, Reverend," the desk clerk greeted him. "May I help you?"

"You're too kind," Tilghman said unctuously. "I'm looking for one of my parishioners, Thomas Wilson. I believe he's a guest at the hotel."

"Yes, of course, I know Mr. Wilson. He stopped by only a few minutes ago to mail a letter. He was on his way to the bath house."

"How would I find the bath house?"

"See that hallway, Reverend?" the clerk said, pointing across the lobby. "At the end, turn right and go down the stairs. You can't miss it."

Tilghman checked his warbag with the bell captain. Down the hallway, he found stairs that descended to what had once been a natural cavern. At the lower level, he tugged his hat low and entered the door of the bath house. There was a lounge out front, with an attendant serving coffee, and a counter where guests were given towels and locker keys. Beyond was an entrance to the dressing room and the baths.

Several men waited their turn at the counter. Others were seated around the lounge, conversing over their morning coffee. Across the room, Doolin was seated in a club chair, reading a newspaper. Attired in a suit and tie that appeared to be newly purchased, he looked much like the other hotel guests. A cup of coffee was on a table beside his chair, and he kept glancing over the top of his newspaper. He was apparently waiting for the line to thin out at the counter.

Head lowered, Tilghman moved toward the men waiting for towels. As he approached the end of the line, he saw Doolin glance at him, then return to the newspaper. He continued on, aware that Doolin had been distracted by the minister's outfit rather than inspecting his face. Quickly, before he was noticed again, he closed the distance to Doolin's chair. He halted a step away, drawing his pistol.

"Doolin!" he ordered sharply. "Stand up and keep your hands in sight. You're under arrest."

A flicker of recognition crossed Doolin's features. He stared over the newspaper, his mouth set in a tight smile. "Where'd you get the preacher's duds?"

"You heard me," Tilghman said. "On your feet."

Doolin rose from his chair. He flung the newspaper forward with his left hand and his right hand flashed inside his suit jacket. On the verge of firing, something stayed Tilghman's finger on the trigger. He grabbed

Doolin's wrist with his left hand, locking it in a fierce grip only inches away from the butt of a pistol. Standing toe to toe, he jabbed his Colt into the outlaw's stomach.

"Let it go," he said in a hard voice. "Don't make me kill you."

Doolin struggled, trying to free his arm. Around the room, the other men suddenly became aware of the wrestling match. They backed away, watching in silence, confounded by the sight of a minister with a gun in his hand. The minister was bigger and stronger, but the second man continued to fight. He clawed desperately at something inside his coat.

"Give it up," Tilghman growled, shoving Doolin into the wall. "Stop now or your wife's a widow."

The warning touched a nerve. Doolin ceased to struggle, the wild look in his eyes abruptly gone. His tensed muscles went slack, and he allowed his arm to be forced aside. Tilghman pulled a pistol from his waistband, then moved back a step. They stared at each other.

"What stopped you?" Doolin said sullenly. "Why didn't you kill me?"

"Let's just say I preferred to take you alive."

"What for?"

"I doubt you'd understand, Doolin. Walk ahead of me."

Tilghman informed the crowd that he was a federal marshal. None of them moved as he marched Doolin across the room and out the door. Upstairs, his gunhand hidden inside his jacket, Tilghman reclaimed his warbag. He saw no reason to alert local law officers, or to undergo a formal extradition hearing. Outside the hotel, he ordered Doolin to lead the way to the train station.

A northbound train was scheduled in at eleven that morning. Tilghman took Doolin into the men's toilet and locked the door. He reclaimed a set of manacles from his warbag and clamped them around the outlaw's wrists. While Doolin watched, he shed the parson's outfit and put on his regular clothes. He pinned the deputy marshal's badge to his shirt.

"Takes the cake," Doolin said, staring at him. "Hadn't been for that preacher's getup, I would've spotted you. You're a lucky man."

"Your wife's the lucky one, Doolin. I almost brought you home in a box."

In the waiting room, Tilghman seated his prisoner on a bench against the wall. Then, after purchasing two tickets for Guthrie, he asked about sending a telegram. He composed a brief message to Evett Nix.

I HAVE HIM IN CUSTODY. ARRIVE THERE ON THE NOON TRAIN TOMORROW.

TILGHMAN

PART THREE

CHAPTER 36

The railway station at Guthrie was mobbed. A crowd of more than two thousand people waited around the depot and along the Santa Fe tracks. Word of Doolin's capture had spread throughout town, and there was an air of celebration among those thronged about on the warm September morning. They were there to greet the most famous outlaw in Oklahoma Territory.

In large degree, they were there as well to greet the man who had captured Doolin. Overnight, with telegraph wires humming the news, Tilghman had become a celebrity throughout the territory. All the more so because he had taken Doolin alive, rather than killing him. None among them understood why he had spared the dreaded leader of the Wild Bunch.

The train rolled into town shortly after the noon hour. The engineer throttled down, setting the brakes, and let loose several blasts with his whistle. As the locomotive ground to a halt, pandemonium erupted among the packed masses outside the depot. Shoving and jostling, they pressed closer around the passenger coaches, fighting for a better vantage point. Slowly, then gaining momentum, a chant went up from the crowd. Their voices built to a drumming roar.

"Doolin! *Doolin!* DOOLIN!"

Tilghman stood in the aisle of the last passenger coach. Doolin was still seated, his hands manacled, staring out the window with a look of raw fear. For all either of them knew, a lynch mob had gathered to perform summary execution on the outlaw leader. Under his breath, Tilghman cursed Evett Nix for allowing the news to leak out. The matter should have been kept quiet, he told himself, at least until Doolin was locked in a cell. There was no way to control a crowd that large.

The train shuddered to a halt. Through the window, Tilghman saw Nix on the depot platform, surrounded by Thomas and Madsen and several other deputies. He took Doolin by the arm, got him on his feet, and walked him to the rear of the coach. After opening the door, he moved onto the observation platform, motioning for Doolin to remain inside. Behind Doolin, he noted that the other passengers were hurrying toward the front of the coach. He leaned out across the rear steps.

Heck Thomas spotted him. Gathering Nix and the other deputies, he bulled a path through the crowd. A moment later Thomas clambered up the steps, followed closely by Nix. Madsen and the remaining deputies formed a wedge at the bottom of the steps. The mob surged toward the rear of the train, their chant now raised to a deafening beat. Thomas waved Tilghman and Doolin back inside the coach. Nix hastily slammed the door.

"You ol' scutter!" Thomas said with a wide grin. "Did it all by your lonesome, didn't you?"

Before he could answer, Nix pushed forward. "Congratulations, Bill! You're the talk of the whole territory."

Tilghman accepted his handshake. "Thanks," he said evenly, nodding out the window. "Where'd that reception party come from?"

"No way to stop the news from spreading. Those folks wouldn't have missed this for the world."

"He's right," Thomas added quickly. "You'd think it was the Fourth of July all over again."

Tilghman looked at him. "Will we have any trouble getting Doolin under lock and key?"

"From that crowd?" Thomas laughed, shook his head. "They're not gonna do anything but bust your eardrums. They're here for the show."

"Why do they keep yelling for Doolin?"

" 'Cause he's the show." Thomas glanced past him, at Doolin. "You're the luckiest feller that ever lived. If it'd been me, I'd have brought you back across a horse."

"If it'd been you," Doolin said with a sarcastic smile, "you wouldn't've brought me back. Tilghman's likely the only man that could've done it."

"You sorry sonovabitch. I'd have—"

"Enough of that," Nix broke in. "Mr. Doolin, it's a pleasure to meet you at last. I think you can rest assured of a swift and speedy trial."

"Got a rope handy, have you?"

"All in good time," Nix said jovially. "But first, we have to get you through that crowd. Heck, lead the way."

Thomas went out the door. He was followed by Nix and Doolin, with Tilghman acting as rear guard. As they came down the steps, the mob around the depot spotted Doolin and went wild with a renewed burst of excitement. Madsen and the other deputies formed a phalanx to the front, their Winchesters held at port arms. They moved forward as the chant of the crowd raised to a thunderous pitch.

The lawmen wedged a path through the massed throngs. Doolin was in the middle, protected on all sides, with people screaming and shouting and lunging forward for the chance to touch him. Slowly, often a step at a time, they shouldered their way across the platform and past the depot. On the street, other deputies waited with a buggy and several horses. Doolin was quickly loaded onto the buggy, along with Nix and Tilghman. Thomas swung aboard a horse and motioned for the deputies to mount. They formed a shield around the buggy.

On the way uptown, the crowd surged along, steadily growing larger. Tilghman gradually realized that Thomas was headed for the marshal's office rather than the jailhouse. He turned to question Nix, who was seated on the opposite side of Doolin. But the noise from the mob was too great to be heard, and he let it go. Some minutes later the driver brought the buggy to a halt outside the Herriott Building. Their mounted escort swung around to block the swarms of onlookers.

Tilghman hustled Doolin from the buggy. Thomas and Madsen dismounted, hurrying forward with Nix, and followed them inside. Upstairs, with Tilghman guiding the prisoner, they proceeded along the hallway to Nix's office. When they entered, a pack of reporters, with cameras mounted on tripods, was ganged around the desk. Tilghman stopped just inside the door.

"What's all this?" he said, looking at Nix. "You didn't tell me anything about reporters."

"Too crowded at the depot," Nix said. "The gentlemen of the press want to interview you and Doolin."

Tilghman stifled a response. There was nothing to be gained in airing their differences before reporters. Nix clearly intended to reap a harvest of newsprint, and an obstinate deputy marshal would merely result in bigger headlines. Tilghman and Doolin were quickly positioned in front of the desk, facing the cameras. Nix hovered about like a stage manager orchestrating a theatrical production.

"Mr. Doolin!" one of the reporters shouted as flash pans fired in rapid succession. "After all this time, how did you come to be captured?"

Doolin seemed to bask in the attention. "I practically

gave myself up," he said in a jocular tone. "High time I had a chance to prove my innocence."

"How can you prove your innocence?" another reporter demanded loudly. "There are dozens of witnesses to the robberies and murders committed by you and your Wild Bunch."

"Mistaken identity," Doolin said with a broad smile. "Nobody can eyewitness me for anything. I'm a law-abiding citizen."

That drew an appreciative laugh from the reporters. One of them prompted him further. "Are you saying you were never the leader of the Wild Bunch?"

Doolin spread his manacled hands. "Boys, I wouldn't know the Wild Bunch from a hole in the ground. I'm just a simple cowhand."

"Will you plead not guilty at your trial?"

"Why, being innocent and all, what else could I do?"

"Deputy Tilghman!" the first reporter cut in. "How do you feel about Mr. Doolin pleading not guilty?"

"That's his right," Tilghman said levelly. "A jury will decide his guilt or innocence."

"Do you think he'll get off?"

"What I think doesn't matter. He'll have his day in court like anybody else."

"How'd you capture him?" a reporter outshouted the others. "Where did you find him?"

"Eureka Springs, Arkansas," Tilghman replied. "I tracked him to a hotel there."

"What was he doing in Eureka Springs?"

"Getting ready to take a bath," Tilghman said with a slow smile. "I believe he felt in need of cleansing."

"Do you favor hanging over life in prison?"

Nix stepped on stage, sensing an opportune moment. "Gentlemen," he said, motioning for silence. "You may quote me as saying Bill Doolin will get a swift and impartial trial. All the evidence will be presented then, and we believe a jury will render the proper verdict."

The door opened and Governor William Renfrow stepped into the room with one of his aides. Everyone fell silent as the governor strode forward, nodding amiably to the reporters. Nix rapidly plucked Doolin off stage, and the aide just as quickly positioned the governor beside Tilghman. The reporters waited expectantly.

"Gentlemen," the governor said in a sonorous voice, "I would first like to commend U.S. Marshal Nix and his intrepid force of deputies for bringing law and order to Oklahoma Territory. None but the brave would have undertaken such a monumental task."

The reporters jotted furiously in their notepads. Governor Renfrow turned to Tilghman. "The bravest of the brave stands beside me here today. For apprehending Bill Doolin," he paused, took a bank check from his suit pocket, "I have the distinct pleasure of presenting Deputy U.S. Marshal William Tilghman with a reward in the amount of five thousand dollars. Our heartfelt congratulations, Deputy Tilghman."

The governor clasped Tilghman's hand, still holding the check, and faced the cameras with a nutcracker grin. The flash pans exploded and shutters clicked, freezing an image of the moment for posterity. A moment later, with his aide clearing the way, Renfrow swept out of the room. Tilghman stood there, holding the check, having never said a word. When Nix began ushering the reporters toward the door, he understood that it was curtain time. The show was over.

Outside again, with Doolin in tow, the deputies regrouped around the buggy. The crowd had diminished in numbers, but fully a thousand people trailed them to the jailhouse. There, grinning and waving his manacled hands, Doolin played to the spectators as he was escorted inside. They roared their approval at his display of grit.

"Doolin! *Doolin!* DOOLIN!"

* * *

Late the next morning Tilghman prepared to leave town. An arraignment had been held earlier, and there was nothing more for him to do until Doolin was brought to trial. He planned to take a few days off and attend to personal matters. High on the list was time alone with Zoe.

After the arraignment, he'd borrowed a horse from Heck Thomas. His horse, which was still stabled in Perry, would have to be retrieved when time allowed. But now, before departing, he had a guard escort him back to the central cell block, where prisoners were allowed to gather during the day. He wanted a last word with the man he'd captured.

Doolin was seated at a table with several other inmates. When Tilghman halted in the corridor, he stood and walked to the bars fronting the bull pen. "Just been thinkin'," he said with a wry smile. "You got yourself a real nice payday with that reward. How you gonna spend it?"

"I'll think of something." Tilghman paused, looking at him through the bars. "Wondered if you'd be interested in talking about the rest of the gang? Might work to your advantage when you come to trial."

"Never kid an old kidder, Tilghman. They're gonna hang me no matter what. We both know it."

"Courts have been known to grant leniency before. You've got nothing to lose by cooperating."

"Yeah, I do," Doolin said firmly. "All my life, I never could stomach a turncoat. Too late to start now."

Tilghman shrugged. "Well, you understand I had to try. Guess it's hard to teach an old dog new tricks."

"On that score, I was always a slow learner."

"I reckon I'll see you in court."

Doolin stuck his hand through the bars. "I owe you one for that day in the bath house. You could've shot me easy as not."

Tilghman accepted his handshake. "I didn't do you any favor. Not if you've ever seen a man hanged."

"Hell, marshal, it's not over till it's over. I take it one day at a time."

Outside the lockup, Tilghman walked back to the front office. As he came through the door, he saw Edith Doolin talking to one of the guards. She looked pale and tired, and he imagined she had driven through the night after hearing of Doolin's arrival in Guthrie. The guard motioned to Tilghman.

"This lady says she's Doolin's wife. You ever seen her before?"

"I'll vouch for the lady," Tilghman told him. "She's Mrs. Edith Doolin."

"Thank you," she said. "After all the trouble I put you to in Kansas, that's nice of you."

"You and your baby get home all right, Mrs. Doolin?"

"Just fine, though all that seems a waste now. You caught Bill anyway, didn't you?"

"Yes, ma'am," Tilghman said, nodding. "Took a while, but things have a way of working out."

"I—" She hesitated, searching for words. "I want to thank you for not killing him. I know you could have, and no questions asked."

"Just doing my job, Mrs. Doolin. No thanks necessary."

Tilghman watched the guard escort her into the hallway. He idly wondered if she knew anything about the remaining members of the Wild Bunch. But then he put the thought aside, for in her own way she was as tough as Doolin. Perhaps tougher.

She would have to watch her husband be hanged.

CHAPTER 37

Tilghman sighted the outline of Chandler late that afternoon. Over the past hour he'd become aware of a steady rise in the temperature, unseasonably hot for September. The air gradually became still and close, without so much as a hint of a breeze. Trees along the roadside stood like statues of leafy stone.

A mile or so from town the land suddenly went dark. Tilghman turned in the saddle, staring off to the southwest, and saw a massive black cloud blotting out the sun. Even as he watched, the cloud spiraled earthward in a whirling funnel and swept northeast across the plains. He knew he'd just seen the birth of a tornado.

The funnel skipped along the earth at an astonishing speed. As it approached, the roar became deafening, and in the next moment, hailstones and torrential rain pelted the ground. Tilghman reined his horse off the road, spurring hard, and galloped into the mouth of a nearby ravine. A short distance ahead, hailstones bouncing around him like white cannonballs, he spotted an outcropping of rock jutting over the gully. He brought his horse to a halt beneath the ledge.

Some moments later, as abruptly as it began, the pounding hailstorm suddenly stopped. Tilghman reined about, gigging his horse, and rode to the top of the ravine. In the distance, he saw the tornado plow into the southern outskirts of Chandler, hurling the debris of flattened houses skyward. Timber and shingles, reduced in an instant to kindling, floated downward across the path of devastation. The funnel churned north through the downtown business district. He urged his horse into a gallop.

On the outskirts of town the destruction was complete. All through the residential area, the tornado had blown off rooftops and then battered the houses to flinders. It seemed another world, somehow demonic, the streets dotted with twisted rubble and cracking flames. Fire from cookstoves had ignited homes, and charred corpses, burned beyond recognition, still smoldered within the wreckage. Survivors clawed through the debris with a look of numbed horror, one of them staring blankly at a dead dog skewered onto a tree branch. The stench of death grew stronger.

An eerie calm, without a whisper of wind, had settled across the land. Ahead, Tilghman saw tendrils of smoke drift skyward, then hang there, suspended over Chandler like a dark shroud. Worse than anything he'd imagined, the funnel had savaged the residential area and then torn a swath along the main road leading into town. The business district had simply disintegrated, transformed by titanic winds into a mass of bricks and glass and timber. Virtually every store on the square had been blown down only to be enveloped in a raging holocaust.

Tilghman slowed his horse to a walk. For a moment he couldn't comprehend the enormity of the devastation, and he had a fleeting image of a world turned topsy-turvy. The top of the hotel had been ripped off, and trees bordering the square had been stripped clean of bark and leaves, standing ghostly white against the brown earth. Only three buildings were undamaged: the mercantile emporium, the hardware store, and a saloon on the far side of the square. Throughout the wreckage, people wandered about in a stupor, their clothes in tatters. It was as though some diabolic force had left behind a blotch of scorched devastation.

A scream attracted Tilghman's attention. On the west side of the square, a bucket brigade had formed outside Wallace's Cafe. The building was engulfed in flame, and he saw men dart into the rubble only to be driven back by a wall of fire. He dismounted, hurrying forward, aware that Jane Wallace, wife of the owner, was being restrained by several women. Her eyes were wide with horror and she screamed hysterically, thrashing to break loose. A line of men desperately passed buckets of water from a pump beside a nearby horse trough.

Malcolm Kinney, the town mayor, and Albert Dale, the county judge, were directing the fire brigade. Tilghman halted beside them as they exhorted the men to work faster. Judge Dale turned to him with a desolate look.

"Bob Wallace," he said in a shaky voice. "He's trapped in there."

Tilghman followed his gaze. The roof on the cafe had collapsed, and the stove in the kitchen had set the building ablaze. Bob Wallace, in an effort to escape, had made it only halfway to the front door. A falling timber, the main beam from the roof, had landed across his legs and pinned him to the floor. He struggled to free himself from the beam.

"It's hopeless," Judge Dale muttered. "We'll never get him out."

Tilghman considered a moment. "What about wetting down a path on a straight line? We might be able to reach him."

"Tried it," Dale said. "Not enough water to douse the fire. A bucket at a time won't do it."

The trapped man screamed from inside the cafe. Flames were all around him, fueled by the jumble of timber from the roof. His hair was singed off and raw blisters covered his face and hands. His eyes were stark with terror.

"Don't lemme burn!" he wailed. "Oh God, please, somebody shoot me! *Shoot me!*"

His wife shrieked his name in a wild cry that racketed across the square. The women holding her tried to turn her away as tongues of flame lapped over her husband. Her head twisted around, fighting the women to look back, and then she fainted. She went limp in their arms.

Judge Dale took Tilghman's arm. "Marshal, I order you to shoot him. I'll take full responsibility."

"No," Tilghman said hollowly. "I can't kill a man in cold blood."

"Don't let him die like that, Bill. I beg you, give him a merciful end."

An instant slipped past. Then Tilghman nodded, his features wreathed in sadness, and walked forward. He pulled his pistol, thumbing the hammer, and stared down the sights. From inside the cafe, his face charred and his clothes afire, the doomed man looked into the bore of the pistol. His expression went from one of agony to desperate hope.

"Do it!" he pleaded in a tortured voice. *"Do it!"*

Tilghman touched the trigger. But even as he squeezed, sighting carefully for a clean shot, the walls of the cafe collapsed. The framework toppled inward, burying the trapped man beneath a roaring pyre of timber. Flames leaped skyward in a blinding inferno.

Forced to retreat, Tilghman lowered his pistol. A faint smell, harsher than woodsmoke but mingled with a sweetish odor drifted from the flames. He recognized it as the stench of burnt flesh, and turned back into the street. The men of the fire brigade moved away, some of them slumping to the ground in exhaustion. Judge Dale nodded to Tilghman with a sorrowful expression.

"Terrible thing," he said quietly. "Bob Wallace was a good man."

"Yeah, he was." Tilghman's voice was raspy. "Wish it had turned out different."

"I appreciate what you tried to do, Bill. Thank God his suffering is over."

Mayor Kinney joined them. "We have to get busy organizing a relief effort. Lots of people lost their homes and everything they owned."

"Not to mention the dead," Judge Dale added. "We'll need volunteers for a burial detail. Bill, would you take over forming—"

Tilghman wasn't listening. His gaze was fixed on the north side of the square, where all the buildings had been demolished. Beyond, the tornado had cut a swath along residential streets and then veered off to the northwest, flattening more houses. A grove of trees at the edge of town stood stripped of leaves.

"Bill?" Judge Dale asked, watching him with concern. "What's wrong?"

"Looks like that twister headed northwest."

"What are you getting at?"

"Quapaw Creek's off in that direction."

Judge Dale suddenly understood. "You're worried about the Strattons. Is that it?"

"I'll see you later, Judge."

Tilghman ran for his horse. He gathered the reins and swung into the saddle. People on the street dodged aside as he spurred from a standing start into a headlong gallop. On the outskirts of town, he turned northwest.

He rode toward Quapaw Creek.

The path of the tornado zigged and zagged across the plains. For all its whirling twists, it was nonetheless easy to follow. A swatch of grass some hundred yards in width had been ripped from the ground.

Shortly before sundown, Tilghman spotted the tree-line along Quapaw Creek. The trail of the twister left much the same sign he'd seen in town. Trees were denuded of leaves and bark, and some had been torn by their roots from the earth. A cow, its legs stiff in death, lay sprawled on the prairie.

Tilghman forded the creek a half mile south of the Stratton ranch. To save time he had cut cross-country, rather than taking the road. Yet his horse was laboring for breath, foamed with sweat from the long run. On the opposite bank, the horse lost its footing, then recovered as it reached the barren treeline. He slowed the gait to a steady trot.

When he rode into the compound, Tilghman was struck by the silence. There was no sound, no one in sight, simply an empty stillness that pervaded the clearing. Off to the far side, he saw that the barn had been torn from its foundation and scattered to the winds. But closer to the road, as though the funnel had zagged at the last instant, the house was relatively unscathed. Other than the windows being blown out, it appeared to be intact.

In the yard, Tilghman leaped from the saddle and hit the ground running. He left his horse wheezing for air as he sprinted across the yard and onto the porch. The front door was hanging open, the windows on either side of the house imploded in shards of glass. He stopped in the hallway, listening a moment, straining to catch any sound. The parlor was empty.

"Zoe!"

"Bill?"

Her voice came from the rear of the house. Tilghman hurried along the hall as she stepped through a door at the far end. Her face was smudged with dirt and tears, and the sleeve of her dress was ripped at the shoulder. She threw herself into his arms.

"Oh God, Bill!" she cried. "I've never been so happy to see anyone in my life."

"Same here," Tilghman said, holding her wrapped in his arms. "I was afraid you might've been hurt."

"No, I'm fine," she said. "I've been tending to Daddy. He was hit by flying glass."

"How bad?"

"His arm and chest."

She led him into the bedroom. Amos Stratton was bare-chested, stretched out on the bed still clothed in his work pants and boots. His right forearm was bandaged, and a blood-soaked compress was bound tightly across his chest. He managed a weak smile.

"Hello, Bill," he said. "How'd you weather the storm?"

"Not a scratch," Tilghman replied, halting at the foot of the bed. "How are you feeling?"

"Little woozy in the head."

Zoe moved to his side. "We were in the house when the funnel went past. The windows blew out just as he came through the parlor."

"How deep are the cuts?"

"His arm isn't too bad. The cut on his chest is worse, but I got the bleeding stopped. I think he'll be all right."

"Damnedest thing," Stratton said in a fuzzy voice. "That twister was headed for the house and then it spun away. Just blew the barn clean to hell."

"Barns can be rebuilt," Tilghman said. "Where were your horses?"

"Turned 'em loose when I saw it coming. I expect they pulled through."

Stratton lay back on the pillow, suddenly weary. His eyes closed, and a moment later he drifted off to sleep. Zoe checked the compress on his chest, then turned from the bed. She led Tilghman into the hall.

"He's worn out," she said, walking toward the parlor.

"More from worry about me and the horses than anything else."

"I'm just glad you're safe," Tilghman said, putting his arm around her shoulders. "Things could've been a lot worse."

"Where were you when the storm hit?"

"A mile or so out of Chandler."

She saw his features darken. "What happened?"

"Looked like hell on earth." Tilghman paused, shook his head. "Half the town's gone. Blown down or burned down."

"Good Lord," she sighed. "It must have been terrible."

"Yeah." Tilghman had a sudden image of a man trapped beneath fiery rubble. "Hope I never see anything like it again."

"There must be some way to help them. What can we do?"

"You know what I said about your pa's barn?"

"When you told him it could be rebuilt?"

Tilghman nodded. "We'll help them rebuild Chandler."

CHAPTER 38

A week later Tilghman was summoned to Guthrie. The message, sent by express pouch on the stagecoach, ordered him to report to Nix's office on September 20. There was no reason given, and the terse wording left him vaguely uneasy. He wondered what Nix was planning.

Tilghman was reluctant as well to leave Chandler. At the request of the mayor, he had assisted Sheriff Frank Gebke in restoring order to the town. The day after the tornado, special deputies had been sworn in and assigned to patrol the streets. Their primary responsibility was to maintain order in the midst of chaos.

The toll from the storm was worse than anyone had imagined. Fourteen people had been killed and more than eighty had suffered crippling injury. The Presbyterian church had been converted into a hospital, as well as a temporary morgue for the dead. Doctors from nearby towns volunteered their aid, along with donations of medicines and drugs. The dead were buried in services conducted by local ministers.

Aside from human loss, the damage to property was almost beyond reckoning. The downtown business district, for all practical purposes, was a total loss. Merchants salvaged what they could from the wreckage, and resumed business in hastily constructed board shanties. But there was no way to house the vast numbers whose homes had been destroyed by the tornado. Farmers and ranchers offered shelter to many families, and others built temporary shacks on their lots. Their personal effects were buried beneath the rubble.

Under the direction of Harry Gilstrap, editor of the *Chandler News*, a relief committee was formed. The other members of the committee were Will Schlegel, a storekeeper, and Tilghman, whose name was known throughout the territory. Within days, word went out requesting aid and hundreds of wagons began rolling into town from as far away as Guthrie and Oklahoma City. The raw essentials for survival were needed, and there was an outpouring of donations from other communities. The wagons were loaded with food provisions, bedding, and everyday clothing for the newly destitute of Chandler.

Three days after the storm, Zoe began working with the relief effort. Her father was well enough to fend for himself, and she moved into one of the undamaged rooms on the ground floor of the hotel. A warehouse near the sawmill that had escaped destruction served as headquarters for the storage of relief goods. There, working with other volunteers, she handled the distribution of food and clothing to the needy. The work was demanding, with long hours, but Zoe went at it with energetic cheerfulness and a natural talent for organization. By the end of the week, she was practically running the operation.

After receiving the message for Nix, Tilghman went by the warehouse. He found Zoe supervising a group of women volunteers who were parceling out food at one counter and clothing at another to families who had been devastated by the storm. Waiting until she could break free, he stood off to one side, admiring the way she deftly kept the operation moving. Finally, when the lines began to thin out, she came around the counter. Her dress was soiled from the dusty warehouse and her hair had come unpinned on one side.

"Whew!" she said, blowing a lock of hair off her forehead. "I must look a sight."

Tilghman grinned. "You look pretty good to me. I wouldn't change a thing."

"Why, thank you, sir." She smiled engagingly. "You know how to make a girl's day."

"How are things going?"

"Oh, the usual misery and heartbreak. All these unfortunate people with their lives turned upside down. I just don't know how they bear it."

"You forget," Tilghman said. "These are the folks that pioneered the territory. They're not quitters."

"Yes, you're right." She glanced back at a woman with two small children. "I just hope our supplies hold out."

"Don't worry yourself about that. We got word there's another shipment on the way from Oklahoma City."

"Well, that is good news! Was that what you came to tell me?"

"Not exactly," Tilghman said with a sudden frown. "I've been called to Guthrie. I'll have to leave this afternoon."

She searched his face. "Do you know what it's about?"

"Nix didn't say in his message. I'll find out when I get there."

"Then why do you look so glum?"

"Shows that much, huh?" Tilghman was silent a moment, then shrugged. "Guess I've gotten used to being around you the last week. I'm not keen on leaving."

Her eyes sparkled with laughter. "Will you miss me a little bit?"

"Yeah, I will, and that got me to thinking. Doolin's scheduled to stand trial late next month."

"I somehow missed the connection. What does that have to do with your leaving today?"

"Well, don't you see—" Tilghman knuckled his mustache, clearly fumbling for words. "Fact of the matter is, Doolin's caught and he'll likely swing before Christmas. So there's nothin' to stop us from getting married."

"Yes!" she burst out. "That was the only reason you wanted to delay. And now, there is no reason!"

"Not so far as I'm concerned."

"Oh, aren't you a sweetheart! You didn't come here to talk about a trip to Guthrie. You're here to talk about our wedding—aren't you?"

Tilghman ducked his head, and she sensed that he was somehow embarrassed. Whatever he was feeling, he found it difficult to put into words. He motioned with an offhand gesture. "I'm not much on plannin' such things. You just tell me when and where, and I'll be there."

She laughed. "You knew I planned on a church wedding—didn't you?"

"Figured as much."

"And that's all right?"

"I've got no objections." Tilghman looked at her with a wry smile. "Leastways if the parson doesn't carry on too long. Never could stand a windy preacher."

She knew they were past his moment of discomfort. He was now teasing her, and she was perfectly willing to play along. "I'll speak to the minister," she said. "A short ceremony without the hearts and flowers."

Tilghman chuckled, aware that she was gently mocking him. "Think you've got my number, don't you?"

"Why, mercy sakes, whatever gave you that idea?"

She walked him to the door of the warehouse. Several people on their way inside snickered when she stood on tip-toe and gave him a kiss. She then waved gaily and went back to work.

Tilghman thought she was the sauciest woman he'd

ever met. A kiss in broad daylight would be the talk of the town.

Early the next morning Tilghman, Thomas, and Madsen trooped into the Herriott Building. Like Tilghman, Madsen had been summoned from El Reno by a cryptic message. The three of them had spent a good deal of time speculating on the reason for the meeting. But nothing of any great import had occurred to them, particularly now that Doolin was in custody. They were still in the dark when they walked into the office.

Nix greeted them with a bonhomie normally reserved for close friends. He was positively chipper, shaking their hands with warmth, as though delighted by their company. Finally, after he got them seated, he took the chair behind his desk. He made a grand motion with a sweep of his arm.

"Gentlemen, let me first extend my thanks for a job well done. You three deserve credit for devotion to the law that is truly above and beyond the call of duty. You have my utmost admiration."

The sentiment, as well as his grandiloquence, took them by surprise. His unusually jovial manner lent even greater mystery to the occasion. They stared back at him with slight smiles, thoroughly baffled.

Nix fairly beamed. "I brought you here for a most momentous occasion." He paused for dramatic effect. "Today, I am announcing my resignation as U.S. marshal."

The three lawmen blinked in unison. Whatever else they suspicioned, his resignation would not have made the list. Their bafflement of a moment before had now turned to dumbfounded astonishment. After a moment of profound silence, Thomas was the first to recover his wits. He shook his head.

"Why the devil would you resign?"

"For the best of all reasons," Nix said, striking a pose.

"Doolin will shortly walk the gallows and the Wild Bunch is but a distant memory. My job is done."

"Have to say," Thomas admitted, "you caught me off guard. I figured you'd stay on till there was another political shake-up."

"Timing is everything," Nix replied. "You gentlemen have afforded me the opportunity of exiting on a high note. I couldn't have asked for more."

Tilghman thought there was some honesty in the statement. With Doolin captured, all the glory had been reaped from the office of U.S. marshal. Nix was probably moving on to bigger things, with a reputation as the man who had brought law and order to Oklahoma Territory. He gave Nix an inquiring look.

"Who's been picked as your replacement?"

"Patrick Nagle," Nix said. "One of the finest legal minds in the territory. He's from Kingfisher."

"A lawyer?" Tilghman asked.

"A brilliant lawyer," Nix amended. "I gave my personal endorsement to his appointment."

"From the sound of it," Thomas said dryly, "I take it we can assume he's a Democrat."

"His politics are immaterial," Nix insisted. "Pat Nagle is a man of great integrity and high moral standards. You gentlemen are fortunate to have someone of his caliber in this post."

The three of them were of the same mind. Though unspoken, they realized that it was a matter of politics as usual. The job had gone to a man with all the right connections, and worse, to a lawyer. Based on long experience in courtrooms, none of them held lawyers in high esteem.

For Chris Madsen, who had listened quietly, the appointment forced him to a decision. "I am resigning too," he said abruptly. "Effective today."

"Hold on, Chris," Tilghman protested. "No need for

hasty decisions just because he's a lawyer. Let's give him a chance."

"Not a hasty decision," Madsen told him. "I've been offered the job of chief deputy of the Western District of Missouri. I was leaning toward taking the job, anyway. Today just decided it for me."

Tilghman and Thomas immediately grasped the reason behind his decision. General Joseph Shelby, one of the famed Confederate commanders during the Civil War, was the U.S. marshal of the western district. Madsen, a former soldier himself, would be working for a military man of the first order. Which was far preferable to working for an unknown lawyer with political connections.

"Hell's bells, Chris," Thomas muttered. "The three of us make a damn good team. I hate to see you break it up."

"An excellent point," Nix chimed in, hoping to salvage the situation. "You're the Three Guardsmen, the greatest manhunters ever! You should really reconsider all this, Chris."

"No, my mind's made up," Madsen said, glancing at Tilghman and Thomas. "We were a good team, and I'll miss working with you fellows. But it's the right decision for me."

"Look, Chris," Nix said quickly. "Pat Nagle's waiting in the governor's office right now. At least meet him before you make such a rash decision."

"No need." Madsen stood, unpinning his badge, and dropping it on the desk. "I'd rather leave before he gets here."

He gave Nix a perfunctory handshake. Then, one at a time, he clasped the hands of Tilghman and Thomas in a strong grip. Their parting was short and without sentiment, for their comradeship went beyond mere words. Without saying it, each man knew he could count on the other whenever the need might arise. Madsen went out the door without looking back.

After that, Nix moved things along swiftly. His wholesale grocery business was flourishing, and there were political opportunities on the horizon. Earlier, he'd briefed Nagle on the duties of the office, and he saw no reason to delay in the transition of power. Nor was there any reason to delay his own departure.

Excusing himself, Nix walked up to the governor's office. A few minutes later he returned with the newly appointed U.S. marshal. He performed the introductions, lavishing praise on Tilghman and Thomas, and quickly explained Madsen's abrupt resignation. Then, with a chipper farewell, he left his successor to take charge.

There was a moment of awkward silence as the door closed. Patrick Nagle was young, not yet thirty, with thick glasses and the somber manner of a professor. He was clearly uncomfortable staring across the desk at seasoned lawmen who were both older and far more experienced. Finally, nudging the glasses higher on the bridge of his nose, he attempted a confident smile.

"I'm very pleased that you gentlemen have elected to stay on. You are doubtless aware that I have no background in law enforcement, or in matters pertaining to criminals. So I will rely heavily on your advice and counsel."

"No problem there," Thomas said. "You probably already know that Nix gave Bill and me lots of leeway. We work at our own speed, and we don't always follow the rules. But we generally get the job done."

"Your record speaks for itself," Nagle observed. "With Doolin and the Wild Bunch under control, the situation appears fairly stable. How would you recommend we proceed?"

"There's some unfinished business," Tilghman informed him. "We started out to break the Wild Bunch to the last man. Clifton, West, and Waightman are still on the loose."

"Just so you understand," Thomas added. "Our main assignment was to bring down the Wild Bunch. We'd like to keep it that way."

"By all means," Nagle said agreeably. "We have adequate marshals to attend to other matters. You men are entitled to finish what you started."

"In that case," Thomas said, "we're gonna get along just fine. One way or another, we'll bring those murderin' bastards to justice."

"Gentlemen, you have my full support. Keep me advised of your progress."

After another round of handshakes, the lawmen walked from the office. Neither of them said anything on the way downstairs, seemingly lost in thought. On the street, Tilghman finally broke the silence.

"Not much like Nix, is he?"

"Amen to that," Thomas said. "So what d'you think?"

"Heck, I think we can write our own ticket. He'll go along to get along."

"By God, maybe we finally got ourselves a smart one."

They strolled off congratulating themselves on their new boss.

CHAPTER 39

A town began to emerge from the rubble. Under the constant din of hammering and sawing the framework of buildings began to take shape. Brickmasons were imported to rebuild the bank and start work at last on the county courthouse. The people of Chandler set about putting their lives in order.

Zoe stayed busy at the warehouse. Yet the number of families in need of food and clothing had gradually dwindled off. There was an independent streak about the townspeople, some vestige of the pioneer spirit that had brought them west. Nearly two weeks had passed since the tornado, and most thought that too long to accept charity. They got back to fending for themselves.

Evenings were for Zoe the best time. Tilghman joined her for supper at the hotel dining room, which had returned to full operation. Then they strolled around the square, filled with pride and amazement as the new town rapidly took shape. By now, they were a common sight on their nightly walks, and people greeted them with a mixture of warmth and respect. Everyone in town knew of their selfless efforts in the aftermath of the storm.

Tonight, they paused to admire construction on the bank. The first floor was almost completed, the smell of fresh mortar strong in the still air. After a moment, arm in arm, they strolled on toward the corner. Tilghman was unusually quiet, and Zoe sensed that his thoughts were elsewhere. For the last three days, since his return from Guthrie, she'd known he was wrestling with some inner quandary. To her, his moods were by now an open book.

"Something wrong?" she asked, aware that he might never speak unless prompted. "You're awfully quiet tonight."

Tilghman nodded vaguely. "Just thoughtful, that's all."

"Are you concerned about the rest of the Wild Bunch?"

"No more so than usual. We'll turn up a lead sooner or later."

"Well, something is bothering you." She gave him a long look of appraisal. "You haven't been yourself since you met with—what's his name?—Nagle."

"Not that," Tilghman said. "Nagle's the least of my worries. He won't be any problem."

"So what is it, then? You might as well tell me. I eventually worm it out of you anyway."

"Some things are hard to put into words. Guess it's got to do with the town, and the people. What they lost."

"Their homes and businesses, all that?"

Tilghman shook his head. "I was thinking more of their personal loss. Folks like Jane Wallace."

She glanced at him. "Are you talking about the loss of her husband?"

"Yeah, I am."

Zoe had heard the story from women at the warehouse. She shuddered inwardly, remembering their description of the cafe owner trapped beneath fiery timbers. She recalled as well the awe in their voices, their admiration, when they spoke of Tilghman. Everyone respected him for his attempt to save a man from being burned alive, even though he had never fired the shot. They thought such an act of mercy required a special brand of courage.

Tilghman had never spoken to her of the incident. She knew, after listening to the women, that he'd been dragooned into it by Judge Dale. But only after first refusing, and then with great reluctance, agreeing after it became apparent that the trapped man was doomed. She considered the courage part of his character, the willingness to act when others flinched from the task. Still, reflecting on it now, she wondered what the personal toll had been for him. Perhaps he was trying to tell her something.

"Bill?" she said at length. "Do you blame yourself for the way he died? For not shooting sooner?"

Tilghman was silent as they crossed the street to the opposite corner. Finally, not looking at her, he shrugged. "Maybe I was too concerned with a clean shot. But the walls collapsed and the chance was gone. I don't fault myself for that."

"So it wasn't him so much as his wife. You're talking about *her* loss."

"The last couple of days it put me to thinking that it doesn't matter how a woman loses her husband. She grieves the same no matter how it happens."

"I don't understand," she said in a bemused tone. "Are you talking about Jane Wallace, or someone else?"

"Someone else." Tilghman hesitated, then went on. "I've been wondering about Doolin's wife."

"What about her?"

"Doolin's sure to hang. She'll likely suffer more than he does. Lots longer, too."

Zoe looked at him in surprise. "You're worrying about Edith Doolin, aren't you?"

"Not worrying," Tilghman said uncomfortably. "Just

that she'll be a young widow with a boy to raise. That's a heavy load."

"I see," she said with sudden dawning. "So you plan to help her in some way. Is that it?"

"Figured I might," Tilghman admitted. "Thought I'd give her part of the reward money. Half of it was hers, anyway."

"How could it be?"

"Doolin was wearin' a money belt when I captured him. Had a little better than twenty-five hundred in cash. I turned it over to the office."

"Yes, but that was stolen money, wasn't it?"

"I suppose most folks would say so."

Zoe smiled. "You just want to help her, don't you?"

"That's the problem," Tilghman said, frowning. "I've been studying on a way to pull it off."

"What do you mean?"

"Some way she won't know it came from me. She might look on it as blood money . . . from the reward."

Zoe felt a lump in her throat. She thought it was so like him to take a practical approach to a compassionate act. He wanted no credit, no recognition, no thanks. He was concerned instead with Edith Doolin.

"Why do I get the feeling," she said lightly, "that you're asking for volunteers?"

Tilghman avoided her eyes. "Well, you're due a break from the warehouse. Thought you might be willin' to lend me a hand."

"In other words, you want me to give her the money."

"Figured you could just tell her it came from a friend."

"How do I find her?"

"I'll take you." Tilghman hesitated, cleared his throat. " 'Course, it'll take a couple of days by buckboard. Your pa's liable not to be too happy with that."

"Let me handle him," she said brightly. "We are betrothed, and you have no designs on my virtue . . . do you?"

Tilghman grinned. "None that I can't control."

"What a shame." She laughed, hugged his arm. "Will we be camping out along the way?"

"Tell your pa I'll bring separate bedrolls."

"Omigosh! I can't wait till he hears that!"

On the west side of the square, they turned back toward the hotel. She looked up at the sky and wondered what it would be like to camp with him under starlight. Not the same as being married and snug together in their own bed. Still, she told herself, it was a start.

Two bedrolls were better than nothing.

Tilghman halted the buckboard on the outskirts of Lawson. The trip had taken a day and a night, and he'd timed it to arrive early the second morning. He handed Zoe the reins, then moved to the rear of the buckboard, where his horse was hitched. He planned to wait while she called on Edith Doolin.

"All set?" he said, returning with his horse. "You remember how to find the house?"

"Stop worrying," she said, a glint of amusement in her eyes. "Your instructions were quite clear. I'm sure I'll have no problem."

"Just give her the money and leave. Don't let her get you into a conversation."

"Honestly, Bill, you've told me a dozen times. I know what to do."

She gave him a quick kiss, and drove off. Last night, camped beside a creek, he had behaved like a perfect gentleman. She'd been ambivalent then, and still had mixed emotions, for she wanted him as much as he wanted her. But she had no ambivalence, no reservations whatever about today's mission. She thought of it as a pleasant conspiracy, their own little secret.

Some minutes later Zoe reined up before the house. She stepped down, securing the horse to a hitching post, and proceeded along the pathway. On the front porch, she quickly checked her gaily feathered hat, then knocked on the door. The woman who opened it was her own age, though shorter and plumper. Zoe nodded with an engaging smile.

"May I speak with Mrs. Edith Doolin?"

"I'm Edith Doolin."

"I wonder if we might have a word in private?"

"Who are you?"

"A friend, Mrs. Doolin. My name is Zoe Stratton."

Edith Doolin hesitated a moment, then held the door open. Zoe entered, moving into the parlor as an older woman came out of the kitchen. After closing the door, the girl motioned Zoe toward a sofa. Then she looked at the older woman.

"It's all right, mama," she said in a dull voice. "Would you check on the baby for me? He probably needs changing."

She turned back to the parlor. Zoe noticed that she had dark smudges under her eyes as if she had not slept well, and there was a haunted, fearful cast to her features. She gave Zoe a veiled look.

"What can I do for you, Miss—Mrs.?—Stratton?"

"Miss," Zoe clarified. "Won't you call me Zoe? And may I call you Edith? I feel like I know you already."

Edith seemed disarmed by her open manner. She took a seat beside Zoe on the sofa. "How is it you know about me?"

"A mutual friend asked me to call on you."

"What for?"

Zoe took an envelope from her purse. "I was asked to give you this."

Edith accepted the envelope. She opened the flap and her mouth ovaled with a sharp intake of breath. After a moment, she riffled through the stack of greenbacks.

"God," she said softly, glancing at Zoe. "That's a lot of money."

"Twenty-five hundred dollars."

"Who's it from?"

Zoe smiled. "An anonymous friend."

"Anonymous?" Edith repeated, as though testing the word. "Someone who doesn't want their name known?"

"Yes, that's right."

"Well, it wouldn't be too hard to guess. It's from one of Bill's men, isn't it? Clifton or West."

Zoe realized she was being drawn into conversation. Her instructions were to deliver the money and leave. Yet she couldn't bring herself to allow a false impression. "I'm sorry," she said with some conviction. "The money isn't from any of your husband's men."

Edith tilted her head. "Who's it from, then?"

"I really wish I could tell you. But the donor wants to remain anonymous."

"What do you mean *donor*? Is this some kind of charity?"

"No, no," Zoe said quickly. "It's a gift from someone who has your best interests at heart. A gift for you and your son."

Edith studied her a moment. "Where are you from?"

"What difference does that make?"

"Are you afraid to tell me for some reason?"

"Chandler," Zoe said, not willing to lie. "I live outside Chandler with my father."

Edith sat straighter, staring at her. "The marshal that caught Bill—the one named Tilghman—he's from Chandler, isn't he?"

"What makes you think that?"

"Stop treating me like a fool! I read it in one of those newspaper stories. He's from Chandler, isn't he?"

"Yes, I believe he is," Zoe said evasively. "But what does that have to do with anything?"

"I get it now." Edith's voice sounded brittle. "My husband's going to hang and Tilghman's feeling guilty about the reward." Her gaze dropped to the money in her lap. "This is half the reward, isn't it?"

"Edith, listen to me," Zoe said earnestly. "Your husband had that exact amount on him when he was captured. Marshal Tilghman just thought you should have it, that's all. He feels compassion for you, not guilt."

"Who are you, anyway? What's Tilghman to you?"

"I—" Zoe hesitated, unable to avoid the truth. "I'm engaged to him. We're going to be married."

"I met him," Edith said distantly. "When I went to the jail at Guthrie, he was there. I thanked him for not killing Bill."

"Funny that both of our men are named Bill. We have something in common."

"I suppose you could look at it that way. Do you think I ought to keep this money?"

"Of course you should," Zoe said firmly. "If not for yourself, then for your boy. Your husband would want you to have it."

"Maybe he would." Edith smiled wanly. "When you see your Bill, thank him for me. You've got yourself a good man."

On the way out, Zoe saw the older woman standing in the hall. She assumed the woman had been listening to their conversation. At the door, she impulsively kissed Edith Doolin on the cheek. Tears welled up in their eyes, but neither of them could say anything. She hurried toward the buckboard.

A few minutes later, at the edge of town, she saw Tilghman waiting by the roadside. Her first inclination was to tell him nothing of the conversation that had taken place. But then she thought it only right that he hear everything said by the woman he'd helped.

Edith Doolin would want him to know.

CHAPTER 40

The train chuffed to a halt outside the Guthrie depot. Thomas stepped through the rear door of the last passenger coach, and stopped on the observation platform. He watched as passengers hurried off the train, and those headed north waited to board. His eyes scanned the stationhouse for any sign of reporters.

After a moment, he turned back to the coach and motioned an all-clear signal. Tilghman herded their prisoner through the door, pausing on the observation platform. Dynamite Dick Clifton was bearded, hat pulled low over his forehead, his hands manacled. A short man, wiry in build, his clothes were dirty and wrinkled, and he smelled. He looked like a vagabond in chains.

Thomas led the way to the north end of the depot. Clifton followed close behind, with Tilghman bringing up the rear. Unless someone looked closely, it would have been difficult to identify the man in the middle as a prisoner. A buggy, arranged by telegram earlier, waited for them on the street. The driver was a town deputy who had no idea as to why he was there. Clifton was assisted into the rear seat, positioned between Tilghman and Thomas. They drove toward the jailhouse.

Earlier in the week Clifton had been apprehended in

Paris, Texas. The town was some twenty miles south of the Nations, and Clifton was using the alias Dan Wiley. Arrested for drunk and disorderly, he was quickly identified by local police from wanted posters. Federal marshals in the Eastern District of Texas were notified, and they in turn wired Patrick Nagle, U.S. marshal for Oklahoma Territory. A day later, on October 17, Nagle met with Tilghman and Thomas.

A murder warrant was outstanding on Clifton, and the marshals were ordered to hop a train to Texas. Before leaving, they persuaded Nagle to delay any announcement to the public or the press until Clifton was safely behind bars in Guthrie. Their argument, which Nagle accepted, was to avoid a repeat of the circus atmosphere surrounding Doolin's capture. The following day, after presenting the murder warrant in Texas, Clifton was surrendered into their custody. Late that afternoon, they boarded a train bound for Oklahoma Territory.

On the train, Tilghman and Thomas took turns grilling the prisoner. They were seated at the rear of the coach, with empty seats around them, and no one to overhear the interrogation. Alternating shifts, one sleeping while the other asked questions, they kept Clifton awake throughout the night. At first, he denied any knowledge as to the whereabouts of the last two members of the Wild Bunch, Dick West and Red Buck Waightman. But as the night wore on, the relentless grilling left him in an exhausted state. He eventually admitted that the gang had gone their separate ways, and the last he'd heard, West and Waightman were somewhere in the Nations. Toward dawn, he was finally permitted to sleep.

Today, approaching the jailhouse, Tilghman was not encouraged. The information on West and Waightman was a month old, and they might have skipped the territory by now. His thoughts turned instead to the upcoming elections in Lincoln County, scheduled for November 4.

A week ago, at the ranch, he had been offered the job of sheriff by Judge Albert Dale and Mayor Malcolm Kinney. If he accepted, they promised their support, which virtually guaranteed he would win. After talking it over with Zoe, he decided that it was time he began thinking about their future. As sheriff, he would be home every night rather than tracking outlaws throughout the Nations. There was much to be said for that when a man was contemplating marriage, not to mention his expansion plans for the ranch. Before leaving Chandler, he had informed Dale and Kinney that he would run for sheriff.

But with the urgency of the trip to Texas, he had delayed saying anything to Patrick Nagle. After jailing Clifton, he knew he could delay no longer in breaking the news. He would have to meet with Nagle, and advise him of his decision. He planned to resign his federal commission, effective November 1.

Upon entering the jailhouse, Tilghman and Thomas surrendered their prisoner to the chief jailor. Clifton's manacles were removed, and his arrival was duly noted in the log book. A guard then led them along a corridor to the steel door fronting the cell block. To the left of the door, a row of metal bars rose from floor to ceiling and extended to the far wall. Directly inside was a large bull pen, where prisoners were allowed freedom from their cells in the daytime. At the rear of the cell block, built one atop the other, were two tiers of barred cages, with stairs leading to the upper tier. After the evening meal, the prisoners were locked in their cells for the night.

Doolin was seated at a table in the bull pen, playing checkers with another inmate. For the most part, the prisoners were a motley collection of whiskey smugglers and bandits who preyed on backcountry stagecoaches.

To them, Doolin was a celebrity, leader of the Wild Bunch and a man who had achieved national notoriety. They accorded him the respect due an outlaw whose picture had made the front page of the *Police Gazette*. One of them interrupted the checkers game, directing his attention to the door.

Clifton stepped into the bull pen as the door slammed shut. Doolin rose from the table, moving forward with a sorrowful look. He clasped Clifton's hand in a firm grip. "Too bad, Dick," he said with genuine concern. "I figured you'd got away for good."

"Yeah, me too," Clifton grumped. "Bastards caught me across the line in Texas."

"Hold on a minute. I want a word with Tilghman."

Doolin walked to the front of the bull pen. He stopped at the bars, ignoring Thomas and nodding to Tilghman. "How's tricks?" he said amiably. "Got a line on the rest of my boys?"

"Only a matter of time," Tilghman observed. "They're not bright enough to beat the law."

"You never know." Doolin paused, lowered his voice. "My wife was by to visit last week. I'm obliged for the way you treated her."

Tilghman sensed that the statement was purposely cryptic. With Thomas listening, there would be no direct mention of the money he'd sent to Edith Doolin. "No thanks necessary," he said. "Your wife strikes me as a good woman. She deserves whatever luck comes her way."

"For a lawdog, you're all right." Doolin flicked a glance at Thomas. "Not like some buttholes I could mention."

Thomas bristled. "You smart-aleck sonovabitch. I'm gonna dance on your grave after you're hung."

Tilghman moved between them. The last week in October he and Thomas were scheduled to testify at Doolin's trial. The charges were cut and dried, with an army of witnesses, and the verdict would result in a death sentence. Doolin's fate was sealed, and he saw no reason to push the matter further.

"C'mon, Heck," he said forcefully. "Let's get out of here. We've finished our business."

Thomas seared the outlaw with a look. Then, muttering a curse, he strode off along the corridor. Tilghman followed him out, trailed by the guard. Doolin waited until they were gone before turning back into the bull pen. He clapped an arm over Dick Clifton's shoulders.

"Don't look so down at the mouth, sport."

Clifton grunted. "Why the hell not? They're gonna string me up alongside you."

"Trust me," Doolin said in a conspiratorial tone. "It'll never get that far."

"What's that supposed to mean?"

"Dick, if you had to pick a day to get caught, you couldn't have done better. You played into luck."

"Quit talkin' riddles, will you?"

Doolin walked him off to one side. "How'd you like to bust out of here?"

"What?" Clifton gaped at him. "You figgered a way to escape?"

"Took a while, but it's all set. Tonight's the night."

"*Tonight?*"

"You lucky dog. You got here just in time."

Doolin, ever the strategist, laid out the plan.

In the evening, after supper was finished, the dirty dishes were collected. Inmates were required to stack their dishes in an open cart, which was mounted on wheels. While three armed guards watched, one of the prisoners rolled the cart to the door where it was taken by a fourth guard. The door was then closed and locked.

After supper, the prisoners were allowed the freedom of the bull pen. Some played checkers or dominoes, while others lounged around, talking of better days.

There were thirty-five inmates, only a few of them hardened criminals, and they were permitted to stay in the bull pen until eight o'clock. Four men to a cell, they were then locked up for the night.

There was seldom any official activity during the night hours. Shortly after supper, the chief jailor and the daytime guards were relieved of their duties. The night guards, a skeleton staff of two men, then assumed responsibility for the jail. The head guard at night, Jack Tull, was a man of few words and cold nerves. He was assisted by Joe Miller, one of the youngest guards on the staff.

A few minutes before eight Tull halted outside the bars. "Awright, boys," he rumbled in a sing-song voice. "Time for bed."

The prisoners slowly stood, grumbling among themselves, resigned to the nightly routine. Doolin and Clifton, absorbed in a game of checkers, remained seated at the table nearest the door. George Lane, a burly whiskey smuggler, ambled toward the bars with a tin cup. Outside the bars, to the left of the door, was a water bucket on a wooden stand. Inmates were allowed to take a cup of water to their cells for the night.

Tull, the key in hand, waited at the steel door. Following regulations, which permitted no armed guards in the cell block, Miller unholstered his pistol and placed it in a box mounted on the wall. Watching him, Tull turned, unlocking the door, and swung it open. Miller entered the bull pen with a master key for the cells, motioning the prisoners toward the tiered cages. His job was to lock them away.

Lane, who was reaching through the bars for the water bucket, dropped his cup just as Tull began to close the door. The cup bounced off the floor with a metallic clang, and Tull looked down, momentarily distracted. In the instant his eyes were on the floor, Lane lowered his shoulder and charged the half-open door. The impact drove the heavy steel door into Tull's face, smashing his nose. He staggered backward, dazed, blood pouring out of his nostrils.

On cue, Doolin spun out of his chair and raced for the door. Clifton and another prisoner jumped Miller, hitting him high and low, and took him to the floor. Lane hurtled through the door, grabbing Tull in an iron bear hug, and pinned his arms to his sides. Only a beat behind, Doolin stepped through the door and snatched Tull's pistol from the holster. With no hesitation, he moved to the box on the wall and grabbed Miller's pistol. He turned with a gun in either hand.

"Well now!" he said, grinning broadly. "How's that for teamwork?"

Tull, still struggling to break free from Lane's grip, glowered at him. Clifton climbed to his feet, the master key in his hand, while other inmates hauled Miller off the floor. The majority of the prisoners, stunned by the flurry of action, crowded together along the rear of the bull pen. Doolin motioned with his pistols.

"You boys know the drill. Let's get to it!"

Lane wrestled Tull to the door and hurled him into the bull pen. Under Clifton's direction, several prisoners collared Tull while others manhandled Miller, and marched them to cells on the lower tier. There, Clifton locked the guards into separate cells and hurried toward the door, still carrying the master key. When he stepped out of the bull pen, Doolin handed him one of the pistols. With Lane at their side, they faced the other inmates.

"Here's the story," Doolin called out. "Anybody that wants to run has five seconds to get moving. After that, I lock the door."

There was a rush as ten prisoners crowded through the door. The others, now reduced to twenty-two in number, remained where they were. Doolin slammed the door, locking it, and stuck the key in his pocket. He nodded to Clifton, then led the way along the corridor to the empty front office. The prisoners followed him across the room and abruptly jarred to a halt as he stopped at the street door. Before anyone could react, he and Clifton suddenly turned on them with pistols leveled.

"Listen close," Doolin said with an ominous smile. "You boys are gonna give me and Dick a five-minute head start. Anybody pokes his head out this door beforehand is liable to get it shot off."

"Like hell!" Lane bellowed. "You and me worked all this out before Clifton ever showed up. You're not leavin' me behind."

"Count your blessings, George." Doolin gave him a hard stare. "I sprung you and the rest of these boys, and you're free to run. Try to follow me and I'll kill you."

None of the prisoners, Lane included, doubted his word. While Clifton kept them covered, Doolin cracked the door open and peeked outside. The street was deserted for a block in either direction; farther downtown he saw the usual evening traffic. He stepped through the door, followed closely by Clifton. They walked west along Second Street.

Doolin's original plan had been to jump the evening freight train. Every night shortly after being locked in his cell, he'd heard the whistle as the train rolled through Guthrie. But as they approached the rail yards, he made a spur of the moment decision. George Lane, who'd been his new partner until Clifton appeared, was aware of the plan. Should Lane be caught, there was no question that he would betray them. His decision was influenced as well by unexpected opportunity.

Ahead, Doolin saw a buggy slow for the Second Street rail crossing. There was no one else about, and he quickly explained the new plan to Clifton. They separated, Doolin moving to the other side of the street, and approached from opposite directions. As the buggy

cleared the rail crossing, Clifton scurried forward and
grabbed the horse's bridle. The driver hauled back on
the reins, and the woman beside him uttered a startled
shriek. Doolin stuck a cocked pistol in the driver's face.

"Keep quiet and you won't get hurt. Climb down out
of there."

The man obeyed with alacrity, and the woman, her
eyes filled with terror, clambered out the other side.
Doolin took the reins, hefting himself into the driver's
seat, and waited for Clifton to scramble aboard. Lowering the hammer on his pistol, he stuffed it into his waistband and reined onto the road beside the railroad
tracks. The man and the woman heard the reins pop,
and the horse broke into a run. The buggy rattled south
out of town.

"Shoulda shot 'em," Clifton muttered. "They'll high-
tail it to the law."

"Don't matter," Doolin told him. "First farm we spot,
we'll steal ourselves some horses."

"You aim to head for the Nations?"

"Straight as a string."

"Then what?"

"Dunno yet. I'm thinkin' on it."

They drove on into the night.

CHAPTER 41

The press treated Doolin's escape with more sensationalism than had been devoted to his capture. The chief jailor, along with guards Jack Tull and Joe Miller, were crucified in front-page articles. Doolin was portrayed as a mastermind who had engineered a daring getaway.

Patrick Nagle emerged relatively unscathed. On the job less than a month, his performance as U.S. marshal drew little criticism from the newspapers. Yet enormous pressure was brought to bear by Governor Renfrow personally, and by way of stinging telegrams from the attorney general in Washington. Additional rewards were posted, and Nagle was ordered to find and kill the remaining members of the Wild Bunch. Failure would not be tolerated.

Nagle had anticipated the firestorm. On the night of the breakout, he had summoned Tilghman and Thomas to his office. In total, thirteen prisoners had escaped, and he sought their counsel in organizing a manhunt. Federal marshals, working with county sheriffs, were ordered into the field. By late the following morning, squads of lawmen were raiding known outlaw haunts throughout the territory. The heaviest concentration of peace officers was positioned along the border with the

Nations. There was general consensus that Doolin and Clifton would make a run for their old sanctuary.

Tilghman and Thomas spent a full day interrogating witnesses around Guthrie. Their first session was with the couple whose buggy had been stolen at gunpoint the previous night. From the description, the lawmen felt reasonably certain that the thieves were Doolin and Clifton. But then, late that morning, George Lane and three other inmates were returned to jail after being caught near the railroad tracks outside town. Lane, who was furious at Doolin, readily agreed to cooperate. The story he told merely muddied the waters.

According to Lane, Doolin had planned to hop the southbound freight train the night before. Yet that in no way gibed with the theft of the buggy just minutes before the train passed through Guthrie. The lawmen hardly thought Doolin would attempt flight in a buggy, which confined travel to roads and could be easily spotted. They were left to ponder if he'd ditched the buggy and hopped the train somewhere south of town. That seemed the more likely prospect.

Wires went out alerting officers at stops along the train line. But then, shortly after the noon hour, a farmer added a new twist to the manhunt. His farm was three miles south of Guthrie, and he reported that two saddle horses had been stolen from the barn sometime during the night. Further, the thieves had left behind a buggy and horse, found not far down the road from the farmhouse. The farmer, who fancied himself a deer hunter, had tracked the horses east from the barn. He'd lost the trail where it crossed a wilderness stream.

For Tilghman and Thomas, the farmer's story removed all doubt. It was now apparent that Doolin, fearing Lane would be captured and talk, had hastily improvised a new plan. The stolen buggy had been dumped, and the fugitives had switched to saddle mounts capable of traveling overland. There was no question in the lawmen's minds that their first hunch had been dead on the mark. Doolin and Clifton were headed on a beeline for the safety of the Nations. With a head start of some sixteen hours, the outcome seemed a foregone conclusion. They had probably already crossed into Indian Territory.

Thomas was all for a manhunt centered on the Nations. He wanted to alert his informants and put the backwoods grapevine to work. But Tilghman had been down that road several times over the last year. Though they had caught gang members in the Nations, they had never once gotten a lead on Doolin. To the contrary, he argued, Doolin was a will-o'-the-wisp who left no trail. Instead, virtually every time, the outlaw leader had doubled back, usually picking a hideout far removed from other members of the Wild Bunch. There was no reason to believe he would do otherwise this time.

Tilghman thought their search should be centered around Ingalls and Lawson. He was convinced that Doolin's primary concern was his wife and child, rather than an attempt to resurrect the Wild Bunch. There was a remote likelihood that the outlaw would contact the Dunn brothers. The ranch was a known hideout, but he was wily as a fox, and often relied on the unpredictable to throw off pursuit. The greater likelihood was that Doolin would somehow spirit his wife and child out of Oklahoma Territory. All the more so since he'd tried once before to take off with his family. The high probability was that he would run and keep on running.

Thomas was finally persuaded. He found it hard to differ with the only man who had caught Doolin, and one who clearly understood how the gang leader thought. They rode out the next morning, and arrived at the Dunn ranch late that evening. A quick check confirmed that Doolin was nowhere around, and they sat down with the Dunn brothers. The Dunns were cooperative, reminded that the charges against them would be dropped only when Doolin was imprisoned or hanged. But they knew nothing of his whereabouts, and swore they hadn't seen him since his escape. Nor had they heard anything on the grapevine from their horse-thief friends. There was simply no word on Doolin.

They stayed the night with the Dunns. The following morning over breakfast, Tilghman casually asked Bee Dunn if he knew anyone in Lawson. To his amazement, Dunn remarked just as casually that his sister lived there. Dunn went on to say that she was married to Charlie Noble, who had settled in Lawson rather than Ingalls during the territory's first land rush. Noble was a blacksmith and operated a shop jointly owned with his brother, Tom. Under questioning, Dunn grudgingly admitted that the Noble brothers frowned upon their in-laws' dealings in stolen horses—their major reason for settling in another town.

Upon riding out that morning, Tilghman and Thomas were still astonished at the turn of fortune. They agreed that a simple, off-the-cuff question often resulted in a payoff far larger than expected. Tilghman was prompted to ask the question in the unlikely hope that Dunn had shady business dealings with a livestock dealer in Lawson. A thief turned informant sometimes led to another thief who could be persuaded to turn informant. What neither of them ever expected was that the Dunns had a sister, and two brothers-in-law, living in Lawson. The joker in the development was that the brothers-in-law were honest men. They decided to appeal to greed.

Early that afternoon they rode into Lawson. The Noble brothers' blacksmith shop was located at the south edge of town, on the west side of the street. As they dismounted, Tilghman and Thomas noted that the back window of the shop afforded a clear view of John Ellsworth's home. The Ellsworth house was two streets over on a corner lot that jutted southward farther than the houses in between. The window was a perfect spyhole on the activities of Edith Doolin.

The Noble brothers were busy shoeing a plow horse. No one else was in sight, and the lawmen assumed the horse's owner had stepped uptown. Tilghman quickly took the lead, explaining that they were there at the suggestion of Bee Dunn. The brothers paused, frowning at the mention of the name. Tilghman related in a confidential voice that the Dunns were informants for the government. The revelation seemed to shock Tom, the younger brother, whose shoulders bulged with muscle. Charlie, married to the Dunns' sister, was apparently beyond being shocked by his in-laws. A man of some girth, heavier than his brother, he seemed unfazed by the news. He appointed himself spokesman for the family.

"Why you tellin' us all this?" he said, when Tilghman finished. "We don't have no truck with the Dunns."

"They're still your wife's brothers," Tilghman observed. "Would you want them to go to jail?"

"Don't make no never mind to me. Jail's where they belong."

"Unless you assist us, they might still wind up in jail. Or maybe you'd be more interested in the reward."

Noble's brow wrinkled. "What reward?"

"We're after Bill Doolin," Tilghman said. "His wife lives here with her father. John Ellsworth."

"Whole town knows about Edith Doolin. Saw her on the street with her baby only this mornin'. So what?"

"There's a five-thousand-dollar reward on Doolin. You lend a hand and we'll split it with you."

"Twenty-five hundred dollars?" Noble squinted, head cocked to one side. "Whadda we have to do?"

Tilghman pointed through the rear window. "Keep your eye on the Ellsworth house. Let us know when it looks like Edith Doolin's headed on a trip."

"That's all, jest get word to you? Nothin' else?"

"Tip us in time to catch Doolin and that's the end of it. You get the money."

Noble's mouth curled in an ugly smile. He glanced at his brother. "What you think, Tom? The Dunn boys're family of sorts. Wanna help 'em stay outta jail?"

The younger Noble grinned. "Hell, Charlie, you know me. Family always comes first."

"Thought you'd think so," Noble said, turning back to Tilghman. "We'll keep an eye peeled, marshal. Anything happens, you'll get the word."

Tilghman explained where they could contact him, and how to get hold of Thomas. They shook hands on the deal, and the lawmen walked from the smithy. After they were mounted, they rode south on the wagon road. Thomas was silent for a long while, then he grunted.

"Bet those boys never saw twenty-five hundred all at once."

"Let's hope they get the chance this time."

"Amen to that, Brother Tilghman. Amen."

The men were hidden in tall weeds beside the tracks. Their horses were tied in a grove of trees fifty yards west of the Edmond depot. Across from them, outside the Santa Fe stationhouse, the agent waited with a mail sack for the midnight train. He paced the platform to warm himself against a brisk wind.

Dick Clifton kept his hands stuffed in the pockets of his mackinaw. Beside him, stiff from squatting in the weeds, were Dick West and Red Buck Waightman. On his other side were Al and Frank Jennings, and beyond them, Pat and Morris O'Malley. They waited, watching the station agent, wondering if the train would be on time.

A week ago, after busting out of jail, Clifton had thought it would be like the old days. He knew where West and Waightman were hiding out in the Creek Nation, and he'd assumed Doolin would reform the gang.

But shortly after crossing into the Nations, it became apparent that Doolin had other plans. With hardly more than a handshake, Doolin had left him at trailside and turned north into the Cherokee Nation. There was no invitation to come along, and no mention of future jobs for the Wild Bunch. Clifton knew then that he would never return.

A day later Clifton had rejoined West and Waightman. He found that they had long since given up hope of Doolin's return. Instead, they had been recruited into a new gang, formed by Al Jennings. Short and wiry with a thatch of red hair, Jennings was a man with grandiose ideas. Over the past month, he'd led the gang in a series of holdups on backcountry general stores. The raids, according to him, were a training ground for their first big job, a train robbery. He meant for them to become the new Wild Bunch of Oklahoma Territory.

Clifton immediately pegged him as a penny-ante bandit. But West and Waightman, who were short on brains, had accepted him as their leader. To compound matters, Jennings was backed by his brother and the O'Malleys, who were none too bright themselves. With the odds stacked against him, Clifton saw no choice but to fall in line. A train holdup was already laid on at Edmond, which was some fifteen miles north of Oklahoma City. He planned to go along, collect his share of the loot, and then strike off on his own. He thought Al Jennings would sooner or later get them all killed.

But now, waiting in the weeds beside the tracks, Clifton was intent on the job at hand. He watched as the train approached from the north and ground to a stop before the depot. On signal from Jennings, the O'Malleys boarded the locomotive and covered the engineer. The rest of the gang followed Jennings around the front of the locomotive, rushing toward the stationhouse. The guard opened the door of the express car, leaning out to collect the mail bag, just as they scat-

tered across the depot platform. West, Waightman and
Frank Jennings, their guns drawn, spread out to cover
the passenger coaches. Clifton and Al Jennings halted
in front of the express car.

"Don't try nothin'," Jennings barked, waving his pistol back and forth between the station agent and the
guard. "I'd as soon shoot you as not."

Clifton vaulted into the express car. He disarmed the
guard, motioning to the safe. "Get it open and be damn
quick about it."

"I can't," the guard said in a shaky voice. "They
stopped givin' us the combination back in July. Nobody
can open it till we get to Oklahoma City."

"You lyin' sonovabitch! Open it or I'll kill you where
you stand."

"Honest to God, mister, I'm tellin' you the truth. The
Santa Fe wires the combination on ahead to the stations. Only Guthrie and Oklahoma City get it any
more."

Clifton suddenly realized that it had been three
months since he'd pulled a holdup. He thought the
guard's story made sense, particularly from the Santa
Fe's standpoint. An express guard without the combination was of no use to train robbers.

"Climb down outside," he ordered, waiting until the
guard jumped from the car before he nodded to Jennings. "I'm gonna have to blow the safe."

"Holy shit!" Jennings protested. "That'll wake up the
whole gawddamn town."

"Told you a town wasn't no place to rob a train. You
should've listened."

"Stop sayin' I told you so and get it done. We're not
leavin' empty-handed."

Clifton pulled two sticks of dynamite from inside his
mackinaw. He found twine inside the express car and
used it to tie the dynamite to the safe door. Then he

struck a match, held the flame to the fuse until it sputtered. He bolted from the door.

The explosion rocked the train. Debris and dust drifted through the open door as the conductor popped out of one of the coaches. The gang drove him back inside with a flurry of shots, and began peppering the coaches to keep the passengers inside. Clifton hefted himself into the express car.

The safe door was scorched but otherwise undamaged. A section of the floor was buckled and tongues of flame leaped along the wall opposite the safe. Clifton tried the handle on the safe door, then stepped back and kicked it in frustration. After a moment, muttering to himself, he turned away. He hopped down beside Jennings.

"No soap," he said glumly. "Hardly touched the damn thing."

Jennings glared at him. "How the hell'd you ever get the name Dynamite Dick?"

"Never blowed a safe!" Clifton said sharply. "Just used it for express car doors."

"Some sorry state of affairs, you ask me. Let's get outta here before the town throws us a necktie party."

The gang beat a hasty retreat across the tracks. The men cursed and grumbled as they ran toward the distant treeline. There, after swinging aboard their horses, their leader set a course for the Nations. Clifton brought up the rear as they thundered off into the night.

He told himself it was time to get far away from Al Jennings.

CHAPTER 42

The aborted robbery made headlines. Not as large and not as bold, but nonetheless a front-page story in the Guthrie *Statesman*. Though unsuccessful, in many ways laughable, the raid was still hot news. There had not been a train holdup in more than three months.

Tilghman and Thomas had returned from Lawson the night of the holdup. At first, when they met with Nagle, there was some speculation that Doolin had given fresh life to the Wild Bunch. But by early morning, details of the raid began filtering in over the telegraph. They were somewhat mystified by the reports.

The express car guard positively identified Dick Clifton. The Edmond station agent was equally positive in his identification of Dick West and Red Buck Waightman. Wanted posters on the three outlaws were plastered on the walls of train stations across the territory. Yet the witnesses were no less familiar with Bill Doolin, whose image still decorated wanted dodgers. None of them could place him at the scene of the holdup.

Their descriptions of the other gang members added still more confusion. Three of them were nondescript in appearance, the type of men who would blend in with a crowd. But the fourth man, according to witnesses, would be a standout in any crowd. He was described as short and slight of build, a bantam of a man with flaming red hair. The witnesses reported as well that he was the leader of the gang.

Thomas and Tilghman were of the same opinion. With the demise of the Wild Bunch, someone had stepped into the breach and forged a new gang. In the process, the man had somehow recruited Clifton, West, and Red Buck Waightman. Which meant that Clifton had joined the gang within days of his escape from jail. In turn, that meant Clifton had known all along where to contact West and Waightman.

Hard as it was to admit, the lawmen had to conclude that Clifton was a skilled liar. On the train from Texas, when they'd interrogated him throughout the night, he had convincingly denied any knowledge of West and Waightman. For Tilghman, the fact that he'd been fooled was of no great consequence. He was intrigued, instead, that Doolin was no part of the Edmond holdup, or the new gang. All of which seemed to bear out his original hunch. The key to Doolin was his wife and child.

Thomas was more intrigued by the new gangleader. Something about the man's description bothered him, tickled his memory. He began rummaging through a stack of field reports from marshals around the territory. At last, he came across a report about a pint-sized bandit with bright red hair, who led a band of misfits in looting general stores. The man had been identified as Al Jennings, and the band he led included his brother Frank and the O'Malley brothers, Pat and Morris. They operated out of the Creek Nation.

When Thomas and Tilghman put their heads together, the conclusion was obvious. West and Waightman had apparently taken refuge in the Creek Nation, and somehow run across Al Jennings. Clifton, after his escape, had joined them and fallen in with the new gang. With Doolin out of the mix, the whole thing made perfect sense. Jennings had absorbed the dregs of the Wild Bunch into his own gang, and gone from looting stores to robbing trains. The question that remained was where Jennings and his men might be found.

A wire late that afternoon brought the answer. Federal Marshal George Bussy, who was stationed at Chickasha, had been contacted by one of his own informants. For the reward money involved, Clifton, West, and Waightman had been betrayed by a Creek tribesman. Al Jennings, along with his brother and the O'Malleys, had been betrayed as well. The gang was scattered throughout the Creek Nation, but their locations were known. Marshal Bussy requested instructions.

Patrick Nagle wired him that Tilghman and Thomas were on the way.

Deputy marshals George Bussy and Andy White tied their horses in a stand of trees. Armed with Winchesters, they moved forward through the timber and halted at the edge of a clearing. Their position overlooked a farmhouse.

The farm, according to Bussy's informant, belonged to Wallis Brooks. A white man, Brooks had married a Creek woman and thus gained the right to property in Indian Territory. Located outside the town of Eufaula, the farm was a couple of miles north of the Canadian River. Dynamite Dick Clifton was reported to be staying with Brooks.

Bussy had met yesterday with Tilghman and Thomas, and several other federal marshals. There were ten lawmen in all, and Nagle had ordered that Tilghman and Thomas were to direct the operation. Three raiding parties were formed, with Tilghman and Thomas in one, and the largest party, with six marshals, under the command of Bud Ledbetter. Bussy and White were assigned to capture, or kill, Dick Clifton.

Their information was that Clifton had a Creek lady

friend in Eufaula. He apparently spent his nights in town and returned to the farm every morning. Bussy and White, traveling through the night, had timed their arrival with sunrise. There was no way to determine if Clifton was in the house or still with his lady friend. They settled down to wait beside a wagon road at the edge of the clearing.

Bussy was a large man with a handlebar mustache. He shook his head, watching the house. "Way Thomas talked, we ought to kill him and have done with it. Tilghman tended to favor taking him alive. Funny the way men think different."

"Not so different," White remarked. "I recollect Tilghman's killed his share. Doolin's the only one he ever brought in alive."

"Wonder what the hell's the score with Doolin. They didn't say nothin' about him."

"Doolin's like their own private grudge match. You can tell, they want him real bad."

"I'll bet you one thing," Bussy said. "Next time, they'll stop Doolin's clock."

"Yeah, he's already dead and just don't know it."

The conversation dwindled off and the lawmen waited as the sun rose steadily higher. Toward midmorning Bussy nudged White with his elbow, nodding in the direction of the farmhouse. Clifton, mounted on a horse, had taken a shortcut through a cornfield to the north. He was broadside to them, already halfway across the clearing.

"Clifton!" Bussy yelled, shouldering his Winchester. "Hold it right there!"

Clifton reined his horse about, drawing his pistol. He winged a shot at the trees as he booted his horse into a gallop. The lawmen fired an instant apart, the reports of their carbines blending into one. White's shot struck the horse, and it plowed nose first into the ground. The slug from Bussy's carbine broke Clifton's left arm as he was thrown from the saddle. He hit the dirt with a hard thud.

Bussy and White stepped from the trees, levering fresh rounds into their Winchesters. Clifton scrambled awkwardly to his feet, his left arm dangling at a grotesque angle. He hobbled toward the cornfield, triggering two wayward snap-shots as he moved. The lawmen fired simultaneously, one slug drilling Clifton through the chest and the other shattering his shoulder. He dropped three steps short of the cornfield.

White spun around, leveling his carbine as Wallis Brooks ran out of the house. He kept the farmer covered while Bussy walked forward to inspect the body. After a moment, Bussy waved his Winchester overhead.

"Dynamite Dick won't dynamite no more!"

Shortly before noon Bud Ledbetter and his squad of five marshals were in position. Throughout the morning, he had waited in the woods while the lawmen, one by one, took their assigned posts around the clearing. They now had the farmhouse surrounded.

The farm belonged to Sam Baker, brother-in-law by marriage to Wallis Brooks. Located some five miles farther along the Canadian, the house overlooked the river. George Bussy's informant had reported that the house was occupied by Al and Frank Jennings and the O'Malley brothers. So many outlaws were difficult to conceal, particularly when they made nightly trips into Eufaula. Their presence was apparently known to everyone in town.

Bud Ledbetter had saved the most critical task for himself. The gang had posted a lookout, armed with a rifle, seated in a wagon near the barn. Ledbetter surmised that the outlaws' horses were stalled in the barn, for there was no outside corral. He stepped out of the woods, on line with the back of the barn, which screened his movements from anyone in the house, or from the lookout. A few moments later he paused at the corner of the barn, less than five yards from the wagon. He shouldered a 10-gauge double-barrel shotgun.

"Hey, mister," he called out in a low voice. "Over here."

Morris O'Malley looked around. He found himself staring into the twin bores of a scattergun. The man behind the gun stared back with a grim expression. "Climb down off that wagon," Ledbetter ordered. "Walk over here slow and easy. You open your mouth and I'll kill you."

O'Malley gingerly moved off the wagon. For a moment, staring into the shotgun, he thought he would wet his pants. But he made it to the corner of the barn, where he was yanked out of sight, quickly disarmed, and his hands manacled behind his back. Ledbetter motioned with his hat toward the woods west of the clearing. In turn the marshal posted there signaled a marshal covering the front of the house.

"Al Jennings!" the marshal out front shouted. "This is a federal marshal speaking. I order you and your men to surrender!"

The back door burst open. The Jennings brothers and Pat O'Malley boiled out of the house in a headlong rush for the barn. Their pistols were drawn, and in their panic to escape, they failed to notice that their lookout had disappeared. Ledbetter moved around the corner of the barn, his shotgun leveled.

"Halt or be killed!"

Al Jennings and his brother fired in what sounded like a single report. Ledbetter triggered both barrels of his shotgun in a thunderous roar. From either side of the house, marshals cut loose with a rolling volley from their carbines. Jennings went down with a slug in his shoulder, and O'Malley collapsed, his legs shredded by buckshot. Frank Jennings froze, dropping his pistol, somehow unscathed in the hail of lead. He raised his hands.

The marshals converged on the house. Ledbetter shifted the shotgun to his left hand and drew his pistol as he moved forward. Al Jennings clutched at his shoulder, his eyes watering with pain. O'Malley writhed about on the ground, his trousers soaked with blood. Frank Jennings stood as though struck by sudden paralysis.

"Helluva note," Ledbetter grunted, inspecting them with a bemused look. "I think you boys are gonna live."

The grass was crisp underfoot. A glazy afternoon sun shed splinters of light over the swift-running stream. Tilghman and Thomas ghosted through the woods, halting deep within the treeline. To their front was a dugout at the bottom of a stunted hill.

The dugout bordered a creek that fed into the Canadian. A battered wooden door was framed as an entrance, and smoke drifted from a stovepipe protruding through the roof. Off to one side was a log corral, with two horses standing hip-shot in the sunlight. There was no sound, no one in sight.

Tilghman and Thomas had elected to raid the dugout themselves. So far as they were concerned, the other marshals were fully capable of handling the rest of the gang. But the informant had reported that Dick West and Red Buck Waightman could be found at an abandoned dugout burrowed from the side of a hill. They hadn't forgotten the farmer gunned down by Waightman some three months ago. Nor had they forgotten burying the farmer while his grief-stricken wife and little girl looked on. Waightman was theirs, and West was icing on the cake.

The congregation of outlaws around Eufaula was to them a matter of blind luck. According to the informant, who had finally let greed overshadow prudence, West and Waightman had used the dugout off and on for over a year. Clifton, whose Creek girlfriend lived in town, was a frequent visitor as well. Jennings and his men were apparently regular guests at the farms of two white men married to Creek sisters. By whatever quirk of fate, the demise of the Wild Bunch had brought them all together. Their mistake, the blind luck, was that they'd opted to stick with hideouts around Eufaula. Old habits had played into the hands of the law.

Thomas hadn't taken his eyes off the door of the dugout. "What d'you think?" he said in a graveled whisper. "Do we call 'em out or do we wait?"

"We wait," Tilghman replied. "They can't stay in there forever. Let's catch 'em in the open."

Looking back, they would remember the words as somehow foreordained. The door opened and Red Buck Waightman stepped from the dugout, followed by West. They were freshly shaved, their hair slicked down, apparently set for a night in Eufaula. Waightman still in the lead, they turned toward the corral.

"Federal marshals!" Tilghman yelled. "Don't move!"

Waightman whirled, pulling his pistol, and fired. West crouched and ran, dodging back toward the dugout, snapping off a hurried shot. The slugs whistled through the trees an instant before the lawmen opened fire with their carbines. Thomas levered two rounds and Waightman fell spread-eagled, his shirt splotched with blood. Tilghman let off only one shot, dusting West front to back, and the outlaw dropped just as he reached the door. His right leg kicked in a spasm of death.

The lawmen walked forward, their carbines at the ready. They inspected the bodies, satisfying themselves that both men were dead. At length, Thomas looked around, his eyes still cold with anger. A hard smile touched the corners of his mouth.

"Scratch Red Buck Waightman off the rolls. Sorry bastard won't kill any more farmers."

"No, he won't," Tilghman observed. "We've done a good day's work here."

"Still got one to go. The he-dog himself."

"Heck, I just suspect we'll get our chance."

They both wondered where they might next meet Bill Doolin.

CHAPTER 43

The washed blue of the plains sky grew smoky along about dusk. A stiff breeze fell off, but there was a lingering nip in the sharp, crisp air. The lawmen rode into the ranch as twilight slowly gave way to dark. Neal Brown helped them unsaddle their horses.

Tilghman had convinced Thomas that they should make another scout around Lawson. Two days past, at a prearranged site on the Canadian, they had rendezvoused with Bussy and the other marshals. The time and place of the meeting had been part of their overall plan for the raids. Any of the gang who had slipped through the net would be pursued from there.

Yet, after everyone arrived at the rendezvous, pursuit proved to be unnecessary. The last three members of the Wild Bunch had been killed, and the Jennings gang had been taken alive. Wagons confiscated at the farms providing refuge had been loaded with the dead and the wounded. Bussy and Ledbetter, both senior marshals, had escorted the wagons on to Guthrie.

Thomas and Tilghman had then turned their attention to the unresolved matter of Bill Doolin. From the Canadian, they had angled northwest through the Creek Nation, headed for the ranch. News of the raids rushed ahead of them, spreading along the grapevine from town to town. Tilghman became increasingly concerned, for newspapers were certain to headline the violent end of the Wild Bunch. He was worried that Doolin would take it as an omen and run.

Their two days on the trail had cost them precious time. Tonight, walking toward the house, Thomas was no less concerned that they might be too late. For all they knew, Doolin might already have heard the news, and made arrangements to flee the territory with his family. But they were weary from the grueling manhunt, and they both felt it would be a mistake to push on without rest. They needed a hot meal and a good night's sleep, as well as fresh mounts. They agreed to leave at dawn.

Brown got busy in the kitchen. While they washed and shaved, he fired up the cookstove and began slinging together a meal. By the time they were finished, he had the table laid out with charred beefsteak, fried potatoes, and warmed-over biscuits. They wolfed it down while he peppered them with questions, whooping loudly about the last of the Wild Bunch. When their plates were clean, he served them large wedges of Dutch apple pie. Their bellies full, they lingered over a final cup of coffee.

Finally, thinking about sleep, they rose from the table. As they walked from the kitchen, they heard hoofbeats, the sound of a horse being ridden hard. Tilghman moved through the parlor to the door, and saw a man dismount outside. His features were revealed in a spill of lamplight as he stepped onto the porch. Tilghman realized it was the young blacksmith from Lawson, Tom Noble. He held the door open.

"Way you pushed that horse, you've got news. What's up?"

"Charlie told me not to spare the whip." Noble entered the parlor, nodding to Thomas. "We think Doolin's about to make his move."

Tilghman looked at him. "Why so?"

"Edith Doolin bought a wagon and horse from the livery stable this mornin'. She's got it parked out beside her dad's house."

"How'd you get wind of it?"

"Saw her drive by in the new rig," Noble said. "Last time she left town, we remembered she'd done the same thing. So Charlie talked to the feller that owns the livery."

"Yeah?" Thomas coaxed. "What'd he find out?"

"She didn't dicker none a'tall about price. Agreed right off, like she's in a powerful hurry."

"Tell me," Tilghman said casually. "Has the news hit Lawson about the Wild Bunch?"

"Has it ever!" Noble wagged his head. "Everybody in town's been talkin' about it 'cause there was no word on Doolin. We heard the others was all killed."

Tilghman and Thomas exchanged a glance. Their fears were confirmed that the news would goad Doolin into hasty action. The fact that Edith Doolin had bought a wagon was all the corroboration they needed. She was planning on leaving town.

"Let's get back to the wagon," Tilghman said. "Has she loaded it, or is it just sitting there?"

"Just sittin' there." Noble paused, then went on. " 'Course, I lit out to bring you the word. She could've started loadin' up after I left."

Tilghman considered a moment. "Where's a good place to keep watch on the Ellsworth house? Your smithy won't do, not for us. Too much chance we'd be spotted."

"Lemme think." Noble studied on it, scratching his jaw. Finally, with a quick smile, he bobbed his head. "There's a big patch of woods off to the west of town. Starts maybe a quarter-mile behind Ellsworth's place."

"Yeah, I remember," Tilghman said, nodding. "I was checking on the Doolin woman at the time and didn't pay much attention. Do I recollect a trail leading into the woods?"

"You sure do," Noble affirmed. "Old logging road that cuts through there to Eagle Creek. Anyplace in them woods, you'd be lookin' right at Ellsworth's back door."

"No rest for the weary," Tilghman said, glancing at Thomas. "We'll have to leave tonight."

"Suits me," Thomas agreed. "I've done without sleep before."

An hour later, mounted on fresh horses, the lawmen and Tom Noble reined away from the corral. They rode north under a star-studded sky.

John Ellsworth looked stricken. Seated in the parlor, he nervously clasped and unclasped his hands. He stared blankly at the wall, avoiding his wife's steely gaze. She glowered at him from the sofa.

A plain dumpling of a woman, Sarah Ellsworth was stout, with sharp, beady eyes. She had the formidable manner of a drill sergeant, and she ruled her household with an iron hand. Tonight, watching her husband, she was incensed by his attack of nerves.

"Stop twitching," she said angrily. "Any minute you'll start having conniption fits."

Ellsworth winced. "Sadie, you know the law's not far behind whenever he shows up. How'd you expect me to act?"

"You've got no spine, never did. Edith loves him and he's the father of our grandson. Now, let's hear no more about it!"

Doolin had appeared at the back door late last night. The word was out that his gang had been eliminated, and Ellsworth knew what his sudden arrival meant. All the more so when Edith had gone out this morning and bought a horse and wagon. Yet he wasn't able to summon the strength to contact the federal marshals. Nor was he able to defy his wife.

"How did it come to this?" Ellsworth said heavily. "When he showed up again tonight, that was the beginning of the end. You know he plans to take Edith and the boy . . . don't you?"

"What did you expect?" she said with a nettled look. "They're man and wife, and they want to be together. You just keep your nose out of it."

Ellsworth slumped down in resignation. At the end of the hall, a bedroom door opened and Edith walked to the kitchen. She filled a glass with water, then paused in the dining room, looking into the parlor. She smiled at her father.

"Don't act so glum, Daddy. The world's not coming to an end."

She disappeared down the hall into the bedroom. Doolin was seated at the foot of the bed, holding the baby. She gave him the glass, then took the baby from his arms. As he drank the water, she gently nestled the baby between pillows at the head of the bed. She laughed softly.

"Daddy's such a fussbudget. He can't bear the thought that you've finally come for me."

"Don't worry about it," Doolin said, placing the glass on the floor. "Your ma will bring him around."

"I'm sure," she said, seating herself beside him on the bed. "Whatever tune Mama plays, Daddy hums along."

"Well, let's let them work it out for themselves. We've got plans of our own to think about."

She hugged herself with merriment. "I still can't believe it! We're really on our way this time, aren't we?"

"For a fact," Doolin said earnestly. "Come tomorrow night, we're Californey bound."

"And we'll make it." She took his hand, pressed it to her cheek. "Nothing's going to stop us this time."

"Nothing or nobody," Doolin said with a determined

edge to his voice. "We're gonna get there come hell or high water."

"You're sure the law has no idea you're here?"

"Honey, they don't have the least notion of where I'm at."

Doolin had spent almost two weeks covering his trail. He'd stuck to the backwoods, living off the land, as he slowly made his way from the Cherokee Nation to Lawson. After scouting the area, he had made camp on Eagle Creek, some three miles west of town. Then, certain his wife wasn't being watched, he'd left his horse in the woods last night and approached the house. Walking still bothered him, but he was happy to endure the pain. By tomorrow night, they would be long gone. On their way at last.

"Bill, would you tell me something? It's been on my mind."

"I've got no secrets from you."

She lowered her eyes. "Why didn't you just send for me . . . like you did last time?"

"Last time you was followed." Doolin smiled indulgently. "I aim to make sure you're not followed this time. That way nobody'll ever know where to find us."

"Oh, I love the sound of it! No more worrying whether we're being spied on. Just the three of us—a new life!"

"But we gotta do it right. You don't start loadin' that wagon till it gets dark. No sense tippin' our hand."

"I'll remember," she said with a vigorous nod. "We've got supplies enough to last till we're out of the territory. Won't take long to load."

Doolin patted her hand. "Don't worry if you don't see me right away. I'll be waitin' somewhere on the trail to Eagle Creek. Anybody tries to follow you, I'll take care of it."

"I know you will." She paused, her voice suddenly

husky. "Couldn't you stay the night? It's been so long since we . . . were together."

"Plenty of time for that later. Better safe than sorry, and I'm lots safer back at my camp. One more night won't matter."

She walked him through the hall. Doolin waved to the Ellsworths and followed her into the kitchen. At the back door, she melted into his arms, gave him a long, passionate kiss. He gently stroked her hair, then stepped into the night.

After closing the door, she danced across the kitchen, her skirts flying. John and Sarah Ellsworth looked up as she hurried into the parlor. Her eyes were bright with happiness, her smile radiant.

"Only one more day! We leave tomorrow night!"

Shortly after sunrise the lawmen parted with Tom Noble south of Lawson. They skirted west a mile, then entered the woods and worked their way back in the direction of town. A half hour later they found the old logging road.

The Ellsworth house was visible from the trees. Outside, they saw the wagon, the horse loosely tied to the rear. After scouting the area, they picketed their own horses deep in the woods, away from the road. At the edge of the treeline, they settled down to wait.

Throughout the day, one slept while the other kept watch. The telescope from Tilghman's saddlebags brought the house into sharp focus. They saw John Ellsworth depart for work shortly before eight o'clock, and later, Edith Doolin came out with a bucket of oats for the horse. The morning passed uneventfully, and as the afternoon dragged on, there was still no sign of activity. They continued to watch.

Tilghman and Thomas were both of the opinion that Edith Doolin would head for the Nations. Once there, knowing she'd been trailed the last time, she would probably attempt some new dodge to throw off pursuit.

They surmised that she would not turn north toward Kansas, for Doolin never used the same plan twice. Instead, they thought she would meet Doolin at some backwoods whistle stop, where the Katy railroad bisected Indian Territory. A train from there could take them north or south, possibly Missouri or Texas. Where they planned to travel after that was pure conjecture, and of no great importance. The lawmen intended to waylay Doolin in the Nations.

Late that afternoon Tilghman was on watch. As the sun dropped below the horizon, he saw Ellsworth return home from the store. Lamps glowed in the house, and within minutes twilight faded into darkness. The night was crisp and clear, the sky brilliant with the glimmer of stars. Another hour passed, and when Thomas came to relieve him, he suggested that they pitch camp by their horses, fix a pot of coffee. There seemed little likelihood of anything happening tonight. Thomas agreed.

But then, as they started to turn away, Tilghman caught a flicker of movement outside the house. He extended the telescope, training it on the wagon, which was dimly visible in a spill of lamplight from the windows. Looking closer, he saw Edith Doolin, assisted by her father, loading bundles into the wagon. When they finished, her father went to hitch the horse as her mother came out the back door with the baby. Finally, after a quick round of hugs, she climbed into the wagon seat. Her mother handed up the baby.

Tilghman was on the verge of sending Thomas to fetch their horses. But he hesitated, somewhat astounded, watching as Edith Doolin swung the wagon around and headed in their direction. Taken off guard, he and Thomas discussed their options, and quickly formulated a plan. They retreated roughly a mile deeper into the woods, and posted themselves on either side of the road. When the Doolin woman passed by, Tilghman would trail her on foot and Thomas would follow along with their horses. The logging road ended at Eagle Creek, some two miles farther on, and beyond that were open plains. They would have to trail her at a distance.

Some while later, hidden behind a tree, Tilghman watched as the wagon approached their positions. He readied himself to follow along, but suddenly froze, listening. From the opposite direction, toward Eagle Creek, he heard the slow clop of hoofbeats on hard earth. He craned around, looking over his shoulder, and saw a man on foot leading a horse. A shaft of starlight flooded the road, and as the distance closed to less than ten yards, the man's features became visible. Directly across from his position, he picked up a blurred shadow out of the corner of his eye. Thomas stepped into the road.

"Doolin! Surrender or be killed!"

Doolin's pistol appeared in his hand as though by magic. He fired from the hip, and the slug thunked into a tree behind Thomas. A split-second later, the carbine at Thomas's shoulder spat a streak of flame. Doolin staggered backward, arms windmilling, and his horse bolted down the road. His knees buckled and he dropped to the ground, the pistol skittering from his hand. His chest rose and fell with a last shuddering breath. Then he lay still.

"Ooo God no!"

Edith Doolin's scream echoed through the woods. Tilghman moved into the road and saw her tumble over the side of the wagon. He hurried forward as Thomas levered a fresh round and walked toward the body. She scrambled off the ground, her eyes wild with terror, and Tilghman caught her in his arms. She struggled to break free, wailing a low, keening moan, but he held her tighter. Her mouth opened in a tormented cry.

"I have to see him! Please, God, let me see him!"

"Later, Mrs. Doolin," Tilghman said in a quiet voice. "There'll be time for that later."

Her features sagged, tears spilling down her cheeks. She went limp in his arms, her body shuddering with soft, mewling sobs. Tilghman held her close, saddened by her grief, knowing it could have ended no other way. Unbidden, a wayward thought came to him, something out of the past. A remark once made by Heck Thomas, and now come true.

One of them would be renowned as the man who killed Bill Doolin.

EPILOGUE

The Wild Bunch was no more, and Bill Doolin was dead. A mood of celebration prevailed, and the Three Guardsmen were once again summoned to Guthrie. The Capitol Building was at last under construction, and on November 14 a crowd of some five thousand people gathered before the capitol grounds.

The capitol was located at the east end of Oklahoma Avenue. A tall speaker's platform had been erected in front of the construction site, the railings and stanchions festooned with bunting in patriotic colors. Behind the podium there were rows of chairs, occupied by legislators, judges and other dignitaries. Seated among them were Bill Tilghman, Heck Thomas, and Chris Madsen.

Governor William Renfrow had proclaimed it Marshal's Day. His proclamation, circulated throughout the territory, had set aside a day to honor the men who had brought law and order to a new frontier. Foremost among that number were the three men seated on the dais today. Their names were household words across Oklahoma Territory, and people had traveled by train and buggy and horseback to be there for the occasion. Men sat children on their shoulders so that they could one day say they had seen the greatest lawmen of an era.

Zoe stood with her father in the front rank of spectators. The crowd stretched westward along Oklahoma Avenue and spilled out onto sidestreets. Newspapers from throughout the territory were represented by reporters and cameramen positioned directly before the speaker's platform. Off to one side, a uniformed band played rousing tunes made popular by John Philip Sousa, bandmaster for the U.S. Marine Corps. The music and the patriotic trappings lent a holiday atmosphere to the occasion.

On the platform, Governor Renfrow and U.S. Marshal Patrick Nagle were seated beside the three lawmen. The governor nodded to one of his aides, who in turn signaled the bandleader. The air filled with the blare of trumpets as the band segued into ruffles and flourishes to open the ceremonies. The crowd broke into lusty cheers as the governor made his way to the podium. A consummate politician, he spread his arms high and looked out over the throng with his trademark nutcracker grin. Finally, lowering his arms, he motioned for silence.

"Good people of Oklahoma Territory!" he boomed in a resonant voice. "We gather today to honor the men who brought law and order to our great land. We commend in particular the three men who again and again risked their lives in stamping out that infamous gang of killers, the Wild Bunch." He paused, an arm thrust out in dramatic gesture toward the lawmen. "I speak of peace officers whose deeds have made their names legend across this land—the Three Guardsmen!"

The crowd burst out in a spontaneous roar. After a moment, the governor quieted them with outstretched arms, and went on with his speech. Thomas glanced at Tilghman, then at Madsen, who had returned from his post in Missouri for the occasion. They exchanged the slight smiles of men unaccustomed to the fanfare and hyperbole of public acclamation. The governor's rich baritone continued to extol their deeds, playing on the theme of good versus evil, lawman against outlaw. The spectators stood as though mesmerized by his words.

Tilghman listened with only mild interest. His mind drifted back over the people and events that had brought him to this point in time. He recalled every manhunt, every shootout, all the death and suffering that littered the past. His most vivid memory was of Bill Doolin, who somehow seemed the last of a breed. Far more clever, and deadly, than the likes of Al Jennings, who awaited trial in federal court. He saw it as the end of an era, horseback marshals pitted against outlaws who ran in packs. Oklahoma Territory would soon absorb Indian Territory, and the sanctuary of the Nations would be gone forever. The outlaw days were finished, and with it, a moment in time. A new era, far different from the old, lay ahead.

Watching from the crowd, Zoe was overcome with pride. Only ten days ago, Tilghman had been elected sheriff of Lincoln County by a landslide vote. Yet she knew, looking at him now, that he would be remembered most for his work in eliminating the Wild Bunch. Historians would one day write of him and Heck Thomas and Chris Madsen, and all the other men who had worn the federal badge. Their courage and dedication, their iron determination, would be recorded for future generations. She thought the record would accord them their due, their rightful place in history. They were, indeed, the stuff of legend.

"So I say to you," Governor Renfrow told the crowd. "Never before in the annals of crime have peace officers faced such a daunting and bloody challenge. These men fought a war, a long and unrelentless war for the rule of law in Oklahoma Territory. And they won!"

Hands upraised, the governor stilled the crowd, promising more. "These are valiant men, each one by any measure, a man of valor. Accordingly, we are here today to recognize their devotion to duty with a special award. The Medal of Valor!"

The band broke out in a stirring tune and the crowd went wild with cheers and applause. Aides got Tilghman, Thomas, and Madsen positioned beside the podium, on line with the cameras. The governor moved from man to man, pinning a beribboned gold medal to the breasts of their suit coats. Flashpans exploded as he paused before each of the lawmen, shaking hands, smiling broadly for the cameras. Then, with a final word of praise, the governor was whisked away by his aides. The band played on as the crowd raised a last, rousing cheer.

"How 'bout that?" Thomas said, fingering the medal on his chest. "You boys ever expect to be heroes?"

"I don't know about heroes," Madsen said in a wry tone. "But the governor was right about one thing. We took on a dirty job and we got it done. That goes for you and Bill, especially."

Tilghman laughed. "Truth be known, none of us deserve medals. Nobody forced us to wear a badge."

"Nobody but ourselves," Thomas said, grinning. "Otherwise you wouldn't have run for sheriff. Told you once, you're a born lawman."

"You should talk," Madsen heckled. "All the badges you've worn, you've lost count by now."

"Chris, I found my calling, that's all. Took the gospel to the heathens."

Patrick Nagle interrupted their bantering to offer his congratulations. He wished Tilghman well in his new job, and thanked Madsen for having made the trip from Missouri. They chatted for a while and after a final round of handshakes, he drifted off. Thomas suddenly looked somber.

"Just hit me," he grunted. "You boys are leavin' me all by my lonesome. Don't know what I'll do for laughs."

"Door's always open," Tilghman said. "Come visit me

over at Chandler. Maybe we could catch ourselves some whiskey smugglers."

"Jesus, I don't know as I need laughs that bad."

Their good-natured joshing continued as they moved off the platform. Zoe and her father joined them, and Tilghman introduced the other two lawmen to Amos Stratton. Thomas shook his hand with an expression of mock concern.

"Guess you know your daughter's marryin' a drifter."

"Drifter?" Stratton repeated, missing the humor. "Bill Tilghman?"

Thomas nodded solemnly. "Drifts from one job to another real regular. One day a marshal, the next day a sheriff. Never know where he'll end up."

"Oh yes, I do!" Zoe interjected gaily. "He'll end up at home every night, right where he belongs. No more wild chases with you, Heck Thomas."

"With me?" Thomas sounded hurt. "Bill's the one that was always draggin' me off to the Nations and such. I'm strictly a stay-at-home sort."

Zoe laughed, taking Tilghman's arm. "Well, I've removed temptation from your path. You can stay at home all you care to."

"Yeah, I know," Thomas said sadly. "Gonna be awful dull around here."

Tilghman said his goodbyes there. He and the Strattons had a long drive, and Madsen was scheduled out on the evening train. The lawmen were kindred spirits, and there was a strong sense of loss when they shook hands. They realized they would probably never work together again, and their parting was all the more difficult. As Thomas and Madsen walked away, Tilghman felt an inward tug of regret. He would miss them.

Later, on the road out of town, Tilghman was in a quiet mood. Stratton was driving, and Tilghman and Zoe sat close together in the back seat of the buggy. Zoe sensed that his thoughts were on the parting with Thomas and Madsen. Yet her thoughts were on an altogether different matter, one she had never before put into words. She understood that a lawman's work was often cold and hard, sometimes brutal. Today, watching the three marshals shake hands, she was reminded that a badge brought with it a burden. She wondered how it affected the man she was about to marry.

"Bill?" she said, unable to resist curiosity. "Would you tell me something if I ask?"

"I'll do my best."

"When you face someone like Doolin, a killer? Does it change you—inside?"

"Never thought about it." Tilghman was reflective a moment. "Guess I've been at it so long, it's like second nature. I do what needs doing to get the job done. What makes you ask?"

"Well—" She hesitated, selecting her words. "I've never seen that side of you, and I'm curious. What you're like when you . . ."

"Zoe, I'm just me," Tilghman said with a crooked smile. "Told you before, I'm only good at two things. One's raising horses and the other's enforcing the law."

She was silent a moment. His statement was his way of telling her that however things might appear, in the end he was simply himself. She snuggled closer, hugging his arm.

"Let's hope you're good at one other thing."

"What's that?"

"Oh, you know," she said in a throaty voice ". . . being a husband."

Tilghman burst out laughing. "We'll know soon enough."

"No," she whispered in his ear. "Not nearly soon enough."

Amos Stratton strained to hear her reply. Then he

realized that he wasn't meant to hear, even if she was his daughter. Some things, and rightfully so, were between a man and a woman.

He drove on toward Chandler.

MATT BRAUN is a fourth-generation Westerner, steeped in the tradition and lore of the frontier era. His books reflect a heritage rich with the truths of that bygone time. Raised among the Cherokee and Osage tribes, Braun learned their traditions and culture, and their philosophy became the foundation of his own beliefs. Like his ancestors, he has spent most of his life wandering the mountains and plains of the West. His heritage and his contribution to Western literature resulted in his appointment by the Governor of Oklahoma as a Territorial Marshal.

Braun is the author of thirty-six novels and four nonfiction works, including BLACK FOX, which was recently made into a CBS miniseries.

BEFORE THE LEGEND, THERE WAS THE MAN...

AND A POWERFUL DESTINY TO FULFILL.

On October 26, 1881, three outlaws lay dead in a dusty vacant lot in Tombstone, Arizona. Standing over them—Colts smoking—were Wyatt Earp, his two brothers Morgan and Virgil, and a gun-slinging gambler named Doc Holliday. The shootout at the O.K. Corral was over—but for Earp, the fight had just begun...

WYATT EARP

MATT BRAUN

For decades the Texas plains ran with the blood of natives and settlers, as pioneers carved out ranch land from ancient Indian hunting grounds and the U.S. Army turned the tide of battle. Now the Civil War has begun, and the Army is pulling out of Fort Belknap—giving the Comanches a new chance for victory and revenge.

Led by the remarkable warrior, Little Buffalo, the Comanche and Kiowa are united in a campaign to wipe out the settlers forever. But in their way stand two remarkable men...

Allan Johnson is a former plantation owner. Britt Johnson was once his family slave, now a freed man facing a new kind of hatred on the frontier. Together, with a rag-tag volunteer army, they'll stand up for their hopes and dreams in a journey of courage and conscience that will lead to victory...or death.

BLACK FOX

A Novel by

MATT BRAUN

Bestselling author of *Wyatt Earp*